DEMONS OF OBENIN

By Alford Kerry Hardy

Design by Alford Kerry Hardy

Lettering by Tony Hardy

Published by Alford Kerry Hardy through
CreateSpace
ISBN-13: 978-0975360279
ISBN-10: 0975360272
BISAC: Fiction / Religious / General
gsawriter@gmail.com

DEDICATED TO:

My wife Stascia, my son David, and my daughters Aijalon and Iman, I love you all truly.

Earl, the late James Riley, and Keith, you remain my fellow Earth Protectors.

My gray and black, water-resistant, enclosed binder that protected this story for 3 years B.M. 286 (Before My 286 Computer).

My 286 computer that found a third life with another user

Marty Rittman, my 7th grade biology teacher, her homework assignment got me to research and write my first science fiction short story.

ACKNOWLEDGEMENT

Huge thanks to Renee Ryan! It's great to have someone in your corner who has been there, done that, and is still going strong.

Holly McClure, thanks for the strong right cross to my manuscript.

Margret Thompson, you are a great friend. For over a decade you have remained my most faithful reader.

Table of Content

KINGDOM OF OBENIN

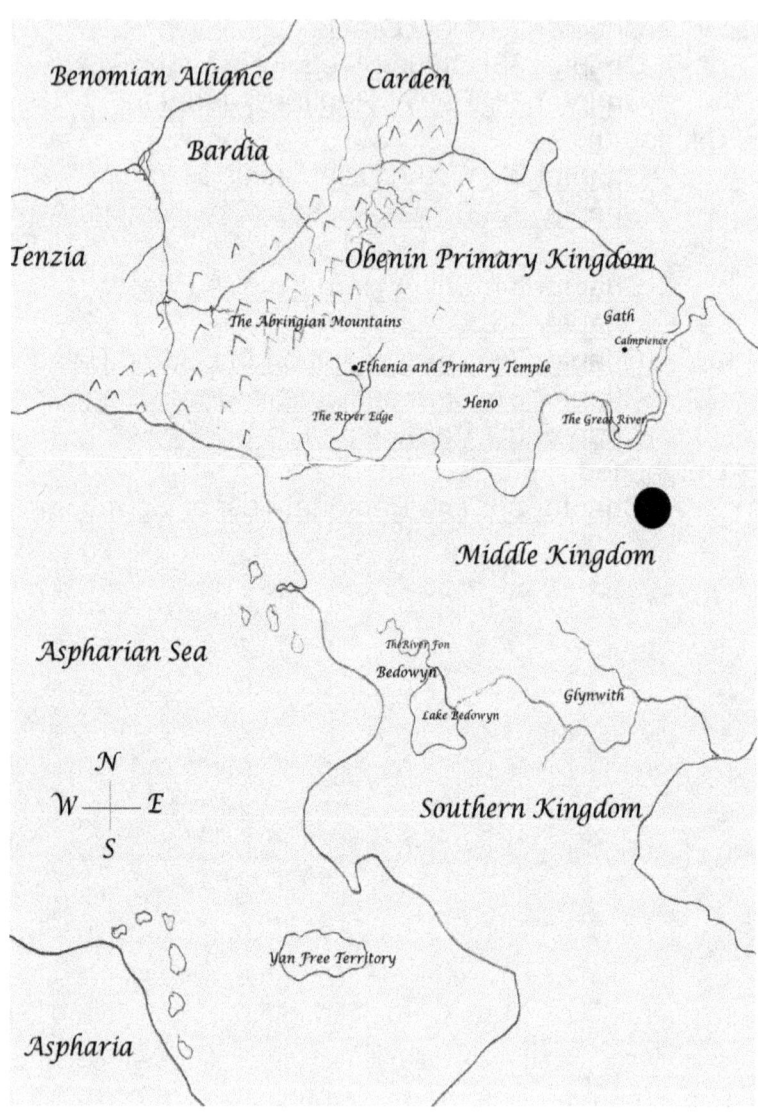

CHAPTER 1
Lord Cuere Wizard and Master of The Barren Lands

Lord Cuere aligned his bony index finger with the pupil of his subject's right eye. "Dead. They have to be dead?"

With a quick jab, he poked the pupil firmly. His fingertip left a depression. No blink, no tears, no blood, the wide-eyed stare of amusement remained on his subject's face.

Cuere continued whispering as if someone might be eavesdropping, "There are hundreds of them here in the Barren Lands. They slump over meals or have fallen in mid-stride. Some of them smile while others cower in terror, an entire village frozen, for who knows how long, right in the middle of their everyday lives. They do not smell. No bird, scavenger, or bug disturbs them. They are neither cold nor warm to the touch. And, there are no children, not one."

He jabbed the eyeball again. "Humpf."

Cuere took a couple of steps over to a female subject. Her nostrils flared. Her mouth gaped open. Her

1

teeth flashed threateningly. Anger distorted her, otherwise, beautiful face. Her finger poked the chest of a bewildered man. The fabric of his blue shirt covered half of her fingernail.

"Her teeth are so white and straight."

Cuere leaned forward to smell her mouth. He took a couple of quick whiffs.

"Um," he grunted. He smelled only the damp cave air.

He put his hand under the nape of her neck. Lifting her hair, he let loose a few strands at a time. When no strands remained in his hand, her hair made a stationary wave in midair.

His fingers felt fat and numb. He watched her hair while wringing his hands until they felt normal again. Nothing happened. The woman's hair did not fall even the width of one strand.

"One question at a time. Oracle is the question at hand. Figure out Oracle and this magic may come to light." He tore himself away.

Cuere dreaded the lonely walk through the caverns; however, loneliness was nothing new to him. Though he accepted the pariah's life, he never embraced it. The soldiers in the flats below despised him. They dreaded their post in the Barren Lands. Though they were necessary, he hated their presence. He needed protection from allies as well as enemies.

The king did not allow the soldiers in the caves. So, they selected the best campsite.

"Major Gremal had no right to bury my subjects." He gritted his teeth.

Despite Cuere's threats, the major, with a rather cheeky insubordination, had leveled his objection, "There were only a few of them outside the caves. But, I could care less if there were a hundred. Execution is better than to bivouac with undead eyes staring at you all the time.

Even when you can't see them, you feel those soulless things damning you to the underworld."

Through poorly lighted, manmade passages, Cuere trudged toward his obsession. He ignored the dozen or so of his rigid subjects as he mentally prepared for the work ahead, his twentieth attempt in two days.

"Raise the staff and speak to the hole." He sighed, releasing air through loose lips. The resulting noise sounded more like that of a horse than a man.

Emerging into the chamber that housed Oracle, he picked one of many scrolls from an open chest and took a deep breath of hope. From memory, he placed the symbols together and ran through the incantation in his mind before he fully extended the scroll.

Cuere knew that Oracle's benign appearance belied its latent power. No ancient inscriptions adorned its face. No statues guarded the entrance. No fiery blasts erupted from its belly, nothing. It

appeared to be a naturally weathered or water-formed hole through solid rock.

The scroll was another matter. The ink looked wet. The parchment, if it was parchment, did not flake or crack when he handled it. Cuere surmised its age as over a thousand years. The history of the Barren Lands reached back for at least a millennium. The mysterious and sudden end of this civilization escaped legend long before the Obenites conquered the land and made it their own kingdom.

He knew of no evidence that a similar culture existed in the known world. No other people had the same anthropological features, the same writings, the same religion, the same strange artifacts, or the well-kept perfect appearance of the pampered. Yet, evidence of this colony's influence reached across many other cultures, their own and even much older cultures like the Aspharians. From where they traveled and why, clues winked at him from every place he visited. Still, he could not piece them together to form conclusive evidence of their origin. Cuere knew one absolute. To become truly powerful, he must decipher the code to Oracle.

Even as a child, Cuere wanted to explore the Barren Lands. Every detail fascinated him.

He first read the words at nine years old: *Pure desolation protected by a perfect circle of petrified trees 20 kilometers thick, their stony roots gouge into venous red soil. The howling winds serve as harbingers of death and judgment for those who enter. In the midst of hell stands a city of caves dug into the cliffs by an ancient civilization. The ancients are still there. They are waiting... waiting for someone to solve their mystery.*

Cuere was hooked. He had used every piece of money he possessed, found, or stole to get more books. Born into privilege, he learned to use that status to get what he wanted at an early age. Cuere's father avoided him, except for the frequent beatings. His addict mother died when he was four. His stepmother ignored him. For all practical purposes, he had cared for himself. The books were a comfort. The fact that they were forbidden didn't matter. It seemed rather fitting to him.

Eventually, Cuere had gotten careless. His father found the books. He made Cuere burn them. That was after the beating, of course. Cuere wept over the ashes of his books. The beating was a common thing. He disliked his father before the book burning. Since then, dislike had developed into loathing.

Six years ago, the king gave him permission to live in and study the Barren Lands. The High Priest, Keeper of Obenin's Primary Temple, Iberius Octun, objected vehemently. He quoted religious text forbidding a repeal of the three hundred and ten year ban prohibiting anyone from venturing into the area. Keeper Octun emphasized that breaking the law meant the gallows. King Saroth lifted the ban anyway. Prince Seth, the heir to the throne, provided money, soldiers, and supplies. For the moment, that was all Cuere needed from the king and prince.

Though a man traveling by horse could ride around the Barren Lands in twenty-six days, it had taken Cuere two years to reach the caves. He had to recreate portions of the single path that led through the many booby traps. It took him another year to find the scrolls.

Curious about a covered cistern, Cuere pushed the lid off and looked inside. The sight startled him but his curiosity kept him planted in place. A mummified body clutched a bundle of scrolls against its sternum. This mummy was the only figure who appeared to be hiding and the only unquestionably dead body he had found. Cuere pulled seven scrolls from the mummy's clutches.

The scrolls were not even yellow. They were fresh. The paper still smelled. The ink looked as if the author wrote them only an hour earlier. Keeping them a secret, Cuere studied them and pieced together the symbols by finding similarities in other writings he believed the ancient people influenced. Three months after discovering the scrolls, he uncovered strange tools, more scrolls and all sorts of artifacts that, if he believed in a god, were truly godlike. By using the knowledge acquired from the scrolls together with the artifacts, he reinvented himself and won greater trust of the king. Cuere studied the scrolls religiously and compiled a lexicon. He constantly added to and corrected the lexicon. The scrolls served as his instruction books for the various artifacts. Each scroll held more secrets than he could uncover in a lifetime. However, he was well aware that he did not have to learn them all.

Cuere tried to relax, to force everything out of his mind, and to still the nervous shivers that ran through his tall, lanky body. His bushy brows crumpled together into one hairy line that wriggled from temple to temple. His eyelids were without lashes, plucked from the root. With protruding cheekbones and an insufficient chin, Lord Cuere looked much like a brown-eyed, malnourished, bearded billy goat.

He focused intensely, carefully enunciating each word according to his lexicon. He believed his lexicon was the major reason that his prior attempts failed. Minor inflections, peculiar accents, they all made a difference. Of his enunciation, he reassured himself the best he could. He tried to speak with a commanding voice. His words echoed within the endless chasm that he had named Oracle.

He finished the incantations, "Come, the heavens are your house. Come, the elements are your destiny."

He picked up one of the artifacts, a fluted rod with a knurled top, and knocked on Oracle. The rod looked like black metal, only much harder than anything he knew.

Cuere waited until his last words echoed into the most nothingness he had ever seen, or, as it were, not seen. Anxiety washed over him. With each breath, his hopes dispelled. He waited. Still... nothing.

Downcast, he trudged to the wall opposite Oracle.

He flopped down and propped his back against the wall. He glared perplexedly at the hole in front of him. "...the gaping hole in which I have placed my hopes." Despair lowered the normal pitch of his voice.

Cuere wrapped his thorny fingers in his gray streaked beard and pulled in frustration. "Aahhh!" he yelled at the top of him lungs. In a flash of anger, he leapt up, spitting profanities in three different languages. He raged about the cave kicking objects.

This did not satisfy his fury. From a burlap sack, he grabbed several artifacts and shattered them against Oracle. Rays of lights flashed. Smoke rose. He swore at Oracle and cursed it. He paused, still nothing. He neither invoked nor destroyed his obsession.

He flopped to the ground again. Eventually, he knew he would regroup and come to his senses. For now, he settled for vacillating between anger and self-pity. He pulled his beard.

"What am I doing wrong?" he yelled.

He recounted his preparations and translation of the passage from which he read. "It is correct. I am certain of it," he declared. Yet, he failed to invoke the power of Oracle.

Cuere pulled at his beard.

"Damned hole... damned whole lot of nothing! Time is more precious than gold. I cannot fail, not after I assured King Saroth that following my plan will crush the invading Benomian Alliance and restore the kingdom to glory. He made promises to me, appointment to Grand Advisor to the Monarch, regent of a province or two. And Prince Seth promised me even more when his father dies and he becomes king.

"This victory, my wealth, and close association with the king will become my revenge, my mountain to look down upon the miserable, blind insects that pester me because of what they call strange ways and my disinterest in things they deem so important... like belief in a god, useless nonsense. Look where it has gotten them. The Benomian Alliance will control the mountains by fall. By this time next year, the snow will start to melt and a full-scale invasion will begin. But, I will be ready by then and I will defeat them."

The light in the cave flickered. He figured that he might as well do something about it. From a sack, he pulled out a crystalline sphere about the size of a small melon. His people called them glows.

Wrapping it in leather, he banged it violently against the floor several times, "I wish I had never come into this place. It is a curse... <thud>... <thud>... every time... <thud, thud>... <thud>.... I get so close...<thud> but each time... <thud>... I fail <THUD>."

The glows grew hotter by the moment. Despite the leather wrap, his hands burned. In his anger, he neglected to place the glows quickly enough into the claw shaped holder. He dropped it. The wrap opened, refreshing the cave with light.

A new fury surged into him. He swept up the knurled staff and attacked Oracle with all his might. He beat it as long as his strength allowed. The beating left no mark on Oracle or the staff. He heaved to regain his breath. Anger still charged the air.

"What else needs a beating? I must break something," he shouted.

With his last bit of strength focused into one fuming dash, he smashed the knurled end of the staff against the glows. The glows burst in a flash of brilliance and sound that sent him diving to the floor. The glows formed an iridescent cloud of dust that hovered formlessly in midair. He guarded his eyes with his arm. The staff, which remained in his hand, grew warm and vibrated rhythmically. The cloud of particles formed an aura around the staff, then, entered it.

The staff's weight increased. Cuere tried to throw it away. The staff locked his fingers tightly around it. He tried to break his grip with his other hand. It stuck to the staff, too. Then, the staff lifted him to his feet. His feet seemed to become a part of the ground and he felt as immovable as a mountain. The staff hummed mightily. The hum got louder and louder. Another explosion seemed imminent. The heat dried his eyes and the inside of his nose. Something big was happening and he was along for the ride.

"Please let me live through this," he moaned, refusing to consider that the request sounded anything like a prayer.

The knurled end of the staff emitted intermittent and concentric rays of light that, at their greatest width, struck the face of Oracle just around the opening. The colors and patterns appeared random.

Then, awakening from an eon of hibernation, the entire Barren Lands groaned and a silvery mist belched from the twisted guts of Oracle.

Cuere heard faint cries from inside Oracle and a stiff wind picked up. Debris blew around the cave. The wind did not disturb his clothing. He did not feel it blowing against him. He did feel the temperature drop from eternal punishment down to volcanic. Cuere thought he heard singing in the same tongue as the scrolls. A sudden jolt shook the entire place violently. After which, like a heartbeat, it pounded faster and faster.

He thought he couldn't be any more terrified. He was wrong. Running for his life was not an option. The staff fixed him so that he could not move a finger.

Reason edged its way through his fear and pain. "Surely this is what I have been waiting for. I don't know exactly what I was expecting but surely this is it!"

Again, mist erupted from Oracle's mouth. This time, it enveloped Cuere to the point that he no longer saw his staff. His lungs filled with moisture. He labored to keep his breath. He felt cooler. The fog carried a stench that churned his stomach. He needed to vomit. He felt lightheaded, almost fainting from shock. He wondered why he still lived.

As a man who has thoroughly enjoyed his dinner belches, so did Oracle; a belch that comes in stages from the deepest parts of the stomach and just when you think it is over, another short, full belch follows signifying the end.

In the blink of an eye, the mist, along with the overpowering stench, vanished, leaving Cuere in a momentary stupor. His mind reeled when he realized that he looked down at Oracle. Some time during the phenomenon, he had levitated. Now, as the staff cooled, he descended. When he touched the floor, the staff went dead. Except that steam rolled away from his body in large, rapidly swirling eddies, he felt normal. He recounted the sequence of events in which Oracle performed. In thought, he lowered his eyes to his left and realized that a body lay on the cave floor.

Cuere shook himself. Afraid to approach, he tried to study the body from where he stood. Its naked torso was the color of old horse leather. With great reservation, Cuere crept toward the body. He watched for any movement. He feared that the person might suddenly leap up and hurt or kill him. Finally, he knelt by the body and watched its back expand and relax with shallow irregularity. He turned it over.

"A boy, not more than fifteen or sixteen, just like the scrolls implied," he spoke.

"Skin color, stocky frame, thick wooly hair cut close, an Obenite," Cuere guessed.

He examined the lad more carefully and found a huge ring on his left hand. "An Obenite wedding ring," remarked Cuere.

The youth's face flinched in pain and the nostrils of his noble nose flared. Cuere propped up the lad's back. He continued, "And he smells of perfume. How can this be after that rank smell just filled this place?"

"I've done it," Cuere exclaimed repeatedly. He grew louder and louder as excitement took hold. Worriedly, he touched the boy's clammy forehead.

"Surely all this was not in vain, to conjure up a person from nowhere just to have him die on me. He must survive for the next phases: Empty this vessel. Fill it with faith in a god. Time for the high priest to carry out the king's mandate. Iberius Octun, Minister and High Priest of Obenin's Primary Temple, humph, High Priest and Minister Nonsense is more like it. He will serve my purpose. Three more, that's all I need. Three more lives on different paths, deflected to converge for one purpose, my purpose. Three more, one at each new moon, after that; I will finally have my revenge."

CHAPTER 2
Parmos of the Gaksoma

Scila scowled at Ax, her lumbering, egg-headed, hulk of a husband. He pounded his burly chest, a clear sign of a highly disagreeable offer from a fat man with a crushed hat. She knew the boy's worth. Ax did, too. With his right hand, Ax slapped the calf of the boy who stood barefoot on blankets and loose hay in the back of the cart. He gestured that the rope tied around the boy's neck and wrists could belong to anyone in the crowd. Next, he held up a silver Llangenthorn coin and shook three fingers. The small crowd of barters murmured in disagreement.

Most of the crowd could not afford to buy the boy; however, they played an important role in helping to determine the final price. With sneers and jeers at ridiculous prices, especially from outsiders, they often lowered the final price.

Scila's hopes of selling the boy for the price they desired waned as some of the Llangenthorn villagers turned to leave. Looking at her old, soiled garments and clumsy boots, she swore under her breath. The village women wore plain dresses, mostly black or different shades of brown or gray and so much nicer than her rags. They acknowledged her as they would any other Gaksoma woman, only with sideways glances and whispers. She glared at the village women as they pulled their shawls or scarves over their neatly groomed hair. They walked playfully through the market, peeking at this or that, toying with things and putting them back, buying and placing frivolous trinkets among their snacks. "Childish," she told herself.

She considered the men as rogues not to buy the boy for the price Ax asked. She wanted to break their thieving little fingers.

Scrawny bastards. She pictured how their skin sagged from their bones. Ax is worth two of 'em in body heat, Scila thought. *"Llan men and women, they fit each other. A cold bed for 'em in life, pain and mis'ry in death.*

This unusually long and cold winter gave no room for thin people. She should know. Scila snorted and wiped her witch-like nose, leaving a wet trail of mucus on her sleeve. She spat on the back of the cart.

"Show 'em how stron' he is," she snapped at Ax in their language.

Ax picked up a stick and rapped it loudly against the rear of the cart near Parmos' feet. Some of the villagers turned again. Others ignored him and continued on their way. With an unyielding stare, he met the irritated scowl of each man.

"Show 'em," her tone sharp and impatient.

Jerking the rope, Ax ordered, "Git down 'ere, Parmos." When Parmos did not react fast enough, Ax pulled him from the cart to the ground. The boy lost his balance and stumbled but recovered quickly. Ax removed the furry knee-length, poor excuse for a coat draped over the boy's shoulders. With only a loincloth remaining to cover his private parts, he shivered dreadfully in the morning air.

Scila hissed disapprovingly, "Damaged goods brin' less at ma'ket, you pig!"

His face flashed hot with anger. Ax shot her a simple glance that conveyed his meaning all to well. "I know what um doin', so shut up or I'll shut you up."

Scila ignored his threat. Wrinkling her nose and crumpling her wild brows, she snapped, "Like a dead man you will."

Ax tapped the hub of the oxcart and ordered, "Parmos lift!"

The boy hesitated. Ax tightened his grip upon the stick and moved his arm ever so slightly.

Umph, 'at'll make 'im move. Ax gives a good beatin'. *"He'll remember not to be so stubborn.*

Straining, Parmos gave a mighty grunt. He lifted the cart nearly pitching Scila from it. She clutched the seat.

Ax turned to her and snickered. She cursed him in her heart.

As Parmos held up one side of the cart, Ax turned to his audience and chanced a snaggletooth smile. Old men bit their lips in envy and wished for their youths again, while the women, who watched the trembling, half-naked lad, blushed in shame as they studied each sinewy muscle rippling in his body.

Eight men made their way from the rear to the front of the crowd. Everyone stepped aside for them.

They stood in front of Ax at a respectful distance -- close enough to see how Parmos looked but far enough away to comfort their own fear of catching a disease from either of them.

A pale man, taller than the rest, dressed in black and sporting a neatly groomed black beard stepped closer than the rest. He looked directly into Ax's eyes for so long that Ax took a step backwards. To Scila's surprise, the man spoke to Ax in their language. She knew that he was either a smuggler or mercenary, possibly both.

"Major Kyln sye um. Qe ist lo adoles?", the man asked.

Ax motioned for the boy to put the cart down, then responded, "His name is Parmos. He is mine to sell."

Major Kyln examined Parmos more closely, from his shaggy blond hair and slightly hooked nose to his cleft chin, down to his long poorly kept toenails.

"Does he fight?" asked Major Kyln.

"Not me. He's broke. Look at 'em hollow eyes." Ax paused then started slyly, "Fill 'im with the soldier for 'ire sp'rit, uh?"

When the bidding finished, Ax exchanged the rope with Major Kyln for four of the silver coins, some change, and three red hens in a wooden cage.

Just as Ax turned to leave, he struck Parmos across the back of both of his legs with his stick. Parmos went to his knees before his new master. The uneven cobblestone dug into his skin.

Scila smirked. Ax knew how to say goodbye and good riddance.

The buyer chastised Ax, "You have no right to touch him, barbarian. He is my property now."

In one motion, Ax climbed aboard the cart and cast down Parmos' belongings. He flopped onto the wooden seat with his back to the crowd. He leaned back and placed the pouch of coins into a pocket sewn inside the crotch of his breeches. He slapped the reins against the ox's back.

Butterflies flitted in Scila's womb. She desired soured milk and hard bread. Instead of giving way to the memory of prenatal urges, she seared the tiny bit of remorse for her part in the selling of their firstborn with the red-hot iron of rationalization. *He makes trouble for us,* she thought.

Their chieftain feared Parmos for reasons she did not understand. She did know though, that the chieftain knew no reasoning but his own. It was simply comply or die. Her family learned that the hard way. She looked back at his new master. There was something familiar about him.

"'is turned out good," remarked Ax. "'at boy was good for somethin', af'er all. I got more 'an I wanted."

He stopped talking for a few seconds. "Maybe we sell one of our daug'ers. 'Ataways we could make more money and save givin' a dowry to marry 'er off."

"Maybe," Scila returned. "We talk on the morrow."

As the cart turned the corner, she lost sight of her only son.

****

Meanwhile, Parmos watched as Scila looked back at him. He desperately wanted some sign that she felt for him. After all, she birthed him. He hoped for some expression to disturb her empty stare, anything, a blush, the flutter of her eyes, a final wave, even a laugh, anything but that void face.

Major Kyln yanked the rope.

Still on his knees, Parmos turned toward him.

The major nudged Parmos' clothes with his foot saying, "Put them on."

Salty tears filled Parmos' eyes and ran down his dirty cheeks, cleaning paths to the corners of his mouth. He wanted to run after his parents. All he managed to do was kneel, weep, and shiver. He did not even have a god to pray to for vengeance or deliverance. He felt himself lower than the mongrels that hung around his peoples' camp.

"'ey even fight to p'otect their young," he wept aloud.

Major Kyln moved closer to him. Parmos didn't care if the man kicked him or beat him. He closed his eyes and tried to banish his parents from his mind.

Parmos realized that Major Kyln knelt near his ear. A blanket covered his shoulders.

"Mumo und Dido urm de?" whispered Major Kyln, hate festered in his voice, changing his accent.

Unable to open his eyes, Parmos nodded.

"Then you are better off with me. I hate those people. I hate myself because they are me. I never thought those people could get anymore base. I escaped when I was ten. A religious family took me in. I have passed for Llangenthornian ever since. At least you will have a life and death of honor. Whatever you feel for them, lose it here. Lose it now."

Parmos' spirit melted like fat in a hot skillet. It dripped out his chest. Every remnant ran down his belly onto the cobblestones. He did not understand the language. He stifled on smoke and the smell of strange foods mingling with the smell of fish, rudely taken from their murky homes to die and fill the bellies of them all. There in the midst of traders calling prices for their goods, with nothing left but a distant void where his heart once beat, he became an empty space.

****

From the mountains along its northern border, where the ground only thawed for two months out of the year, to the white cliffs of the southern shores, all Llangenthorn cursed the lingering winter. Everyone prayed for the last freezing spells to pass, everyone except the Gaksoma. The Gaksoma, those people, kept moving regardless of the weather.

Llangenthornians did not see the Gaskoma as countrymen. They looked upon the Gaksoma as foreigners, nomads and barbarians. For as long as Ax could remember and as long as his father could remember, several loosely associated Gaksoma bands traveled within Llangenthorn, wandering the borders. As an entire tribe, they seldom wandered into any of the surrounding kingdoms. They sent a few men out to trade while the rest of them camped and anxiously awaited the trading party's return. His people existed on the land, bartering, smuggling, and trading for new blood to avoid inbreeding.

The nomads puzzled the commoners of Llangenthorn. No one knew where they came from, not even the Gaksoma. Their origin was not important to them, anyway. Each Gaksoma satisfied him or herself to eat, sleep, and gratify their insatiable desire for heat.

No proper Llangenthornian ever spoke to them cordially at the markets. They agreed upon a price and made the exchange without so much as a head nod. That began and ended the Llangenthornian's public involvement with the Gaksoma.

Those who bought contraband from the Gaksoma dealt with several go-betweens as buffers to cloak their involvement. Many of the more lawful citizens petitioned the emperor to rid the empire of the Gaksoma, or at least confine them to some desolate area of the country where no one saw them. Thus far, no emperor had ever taken the initiative to rid Llangenthorn of *Those People*.

Only a half-day's ride from the village in which Ax sold his son for a few coins and poultry, he and Scila camped in an opening along a forest road. He hoped to catch up with their band in a day or so.

With waking snorts, Ax stirred reluctantly and missed the little heat Scila's body offered. *Not enough*, he thought. *I'm gettin' ol'er and my bones get col'er, I'll 'ave to fatten 'er up for next winter.*

Aroused by the smell of hot food, he opened his eyes to a gray sky. Clouds lingered low and moved southwardly into a darkening storm. Ax flung off layers of furs and slid down from the rear of the cart. Walking over to where he hitched the ox, he untied the rope that held up his breeches and reached inside the pocket for the pouch of money. He studied it carefully, smiling and figuring on where to hide it from their chieftain. The chieftain was bound to question and search them after they returned. He always demanded his share.

After he assured himself that Scila had not taken or swapped any of the money, Ax relieved himself on the hind leg of the ox. The ox turned its head and looked at Ax. With a quick swish of her tail, she slapped Ax's hand and manhood. He cursed the ox, lost control of the direction of his stream and peed on himself. He finished and without wiping his hands dry, turned around toward the campfire.

He watched Scila stooping over her small pot stirring his usual breakfast of bits of dried meat and roots, called grot. In vain, she kept brushing her stringy blonde hair from her face. Finally giving up, she wiped her nose with her hand. She wiped her hands on the fur skins -- the very same hand, moments later, she stuck into the pot to test her stew.

Scila stopped stirring her pot and listened intensely to sounds carried by the morning air. Ax heard it too, horses, five or six, at a gait. He hurried back to the cart. The rope loosened around his waist. He clutched his pants, pulling them up before they dropped lower than mid-thigh, and tied the rope tighter. Reaching the cart, he crawled up and sat with his legs dangling from the rear like a little boy waiting for his playmates.

Six horsemen, riding proudly, came over the little knoll and each broke their mounts spirited gait into a trot. As they approached, Ax's heart raced. He recognized the man riding out front as Major Kyln, the one who bought Parmos.

What does he want?

The fact that Major Kyln had spoken Gaksoma nagged at him. The major seemed to tease him by letting the thick-tongued Gaksoma accent slip through when they settled up. Now, darkness radiated from his pale face.

Major Kyln halted his men. He pointed to one side of the road and then to the other, directing them to search the forest. Immediately, four men spurred their mounts, two to each side of the road. They headed off into the leafless wood. Birds fluttered out of their way and resettled nearby. The soldiers returned, shortly, shaking their heads negatively.

As Kyln approached, Ax slid from the cart and leaned against the ledge.

Flanked by his five soldiers, Kyln spoke, "I came for my money."

Ax objected vehemently. The outburst sent birds fluttering from the wood again, "We 'ad a fa'r price and you 'ave what you bought. Why do you cheat me?"

"The boy is gone and I am convinced that you had something to do with it. His disappearance was too strange. I put him in a room. I locked the door. I came back moments later and he was gone. No one saw or heard a thing."

"I can't 'elp it if you can't keep up with one boy!"

"I come for my money and I will have it," Major Kyln threatened.

Ax shoved his right hand into his pants. He twisted and contorted his face. His entire body squirmed and he pumped his hips. He made sure the horsemen saw his hand bulging in his crotch. Major Kyln and his men watched in disgust.

Ax squeezed the pouch from between his flopping belly and his pants.

"Is 'is what you want?" he jested.

The horsemen shook their heads at one another. Major Kyln would have to choose which one of them was going to check the money.

"'ere, take it if you still want it!" Ax spat. He pitched it high into the air over the soldiers' heads.

They drew back in disgust refusing to catch it. Major Kyln reached for the pouch, but before he caught it firmly in his leather riding gloves, he fell. His beautiful black steed lay dying, pinning his right leg from the knee down.

Ax's quickness and agility defied his lumbering appearance. He, with skillful ease, wielded a huge battle-ax. By the fearful expressions on the soldeirs' faces, he knew it must be the most gigantic battle-ax that any of them had ever seen. If placed on the ground, the head of the battle-ax stood waist high and ran shoulder-width from razor sharp edge to razor sharp edge. A counter balance graced the opposite end of a thick shaft.

Ax had slept with it for years, thus earning his nickname. Letting no one touch it, he cared for it better than any living thing.

Unable to withdraw for fear of losing their master to a beheading, the soldiers drew their swords to face him. Ax looked at each one of them. Their hearts burned furiously at their carelessness.

Thump! A rock hit one of the soldier's head, opening a gash just behind his left ear. He plummeted to the ground. The soldier wallowed in pain, barely able to catch his breath.

More carelessness, Ax knew the soldiers were better. Their overconfidence undid them. They completely forgot about his woman. Both he and Scila knew they fought for their lives. Even if the major got double his money back, Ax knew their fate. To survive, he needed to take advantage of their faltering behavior before they recovered.

"Every Gaksoma girl knows 'ow to pitch rocks. Mine's don't miss much," Ax taunted.

One of the horsemen turned to face Scila. As he turned, another rock hit his horse square in the white spot between his eyes. The horse reared and bucked wildly, throwing the soldier. He, skillfully, rolled to his feet.

"Enough of this!" he screamed at Scila.

She approached him with two fiery torches.

Scila screamed and swung at him. The mercenary faded back and kicked her down. She got back up and ran toward the campfire. The mercenary pursued her. He raised his sword. Scila tripped and lurched to the left. He missed his target and ran into her. They stumbled into the scalding stew and fire.

"So which of you lit'le runts gonna teach the ba'barian a lesson?"

The soldiers did not understand Ax, but Major Kyln did. For those were almost the exact words he'd spoken at the start of their hunt.

Now dismounted, the soldiers thought soberly. They did not let Ax dupe them. They needed to attack together and maybe one of them could give Major Kyln a hand with getting from under his horse.

"Come on! Come on! You ain't nothin' to me," Ax roared in broken Llangenthornian.

The soldiers advanced, taking small steps, careful not to rush, checking their balance.

Ax studied each of the men. "Who'll I kill?" he taunted.

He chanced a glance at Major Kyln. Ax saw that only his ankle and foot remained under the horse.

"I should've finished 'im," Ax cursed, under his breath.

He faced the three men in front of him.

The man in the mi'le looks tougher 'an the other two. The one on the right looks the scaredest Ax reasoned.

With a loud battle cry, he charged at the scared soldier. As he figured, his quarry stumbled backward in fear when he saw the huge ax fall towards him. The others sought to take advantage of Ax's seeming single-mindedness. Instead of killing the soldier who stumbled, Ax twisted his body. With one hand, he buried his weapon into the arm of the soldier who seemed so determined to kill him. The soldier's arm hung from his shoulder. When he hit the ground, it came off completely.

Ax never considered that soldier, who had been so fearful, might fall in his path and manage to stun himself in the process. Ax stumbled over him and lost grip on the battle-ax. The scared soldier's sword fell out to Ax's left. Ax hit the ground and rolled a couple more paces. Scrambling desperately for anything with which to fling, cut or strike, he found a soldier's sword. Major Kyln freed his boot. Ax growled when he saw the Major pick up the battle-ax.

Slashing at the soldier's clumsily, Ax snarled and snapped his teeth like a beast cornered by hounds, lunging out then back, hoping to cut out a chunk of flesh from one of them. With the scared soldier recovered and armed, they circled him carefully, the points of their swords hungry for vengeance. Ax jumped out at a soldier and slashed him across the chest.

The sharp pain of cold metal in Ax's back stunned him. When the blade withdrew, the blood warmed his skin for a moment. It felt good to Ax. Then he grew colder by the moment.

"Damned barbarian! You are not me."

Ax, panicky with desperation, turned at the words.

"I'll cut you to..." He saw his own battle-ax falling toward his face.

****

Meanwhile, Scila clawed and bit her mercenary. Though the fire and stew burned them both severely, they brawled. The mercenary tried to break free from her filth.

Every way he rolled, she ended up on top of him biting, scratching and kneeing any place convenient.

Finally, he landed a solid punched to her jaw. Scila looked at him. He punched her again. Her eyes narrowed. She spat in his face and beat him with renewed ferocity. He struck her several more times and, finally, heaved her to his left side. He looked hastily for his sword. Spying it, he dived just in time to dodge a large stone Scila flung at his head. Painfully, he got to his feet.

From her position, she witnessed Ax's gruesome end. With a scream, she charged toward her foe, who, simply stepped aside and stuck his sword into her womb. Scila slammed into the earth and ended up on her back. The soldier waited for her to move. When she didn't, he turned to nurse his wounds.

Scila crept back into consciousness, her thoughts hazy, her vision blurred.

She heard someone ask, "Is she still alive, Major?"

"Only for a moment longer. Give me that."

Someone stood over her, someone with a sword.

A little more aware, the major seemed to float over her. "Cheatin'... cough... bastard... cough." Pain pushed away the numbness in her body.

As she tried to focus, Major Kyln's face blurred and transformed.

"Parmos no. Parmos, don't kill me," she begged. "That was your son's name, wasn't it?" Parmos thrust his sword into her heart.

CHAPTER 3
Ulthea and Ictheos of Lompolosona

Ulthea watched Brother Fordham rebuke one of the new Spirit Men. Spirit Men, *Eesdios*, in her native tongue, lived among the tropical rainforest tribes preaching, teaching, and healing with medicine. Brother Fordham looked different from the other Spirit Men. As a matter of fact, he looked tougher than the secular explorers who arrived every year or so. His big, leathery hand swatted the air as if he knocked swarming bugs out to the middle of the sea. The new Spirit Man cringed, afraid to meet Brother Fordham's eyes. When angry, Brother Fordham always fussed a long time, turning a one-way conversation into a history lesson, a testimony, a scolding, and an uplifting sermon.

Brother Fordham served as leader of all the missionaries in the rainforest. Yet, he opposed the increased missionary presence. Two new Spirit Men stayed when the last supply ship sailed away. They both came to Ulthea's village. Brother Fordham complained that he did not need any more help. He dared not outright reject the directions of his elders back home, though. Instead, the new arrivals took the brunt of his dissatisfaction. This was the third time Ulthea heard the speech. He rearranged the words but all echoed the same themes.

Ulthea liked the Spirit Men. She trusted Brother Fordham. He taught her of far away wonders. He taught her how to read and write, and showed her paintings and sketches. Though the stories inspired her curiosity, the thought of living outside of the rainforest scared her, especially in a desert. She shuddered. Her mother insisted that he had arrived on one of the first ships, years before Ulthea's birth. He befriended her tribe, the Emas, within days after his arrival.

Lompolasona, all the known native tribes used some form of that word for the entire rainforest. Though the Spirit Men truly sought to understand, they undervalued the meaning of Lompolasona, the forest is life. The Spirit Men agreed, wholeheartedly, that the forest teemed with life; however, this did not reflect the meaning her people intended. To her and her tribe, the rainforest not only provided an endless supply of food, it served as the beginning and the sustainer of every form of life, even the fish in the sea.

As long as the forest thrives, the world lives. When the forest dies, man dies and the world will end, Ulthea thought.

The rainforest's canopy sheltered millions of acres and its inhabitants from the glaring sun. Most of the explorers, acting independently of their native country, were religious men who embarked on a sincere mission to proselytize the natives.

Her mother told her that, in the early days, soon after the Spirit Men established a port and a mission, secular explorers came by the hundreds. At first, the secular explorers did not trust the Spirit Men. They insisted on independent exploration. They wandered off into the rainforest with weapons and heavy gear and without the religious sect's guides. They never returned to their ships. Now, secular explorers hardly ever sailed into the port. While Brother Fordham could not control who and what came into the port, he definitely controlled what and, often, who left the port.

The Spirit Men grossly underestimated the vastness of the rain forest. Sixteen years after they built their port at Lands End, the immensity and density amazed them.

The incredible dream they possessed awed and excited them. No one had traveled the breadth or the width of the jungle by land nor had anyone found a sea route around it.

Rainforest tribes were isolated, but each tribe knew the approximate whereabouts of dozens of other tribes, even those two months' travel by land. The Spirit Men built small missions in many of the villages and furnished them with only a few comforts from their native land.

Even with harsh conditions, the Spirit Men seemed content-- and not just out of religious conviction. They found a strange calmness and refuge there. Life was simply simple. Brother Fordham preached bold long-winded sermons about escaping the threats of his king and the persecution of his sect.

Ulthea's tribe did not care one way or the other about the Spirit Men's presence as long as they did not force change on them. That is, everyone except the shaman. If the Spirit Men wanted to take the role of the fly on the wall, the tribe took no offense. If they wanted to participate in a ritual, that was fine, too. At night, the old men, shaman, and tribal leaders spun stories about mysterious encounters during their journeys. The light from the fires brought further enthusiasm as wondrous words filled Ulthea's ears and made her heart skip a beat. The shaman, Qetoo, retold stories from other tribes that no one else knew. Though they tried to resist, the stories intrigued the Spirit Men. They all doubted. They all listened.

One particular story fascinated even Brother Fordham. Whenever he heard it, he sat like a mesmerized child listening to the shaman. This was the only time he ever really acknowledged the shaman. The story scared Ulthea. The shaman told the legend of a strange people who lived further away than an Emas man could walk to and from in his lifetime. These people appeared from nowhere and claimed four hundred villages worth of land as their kingdom. They possessed the power to change forest creatures and disguised themselves as anything they wanted.

Bored with animal transformation, the strange people changed themselves into beings with no earthly needs. But, they made a mistake. They gave up their souls in the transformation. With no soul and no earthly desires, they possessed no will to eat, to love or to hate. They were unable to undo the change. The only thing they could do was stare back at the life they once lived and the power they once wielded. Soon after, they turned the forest around the area into stone to keep others from witnessing their misery.

Ulthea's tribe, the Emas, the peacemakers in Brother Fordham's language, acted as judges to resolve disputes between different tribes.

Over the centuries, the Emas had developed a system by which each Emas village judged an assigned area. The entire Emas village played a part in these trials. Some acted as lawyers, some hosted the witnesses, and others investigated the incident and so on. The accused and the accuser took the Emas' decision as binding.

If a tribesman defied their decision, the rest of his own tribe made him a social outcast within their village. Most communities depended upon the skills and dedication of each villager. Living as an outcast was unbearable. Even if the guilty tribesman escaped, the other tribesmen hunted him down, brought him back and tied him to a pole. He became a non-person until he surrendered to the will of justice and paid recompense for the crime.

Peace abounded within the regions where the Emas judged. The Emas knew no tales of battles between those tribes, even in fables. They knew no word for "war"; that is, all-out war between tribes. Fights broke out between men, but the tribesmen could not imagine why any one tribe would rise up to kill others. To them, killing men, as one kills a tree sloth or thrusts a gig into a school of fish, appalled them.

"There is more than enough to fill everyone's hut to the top," the tribesmen would say.

Ulthea agreed. She never really got hungry. Gold and silver did not cause conflict between the tribes. No one bartered the raw material. They traded in things made from it.

The Emas wore gold necklaces, bracelets, earrings, and toe rings. They pierced their skin with small gold barbs in every place imaginable. Only tribal leaders wore gemstones. They marked their positions with large gemstones that dangled from their necklaces and earrings, the higher the position the larger the gem. Of course, the chief wore the most and the largest gems.

Brother Fordham tried to discourage Ulthea from wearing such ornaments. That's what he called them, ornaments. He said that such things brought out the worst of the civilized world, whatever "civilized" meant. He never used the word to describe the rainforest tribes.

Whenever secular explorers came, the Spirit Men begged the tribesmen to remove and hide the ornaments. The Spirit Men took the secular explorers only to certain places and to tribes they knew very well. They always forewarned these tribes.

So far, the Spirit Men kept knowledge of the great wealth of Lompolasona from getting outside the rainforest. Brother Fordham insured that the secular explorers returned with various curiosities but nothing that assured a return of the "hordes," as he called them. Yet, Brother Fordham confessed that, sooner or later, others would discover the vast wealth of the rainforest. Almost everyday, Brother Fordham warned them, "The day that happens, civilization will come. War will surely follow."

This was why Brother Fordham fussed at the new Spirit Man. Someone had left an unfinished letter on the table. Not knowing to whom it belonged, Ulthea brought it to Brother Fordham, who wanted to stop the "deluge of missionaries". The letter written by the new Spirit Man said otherwise. Brother Fordham sent him off to fifteen days of fasting and prayer. Ulthea went to find something else to do.

"Ulthea . . . Ulthea," her mother, Blaia, called, "go balla sei."

Ulthea wanted to examine the insect she held firmly between forefinger and thumb. She looked carefully at the two blue spots on its head where its eyes should be. If she got caught playing with the bug, a switch to her backside followed. Parents taught their children from an early age not to play with the sick-head bug. Her twin brother, Ictheos, at the age of ten, collapsed and did not wake up for two days after the sick-head bug gave him an unrestrained blast of perfume.

The men used the sick-head bug for entertainment during their hunting parties. If harassed enough, it raised its wings and sprayed its perfume in your face. The men knew how to caress it just right and in the right place so that it released only a small amount. The perfume didn't smell bad, but it made you a staggering drunk in the snap of a finger. Though Ictheos went on the hunting parties, their father did not let him take a whiff of the sick-head bug. Her father stopped using it after Ictheos' accident.

Blaia called again and Ulthea put the bug back on the branch gently.

As Ulthea approached her hut, she saw her mother already stretched out in her hammock with her pipe's stem mashed firmly between her lips. Her mother waved a tired arm at her and pointed to the book lying beside her on the hammock. Ulthea picked it up, hugged it to her breasts and snuggled beside her mother. She, then, cleared her throat, opened the book and began to read.

Ulthea translated the words of the Spirit Men into her tongue so that her mother understood. If there were no words in her language to describe the writing, she did her best to explain or find some common ground.

****

Ulthea's soft voice fell sweetly into her mother's ears. Blaia stroked her daughter's straight black hair. She saw the eagerness in her brown eyes. She was sure that Ulthea must be the most beautiful girl in all Lompolasona. Her hair draped down to her hips. Ulthea's eyes reminded Blaia of some of the animals that came out only at night. As soon as her body filled out a little more, she would put other young women to shame.

Blaia stretched and yawned. The air smelled thick and wet. Ulthea read a few more pages.

Sleepily, Blaia thought of the night her precious twins were born. An-out-of-season storm raged that night. The storm was merely a rain shower compared to the typhoon that battered the inside of her body. Thunder rattled the world and the wind screamed through the trees like wayward spirits fleeing judgment. In fact, every tree and animal seemed to scream along with her.

She screamed as a storm surge of labor contractions drowned her. The shaman screamed back. His screams and chants worsened her pain. No one else had a right to scream. No one else felt the torment. Brother Fordham chased the shaman outside. His rattling bones and painted face aggravated her, anyway.

[Make the pain stop.]

No comfort, their touch, their talking, attempts at comfort, all agony.

[Kill me and let the baby live.]

For so long I wanted to bear a son for my Shunie. In the throes of labor, however... *[Curse the day I prayed that prayer and curse me for praying it.]*

Push, push. I sank into the unthinkable fathoms of the underworld to await rebirth into the rainforest as an evil spirit. Then, it was over, but no.

So soon after the happiness in sheer exhaustion... *[Curse the pain again. Push! Push!]*

I died. I was resurrected.

Late the next evening, when I woke up, the light of resurrection shone through the door. Fading scents of the storm put breath into my nostrils. The storm passed. Shunie laid the twins to suck. The love was worth the pain, Ulthea and Ictheos, daughter from the gods, son from the gods.

Because I bore twins, I am special in the eyes of all the villagers and so are Ulthea and Ictheos.

****

Ulthea awakened to several high trills echoing through the ancient trees. Three hunting parties went out a day ago and now one returned. She listened intently for her brother's and father's distinct calls.

"Mama," she nudged her mother awake from her dream. "Ictheos and Father come."

Ulthea rolled from the hammock and stretched the stiffness from her short frame, her stature characteristic of her people.

Ulthea answered the calls with three short warbling bursts followed by a waning trill. She heard Ictheos return her call. By now, other reclining figures stirred to greet the returning party. Calls erupted from everywhere, each distinctly recognizable by family members, even among the cacophony of whistles and trills.

Ulthea rejoiced. Her father and brother returned safely. As she ran to meet them, she saw the worried faces of others who did not hear their loved ones' calls. She hoped deeply that they were well, too. Excitement filled her heart. She expected some token from Ictheos, a strange stone with the imprint of an insect or plant in it or maybe a beautiful flower she had never seen before.

Today, he may even bring a lost necklace or bracelet from some other tribe, she hoped.

Swift, frightening, consuming darkness engulfed her. She stumbled headlong. Searing pain uprooted her very soul. She cried out but no words came from her mouth.

****

Immediately, Ictheos reacted to his father's quickened pace. When the replies to the hunting party's calls ceased, they knew something was wrong. Hoisting their blowguns, spears, and bows, they ran. Maybe a beast stalked into the village. Some of the hunters with large game dropped it. Others with smaller game grasped it firmly and hurried forward. As the party approached, the entire village massed around one spot. Ictheos heard his mother's wails. His father forced his way through, Ictheos following in the wake.

"Bandie! Bandie!" Shunie yelled, until they reached where Blaia wept over Ulthea.

Ictheos grasped Ulthea's hand. She lay supine, her head in their mother's lap. Her body quivered spasmodically and her hand grew incredibly warm.

The shaman screamed furiously at the Spirit Men. As usual, they usurped his inherited craft and authority when someone took sick. Brother Fordham and the new Spirit Man looked at one another in puzzlement over

Ulthea's sudden distress. They examined her ears, mouth, and pressed her belly. Ictheos watched their every expression. When Brother Fordham shook his head, his heart dropped like a stone.

Ictheos looked toward the shaman. The crowd gave the shaman room to work. After jumping and chanting, the shaman poured dark liquid from a bottle onto Ulthea's forehead. Ictheos recognized it as the fever healing medicine the Spirit Men used.

The shaman poured a little on the ground and then drank some. He rubbed Ulthea's forehead with his index finger.

Next, he reared back as if he struggled to pull some unseen spirit from Ulthea's body. His muscles flexed as he battled the invisible force. He reached and pulled like a fisherman pulling in a full net. Finally, he gave a strong yank and fell backwards. He opened a charm-covered basket, wrestled the invisible force inside and slammed it shut. He secured it with more charms that kept it retrained for later banishment. After which, he watched Ulthea closely and waited for her to come around.

Nothing happened.

"Ulthea!" sobbed Ictheos. "Qetoo, Brother Fordham, don't let her die!"

Brother Fordham wiped Qetoo's dark liquid spell from Ulthea's forehead with a wet cloth.

Qetoo whirled around. With one hand, he picked up the basket containing the bound spirit. He beat the basket with his staff. "Roots o' the evil dead damn ye, Fordham, body and soul. Rise f'om the dirt ye roots. Drag ye down, Fordham. Let 'em beetles tear you up, starting with ye eyeballs. Many worms, suck ye soul, curl 'em up in a knot. Keep ye f'om Lompolasona."

He shook his staff and kicked dust on both Spirit Men. They paid no attention to him and concentrated on Ulthea. The shaman began a throaty scream that increased in volume. He raised his head slowly toward the heavens. Right in the middle of the blood-curdling peak of his cry, he fell silent. His mouth locked open. His eyes went cold.

Ictheos looked up. So did everyone else. The shaman fell flat on his back. Not a breath expelled. A silvery cloud descended through the tree canopy to the forest floor. It engulfed all those closest to Ulthea. As quickly as it appeared, it disappeared, rising out of sight in the blink of an eye.

Several villagers screamed, drawing his eyes to where Ulthea had fallen. She was gone. Blaia lamented pitifully, her arms extended, still reaching for her lost child.

Ictheos shook himself from misery. His skin crawled. His hairs stood on end. He looked around. Every piteous eye studied him. No one breathed a word. Yet, he knew their one thought. The overwhelming revelation caught him by the throat and choked the breath out of him, *Ulthea was rightly named. Now the gods wanted her back. When will the gods take, Ictheos, son from the gods?*

CHAPTER 4
Ictheos Meets the High Priest

Shadows, watery images, strange voices he did not understand, impressions of traveling a great distance, painful cramps in his abdomen and the stifling sense of entrapment, Ictheos drifted in and out of consciousness.

Death lingered in the seat of his mind. In his brief moments of consciousness, delirium shrouded him in an impassible gulf, separating him from the world. He heard distant voices. Occasionally, the voices seemed concerned but no one helped.

Reptitious memories, especially his last, swept past him like leaves blowing across his narrow field of view. Dreams altered some memories. Things that never happened wove themselves inextricably into his memories, threatening to confuse him forever. A void always followed. After a while, the same dry leaves rustled past him again.

Ictheos sat halfway down the rocky bank of a waterfall near his village. His parents tried to discourage him from going off by himself. Despite their warnings, he slipped out of the village often. From the moment the clouds snatched his sister, he banished happiness. He accepted no comfort from his parents, the shaman, or the Spirit Men. Each day the memory of Ulthea stood fresh in his mind and he often found himself calling for her.

Cool water dripped from his face. Deep in thought, he blocked out the mighty roar of the falls plummeting into the tormented river beneath. At first, terror kept him close to his father's side. He figured that he was next.

Everyone expected it. Soon though, his terror turned into a festering sore that hurt when touched. He drew satisfaction from the pain. As he scratched it, his lesion grew more and more until it consumed his soul. It immobilized his normal everyday life. He cursed the heavens for taking his sister and concerned himself only with her rescue.

He removed the shaman's protective talisman from around his neck and shook it at the sky, "Take me," he shouted. "What are you waiting for? You take a helpless girl from her mother. Take a man."

His fourth attempt that day ended in another failure to provoke the gods into action. He replaced the talisman around his neck. He wanted to be ready, so that if they took him, he could be aware and prepared to rescue Ulthea.

He pulled out his metal knife, a gift from Brother Fordham on his fifteenth birthday. He whetted it on a smooth stone developing a scheme. The old tribesmen of his village told the legend of a mountain that reached beyond the sky. There, a man could look down upon the clouds and walk on them to meet the gods.

"I will go to the mountains and find her. I will make the gods give her back."

One full moon had passed since Ulthea's disappearance. He decided to leave on the next one.

He stood on the rock and vowed, "No man, or any god will stop me!"

That's when it happened, the terrible agony that turned him inside out. The gods punished him for such contempt. He clutched his sides but that brought no relief or comfort. He fell from the rock screaming in fear of being lost in the foamy depths of water.

Now, weak as a newborn babe and aching from head to toe, Ictheos groaned. He smacked his lips and tongue, trying to remove the foul taste that clung to every corner and pocket in his mouth.

"A nightmare," he thought.

Then, before he opened his eyes, he felt completely out of place. He felt closed in. The bed upon which he slept had no straw; instead, cloth lay against his face, softly and smoothly. His face felt cold, like the inside of a cave. A mad man with a club pounded his head. His stomach churned. *This feels worse than getting sprayed with the sick-head bug*, he thought. Drowsiness, eventually, made him sleep.

This time, he dreamed of hunting a tree sloth. His bow twanged and the line followed the arrow finding its mark, between the shoulder and ribs of the animal. His father smiled at him and patted him on the back.

Ictheos lay silently, the salty taste of tears fresh in his mouth. He kept his eyes shut, listening carefully, taking in deep breaths, stretching the limits of his perception. Maybe he made a mistake. He listened for birdcalls, the smell of the women cooking, or the occasional breeze that brought the smell of wild flowers that the Spirit Men called orchids. He heard, felt, nor smelled anything familiar.

I must be dead!

He pulled the covers over his head.

Whose death was this, Emas or Spirit Man? He didn't know. He thought he knew both descriptions of death pretty well. This did not fit either of them.

Ictheos considered his tribal elders. They taught that when a man dies, his spirit joins with the gods of the forest. Gods of blessing and gods of evil exist in the rainforest. The gods of blessing inhabit the trees and other sacred plants. The gods of evil roam from place to place seeking to cause trouble and throw things out of balance. The spirits of the good dead people join with the gods of blessing to help nurture the forest. As the forest thrives, it provides for and blesses all the inhabitants, man, animal, and bug. The forest even helps the creatures that live in the ocean.

Sometimes too many spirits of the evil dead enter into the forest and harm parts of it, he thought. *We have rituals for those occasions, though. The most important thing is, so long as that forest lives, man lives. When the forest dies man dies and the world will end.*

In contrast, the Spirit Men taught differently. Ictheos sincerely wanted to believe, but his tribal religion put up a barrier that he found hard to overcome. The Spirit Men did not make anyone carry out religious ceremonies in which they did not believe. They taught that there is one god, God. God created everything living, every spiritual thing, everything that has never lived, and even the very imagination of man. They taught that God was God and then he became a man and then God again. When a man died, his spirit went to rest with God until the end of this world.

A sound outside his room startled him and his eyes opened wide. Two different voices, men, angels, demons, he could not tell, mumbled unintelligible words. His heart raced. Another voice joined the others. He heard a rusty squeak.

"Oh, god, someone is coming." He shook under the covers.

He heard another squeak, only this one ended with a solid thud.

He turned over and peeked from beneath the covers. Startled, he jerked the covers over his head. He peeked again only to stare at himself in a mirror beside the door. Ictheos remembered that the Spirit Men said that a mirror was made of glass. With the green bed covers wrapped snugly around him, he saw only his face.
Studying the image in the mirror, he surveyed his

whereabouts and compared them to each description of death he knew.

"Well, I'm definitely not part of the forest. This is like some stone hut that a man has carved from rock."

He remembered the words of the Spirit Men.

"I must be resting with God," he reasoned carefully. "I am resting and . . . I am resting . . . Maybe I should pray," he thought.

He prayed with fervor but soon his weakened body drew him into a restless sleep.

Sometime later, he sat up in his bed and rubbed sleep from his eyes. He tried to figure out the length of his death. The tumble from the waterfall served as his only reference. There were no windows to let in the sunlight. The light in the room came from two glowing spheres held by what looked like iron condor talons. It hurt his eyes if he looked at it directly.

He thought with amazement, "I must be in the Spirit Men's heaven. They said that there would be no sense of time."

Confident that he knew which death he suffered, he further acquainted himself with his surroundings. The room was not as large as his hut in the village. He started at the door, a few steps to his left, and worked his way to his right. The room contained a table with a basin, the mirror, and his bed. The bed and table looked powerful. Everything was big and square, making the room look smaller than its actual size.

He bounced on the bed. He found it springy as the branch of a tree.

The same sound as before startled him. When he looked at the door, he saw eyes at the little window within it. The eyes stared like a dog watching a stranger, wary and watching his every move. The first pair of eyes moved back, a different pair appeared. These eyes were strong, quiet, and troubled. They moved away and the window closed.

Cornered, Ictheos tried to calm himself. *If this is truly the Spirit Men's Heaven, they always spoke of this place with great joy and hope.*

His heart pounded against his chest as the door opened. A man, seemingly twice as large as the biggest man in his village, stepped over the threshold. He thought his guest bald, but as he turned to close the door, Ictheos notice a wolly braid grew from the back of his head. The braid was about as thick as three of Ictheos' fingers and as long as his forearm. The braid hung stiffly. Unruly hairs sprouted out from it all over the place.

Clinging to the covers, he closed his eyes and waited. He tried not to look directly at the man's eyes, but they drew him.

His guest's green eyes wilted like the leaves of a thirsty plant. They studied him. His guest had a thick nose and a mouth that resisted anything that resembled a welcome. Despite, his size, the man's eyes did not seem threatening at all. In fact, he looked a little lost.

A rainforest tree reborn into form of man, he thought, while observing the man's rugged skin and dark brown complexion.

He pictured a lost purpose floating somewhere between his guest's eyes and his soul. It was not so much as, a why *am I here look*, that affected his countenance; rather, a *what is the meaning of my being here* bewilderment.

Ictheos started to speak but found his mouth, tongue, and lungs did not cooperate with each other. He tried again, slowly and with determination. He could not bear the thought of not knowing any longer.

"Are... you... Jesus?" Ictheos asked, his voice cracking.

His visitor did not respond.

"Are you... an angel?" entreated Ictheos, thinking that he had somehow offended his visitor by exalting his status. Not even in the hunting and trading parties did he encounter anyone who looked like this. "Do you know Brother Fordham?"

Ictheos mouth dropped wide when his visitor spoke his native language.

"Good morning." He held out a hand large enough to cover Ictheos' face from ear to ear.

Ictheos cowered against the headboard.

"Don't be afraid. I am a friend. I am Keeper Iberius Octun, Minister and High Priest of the Obenin's Primary Temple."

CHAPTER 5
Ictheos: I'm Dead

Ictheos stared blankly into his host's eyes. His mind scanned quickly through every name of the Spirit Men's religion that he could remember.

"Obadiah?" he attempted.

"No," Keeper Octun corrected. He pronounced each syllable and emphasized appropriately, "I-beer-re-us Oc-tune."

They still did not make sense to him. Neither O...be...nin nor I... B Oct... something-or-the-other seemed familiar.

Without hesitation, another question popped to Ictheos' lips. "Am I dead?"

"No," Keeper Octun answered directly. "You are not dead."

Ictheos' eyes narrowed into slits of doubt. He wasn't sure that this I... B...whoever was alive.

"Are you sure I am not dead," he entreated nervously, "and you are not a spirit?"

Octun did not answer but turned as a fat jolly man with a small nose and tight, puffy cheeks, carried a tray that bore a cup, bread, and a bowl. He set the tray in front of Ictheos.

Octun dismissed the man, who withdrew still staring at the tray as if he wanted another small taste.

Ictheos looked at the food in front of him. Nothing looked or smelled familiar. The bread felt hard. It looked and sounded like a piece of wood. After sipping the broth, he found it good. When he took a large gulp, his stomach knotted.

Slowly," instructed Octun.

CHAPTER 6
Iberius Octun, High Priest of Obenin

Keeper Octun watched Ictheos tear the thick, log shaped roll of bread with his teeth. He chomped on it for a few moments then forced it down with more broth.

The Keeper found it just as hard to swallow his own food-for-thought, the renewed success of Cuere the mystic. Even though the Archeological Guild once lauded Cuere as their principal young scholar, now, they wanted nothing to do with him. For, in the last year of his exploratory studies, Cuere ruined his own reputation; something his father had said was inevitable. After all, his father had nicknamed him Cuere.

After a decade of dedicated study and his far-reaching translations of ancient foreign text, Cuere had distanced himself from his father's relentless rebuke. People had started calling him Young Master Amrion.

But, Cuere's secret obsession with the Barren Lands brought his father's predication to fruition. While addressing the Guild, one of the last steps of his exploratory studies, Cuere asserted that the Barren Lands should be the source of Obenite power. He wanted the Archeological Guild to tell the king to pull back most of the army and attack the Barren Lands. The name Young Master Amrion Vymeriqus sank into the grave and Cuere resurrected itself. The Guild threw him out and ridiculed him so that he became a recluse.

No one knew his whereabouts for almost eight years. Some say he lived like a hermit in the lower region of Aspharia. Others say he sailed farther across the ocean than anyone dared before. Octun believed the reports of Cuere in Aspharia but not those about the ocean. Cuere did not seem the type. While his curiosity spurred his desire to seek out the unknown, his physical ability caused Octun serious doubt about any seafaring days. Soon after his return, Cuere started studying the Barren Lands. How he got King Saroth to give him passage remained a true mystery.

Despite his doubt, Octun acknowledged that Lord Cuere brought this boy and other curious youths into the temple. And there were the magic artifacts. By them, Cuere's power grew stronger over time. The entire matter stuck like a fishbone is Octun's throat. No matter how hard he coughed, no matter what remedy he tried, he could not dislodge the bone.

Everything Cuere did conflicted with generations of religious teaching. The children were no exception. Only the King, Prince Seth, and Lord Cuere knew the full story.

Octun crossed his arms over his chest and rubbed his chin with his right thumb and index finger. He certainly did not know anything about their purpose or how these strangers were to help with the war.

This lad and the young girl resembled one another. Their features were similar and possibly had a family resemblance; only, Ulthea did not look so much like a frog. Octun attributed their resemblance to two possibilities: no one had seen their kind before, so they all may look alike to the Obenite, or they were related. He watched over the boy's rambling and moaning for three days. In his delirious mumbling, Octun noticed that the girl's language and this boy's language sounded similar. A few times the boy muttered something that sounded like Ulthea. Then, just moments ago, that Fordham name came up again.

CHAPTER 7
So I'm Not Dead

Ictheos ate everything, even the twig-like garnish beside his bread. He ignored the large spoons, like the one the Spirit Men used, and drank from the bowl. Finished, he belched with loud satisfaction.

He watched as the man named Octun removed a strange object that hung from inside his belt. He placed it on the tray. The object looked like a round stick. It was about the thickness of two of his fingers and about four times as long. He watched nervously as Octun pressed four round spots of the shaft. The thing buzzed like a large bug flying by his ear. It morphed into a narrow goblet with a long stem that looked more flower blossom than something from which to drink.

Nothing the shaman ever did matched this, he thought.

Ictheos did not see him pour anything in it, yet Octun drank from the cup and placed it back on the tray. When Octun reached for Ictheos' hands, Ictheos withdrew.

Octun moved more slowly and determinedly and took both Ictheos' hands. He put them gently on the cup. Though Octun assisted him, the cup felt three times heavier than its size suggested. Instead of the cold of metal, it felt as warm as Octun's hands. It was flawless, not a nick, a chip, or worn spot, just a perfectly smooth, perfectly comforting surface. He sipped the liquid from the cup. Octun kept him from finishing it off.

Ictheos did not understand Octun's words. They weren't spoken to him anyway. Octun looked directly at the cup. The instant after he stopped talking, the cup glowed softly and hummed faintly.

The aftertaste of the drink turned from honey sweet to disgustingly bitter. It lingered in his mouth.

Octun placed both their hands back on the cup and explained.

"I don't know much of your language. This," Octun nodded toward the cup, "helps us overcome the differences in our languages."

"No you are not dead, far from it. You are as alive as I am."

Ictheos drew his head back to get a better look at Octun's lips. They did not match the words he heard. Octun seemed to speak two languages at once, but he understood what he said despite the garbled mess of words.

"I am sure that I am alive and not a spirit. And if I know that I am alive, then I can vouch for your well being," replied Octun matter-of-factly.

"Then where am I?" asked Ictheos looking around.

Octun put one hand on Ictheos' shoulder to regain his

attention, then returned his hand to the cup.

"Don't struggle against the talisman. We call it the Strangers' Cup. It helps us to speak freely without confusion. It leaves a permanent understanding of the words we speak. If used enough, we will eventually remember how to speak each other's language. I know you have many questions, and I will do my best to answer most of them. Those I don't will be answered in due time."

Ictheos hesitated, then, asked again, "If I am not dead, then where am I?"

He heard himself speaking, but his words were not the ones he spoke. Strangely, his throat felt much better. His body aches subsided.

"Just relax. As long as you know what you are saying,
everything will be fine. You are in a land that we all assume is far away from your own. Our land is called Obenin, named after our forefather who founded it. Amrion Vymeriqus brought you here. He is an archaeologist and mystic."

"Arko...?" questioned Ictheos.

"One who studies the remains of dead people and animals," returned Octun.

Ictheos shivered. Already, he wanted nothing to do with this. Magic and the dead did not make a very good mix. If he was not dead, he wanted to go home. A veil of sadness lowered over his body. He cried.

Keeper Octun patted him on the head. Ictheos sniffled and looked up. He found himself on his feet. Octun held him until he found his balance.

"You must move around," Octun said, "it will help you regain your strength."

Ictheos felt weak and helpless. While he was not big, he never considered himself a weakling. His legs always carried him swiftly through the rainforest faster than anyone else. He carried more than his share of game, too. Now, he wanted to wail loudly and shamelessly. The spirit of strength projecting from Octun's huge body scared him and comforted him at the same time. He dammed his tears and dried his eyes with his sleeves.

"Where are you from?"

"From?" questioned Ictheos. No one ever asked that before. The Spirit Men knew his village. The tribes with which they traded knew his village. He thought hard for a moment and then with an unsure look answered, "Lompolasona."

Ictheos saw the recognition and surprise in Octun's eyes. "You know Lompolasona?"

"Do you have a family?" asked Octun.

"Yes," answered Ictheos. The dammed up tears broke free, flooding his cheeks.

"My mother's name is Blaia and my father's name is Shunie. I had a sister...."

Ictheos froze. He regretted the words.

"I *have* a sister, her name is Ulthea," he continued. The tears flowed harder. "The heavens took her, but I have vowed to bring her back and now I am lost too."

"Tell me," asked Octun curiously, "what is your name?

He sniffled, "Ictheos."

Ictheos rambled on about the day Ulthea disappeared. The tears kept coming. Nothing stopped them. Octun steadied him as they walked around the room. Ictheos talked and cried until he became hoarse. He gestured back to the bed and flopped onto it. The walk tired him out but his mind cleared a little. He picked up a cup from the tray.

"Drink all of it," instructed Octun.

Ictheos, lifted the cup cautiously and looked at it contents. He took a small sip, expecting it to turn bitter. It tasted a little like his mother's boiled root medicine but not too bad. He drank thirstily.

"I will leave you to rest now. You must regain your strength quickly," Octun announced. Octun's tone of voice made him feel that neither sleep nor rest was an option.

Ictheos watched Octun close the door behind him. A thousand questions rushed into his mind, questions that he should have asked. How could he rest? All this overwhelmed him in what seemed like one day. His head ached. A sluggish unnatural drowsiness crept into his mind. He turned onto his back. A face looked down at him. The painting on the ceiling looked so real. In comparison to his bare and drab surroundings, it was vivid with color. It covered the portion of ceiling directly above his bed. The saintly face smiled down at him as if looking down from heaven. Maybe Octun meant the painting to comfort whoever slept in the bed. Ictheos rolled onto his side to keep from looking at it. He believed the painting would keep him awake. It didn't.

CHAPTER 8
The Reunion

His legs felt like stone and they ached. Rubbing them did not help much. How long did Keeper Octun say he had been here? Or, did he mention it?

"Three or four days, maybe," he reckoned.

Looking up at the painting on the ceiling, he continued kneading his muscles. The painting was so real, nothing like his own people painted. The Spirit Men had something similar. Even they did not measure up to this. A thick black beard covered a face as round as the river stones that he liked to skip over the water. Despite his saintly looks, a trace of anger affected his features when looked at in a certain way. Probing eyes followed him no matter how he moved.

He prepared himself for Keeper Octun's return. There were questions he needed answered. The fall from the cliff did not kill him. If he was not dead, then maybe he was in the same place as Ulthea.

Furious with himself, he accepted and repented of the self-pity that kept him from thinking of Ulthea. He thought more clearly now. This Amrion brought him here. Maybe he brought her as well.

He had made a mighty vow. Faced with this mountain of a man, his vow seemed a wisp of smoke rising from a doused campfire.

"You can't eat smoke," he whispered.

How could he ask Keeper Octun about Ulthea? The question might offend him if he had something to hide. The nice treatment might stop. The trouble in the Keeper's eyes may just as well be restrained viciousness.

The lock clanked. Keeper Octun entered the room. Ictheos noticed he had changed clothes. Instead of the thick shirt and loose fitting breeches, he now wore a bone-colored woolen robe that dragged the floor.

Before speaking, Keeper Octun activated the Stranger's Cup. It impressed Ictheos just as much as the first time. Hesitantly, he took a sip. Keeper Octun's hands engulfed his own. He put the cup to his lips and took a swallow.

"How did you sleep?" Octun asked.

"Good," returned Ictheos simply.

"Put these on." Octun placed a robe and boots that closely matched his on the bed.

He put them on. The robe warmed him but scratched the back of his neck.

Octun motioned toward the door.

"Where are we going?"

"For a walk. You must move around."

He waited for Keeper Octun to help him. When he did not, Ictheos tried on his own. Finding balance, he took an unsteady step, then another. His sore legs stiffened but he kept going, constantly looking at Keeper Octun for help.

"Our walk is not far. If you tire, just say so and we will rest."

As they walked over the threshold, a heavy spirit lifted off Ictheos. He was glad to leave his room. The long corridor stretched forever. The same glowing balls that lit his room lined the corridor. Keeper Octun talked to two men who stood by the door. When he finished, they snapped their heels together and looked forward. Keeper Octun acknowledged them with a simple nod. Ictheos got the impression the title of Keeper meant more than watching over a place to worship.

The surroundings awed Ictheos. He looked up, following one of many huge arches reaching out of sight in to darkness. He didn't know whether it was late evening or early morning. Statues stood on each side here and there; every few paces he passed another figure. With solemn expressions chiseled upon their faces, Ictheos believed they represented some virtue.

Their virtue gave him no comfort. Ictheos grew afraid and walked closer to Keeper Octun, causing him to stumble. Keeper Octun turned him with one hand. He held the Stranger's Cup between them. Ictheos touched it.

"Don't be afraid," Octun directed. "These statues are the actual likenesses of heroes of Obenin, those who carry the tenets in their hearts and live by them. Look there." Octun pointed.

Ictheos looked over at the figure of a man lying on his back on top of a huge stone box.

Octun put his hand upon Ictheos' back to guide him over to the coffin. He resisted. He did not want to go near the thing.

"It will not hurt you. It is only stone."

He looked down at the man's effigy as Octun explained, "This is the death effigy of Lord Materu."

He looked up at Octun blankly.

"At his death, a mask was made of his face."

Ictheos shivered.

"In the year 42 of the Obenite calendar, Lord Materu reasoned that the best way to stop the spread of a dreadful plague that ravaged our country was to clean up the unsanitary conditions. Because of him, channels, aqueducts, and refuse pits help keep our cities clean. There have been no widespread reports of the plague within our borders since Lord Materu's discovery."

"How long ago was that?" questioned Ictheos.

"Over three hundred years."

Soon after they resumed their walk, Ictheos complained that he was tired and they sat on one of the benches placed sparsely along the walls of the corridor.

"This is a frightening place!" Ictheos said aloud without thinking.

"Some might think it so," confessed Octun.

"It's just so dark and cold and dead people are buried here. I wouldn't want to live here."

He thought over his own words. He was living here, temporarily anyway. He would not rest well tonight surrounded by all these dead people.

"Yes," explained Octun, "but this is our history. The people in this temple, living or dead, are those who have proven themselves valorous or done great deeds of compassion for the kingdom. Some are soldiers, who in the face of certain death, held their ground so that the tide of battle turned, or lords who showed mercy to those who lived upon their land. Others are our best scholars or even common people who have done willingly what others could not be paid to do.

"We look upon all of them as examples of the epitome of our faith. They worshipped Obenin, our god, and they lived by his tenets. Some say there are those who paid their way in. I can truly say that since I have been placed here as Keeper, not a single coin has been accepted to assure anyone's burial in Obenin's Temple."

Octun declared the latter with such strength and sincerity that Ictheos believed him without question.

"What did you do to get here?"

Octun raised a brow. The response did not come as quickly as Ictheos expected.

"Well, that is a long story and a troublesome one at that."

Ictheos waited for him to continue. Instead, Octun stood and motioned for them to continue their walk.

Ictheos' legs were not as sore but he was tired. They came to a door. He hoped that whatever was behind it was their destination and that there would be a place for him to take a long nap.

Keeper Octun spoke to the two men in plain brown robes standing beside the door. They showed the same air of confidence as Octun. Ictheos noticed the respect in their eyes, almost admiration, as they listened to Octun's instructions.

As Octun spoke, they simply nodded their heads and replied with an enthusiastic, "Yessir."

Turning back to him, Octun announced, "We are here."

Then, he opened the door and let it swing wide.

Ictheos recognized the place as some sort of chapel, similar, but much more spectacular than the one of wood and brush that the Spirit Men built in his village. A tall, thin, owlish looking man stood before a large window of colored glass that almost took up the entire wall. Ictheos saw daylight. He felt lighter.

He studied the window. Colored glass made several pictures of soldiers riding large animals.

The man stopped talking and looked up at them. Three children to whom the man spoke turned and looked at him. Their expression struck him as unusual. Their eagerness seemed detached and no zest reflected in their eyes.

Ictheos' heart quickened. His thoughts raced. The girl sitting in the middle, she looked like Ulthea. Her hair looked prettier, neater and straighter. She looked more yellow, as if she had not seen the sun in months. The thing she wore, the Spirit Men called it a dress.

"Ulthea!" he shouted. She was here all this time.

****

The boy stunned Ulthea. He knew her name but she did not remember him. Yet, she realized that she should know him.

His name, his name, I am supposed to know it, she concentrated in thought.

She focused hard, closing her eyes, digging and digging until she uncovered one word.

"Ictheos?" she whispered.

Her face went flush with frustration. She brought her hands up to her mouth.

"Ictheos," she whispered again.

The distant memory surged and sprung alive.

With joy, she screamed, "Ictheos!"

Suppressed memories flooded her mind. Another world, another time or maybe a vivid dream, something did not measure up. She should not be here. She did not want to be here but something or someone made her want to. She began to weep and her body shook. Even now, she felt herself slipping back, starting to question why she felt the need to cry.

Ictheos attempted to rush toward her but stumbled. Octun caught him by the arm and kept him from falling face first unto the stone floor. He helped Ictheos to Ulthea. She stood sobbing in joy, moaning his name over and over again. Consciously, Ulthea's mind and feelings clashed. She fought desperately to reach the edge of the mental quicksand.

"Ictheos my twin bother... Shunie, my father... Blaia, my mother... Where is Brother Fordham? Can he help us?"

In the middle of her fight, an almost audible voice comforted her, reminding her of the tenets and obedience to Obenin.

With Ictheos' arms around her, she wept for a long time, sobbing a spot in his robe. Her memories seemed to have lost their value. Though the voice told her that her current life was more important, she wanted out. With each advance, something pushed her back to the middle of the quicksand. Her mind dipped below the surface into the darkness. She locked her fingers together, hoping that

Ictheos could help her, hoping that he could pull her up and out because there was no way she could save herself.

CHAPTER 9
Jared of Yan-Free

Jared hardly remembered that he came through Oracle first. He remembered Cuere looking into his eyes, blowing in his ear, snapping his fingers and poking him. He did this several times a day. One day Cuere was gone. Since then, Jared's daily routine consisted of reading, praying, lectures, more praying and the curious presence of Octun. He never really thought of anything else until this moment.

Like a disembodied spirit not sure of whom to haunt, the memory of his wedding day drifted into his thoughts. He recognized this memory as if it were the ghost of a dear friend. The hovering ghost beckoned him to follow.

Jared married on his fifteenth birthday in the Yan Free Territory. The wedding was lovely but not as lovely as Lady Jacosta, his arranged bride. Both he and Jacosta were victims of the hope of one man, Yan Usamdi. Centuries ago, he sought to restore the relationship between the kingdoms of Aspharia and Obenin. So far, this hope succumbed to the greed of men. No one he knew believed that true peace would ever return between these kingdoms. Yet, the island and the marriages kept going.

Anxious to get the honeymoon started, he pulled Jacosta away from the wedding ball immediately after it started. Many of his guests turned up their noses and considered him rude because he left the ball before all the acknowledgments and traditional presentations were complete. His mother-in-law got so upset that she felt faint. His father-in-law just stared at him sternly, watching his every turn. Even as they rode away in the carriage, he felt the man staring at him. Evidently, knowing for years this day would come did not help Jacosta's father with the matter.

When the newlyweds arrived at the cottage and entered their bedroom, his valet excused himself in embarrassment.

But, what had his womanizing tutor, Kymes, said. "Take it slow, don't ravish her, make her feel confident that you know what you are doing. Woo her. Win her prize so that she gives freely, willingly. Though by custom she is yours, don't take, wait for her to give and she will be truly yours for life. Sadly, you are going to waste such good advice upon a wife. Why don't you practice on some other women first?"

This latter, Jared refused, at least to the point of sex anyway.

Jared removed his hand from her trembling thigh. He rang twice, the signal for the butler, who came all too soon, as if he might have been listening at the door. The butler returned with wine, sweets, and fruit. Afterwards, Jared dismissed all the servants from the grounds and ordered the valet to put them up somewhere in the village nearby.

He unbuttoned Jacosta's dress and loosened her corset. She shied away at first, but thanked him wholeheartedly as she took a freeing breath.

They talked for a long time, which took a great deal of effort on Jared's part. They talked about the wedding and their mothers' tears. He waited and waited until he saw the fear fall from her eyes. Then he knew that it was all right for him to make a move.

He stroked her arm again as he had been doing infrequently for the past hour. She sensed something different in his touch and shot him a glance. He hoped that she would have drunk more wine, but she hardly touched it. Most of her clothes were off and that was something. Her bare arms seemed to beckon for his kisses. He caressed her shoulder softly. Her breaths became shallow. Slowly, he moved down her arm and grasped her hand, brought it to his lips and kissed it. Then he gave a deep sniff and let it out slowly and with savor as if the smell of her hand gave him pure bliss.

"Ah, what are these?"

"Hands," she panted, "what a strange question to ask."

"No, not hands, but fragrant blossoms whose tender petals touch me and burn fire into my heart."

He kissed her forearms and shoulders. "And these?" he asked.

"Arms?" her response a mere wisp of air between drying lips.

"Yes, but they are so warm and loving, soft and tender, too precious to embrace such an unworthy soul as I."

He kissed the lace garment that covered her thighs. "And all these belong to such a stunningly beautiful woman, who must be the high princess unawares. I know that suitors must have come from the ends of the world, through many dire perils to catch the slightest glimpse of you. Nevertheless, you were destined for me.

"Now, my wife, don't fear. If you wish, let the loving tide of my kisses wash away the apprehension of your innocent heart and my arms still the shivers of the unknown. Then, my cherished rose, no love shall equal ours." He held her closely, tightly, without caressing trying to let her know what he wanted but did not demand anything. Sincerely, he wanted the choice to be hers.

It worked just as his tutor said it would. Jacosta was all kissing lips and groping hands. Desire drove away her fear. She rolled on top of him. Her legs locked around his as she entangled herself in him.

She had received advice too. Her words fell sweetly to a receiving heart. "From a child I have loved you. Though we did not see much of each other, I loved you. I loved your ways. I loved your arrogance towards my father. I loved the smell of you, everything."

Then there was pain. At first, he thought Jacosta had grabbed him too hard. Then he felt her slipping away. Jacosta's loving arm-lock around him broke. Cold death-like shrouds replaced her hot body. After that, everything went black.

Jared stood up. He looked at Parmos, the wild looking, blond lad sitting next to him. He expected Parmos to join him. Instead, Parmos turned away and folded his arms.

"Chancellor," Keeper Octun motioned.

As Chancellor Levid moved to intervene, Jared turned walked to the wall and then stopped.

Chancellor Levid Beine, the foremost historian from the King's Academy of Cultural Affairs, spoke to him with concern. The Chancellor turned him around. Jared reacted to the Chancellor's outstretched arms and let himself be herded like lamb into a corral.

"Master Jared, calm down," Levid guided, his tone refined and confident from many years of travel and study.

To Octun, Levid said, "You found out they were twin brother and sister, didn't you, Keeper? So, you brought them here just to see the reaction. You could have warned me you were coming. Do you think it will hinder our mission?"

Octun rubbed his chin. The lines of worry straightened minutely.

"We shall see. I will report this and wait for King Saroth's instructions."

"I don't think," Levid continued, "that we should finish lecture today and, if you don't have any objections, I will let them retire to their quarters."

"Do as you wish Chancellor. I will escort Ulthea and Ictheos, let them spend some time together."

"But . . ." the lecturer started to object. Instead, he ushered Jared and Parmos away.

Jared looked back at Ulthea and Ictheos still embracing. He managed a weak smile.

CHAPTER 10
The Kingdom and the Primary Temple

Finally, Octun separated Ulthea and Ictheos. He directed them out of the chapel.

Ulthea looked up at him, her eyes still watery. "Keeper Octun, I am so grateful that you brought Ictheos to me. He can help us."

Ictheos looked at Octun, then at Ulthea. He kept silent. For one thing, he did not understand her. He recognized that she spoke the same language as Keeper Octun just as well as she spoke her native language. Seeing his confusion, Ulthea switched back and forth, translating. They no longer needed the Stranger's Cup.

"Can I show him the sanctuary, Sir?" asked Ulthea.

"That would be fine, if he is not too tired."

Ulthea asked him.

Truthfully, he was exhausted, but he was not about to let Ulthea out of his sight for fear of losing her again.

"I am not tired," he lied.

Octun looked at Ictheos and sent for a rolling chair. The chair, shaped like a small cart with handles in the back, smelled of old wet wood. He fought off his fatigue as Octun pushed him. In the morning, he would pay. The elation of spending time with Ulthea was well worth every exhausting second.

With his body relaxed, his mind began to wonder about the temple.

"This is such a sad place. Not like the forest which is alive and open... this is a place for the dead," Ictheos stated.

"Don't say that, Ictheos," objected Ulthea. "The Primary Temple is very important to our faith. Each Obenite is required to visit the temple during the summer solstice to stay in good faith. Isn't that right Keeper Octun?"

"Yes," Keeper Octun replied.

He wished that he would go away and let them alone. When they occasionally stopped to look at something, he walked around them like a shadow trying to find which way the light cast and always within earshot.

They approached a door where another pair of men stood. Only these were visibly armed to the teeth. Both had swords on their belts and daggers strapped to their boots. They wore helmets and chain mail similar to the secular explorers of the rainforest.

"Who are they?" Ictheos asked.

"The temple guards, they help Keeper Octun and take part in various ceremonies," answered Ulthea.

They didn't look ceremonial to him.

Once Keeper Octun pushed Ictheos over the threshold of the door, they stepped down onto the top landing. From there, steps led into a large open area. Ictheos held to the chair as it bumped down the steps.

Ulthea called it the People's Courtyard. The area was several times larger than his entire village.

Far to their left, a gate with thick iron bars blocked the entrance. A gigantic wooden gate stood to his right. Four stone horsemen towered before the gate facing away from the temple. Ulthea explained that the horsemen symbolized the four vigils of the faithful. These vigils also served as the first four tenets of Obenin.

Ulthea instructed, "The first horseman wears the cowl of a lion. The lion's front claws drapes over his shoulders. He symbolizes tenacity in battle. The second horseman carries an eagle on his arm for swift lethality. The third horseman carries the hammer to smash all who stand in the way of Obenin. The fourth horseman holds a round shield that blocks his face. The shield bares a blazing sun representing the eternity of Obenin.

As they approached the gate, he saw that, if they were open, about fifty people walking shoulder to shoulder could enter. However, Octun unlocked and opened a smaller door within the gate.

When they entered the sanctuary, it astounded Ictheos.

"Beautiful isn't it?" complimented Ulthea with a reverent hush.

He choked on the words, "Oh!"

Ictheos remembered the Spirit Men spoke of such places, but his imagination was not large enough to come even close to picturing this. He could see why they had walked in a straight line for so long. His room, the corridor, and the small chapel were built along the walls of this huge sanctuary.

"We could have come through one of the side doors but this view is the most breath-taking."

"It is so big. I never knew that something manmade could be so big."

"The sanctuary has room for over a thousand worshippers to kneel and pray," Ulthea stated.

Blue and white slabs of highly polished marble covered the floor. Pillars of black marble, decorated with bands of gold from top to bottom, supported the ceiling. Large brilliant paintings like the one in his room covered the ceiling. Those paled in comparison to these. In every painting men fought with fierce determination upon their faces.

On two sides of each pillars, more glowing balls sat in their holders.

"Do these things shine all of the time?" asked Ictheos.

"No, the Chargers of the Light keep them shining," answered Ulthea.

"I never see anyone doing anything to them," retorted Ictheos.

"You aren't supposed to," she sounded as if he should know.

"The Chargers are those seeking the priesthood, it is part of their duty," she continued.

Along the walls were statues of men with swords and shields facing away from the altar.

As they approached the altar, Ulthea pointed to several oblong white stones inlaid and flush with the surface of the marble, "These are the grave stones of Father Obenin's sons."

Dread filled Ictheos at the thought of rolling over dead bodies.

"Tell me about this Obenin," Ictheos insisted.

He heard that name in almost every sentence. Impatient, he wanted to know more.

"Obenin is not just the name of our kingdom, it is the name of our god. The founder of our kingdom transformed himself to godhood just before the death of his temporal body. His true followers are called Obenite."

"Our god?" Ictheos snapped.

Not only did he object to what she said, but how she said it. Her voice revealed sincere conviction. She believed wholeheartedly.

"What about our mother and father?"

Ulthea did not reply.

Octun started to speak.

Just as he did, Ulthea pointed. "Look at those paintings on either side of the altar. Keeper Octun says it's a picture of the temple... what it looks like from the outside. Stay here and watch the sun shine over it."

As she walked, off Ictheos thought, *"What does she mean 'Keeper Octun says?' Hasn't she seen the outside for herself?"*

Ulthea picked up a wooden mallet and beat a certain place on the frame of the huge painting. Slowly, the sun began to glow and a wave of life seemed to sweep across the entire painting. The sun still shined more brilliantly than the rest of the painting.

Ulthea hurried back to his side to explain, "It's the glows." She pointed to the spheres of light. "They can be cut into small pieces and then put through a process of cleaning and grinding into dust. If it's done correctly, they will still glow."

"Yes it is beautiful, but not as beautiful as the sunrise at home," complained Ictheos.

"Look back there," directed Octun.

Ictheos ignored him, pointing forward instead. "What is behind the gate down there?"

"That is the Resting Place of Obenin's temporal body. Once a year a few worthy people are selected to walk beyond the gate and behold the face of Obenin," Ulthea beamed.

"What do you mean by worthy?"

"You will find out soon enough," injected Octun.

Octun's tone signified that he was ending Ictheos' company with Ulthea.

He rushed to ask, "Are you okay? Have they treated you well?"

"Why, yes. I have never even felt a pang of hunger. Both Keeper Octun and Chancellor Levid have always been here to teach me things."

"But what about the things that we were taught at home?"

Ulthea hesitated. She scratched her head, then urged, "But these things are more important. You will understand soon."

She hugged him. He noticed she smelled differently. She no longer smelled of the rainforest. An unnatural perfume replaced her natural musk. Her hug lacked any sisterly affection.

"What has come over her? It seems she has forsaken everything we know," he questioned silently.

He beckoned her closer.

"We have to talk later, alone," he whispered.

"It's getting toward supper," interrupted Octun. "We are leaving now."

Back in his room, Ictheos nibbled his food. Extremely tired, he fought to keep aware and make plans of their escape. Ulthea did not act like herself. He figured that a spell imprisoned her heart. A burden seemed to weigh heavily upon her shoulders too.

"Octun and Levid are bad men," he reasoned.

After all, if they aren't, why was he in this room eating by himself? Why couldn't he have supper with Ulthea?

"I will steal some food and hide it, just enough to get far away so that I can have time to find our own."

He took a final sip of the sweet-tasting water.

"Somehow, I will find the man that brought us here, Amrion, that's what Octun called him, and make him send us back."

As he sat planning their escape, he became drowsy and fell asleep in his food.

The entire morning wasted away in a fog. Ictheos remembered someone washing him. He remembered eating. The inside of his head buzzed. Every now and then, a sharp pain shot from temple to temple. And what had he been thinking before falling asleep? He couldn't remember. It didn't matter though. Nothing about yesterday mattered.

"Wait, I was thinking about escaping, going home... home." His previous thoughts seemed far removed.

In the same chapel in which he met Ulthea the previous day, he sat listening to Chancellor Levid's lecture. Keeper Octun looked on.

"Ulthea..., she looks so different. The same as yesterday... so different than when we were... we were..."

Ictheos shook his head violently, trying to throw off what ever covered his mind, making him accept the here and now, urging him to forget everything he thought important. He closed his eyes and looked hard for the determination that he felt so strongly only yesterday.

Chancellor Levid stopped lecturing. "Master Ictheos, are you alright? Ictheos... Ictheos?"

Keeper Octun arose and started to approach.

Ictheos reached deep within himself. There he found all the fight that he possessed drowning in the sweet-tasting water he drank the night before. He heard a voice within telling him to give in. He gathered all the shreds of defiance left in his heart.

Grabbing Ulthea's hand, he rose to his feet.

"We want to go home," he whimpered.

The others looked at them and then at their abductors.

Octun acknowledged Ictheos with a bow. Ictheos did not know why. He took it as a sign of respect.

"We want to go home," Ictheos declared much more strongly.

"I am very sorry," apologized Chancellor Levid, "but this is your home now."

Levid flashed an angry glance at Keeper Octun, who still said nothing.

"Where will you go?" Levid persuaded. "Where is home from here? I, for sure, do not know."

"We will find a way to get home!" shouted Ictheos, mentally moving himself to the end of their world and the beginning of his.

Ulthea wept, but he figured, "She will be fine when I get her out of this place."

Ictheos started down the aisle half leading, half dragging Ulthea.

"Wait," shouted Chancellor Levid. "You have no idea where you are going. But more important, we need you."

Ictheos had no idea what Chancellor Levid meant by needing them and it did not matter.

"I don't care. All I care about is that my mother and father are looking for me and crying because I am lost, too. They will be very happy to see us back again!" His sweet rage satisfied him.

He reached to open the door. Suddenly, a finger's width from his nose, the door burst open. Two guards towered over him, their swords drawn. Ictheos froze. Surely, his death met him at this moment.

Ulthea and Ictheos stunned the guards too. Ictheos pulled Ulthea close to him. He wrapped him arms around her and put his back to the guards as if it protected her from the swords. When nothing happened, he chanced a look over his shoulder.

The guards looked nervously at Octun.

"We heard shouting and thought someone breached the guard," one of the guards apologized.

Keeper Octun lifted his hand understandingly. They withdrew.

Chancellor Levid came to Ictheos and Ulthea and ushered them back to their seats, "I am so sorry that happened. They thought that someone was trying to harm you. See how much we care for you. See how much we need you."

"Why didn't you do something?" Levid scolded Octun.

"He inspires me, even if it is in vain," chuckled Octun.

Ictheos did not eat anything the rest of the day. He was determined to break whatever witchcraft threatened his mind. Despite his determination, he grew tired of fighting the powerful urge to give up. He gritted his teeth and tried to hold on to thoughts of home. Something unknown wrestled against his will. When his will waned, he found it again. Each time he fought, he lost ground. His soul drained a little more of all he held dear and he could do nothing to stop it. Before morning, his will caved in. Awake, his empty and idle mind waited for someone to fill it again.

One of the knobs on his headboard clicked. He sat up and looked at it. The knob flashed a soft light in his eyes several times. He got back under the covers and fell into a deep sleep.

CHAPTER 11
Octun's Faith

Octun climbed the stairs to the top of temple's sixth tower. He often came to this particular tower to look beyond the grounds of the temple. From here, he watched over the village of Ethenia, which lay southwardly and nestled cozily in **the** valley below. A chilly autumn wind bit his ears, reminding him that he still lived.

In the rising sun, every shade of orange and yellow filled the valley below. With little rainfall since Ictheos' arrival, the River Edge flowed below its normal level. If the drought persisted, ships would not be able to navigate the river. He considered the spring thaw, too. Octun believed that melting snow symbolized beginning anew and the awakening of dormant ideals.

He turned northwesterly, surveying the temple grounds. He heard the trumpet calls for second muster echo from out past the mall. Barely visible beyond the trees, the cadre gathered the conscripts to stand for inspection by the training commandant.

About two hundred conscripts received training at the temple. Many wealthy men attempted to bribe or politically bully Octun to accept their sons for training. He reserved the grounds of the temple for the poor who wanted to serve and bring honor to the kingdom. Otherwise, they did not get a chance to receive superior training that did not consist of deadly brutality.

Octun taught his men to fight without it. Not only did he teach them to fight well, he taught them perseverance. Despite their feelings and in spite of their pain, he made them fight like there was no tomorrow, because there truly might not be. Even those who could not endure his training had certain grueling tasks to accomplish before discharge. Those few men, who broke mentally, managed to understand that the only way out was to do exactly as they were told. Octun described his training as making a conscript realize that death could be swift or agonizingly slow without actually killing a soldier to prove the point.

Glorious news of his men's feats returned almost daily. He felt good about that. Unfortunately, that was about the only good news concerning the war.

The kingdom busied itself preparing for the pending invasion. Bands of Obenite raiders arrayed themselves, terrorizing and hindering their enemy's movements along the treacherous paths in the Abringian Mountains. In reality, only the threat of winter in the mountain peaks kept the armies of the Benomian Alliance from flowing down from the mountains into their land.

The entire country prepared to repel the invasion.

Unless Obenin provided a miracle, an invasion followed in the spring. For now, the enemy held steadfast and would build their forces throughout the winter. Every man and Obenite male child able to hold a sword dreaded the following spring. King Saroth ordered the preparation and training. Mere children learned swordplay in the morning, archery for lunch and scriptures in the afternoon.

"And here I am, a decorated hero stuck in a highly honored but benign post, working on this crazy plan I know only in part."

The post of High Priest and Keeper of Obenin's Primary Temple carried prestige. Only the most faithful and most valorous warrior-priest earned the appointment, which usually lasted for life. The royal family insured that all the Keepers' needs were met. Octun possessed more than he could possibly use in two lifetimes. Why did happiness avoid him? For one, he did not find the fulfillment he expected from the posting.

He took the vow of priesthood just before joining the army. The dream of Keeper of Obenin's Temple seemed a mere wistful dream at that time. He expected a shrine tender or minor temple at the most. Yet, his wildest dream happened, the apex of the priesthood -- not just Keeper of the Temple but Keeper of the Obenin's Primary Temple. This day, four years ago, he became the high priest of the most powerful kingdom of the known world. Now, he regretted accepting the appointment.

"Happy anniversary to me." He kicked the wall with his boot.

Taking a long breath, he held it in for a second and let it out.

He took in a deeper one and let it out reciting, "Harness your anger. Do not surrender to it. Mold it into a force of will and determination. So says the twelfth tenet."

Octun prepared for prayer and meditation. He kneeled, sat back on his heels, and closed his eyes. The answer resided not within himself but in Obenin's will. Part of his meditation ritual was to clear the mind of contentious thoughts and find a peaceful center.

As Cuere predicted, four adolescents appeared. The potions and devices Cuere left with Octun bent the adolescents' wills in any direction Cuere desired. They possessed unalterable obeisance to the king and to Obenin.

The latent power that the adolescents possessed was not for him to know. Yet, why was it necessary to use mysticism to convert anyone to believe in Obenin? As high priest, this question fell within his rights to seek an answer. No sacred teaching from any era even hinted of such an assertion. Some text even advised the faithful to avoid the use of magic. Yet, the king immersed himself in it.

The dilemma tore at Octun because it railed against the tenets and other sacred writing.

That should not happen, he thought. *The king's actions and the tenets should go together like hand in glove.*

Lately, he found no solace in the teachings of his faith. Though he understood them, lived by them, fought by them and taught others, his meditations on them offered no comfort today, either. The peaceful center avoided him.

"I must have missed something? The answer must be there, somewhere in the tenets or the other writings. I must endure this test of faith."

He tried to relax, to clear his mind and let inspiration from above give him resolve. Instead, the stern face he wore like a mask to ward off doubt and inefficiency transformed into something worse. The corners of his wide mouth drooped. He shut his eyes so tightly that he saw spots of light swimming in the darkness.

Octun tried another religious practice. He stirred his anger. He focused the anger on himself. He needed to use his anger to purify his thoughts, to drive out doubt and questions he did not want to ask himself, let alone the King's Council. He scolded himself, "The king chose you out of hundreds for this appointment. It is one of the greatest honors attainable by someone not of royal blood. That is your sworn duty. Why do you complain about everything like a self-interested bureaucrat?"

He clenched his fists and quenched the yell that burned inside. He breathed deeply. The cool air brought more doubt to his rationalizations. He fought it off.

"Are you not questioning the divine wisdom of the Grand Monarch and all his court? Are you so conceited that you know more than they do? You are a warrior high priest, a servant of the King who protects the faith of the people."

He put his hands on his thighs and rocked back and forth in a higher form of prayer. His motions became extreme, going from sitting on his heels to straight up, all the pressure on his knees. Finally, he just got up and left the tower, inflamed with frustration. His meditations on the tenets seemed more a hindrance than a help.

He stormed down the winding stairs and slammed the door. The guard, whom Octun previously ordered down from the tower, snapped to attention.

"Return to your post," Octun ordered.

The guard threw the door open and sprinted up the stairs.

The Keeper needed something to change his mood. He needed to hit something, hard.

Starting away, he heard someone coming. The Captain of the Guard, Horep, rushed toward him.

"Colonel Octun," he called.

Colonel sounded so much better than Keeper did.

The distance between him and the captain was as good an excuse as any to vent his stress.

"What do you want?" Octun boomed.

Horep broke his stride approaching Octun more slowly and a little warily. "Sir Brock Stannick is here to see you, sir.

Octun noted the look on Horep's face. He reminded Octun of a calf. His face, unusually long and innocent, flicked as if a fly had landed on his cheek. His expression revealed what he chose not to speak, "Why did you yell at me?"

"Sir Stannick. Are you sure?" Octun drilled.

"Yessir. The perimeter guard questioned him and checked his papers. He is still rather angry." Charge

Horep enjoyed the moment. "Besides, I smelled the stench the moment he entered the gate."

Octun's mood lifted. He didn't like Stannick, either. This man never came to worship. He always showed up for more than the stated reason. He hoped that Stannick's security check was completely unpleasant.

"He shouldn't be angry," objected Octun. "The Charge of Grand Palace Security should understand quite well the need for vigilance and thoroughness."

That was a good excuse. By it, he let Horep know that whatever retribution Stannick tried to dish out would never amount to anything.

"Yessir. After he has washed and warmed up, he will be ready to brief you on orders from the King."

"Very well, tell him to meet me in my study."

"Meet you, Sir, but... Yessir," Horep cut his comment short.

"And Charge Horep...."

"Yessir?"

"Have you told Chancellor Levid?"

"No, sir."

"I'll tell him," commented Octun, not giving the customary head nod to dismiss his subordinate.

Charge Horep snapped to attention and waited for acknowledgement. When Octun did nothing, he started to turn away then stopped.

Taking advantage of their long association, he asked, "Are you all right, sir?"

Octun shifted uncomfortably and put his hands into his robe sleeves, monk-like. "What do you mean?"

"It just seems that you are troubled, sir," Horep said, growing uncomfortable with Octun's response.

Octun pulled the hood of his robe over his head shadowing his eyes and walked off leaving Charge Horep with his thoughts.

He felt Horep watching him. He walked faster, putting some distance between the two of them. With each passing month, the corridor seemed longer. Either that or he just moved more slowly.

Octun drifted around his study. He tried to avoid Levid's ever-probing eyes. The man knew him too well not to be a close friend. Levid kept him off balance too.

Occasionally, Octun thumped one of the two huge shields attached to either side of the huge writing table. The shields were spoils of military campaigns. So was the entire room. Touch the wrong thing and it might fall and cost you an arm, or worse. The place could serve as a small arsenal, or a library equally as well.

Chancellor Levid never went on campaigns. But, Levid often told Octun how he admired both the literary and the lethal prizes that packed the study. Levid's guild acknowledged him as the leading expert on most key aspects of their Obenite heritage and on those who helped forge Obenin into a powerful and vast kingdom. Unfortunately, his life sat center focus in Levid's eye of interest.

Each of Octun's monikers fascinated Levid. Iberius Octun, Colonel Octun, Octun the Faithful, Octun the Stalwart, the Lion of Namiberro, those were the nice names. Levid asked him questions and wrote down just about everything. The persistent probing and the occasional compliment grated on Octun's patience. Octun tried to resist, but King Saroth gave the orders. The orders compelled him to obey, allowing Levid to record his life. Levid's one saving grace: the man truly knew his business better than any other scholar he had ever had the displeasure of meeting. Levid knew the tenets. He knew the law. He knew the origins of Obenin's ancestors back when Aspharia was the center of everything civilized.

Levid's study of him seemed downright disrespectful. Yet, sometimes, Octun caught himself obliging Levid with a story or two and found himself sharing more details than he wanted to reveal. He, totally, resisted Levid's drabble concerning his living-legend status. The statues of him, erected in several Glynwith villages were just something people did to make themselves feel better.

"Your story will inspire the peasants" didn't feel like a compliment, especially since he rarely visited his kinsmen. Not to mention that it had been a long time since his family had been considered peasants.

Octun's father, Ruben, served in the Obenite navy, involuntarily at first. Later, he served with distinction. Caught in an ambush by a band of pirates, Ruben cut a swathe to stand and defend his wounded captain.

Ruben carried the captain to safety and dressed his wounds. He never left the captain's side until safely in the hands of a surgeon. Only then did he care for his own wounds. Ruben was tough as nails but cared for his captain deeply. He could read and do figures. This impressed the captain. The captain could not see Ruben returning to a peasant's life and turned the day-to-day running of his estate over to him. Ruben ran the estate as the captain ran his ship, everything in order, every worker with his assigned duties, mess up and suffer the consequences.

Ruben, held to the Obenite religion devoutly. People associated him with the catch phrase, "Go pray." He married a slave girl captured during an uprising in lower Aspharia. Ruben fell in love with her. She bore him two sons. One died as an infant. His mother, who changed her name from Xyali to Milla to fit in with her husband's people, was very quiet and to herself.

No one knew much about her other than she was much smarter than she let on. Levid seemed intent on finding out more about her. Only, Octun knew nothing. She was his mother, not a field of study. All Levid's attempts to find more about her came to a dead end. Both Octun's parents died knowing he had reached hero status. Neither of his parents lived to see the legend develop.

One story Levid told him stuck in his mind. Levid repeatedly hinted at it or used portions of the story whenever he wanted to pry deep into Octun's personal life. The story consisted of Levid's encounter with children playing war in the streets. They had a popular game that essentially re-enacted the battle in which Octun won the shields that hung on his desk. Octun remembered clearly:

The children besiege the city. Octun and his men lead the way. They cut through the rebels like reapers cutting fodder. They break through into the middle of the walled city. Then the children pretend to burst down the doors of the temple and bring down the statue of the enemy's multi-armed god, ripping away the shields it holds. Finally, the lad playing the role of Octun stands on top of the broken idol and laughs mockingly at the non-existent god.

****

Chancellor Levid watched Octun carefully. He considered asking Octun, "What are you thinking?" but he needed something to soften the question. Otherwise, he would get a resounding, "Nothing."

He strolled over to Octun's desk and looked down at a book opened about midway. "Do you mind?" he asked.

"Humph," returned Octun.

"Not a yes, not a no," replied Levid, "usually meaning, whatever I feel like doing."

Octun did not acknowledge his last comment.

Levid read silently for a moment. The passage made him curious. He wondered why Octun would be studying a passage about a high priest who manipulated his way out of the priesthood, yet kept his reputation in tact. "Keeper Dal Taroda and King Bedowyn II... political implications of the High Priest, thinking about leaving the priesthood and going into politics."

"Never," snapped Octun.

Levid summarized Octun's political influence. In these times, people rallied around him. This served to King Saroth's advantage. Also, the posting at Obenin's Temple allowed the king to keep an eye on Octun. Levid felt that the king harbored other reasons, too; what, he did not know. Levid trusted in Octun's loyalty. Many blamed the pending invasion on King Saroth. Octun refused to align with the king's critics, even Lord Mernus, Octun's mentor. Octun found himself between 2 powerfully colliding forces.

If the King doubted Octun's loyalty, the best thing he could do was let him command troops in the field. Here, he thinks too much. Then again, that was one of Levid's jobs, to keep an eye on Octun and report any suspicious activities to Stannick. Stannick reported to Prince Seth. Levid assumed Seth reported to the king.

"It was a jest," replied Levid, putting the book back on the table and turning the pages quickly. He stopped then thumped the book firmly. "You might want to read this passage." There were other passages in other books. He kept that to himself. The idea was to open a narrow opportunity, not slam the door.

The door burst opened and a slim, rugged man with a cleft chin, flat forehead stepped into the room. His eyes revealed that he trusted no one. Despite splotchy patches where Stannick had attempted to clean his boots, cold dusty earth still clung to them. He gripped leather gloves tightly in his fist. He glanced at Chancellor Levid, who avoided eye contact with him.

Clearing his throat, Stannick nodded to each of them. "Chancellor Levid, Keeper Octun."

They nodded and mumbled greetings in return.

"How was your ride?" Levid asked.

"Hard," Stannick returned, slapping his gloves against his right hand.

"Did you come by mount or carriage?" inquired Levid.

"The way that makes your butt hurt, your thighs itch and you doubt if you will ever have any children," he jested in return. Stannick paused for a moment, then continued. "This place always feels the same."

Levid replied by waving his hand in the Obenite fashion, opening his hand like waving good-bye and moving his entire arm out to the right, "Always, always."

Stepping forward, Stannick approached Octun while scanning the walls quickly.

"I see you put up those Aspharian arrows. Seems more and more old spoils fill your study as of late." He remarked before his eyes landed on the instruments. "Near carnage, wasn't it? Arrows, shot from their longbows, fell from the sky like sheets of rain."

"But we prevailed," commented Octun.

"Prevailed we did. I was there. Do you remember?" It was more a statement than a question. "That was the first and last campaign I served under you as a young officer."

"I remember very well," acknowledged Octun.

Stannick grinned, taking Octun's comment as a compliment.

"After that campaign, I transferred to Grand Palace Security. I became charge in eight months. I cleaned up that den of liars and spies. Now the king's business remains the king's business." He slapped the gloves loudly.

"Yes, I remember during the Aspharian campaign you happened to mention you wanted to serve there," Octun returned matter-of-factly, a hint of annoyance in his voice. "So I had you transferred. I thought your suspicious nature and mistrust might at least do some good there."

Levid clutched his belly with both hands and coughed. Stannick's face turned so ashy that a punch in the lips wouldn't have drawn blood. Levid's laughter rebelled, rising to his throat. He tried to swallow. It burst free in a spell of coughing. He turned away from them.

Levid knew that Octun timed Stannick's chastisement like the downbeat of a drum on a forced march. Stannick's vanity marked the left foot down. Octun's slight marked the right foot hitting the ground on the downbeat. Stannick's discovery of an unexpected truth behind his success caught the next left stalled awkwardly in mid-air, unable to come down.

Before Stannick regained his composure, Octun appeared to offer him a way out. "You have some important news for us, I assume?"

Now, his blood pumped. Stannick eyes flushed red. He tried to stick it to Octun. After all, he carried orders directly from the king. "You will speed up the indoctrination of the subjects."

Levid choked on his cough. Turning back, he gasped for air. "What... do you...mean speed... up? What about Amrion's instructions?"

Stannick still looked directly at Octun, "Amrion advised the king to do so. Wean them off the daily dose of the potion. They are only to have it in their meals once every week. Furthermore, the king will be here in less than three weeks. The three lads and the lass will take leave of you then."

Stannick stood toe to toe with Octun.

Octun declared, without the slightest trace of inconvenience, "Tell Grand Monarch Saroth, Ruler of all Obenin, Master of Obenin Proper and Subjugated Kingdoms, that he has my word, they will be ready for his visit."

Levid swallowed his objections.

Trying to find some sign to satisfy his injured pride, Stannick studied Octun's face. He came up empty.

Octun stepped back and turned away from Stannick. "What about King Saroth's health?" Octun inquired.

Stannick stuttered, then answered slowly and deliberately, "He still suffers. No one can do anything for him, not even Amrion. Nevertheless, he still fights it with every fiber of his being, just as you would expect him to. Oh, by the way, Amrion is officially Master of the Barren Lands. You must address him as Lord Cuere, Master of the Barren Lands." He took this one last verbal stab at Octun's back.

Finally, Levid had an excuse to let his laughter fly free. "No doubt as revenge to those in his province, especially his father who nick-named him Cuere. In proper Obenite it means 'unique'. In Amrions's..., er, Lord Cuere's dialect it means 'not all there'."

After Levid's laughter waned, Octun continued without acknowledging Levid's comments, "Tell the king...."

Stannick waited for an ending to Octun's phrase that never came. Finally, Stannick snapped, "That's all for now. I have other important matters to deal with... a few lords to visit."

As Stannick turned to go, Levid saw his mouth, "Iron bottomed, half-breed bastard."

Octun bade, "Good-bye Sir Stannick, Charge of Grand Palace Security."

At which, Stannick slammed the door behind him.

Levid approached Octun, who turned to him.

"What are you grinning about?" asked Octun.

"Feeling better?" Levid chanced.

Octun's features loosened, "That was much better than breaking something."

CHAPTER 12
Centuries Old Hate

Shielding his eyes from the rising sun, Parmos did not remember the outside being so bright. Vapor blew from his mouth. His chapped lips burned.

He and the others stood speechless, marveling at the gardens. Winter flowers blossomed with thick clusters of small purple or blue petals. Bunches of red berries hung from waist- high shrubs. The temple gardeners made sure the garden flourished despite the persistent drought.

A stone wall lined the garden. Several levels of steps descended into a mall. Broad stone landings separated the levels. On each side of the landings, footpaths of tiny loose stones lead off ending at the wall or a pavilion.

Beyond the lowest garden, the mall, with its narrow pool and evergreen trees, stretched into the sun. When the sun rose just right over the pool, it reflected a blinding stream of light.

Jared's shuffling feet put some distance between himself and everyone else. One by one, the others drifted away, too. Parmos looked for Octun or Levid. He did not see them anywhere. This left him feeling like a lost lamb waiting for a shepherd to take him back to flock. Someone always lingered by him, keeping him safe. Now, he saw only the gardeners caring for the grounds.

Parmos closed his eyes and took a deep breath. The fresh air, deep into his lungs, purged the last bit of dusty temple air hiding there.

We shall see him today, he thought. *I hope that I am worthy.*

He started to walk down the landings toward the mall, stopping here and there for no good reason. When certain thoughts came into his mind, he just stopped and stared into thin air.

Earlier, Keeper Octun told them to examine their thoughts and hearts, to make sure each of them trusted in Obenin. Parmos trusted in Obenin and he trusted in Keeper Octun, too. There should have been a difference. Parmos did not find any difference in his feeling of trust for either.

Parmos knew that his feelings were out of line with Octun's teaching. Keeper Octun served the king. The king served Obenin. But, Parmos had not seen the king. Also, the constantly present Octun comforted him more than the god they all worshipped.

He resumed walking. He still did not know their fate, but he strongly believed that when the time came, he would do whatever the king required. *Because Octun told him to.*

Parmos stopped and closed his eyes tightly. Growing a little wobbly, he sat down quickly and closed his eyes again. A confusing sensation stirred inside of him. It wrapped around his brain and squeezed to the point of pain. An egg-headed, demonic face flaunting a snaggle-toothed smile floated out of the pain. Fear, hate and anger filled Parmos. He clenched his fist and gritted his teeth, forcing the apparitions back under the shroud of darkness.

He opened his eyes. For a moment, he thought the demonic apparition had escaped his mind and confronted him in the real world. A shadow engulfed Parmos. A man stood over him. The man was dark-skinned, so black that he looked blue. His egg-shaped head bore an awful scar. The scar ran like a canal flowing from his blinded right eye and disappearing somewhere atop his baldhead.

Parmos let out a little yelp.

"Are you good, young master?" the figure asked, his voice like two stones grinding together.

Unable to reply, Parmos' mouth gaped open. Without a word, the man stepped back. Parmos realized he was a gardener. His expression was not one of anger but of concern. The gardener cupped a small leafless bush with both hands. The roots dangled between his fingers. Parmos watched the gardener's one eye widen in surprise, then harden. The corners of his lips flinched to the left, then to the right, then centered emotionlessly under his nose. Finally, the gardener stared straight through Parmos with numb acceptance. Parmos knew the gardener's thought- his disfigured face and size made him look like a monster.

Parmos meant to apologize but the apology never formed on his lips. He wanted to explain to the gardener that something else haunted him, a nightmare from a previous life. Instead, Parmos stared dumbfounded. The gardener turned and walked away.

Parmos made his way to the mall and kneeled by the water. Looking at his reflection, he studied his wild and unruly, blond hair and thick eyelashes. He looked so different from everyone else, yet he felt a part of them. Ictheos, Ulthea, and Jared were his brothers and sister. Keeper Octun and Chancellor Levid were his parents. Piercing his own image with his hand, he quickly disturbed the water, erasing the pale reflection of himself. He waited. Slowly, the water stilled and his reflection returned. Nothing changed.

****

From the sixth tower, Octun observed Parmos by the pool. He wondered about him. Parmos was the only one from whom they had learned nothing before Lord Cuere's potions and artifacts took control. Keeper Octun saw something each time he looked into those blue eyes:

sorrow, anguish, he could not tell. Lord Cuere's potion should have washed away any nostalgic ties, or reminiscing of their past, he still sensed that Parmos held something.

Perhaps, Octun thought, *pains roots deeper than he can understand, something left unspoken, a long past guilty deed held close to the heart.*

****

Admiration overcame Parmos as he watched his mentors march toward him. The inspiring sight took his mind off his own anxiety. Octun, slightly ahead of Chancellor Levid, radiated like a soldier about to receive honor before his home village.

The cape he wore matched the crimson plume of his open-faced helmet. Chain mail hung from under his gold and silver breastplate. Thick black britches whisked loudly as he marched. On his left arm, he hoisted a huge silver shield with a golden inlay of his family crest, granted to him and designed by the king himself, the ensign of his region, the Lily of Glynwith with a lion above it.

Levid's miter bounced up and down as he hurried to keep up with Octun's impatient pace. Around his neck, clashing with his violet robe, hung a large square medallion, silver with dozens of emeralds placed to form a tree, the Tree of Wisdom from which all men may eat and learn. Over his right shoulder draped a long white sash with thick silver stripes woven into it. The cloth symbolized his position at the pinnacle of his studies. He held a long staff with a metal tip on the bottom that tapped out a cadence for the two men. A silver eagle, with its wings spread, perched atop the staff.

Parmos looked at Ulthea, Jared and Ictheos. They watched just as wide-eyed as he did.

"What a burden," Parmos thought, knowing that the tenets required every attendant to enter the Resting Place with the appropriate attire for his position even for simple maintenance. After a brief ritual, visitors were expected to collect their gear and leave. Those who cleaned, repaired, or performed rituals, like carpenters, priests and the like, were expected to leave everything at the foot of the sarcophagus until they were done for the day. Priests put to death those who defiled the Resting Place even if the offense was by accident.

Ulthea cleared her throat, "Keeper, what about us? We look so plain in these robes and boots."

"They are fitting for now," returned Octun. He motioned Levid forward, "Stay off the altar until we return."

Octun and Levid walked up the steps beyond the low altar. There they knelt and kissed the floor. Octun drew his sword and kissed it. Levid kissed the sash. When they stood, both reached into a basin on their left side and flicked water on their faces. Again, they dabbed their fingers into the basin and touched the bottoms of their boots. Octun unlocked the heavy gate barring the entrance to Obenin's Resting Place. Once inside, they closed the gate, so as not to disturb the dead, and performed the same ritual as before.

Parmos watched the two walk away from them. He strained his neck and eyes as Octun walked into the light of the Resting Place. With the snap of drilling soldiers, Octun and Levid knelt before the sarcophagus.

Octun, on his knees, moved closer to the sarcophagus and kissed the feet of Obenin. Afterwards, he surrendered his gear. First, he offered his shield. Then, he removed his helmet and placed it on the floor. Next, he removed his sword from its scabbard, kissed the blade and placed it on the floor alongside his helmet.

Levid kissed the feet, offered his rod, his miter and medallion. Lastly, he laid down the sash.

The two emerged from the gate like ones who had purged themselves of all their guilt. Parmos wanted to experience the same feelings, happy and free.

"Now you may enter and offer your, body, soul, and spirit," explained Octun.

Octun led the way. Levid walked behind keeping the group tight. Parmos performed the ritual cautiously watching the others, making sure that he did not miss any steps.

Whispering, Levid explained everything. Solemn awe shortened Parmos' breath to wisps. Power filled the place. Power filled them all. At that moment, he understood Octun's devotion.

Levid spoke of the two wooden soldiers, on either side of them, just inside the gate. Cracks along the grain marred the statues.

Ten stone coffins, five on each side, lined the way to the Resting Place. Parmos studied every face.

Levid explained that they were wives of Obenin. Some of them committed suicide when they heard of their husband's death so they could be with him in the afterlife. They believed that the wife who met Obenin closest to his transition would hold the status of the primary wife.

Parmos lost his attention on Levid's lecture as they approached a mural.

"Obenin's life," he whispered.

The mural told the story of Obenin's life from childhood to transition. As they approached Obenin's sarcophagus, the mural gave way to a large painting, an artist's impression of what Obenin looked like after the transformation. Obenin looked nothing like his former self. Parmos thought the picture rather eerie. Obenin's face formed the night sky. His most prominent feature was his eyes piercing out of the darkness.

The black granite floor gave way to one of highly polished alabaster. The Resting Place formed a dome of blinding white and Obenin's sarcophagus was the only thing kept there. When they stepped into the Resting Place, Ulthea let out a little start.

"Someone's in here," she gasped.

She pointed to four motionless figures dressed in white. The figures kneeled, forehead pressed to the floor in separate areas along the perimeter of the dome. It was impossible to see the figures until they walked into the Resting Place.

"These men vowed to the predicant quest," Octun revealed. "They must fast and supplicate here for two weeks before moving on to the quest for fire. They can leave the Resting Place for only brief moments three times a day."

"The predicant quest, five quests that are one, then this must be the quest of weakness, the second quest," replied Ulthea. "I did not know it took place in the Resting Place."

Octun did not answer but ushered them toward the sarcophagus.

One by one, Parmos and his comrades parted with their very selves. Both Octun and Levid smiled devoutly as Parmos and the others wept upon seeing the golden face of Obenin.

Directing them to look up at another mural on a portion of domed ceiling, Levid said, "It took two artists, one for the scenery and one for the likenesses. They worked on it every day for five years. The artists are buried in the sanctuary. You have seen their stones. Would anyone like to tell of the struggle you see portrayed here?"

Parmos wanted to answer the question but feared to do so.

What if I messed up? he thought. *Obenin might strike me down. Better keep my mouth shut.*

Jared cut off Ulthea's attempt to answer and spoke out as if Levid addressed the question to him:

Twin brothers, Benomi and Obenin, locked in a furious struggle. Father Obenin is the one with his hands locked around his brother's throat and the halo above his head. They are identical. They have the same shaggy hair and skin the color of coconuts and just as hairy. The painting shows the physical representation of the struggle. Though there were actual fights between them, this does not portray any specific one of them. This is symbolic of the beginning of our conflict. Here, Obenin defeats his brother Benomi, the forefather of our mortal enemy. The trouble started when Father Obenin started having dreams...

"Prophetic visions," Levid rebuked, looking as if lightning would strike them all.

Jared waited for the impending retribution from above. He looked at Octun. When nothing happened, he continued more cautiously, choosing every word.

"He received visions that showed him that he must unite and lead his father's people. If he did this, he would become a god. Benomi was outraged with jealousy when he found out. He rallied those infidels who would follow him in an attempt to thwart Obenin from fulfilling his mission, thus preventing him from becoming a god. He tried to kill Obenin by night, but failed. Obenin had received his destiny and fate was on his side. After a civil war, Obenin banished his brother and the other rebels to the other side of the Abringian Mountains on our northern border.

"After Benomi's exile, Father Obenin organized his scattered people and purged the other inhabitants from the land. He punished Obenites who did not accept his destiny. He set up regents over provinces of his kingdom and the people believed in him and called him Grand Monarch. He called the land by his own name. Under his leadership, we conquered other lands and increased the size of the kingdom in all directions, except for over the mountains. His brother befriended the people, formed an alliance, and brought them to arms in expectation of Obenin's attack. Also, after the civil war, the people were not ready to fight their brothers again.

"But, as time passed, Father Obenin felt that the kingdom was divided and incomplete without all of his father's people. Reluctantly, he agreed to abide by an arbitrator's decision. "Before the day of the treaty, Benomi corrupted the arbitrator. For on that day, the decision was for Obenin to surrender the greater part of the kingdom. Father Obenin argued that the kingdom was not the same as when Benomi lived there. He had no right to anything but the one or two cities their father had controlled.

"Benomi, with no other ground to tread on but that of a biased judge, insulted Father Obenin. With Father Obenin's honor insulted, they fought. He would have ended the whole matter right there if the arbitrator's forces had not stepped in. Both brothers left there furious. Thus, the meadow, where they met upon the Plains of Gath, is called Calmpience or 'Broken Peace'.

"Father Obenin attempted to make peace with his brother three years later. He tried again to come to some acceptable agreement. He sent an emissary to Bardia, the province in which his brother resided. By the craftiness and deceitfulness of his heart, Benomi held great sway in Bardia.

"Leaving his small escort, the emissary rode by himself into Venzant, the capital city, to offer peace. Benomi sent the emissary's body back to its escort without its head and a declaration of war pinned to the tunic: 'Every man-child of Benomi, born away from his homeland, shall have the head of an Obenite to kick about in the alleys. When we return, we will trample down every stone that Obenin has erected.'

"Obenin declared that Benomi and all those that followed him were no longer his father's people and excommunicated them; therefore, they no longer had any rights to anything. War erupted. Benomi convinced his allies they should not wait for Obenin to come over the mountains but that they should attack first.

"We greatly prevailed in that onslaught and drove the Benomian Alliance back through the mountain passes. Father Obenin did try to invade Bardia. He found opposition much stiffer on the other side of the mountains and had problems supplying his forces. The war broke off in a stalemate. There was no truce signed. For centuries, there have been several clashes, unyielding force against unyielding force but no victor.

"This last war broke out after our present monarch, King Saroth, had concentrated on building his ships to carry traders and armies to far away kingdoms. Bardia saw this as the perfect opportunity to attack us. They claimed we were behind the bandits that raided their villages. Before this, there had been forty years of peace between us.

"Bardia called together the old Benomian Alliance. The better half of our forces were committed elsewhere and there was no warning. Our few soldiers were the more valiant and drove them back into the mountains. However, we could not dislodge them from there.

"King Saroth sent the word to withdraw some forces from Aspharia. Unfortunately, Aspharian pirates attacked a large convoy of our ships. We defeated the pirates, but the cost was dear. The pirates only wanted revenge. They did not have the slightest intention of returning from the battle. They had only one goal in mind: sink as many of the troop-carrying freighters as possible. They fired flaming pitch unto the hulls, not even caring if their own ships burned. After the destruction of so many ships and men, the admiralty decided to let each captain determine the routes back home at the last moment. They never returned in such large fleets again.

"The Aspharians' revenge lowered our troop strength and delayed their return. Now the Benomian Alliance has a stronghold in the mountains, waiting for spring to come. The Benomian Alliance is growing. They will eventually outnumber us three to one. As the spring thaw melts and floods the lowlands, so will they come. Instead of life and fertility, in contrast, they will bring a deluge of filth that will defile our land."

Chancellor Levid gawked at Jared in exasperation, "Thank you for, um, the in-depth lecture on Obenite history. It is much more than I asked for, but it is good to know that you have been listening and studying."

Jared smiled proudly.

Locking the gate to the Resting Place, Parmos stood close to Octun. It made him feel better. Clearly, uncomfortable that he lingered at his shoulder, Octun kept looking at him. Yet, he found himself unable to leave Octun's side.

Ulthea approached them. She looked at Parmos, then at Octun and at Parmos again.

Finally, Octun addressed him. "Master Parmos, the lady clearly has something to say to me. Go on about your way."

He moved a few paces away and tried not to look or listen.

Ulthea, jittery and wide-eyed with excitement, tried to whisper reverently. With her excitement and the acoustics of sanctuary, Parmos heard every word.

"Keeper Octun," she said, "I wish we could hurry up and get the power."

"Why do you say that, Ulthea?" he asked as he hung the key ring over the hilt of his sword.

"I mean, I don't want anyone else to die. If Father Obenin hurries up and gives us power, we can stop them from killing any more of us."

The words moved Parmos. He saw that they moved Octun too. He actually put his hand out as if he wanted to touch her arm. But, he didn't. His hand remained outstretched for a moment, then he dropped it.

Instead, he said, "Father Obenin shines on the faithful."

"Faithful in heart and deed," she returned. "The thirty-first tenet."

"It will all happen in good time. King Saroth will be here soon and after his visit, you will go back to Oracle. We shall see what happens," Octun concluded.

Parmos pulled his hood over his head and trudged away. Ulthea's devotion stood out over his, or any of the others' for that matter. He figured his own faith did not measure up and wondered how he might find more. Jared knew so much about Obenite history, more than he remembered even hearing. Ulthea wore her faith outside like a gold necklace. Ictheos read and wrote in the Obenite language easily. He never got the hang of writing and reading gave him a throbbing headache. Smart people surrounded him. He desired to do more and learn more but struggled even with the simplest things in his studies.

He watched Ulthea leave Keeper Octun and join Jared and Ictheos. Chancellor Levid walked over to Octun. Levid nodded his head in Jared's general direction. Parmos took it as a complaint. He felt ashamed.

Octun is my answer. Mark the path of the perfect soul and follow it, he thought, brightening. The tenet came out of him like a child's song. He did not have to force it out of his brain. He knew only a few words. But they were good words and told the story of the whole thing.

Levid and Octun walked past him. He noted how Octun walked and where he stepped. When they passed, he fell in right behind them placing his feet exactly where Octun had stepped.

Octun and Levid stopped and looked over their shoulders at him.

"I believe the lad is taken with you," Levid quipped.

Octun turned completely around and scanned Parmos from head to toe.

To Parmos' surprise, Octun stepped aside, saying, "All right, let's see it."

Parmos wasn't sure what to do next.

"Well..." Octun spurred him on.

Parmos pulled his shoulders back and held his chin up. Leading with his right shoulder, he stepped off. He checked his gait, lifting his left knee and taking a long stride then, planting his heel firmly on the floor. He stepped with his right foot in the same fashion, swinging his arms like reeds blowing in the wind. He paraded in front of them, turned and came back.

Octun glared at him with a mix of disbelief and shock.

Levid laughed out loud.

"That is not me," objected Octun.

"As sure as the heavens float above us, that is surely you."

CHAPTER 13
King Saroth In Royal Agony

Hofas, the driver, kept the reins taut on the lead horse, Jiataro. Escaping the orange and red horizon, the small black coach raced into the deep purple night. Waning daylight cloaked the multitude of stars. Only the brightest glistened above. A slither of a crescent moon hung in the heavens like a portal, cracking open to reveal a shocking secret. Beyond the horizon, the top of the sun remained visible as if it were a cognizant thing craving to devour what secrets the night revealed.

Of the four horses pulling the coach, Jiataro was the oldest. Most horses his age were either leather or glue by now. Something kept him running. Hofas fancied that the horse loved the night. This phase of the moon sent the horse into a running fury. It gave him strength, strength to steady his anxious heart. Jiataro could run younger horses into the ground and still have the strength to pull a wagonload of corn to market.

The horse sensed something important when the groom fidgeted around, unhitching the old team and hitching up the new one. Hofas saw how the horse looked at him, shook his mane, and neighed constantly before they left the last checkpoint. The moment he released the brake, the entire team reacted to Jiataro's whinny and the coach jerked forward.

****

Inside the coach, dry air bit into the king's nose. King Saroth Seth Moabus Bedowyn, Grand Monarch of all the kingdoms of Obenin, clutched his stomach and gritted his teeth in royal agony. He cursed his nurse for her hesitancy in giving him the foul-tasting liquid that brought some relief from his sudden attacks. His physicians proved useless. Only Lord Cuere's potions and magic helped. There were times when they made Saroth feel well; however, Cuere knew no cure.

King Saroth drank from the bottle and the knots in his guts loosened. He straightened himself a bit, then leaned back against the contraption Cuere built for his coach. It looked like a small chair with fluffy cushions. Cuere placed glows in the seat and back to keep him warm. When it cooled, Seth, his son, placed what looked like a key into the hole on the arm and ratcheted it quickly. The chair purred like a kitten and warmed up again.

Saroth studied Seth's flirtatious contact with the nurse. They both sat across from him. Their shoulders touched in such a way that it made her appear to snuggle against Seth. As his oldest of eighteen children from seven wives, Seth claimed the divine right of accession. No one challenged that. The challenge arose as a result of the war. Powerful people plotted against him. If Saroth died, the alliances he still held would crumble, leaving his challengers no reason to plot in dark chambers anymore.

The people loved Saroth. Keeper Octun, despite his maltreatment, supported him. Lord Mernus, head of the second most powerful Obenite family, owed him service until death.

Seth, on the other hand, lacked all of the above.

Seth was an albino. Superstition surrounded him. It formed his soul as a child despite all that Saroth attempted. No one dared to say anything to his face; he saw it in their eyes. If he lost this war, the centuries old Bedowyn line of kings would collapse. The rich and powerful plotted and argued in shadows about how best to remove power from the king and place it in the hands of the Grand Council. Even more, they argued who would lead the Grand Council. Saroth knew that neither he nor his children were among the possible candidates.

I have a plan too, twofold at that. Get Seth to demonstrate his faith and win the war, thought Saroth.

It sounded simple. As far as winning the war, Lord Cuere's part went well for now. *Of Octun's part,* determined Saroth. *I have to make up for lost time, put the offense behind us, let Octun show Seth the way.*

Seth, wearing a black cloak, pulled it up around his own shoulders. "Father, why do you look at me so?" he asked. "Are you all right?"

"My... son," Saroth replied, the pain easing but by no means gone. He reached out and grasped his son's knee weakly.

Seth grasped Saroth's hand firmly. "To see you in such pain grieves me. I feel so helpless to do anything."

Saroth looked into his son's eyes. "Death is a predator hunting me vengefully. He wants to dine on me only after I suffer and waste away to skin and bones. What have I done to deserve his wrath?"

Prince Seth's grip weakened, then tightened, "Don't speak like that, Father. Lord Cuere will find a way to heal you. I can have him stop what he is doing to work night and day to find some way to help you."

"He has done his best. Besides, what he is doing now is far more important. This victory promises a kingdom more powerful than any of us ever imagined. I do pray that I can bring my plan to fruition. Yet, I fear all hope is vanity."

"You will prevail," Seth reassured. "More duels than one have been won with half a sword. The people are behind you. The pilgrimages to all the temples have increased, especially to Obenin's Primary Temple. This war... this victory is Obenin's fate for you."

King Saroth smiled. Seth's words comforted him. They gave him strength to fight a little longer. He favored

Seth despite the objections of his other wives and their children. They were all suspicious of him because he was an albino and often lied about Seth and expressed no compassion toward him. He put an end to their outright mistreatment of Seth long ago by beheading a nurse who had let him go without food because of a full moon.

Now people were more subtle in their dealings. Saroth believed the superstitions of others caused Seth to withdraw into himself. Although he knew that some things even a king could not change, he truly wished he could make a royal decree banishing superstition from each of his subjects' hearts.

"I am glad you are the eldest and that all the kingdoms will go to you at my death."

"And you, Father, will surely sit with Obenin. May that day be long away," Seth smiled.

****

The horses' hooves thundered into the night. The weather fitted the horses, not too frigid but cold enough to soothe their flexing muscles. Hofas shivered miserably. He wondered why the king hadn't ordered Lord Cuere to build him a contraption, too.

They passed through hill country now. As they raced up and down the hills, the moon occasionally disappeared beyond the trees. They ran around the curve to the next hilltop. Finally, with the twilight fading, Hofas saw Ethenia.

As they started down the hill, Hofas pulled back on the reins to slow their descent toward the bridge over the River Edge. Jiataro ignored him. They hit the bridge with a thud.

Prince Seth cursed at him from inside the coach.

"Infernal beast, if I gets lashes, you will too," Hofas threatened.

The horses neighed at one another.

"Whoa... whoa...!" Hofas bellowed, pulling at the reins and tapping the brake to slow the team for the hard left turn ahead. His heart thumped in his chest. He hit the brake harder. It didn't help.

The horses hit the curve without breaking stride. Hofas grabbed on to the seat thinking a lashing was the least of his worries. "The driver that killed the king and prince, that'll be whats I goes to the gallows for," he moaned.

Jiataro cut short over a smooth patch of grass. The wheels never left the ground. After the next knoll, the team slowed for the long haul up to the Primary Temple.

"I should have just tied these reins and stayed at home. The bloody horse didn't needs me," protested Hofas.

Jiataro whinnied.

Hofas rejoiced that the ride was almost over.

His beard and three scarves were not enough-- the ride was too long for them to keep him warm.

"Just cut the reins and buries me with them because I won't be able to lets go. Or, maybe I'll catches a death of cold and never sees my son again."

When the word came that he must drive the king's coach, it caught Hofas completely off guard. The fact that the king was out on this night or any cold night seemed careless to him. *He still fights like a good king should,* he thought.

Not knowing the reason they were off to Obenin's Primary Temple in such a rush, Hofas hoped it had something to do with putting an end to this war. His son served among the many parties of raiders that hindered and harassed the Benomian Alliance armies in the mountains. He thought of his son sleeping in the frozen terrain, keeping warm the best he could, away from those who loved him and away from the comforting warmth of a loving woman.

Maybe this night's ride would not make his son's effort in vain. While he visited the temple, he would go and pray for him. He waited for the guard to check them and open the gate. They arrived in the nick of time. Unable to resist the inexorable tow of time, the sun dipped into darkness. The night, finally, had its way.

CHAPTER 14
Levid Comes To Understand Octun

Octun and Levid waited for King Saroth in the antechamber to the king's quarters. The fire crackled and snapped, sending small embers onto the hearth. Octun stood with his back to Levid. He stared at a portrait of himself.

Not a particularly good one, thought Levid.

A picture of the current keeper always hung there.

Levid sat quietly behind Octun. He wanted to talk about the king's arrangements even though Octun assured him that everything that could be done was done. Truly, the staff scrutinized every detail. To the contrary, Levid, being a creature of habit, preferred to go over everything again and again, until the last minute. It kept his mind occupied and his nervousness down.

He believed Octun wanted to talk about something. He showed all the signs: talking around the subject, avoiding questions only to make an off-hand comment later, and contemplative silence when certain subjects came up. He detected conflicts within Octun. He speculated that Octun saw no sense of purpose in their mission.

The artist captured something about the eyes and the position of Octun's head. Though the portrait showed only his shoulders up, he looked as if he were inspecting his soldiers before marching to the front. The man in the portrait did not need to talk about politics and succession. The man in the portrait didn't need to ask someone if his assumptions sounded crazy. He knew his purpose. He knew his heart.

The man looking at the portrait searched for truth and questioned his own relevancy. Octun needed to keep the cork on, yet vent to someone. Levid saw it coming.

Octun turned, meeting Levid's inquisitive stare.

He has that look on his face. I am not going to like what I am about to hear, Levid prepared for a direct statement that pulled no punches.

"I don't trust Prince Seth," declared Octun, studying Levid's expression.

Levid's mouth gaped open. Incredulity gripped his mind, so much for his expertise. If the king walked through the door, he would be heard keeping the faith, no gallows for him.

"Surely you don't believe those fairy tales about albinos being evil? And to speak of such things when the king and his son are in their father's house!" scorned Levid hotly. "Why do you wait until now of all times to tell me of your doubt?" Lowering his voice, he glanced at the door, "We should talk about this later."

"Obenin is the father of us all," chastised Octun. "And no, I do not believe in such nonsense. Prince Seth may be king soon and I dread the day that I will have to serve under him."

"What then, deceitfulness, not tall enough, no great victories?"

Octun frowned at Levid's sarcasm. He turned and stepped toward Levid. He uncrossed his arms and widened his stance.

Levid got the message.

Octun continued without interruption and without the sarcasm. "King Saroth and I were close friends once, too close for a king and officer not on the council. We often hunted together at the Shebeth Castle estate on the River Fon. The hunting was exceptionally bad that day. We sat under a willow tree drinking wine casually despite my vows of priesthood. I should not have been so at ease but Saroth always brought out a freer side of me, a side that makes me drop my guard. We talked like brothers. It was too beautiful of a day for me to spoil. I did though. The subject of Prince Seth came up and before I was aware of what I said, King Saroth glared at me furiously."

"What did you say?" asked Levid.

"I said... 'I hope that you live forever because Prince Seth will make a horrible king.' Saroth and I have not talked face to face since."

Well that explains a lot of things, Levid thought. *Mainly, why the renowned Iberius Octun sits here as Keeper. In this position, he garners no real power to himself. When the crown eventually passes to Seth, Octun's duties require him to anoint Seth as king and place the crown upon his head. It explains, in part, why I make secret reports to the king.*

He still saw holes in his argument about Octun's position as Keeper. But that needed to wait. He pried more at the immediate question.

"If not superstition, then what?" tested Levid. He moved around to his right, causing Octun's voice to project away from the door.

"Because I have been told things by good soldiers, those I have trusted in battle."

"Rumors spun by superstitious hearts and weak minds." Levid waved his hands dismissing Octun's report.

"Weak? These are the words of men who have fought alongside me. They have seen things that would make many like yourself lose everything held in your bowels since birth."

Levid's face darkened with anger. "I may not be a military man, but I am no coward either," argued Levid.

Octun paused. For a moment, Levid thought he was going to argue the point. He breathed easier when Octun gave him an explanation.

"Have you ever known Prince Seth to come on a pilgrimage alone since he has become a man?" Octun waited for an answer.

Levid did not respond.

"I have been here for four years and I have never seen him kneel at the feet of Obenin by himself," continued Octun. "Once he tagged along casually with his father. He appeared insincere."

Levid's reason took hold again. Octun was the most devout person he knew. They worked together for over a year. When Levid found out that Saroth decided to remove the previous chancellor, he leapt at the chance. The year flashed by. Levid learned a lot. He wrote a lot. At this instant, all the bits and pieces of the puzzle shattered and came together again in a different picture. Tonight, Levid learned volumes.

"It bothers you that much that he misses the solstice observances and that he never shows obeisance not associated with his father."

"Yes," said Octun flatly. "There are young lads, twelve or thirteen, who travel here on their own. I know one lad, Theron, who travels by himself from a fishing village on the shore of the Aspharian Sea. He walks. He travels by caravan. He even stows away on ships. Seth has yet to take a royal coach on his own."

"Eventually, when he becomes king, you are afraid that his seeming lack of faith will become more noticeable to the people, and that will reflect in the kingdom?"

"Yes," Octun answered. "Or worse."

Levid noted Octun's gratitude for finishing his thoughts.

"No one will fight for the faithless," added Levid, purposely not speaking the remaining text, *Therefore, the faithless shall not rule.*

Octun commented, "Though no tenet states this verbatim, all of the priesthood agrees on this principle."

Levid thought for a moment. He looked at the man in front of him. He looked at the man in the portrait. Though no tenet stated the concept word for word, the tenets did say, verbatim, 'The king is faithful and will spread his faith wherever he conquers.' While most of the Grand Council saw the war as expansion, empire, power and wealth, Octun saw an ordained purpose. Expansion and empire resulted from faith. Octun understood the very reason why Obenin and the early priest wrote the tenets in the first place.

Levid did something he never did before to anyone. He approached Octun face to face, looked him dead in the eyes, placed his palms on each side of Octun's head. Then, he patted him twice firmly on the shoulders, letting his hands stay there. He shook Octun gently.

"*Romala*, my great respected one," remarked Levid.

Octun removed Levid's hands by crossing his arms to fend off the compliment.

"If ever there existed a true moment to use the word in my lifetime," Levid complimented, "this is it."

Octun's reaction did not offend him. The man just did not know how to take a compliment, especially this one.

Romala meant more than just a compliment. By using the word, Levid's words put Octun in a status few attained. At the same time, he revealed his depth to Octun. Octun knew that Levid knew every nuance of the word and meant every one: one who lives and understands the ancient ways, the one that brings every one back to faith. One specific Keeper of the Primary Temple, Romala, brought the people back to the service of the king. Afterward, the king ushered in a glorious renewal and expansion. The name became a metaphor.

Levid made a promise to himself to associate the name with Octun in his version of Obenite history.

"But other things worry me, also," Octun blocked.

Levid focused his curiosity on the two remaining questions that lit his mind like a beacon, *What other things? And, are you planning to do anything about it?*

He contemplated how to keep the question from sounding like an accusation.

They were silent for a very long time. Octun returned to looking at his portrait. Levid stared into the leaping flames, rephrasing his question in his mind.

A knock on the door relieved him of his responsibility, for the moment.

CHAPTER 15
Octun's Heart Trembles

A guard stepped in and announced, "The King!"

Octun straightened slightly to take the actually position of attention. The door swung wide and King Saroth stepped in, leaning heavily on Prince Seth's shoulders. The nurse followed, her eyes cast down as if she avoided Octun's eyes.

King Saroth flopped into the chair closest to the fire. Octun's eyes widened. The king looked frail and thin. His handsome face no longer glowed with vibrancy. An ashen complexion turned his brown skin grayish. He did not sit erect but bent over like a man twice his age. From his appearance, one would think he was senile. Once he spoke, his voice assured Octun that the King retained his personality and wit.

"So you still have feelings for a man you once called friend or is that pity I see in your eyes?" remarked King Saroth partly jesting, but mostly serious.

Kneeling, Octun dropped his head in the customary manner and started to speak.

Saroth cut him off. "Goodness man, stand up. We don't have time for formality. By the time everyone gets through kneeling and bowing, I might be dead."

Humor found no place in Octun's reaction.

"And someone take these boots off so I can put my feet near the fire. They feel like mortar blocks. Cuere should have put foot warmers in that contraption of his."

Seth took the boots and placed them by the king's chair. He put a stool under his feet.

"Ah, that's better." Saroth wiggled his toes.

Another guard knocked and entered after Octun told him to do so. He carried a wide tray with large cups of steaming broth.

Holding a cup with both hands, the king sniffed it deeply and smiled as he sipped the broth graciously.

Octun noted Saroth's trembling hands and his attempt to control them.

"How was your trip, my liege?" Levid questioned.

With a wheezing laugh, the King returned, "Deathly cold out. I would not send the blasted royal cat out on a night like this. I bumped my buttocks for hours in that coach. It was simply grand."

No one laughed. Octun glanced at Levid in silent agreement. He thought, *Mercy, he looks too awful to have such a good sense of humor. Should we humor, respect, or pity this man? He fights to be himself despite the illness.*

Saroth declared, "Goodness, it's not this sickness that's going to kill me, it's the deathly daggers of pity in the eyes of those who see me."

"I urged him not to come," jibbed Seth. "He is stubborn and refuses to stay at home and let me take care of everything."

"I want to see you off tomorrow morning." Saroth glanced at Octun.

"But I could have handled everything, Father." Seth paused. "There is no reason to make your condition worse."

Octun looked at Prince Seth for the first time.

"My son, always thinking of his father.... He will be a good king someday." King Saroth looked directly at Octun.

"You flatter this humble son. I can never replace you." Seth patted his father's shoulder.

Octun didn't flinch.

"Enough!" demanded Saroth. "I want to see them right away so that I can get some rest. We have an early start tomorrow. Stannick has already set things in motion."

"They are ready," answered Octun. "We have followed Lord Cuere's instructions without error. They will honor you and Obenin forever."

"Lord Cuere will be anxious to see them again. I bet he gets more in a tizzy as the day approaches," returned Saroth.

"They are anxious, too," Levid added. "They talk of nothing else of late."

"Do they speculate on what shall happen to them?"

"No, sire. I noted a spark of curiosity in Jared but they are satisfied with the answers we give them," assured Octun.

"And what answers are those?" Seth asked more directly.

Saroth shot him a cautioning glance.

"That...," Octun answered slowly, "only the king, and Lord Cuere know."

"And me," Seth reminded.

"We are among loyal friends, son. Don't question that loyalty with your tone," Saroth returned.

Saroth continued looking at Octun for approval. "Please forgive him. He is just trying to find his way to the throne."

Levid inquired, "Lord King, we have a minor issue. We cannot continue referring to the lads and lass, well, as the lads and the lass. How shall we announce them to the people? It may help if we actually knew what is to become of them."

Seth frowned and switched weight from his left foot to his right foot, them back to his left.

Twisting his mouth and humming for a few seconds, the King admitted, "We are not fully sure what will happen to them. We know they will become powerful. We know that we control them. We know they will control the elements. We do not know to what extent they will be able to do this. Lord Cuere is telling us one thing, but he says less than he knows. At first, we were confident, but my little ears throughout the kingdom tell me that there is more to this than Lord Cuere says."

Octun snapped alert, his adrenalin pumping up.

Before Octun could voice his distrust of Cuere, the King said, "Don't worry, Octun. You have worried enough already. I keep a good eye on Lord Cuere. I know you probably thought he had completely hoodwinked me. Yes, I do have a certain trust in him. That trust is not without foundation. I have seen him do many miracles right before my very eyes that were more than just a sleight of hand, but to trust an entire kingdom on a whim.... I am not that ill. Why do you think we are preparing for the invasion?"

Leaning back on his heels, Octun resigned himself to the king's comments though his doubts still gnawed at him like a rat in a pantry. The monarch effectively avoided Levid's question.

Why wouldn't he tell them? Surely, he knows.

"Now, we must have a fitting name." continued the king, "Let's call them 'the Hands of Obenin'. And I assume they are waiting to see me. Send someone to fetch... the Hands of Obenin."

Octun knocked on the door and a guard opened it and reported, then disappeared down the corridor, leaving his partner alone.

Hands of Obenin, the second ancient reference for the night, thought Octun. *A group of zealot high priests who brought terror to those who did not accept Obenin's prophecy of godhood, Obenin appointed them as the first Keepers. In the early years, they slew heretics and built temples in his honor.*

Four of the more powerful priests garnered power to themselves and corrupted the temples. They became known as the Demon Hands of Obenin. Eventually, Obenin slew them. He removed the other priests even though most of them did not align themselves with the Demon Hands. He appointed new priests, taking away some of their power. He did not want the Hands of Obenin moniker associated with the earlier priests. So, the newly appointed priests were also named the Hands of Obenin."

Octun grew more concerned. Saroth looked worse than when he first arrived. He wanted to ask him to wait until the morning when he would be fresh and look more alive. The lads and lass were still very impressionable.

To his surprise, Seth spoke. "Father, why don't you wait until the morning? You will be more... more...." Unable to find the appropriate word he left it at that.

"Do I look that awful?" Saroth asked sincerely.

No one answered but stared quietly to the affirmative.

"Well, if I look that deathly ill, I definitely should see them tonight. I might not have a tomorrow," the king spat, not caring what they thought. "Nurse, make me look more... kingly."

Octun turned. The nurse stood in the farthest corner from him. She had a path to the king right pass Octun. Instead, she walked along three walls to get to the king. She washed and oiled his skin, put a touch of color onto his cheeks, then placed the crown on his head.

"Better?" he asked reaching to adjust the crown slightly forward, trying to make it feel more comfortable.

The others smiled uneasily, showing that it was only a minor improvement.

"Well, if you can't show a little support, I guess you all will have to leave."

Levid and Octun looked at one another.

"You can leave... now," he reiterated, pointing toward the door, a bit of the fiery Monarch flaring to the surface. "And that includes you, Seth"

"Someone has to stay with you," Seth objected, sounding more like an order than a request.

"Take this crown off my head. It's giving me a headache."

****

With everyone out, Saroth tried to sit himself up and straighten his back. He did not mind looking ill, he knew the lads and the lass expected that, but he did not want to appear helpless.

CHAPTER 16
Saroth Reveals The Mission

Ulthea, Ictheos, Jared, and Parmos, the Hands of Obenin, stood before the king, each embarrassed that their faces showed disappointment. Tears welled up in Ulthea's eyes.

"What's wrong?" asked Saroth, beckoning for her to approach.

About two steps from him, she stopped and curtsied.

Pointing to a spot on the floor near his right knee, Saroth motioned her even closer. She turned to look at the others. Their faces turned blank, offering her no encouragement whatsoever.

Ulthea took a step.

"Why is such a pretty lady crying tonight? Are you afraid?"

"No, my good king," she sniffled, and curtsied again.

He wiped her face with his handkerchief. "Then why are you crying?"

"I don't know, sire. It is... just that... you are so sick."

Saroth sat back and looked at her. "Sincerity dips your words in honey. Cuere brought you here an empty vessel. Levid's teaching may have filled you with the knowledge of our history, but Octun submerged you in faith."

Saroth held her right hand tightly in both of his. He spoke to her as an uncle speaks to his young niece who had fallen and gashed her knee.

"Ulthea, so much concern for her king, I wish others were so easily moved. If being healthy keeps the tears from your beautiful eyes, then I wish I could declare it so."

Ulthea blushed and sniffled. She curtsied again.

"Ah, that's better," King Saroth comforted. "a pretty smile for a pretty lady."

He released her hand and beckoned Jared to approach.

Jared approached and bowed straightaway.

"Master Jared."

He bowed again casting his eyes toward the floor.

Saroth studied him for a moment. "You came from an island off our coast, the Yan Free Territories."

"Why, yes, my liege. Keeper Octun told me so."

"I suppose that these surroundings are not too different from those of your home."

Jared did not reply.

"Yan is a place where cultures blend -- Obenite, Aspharian, Cardian, Bardian, the entire civilized world settled on one small island. It is a place of lost promise, yet the Yan people prosper on that promise anyway. Amazing, isn't it?"

Jared pressed his lips together. He shifted uncomfortably at the King's comments.

"We must seem rather drab to you?"

Saroth stopped and looked into Jared's eyes. A light flickered, remained there for a moment, then faded away into a dull stare.

"Why do you ask me such questions, sire? It is but a dream to me," His tone was direct.

Saroth thought, "This one we need to watch."

He changed the subject.

"I haven't heard anything from you, Master Parmos."

Parmos bowed quickly, not having the foggiest notion how to return such an ambiguous question. He shuffled toward the king and aligned himself behind Jared.

It didn't work. Saroth directed Jared to the side. Parmos moved no further.

"They tell me you are the strong, silent type," the King complimented. Though they looked nothing alike, Parmos' revealing expressions, eyes and movements reminded him of Octun.

"Yes, sire. I mean no sire... I mean...."

"How do you like it here?" Studying Parmos curiously, Saroth figured this was a simple enough question.

"Good, sire," Parmos' eyes buried into the floor.

"How have Keeper Octun and Chancellor Levid treated you? Extremely well, I would hope, or I will have a word with them."

"Oh, sire, they have been both father and mother to us. I have been taught more than my head can hold."

"You are shaking your head Ictheos."

"Yes, my Lord. Keeper Octun and Chancellor Levid have been everything to us."

"Everything," echoed Ulthea. "Them and the guards... oh, and attendants are all that we have seen of our home."

A lengthy silence passed as the king met the eyes of each one. They accepted their fate and their new home without the slightest instinctive rejection.

Straining, Saroth rose from his seat.

"You mentioned that Keeper Octun and Chancellor Levid have been everything to you. Well, I am afraid that is going to change all too soon. It is absolutely necessary."

Checking his balance, he took a careful step. He felt steady, so he took another and another until he worked his way around to the back of his chair. He propped himself up.

He pointed at the gaudy crown sitting on the footstool by his chair. "There are times when that crown gives me a headache from more than just weight."

He turned toward Ulthea. "You called me good king earlier and I'm glad someone thinks so. For it is very hard to be a good king in times like these. Everyone wants answers or thinks they know the answers. My subjects gripe about the drought. The war is going badly. Some say a war brings a kingdom closer. I contest this and I say only if the hardships are brought on by reasons that a nation can rally around.

"The very nature of our kingdom is to expand by force and carry out the vision of Obenin. I will not let that vision dim while I breathe. Some of those who should stand with me cower behind the rhetoric of peace, inviting others to establish diplomatic and religious missions in our land. My detractors shame themselves by surrendering to the outright corruption of our culture."

Saroth continued, "It is for the king to lead in times like these. I am the king and I say 'no'. They have slain too many of our fathers, sons, daughters, and mothers. Vows and pacts of revenge are sworn on both sides, fueling the consuming fires of hatred.

"Furthermore, I agree totally with my forefather. This is not the same kingdom. Guided by the vision of Father Obenin, Obenite blood forged this kingdom. We are not giving up one inch for some treaty that is not our god's will. The only way is to win this war, the only way to peace is to convert the world to our faith and subdue the world to our will.

"Then, Lord Cuere discovered you; rather, those like you, written of in ancient text, and hope filled our hearts. The time of your revelation is near. The time of Obenin's power is upon us. Levid follows. Octun follows. Will you follow your king?"

The king leaned heavily against the back of the chair. He decided to return to his seat. The oration exhausted him.

"Have you understood what I said?" his eyes searched for any sign of understanding in their faces. "Obenin's Primary Temple will become the center of religion for every land known to man, as it should be."

Ulthea stepped forward. Earnest aspiration of a true calling brightened her face.

"Grand Monarch, how can the four of us help? We do not know how to fight," she replied, vexation heavy in her voice.

Dumbfounded by his own neglect, the king admitted, "Ah, in my rambling, I forgot to tell you what you shall become."

He leaned forward and put on his best eager face. "You are the instruments by which Obenin will show his power to the world. Obenin has granted you the power to control the weather. Lord Cuere will teach you how to use it. Our enemies will see that righteousness and power is on our side."

Ulthea looked at him with great admiration. Although he was fatigued, his words rang clear through to her soul. He saw her resolve before it formed her response.

"Grand Monarch Saroth," Ulthea started. She turned to look at the others, motioning her head towards the floor. The others followed Ulthea as she got down on both knees at the king's feet. Her face to the floor, she declared, "I know that Obenin is with us. We are humble servants to be consumed by Obenin's will."

King Saroth rose later than he wanted. Although tired from the trip, he felt stronger than he did the night before. He sat on the edge of the bed and stretched until his shoulder popped and his back cracked. He felt better, almost well.

Mentally, he prepared himself for the first mission of the day, talking face to face with Octun. He wanted two things from Octun, one personal, one political.

"The latter matters most," he determined.

He stood and checked his legs. They felt steady. He walked over to a basin of steaming water.

Looking around the room, he saw the nurse's work. Clothes, medicines, stoked fire, soiled clothes gone, boots shined, new clothes out, and hot food, all while he slept. The nurse's customary stealth always sent a chill down his spine. Getting another would not help. Taught that way as children, all of them acted the same.

He tested the water in the basin with his fingertips, too hot, almost scalding. He cooled it down with water from a pitcher and washed his face. Wiping the steam from the mirror, he winced at his own reflection.

"Ah, Saroth, tsk, tsk, tsk, you may feel better but you don't look better. I pay for my indiscretions."

He washed and dressed himself, wondering why Seth had not come to check on him.

"Let the old man sleep until the last minute," he reckoned.

Saroth sat down and drank his usual two small cups of elixir. This he did every morning without fail.

He sniffed the food. It smelled good. If his appetite held, he might actually finish it all. He took a sip of the elixir. Like the day he and Octun argued over Seth, the elixir left a bitter taste in his mouth. After the bitterness passed... years of bitterness, he repented and admitted that no one supported him more.

Remembering he and Octun's first meeting, Saroth's chewing slowed. He felt such energy and thought so clearly in those days. There were times he felt invincible, like death was unnecessary to earn immortality.

The first words of their conversation grounded Saroth.

He and Octun had met at a ball. No one schemed for them to meet, they just did. Music played merrily, about as merry as Obenite music got. The theme of Obenite music remained the same throughout the centuries. Though some instruments and styles from other cultures influenced them, over all, composers scored grand, stiff, and flowing orchestral pieces with no rhythm.

That night he chased a beautiful woman who teased him mercilessly all evening. She frequently caught his eye, smiled coyly, then moved out of his view. She played hard to get but, he knew that if he persisted she would, eventually, reward him. Saroth saw her go out on the terrace. He didn't follow immediately, not wanting to seem too taken with her invitation. Evidently, she saw Octun there and came back inside. For when he went after her, she was not there. All he saw was a huge man whose uniform fit him well but very uncomfortably. Where she had skirted off to, he never found out.

He turned to go, when recognition sparked a thought. "This man had a strong connection to Lord Mernus. He might be useful."

He approached Octun. Octun bowed.

"You are Field Captain Iberius Octun of the Order of Keepers, aren't you?"

"Yes Monarch, I walk the path of the keepers."

"Your name and deeds have reached my ears. You are with Lord Mernus tonight?"

"Yes, my liege and if there is to be any glory, then let it be Obenin's," Octun replied.

Saroth forgot his pursuit as the man he came to call Iberius talked about the men in his command and their needs. Strangely, even though Saroth didn't think they would become friends, they did. He found Octun's self-possessed appearance was not at all a true indication of what went on in his mind. Normally reticent, except when it came to war, faith, and his men, as their friendship grew,

Saroth found ways to make Octun talk about personal matters. The intention of learning more about Mernus and his dealings faded into the background. At times, when his guard was down, Octun's sharp sense of humor and stories about his soldiers refreshed him and lifted his spirits. He found renewed hope in his subjects. After all, Octun had no royal blood. His father was a peasant whose misfortune turned to good fortune. If there was one truly loyal subject, there may be more. Octun represented the hope Saroth held for all his people.
 Nevertheless, the one both worrisome and admirable thing about Octun was his dogma concerning faith and the Obenite religion. Then, he was a priest.

The aristocracy turned their noses up at their friendship. Saroth took heat from wealthy fathers for giving Octun assignments they thought their son's should have.

For eight years, their friendship remained steady. Octun even came to know Seth and spent time with him.
 He taught Seth swordplay and fencing teachers knew nothing about. Dueling was an important skill. Octun taught Seth that dueling was much different from battling axes, pikes, spears and everything else coming at you in a war; there were many opponents, not only one. Show off like a braggart, you die. Tire too quickly, you die. Fight as if you are alone, you die. Octun taught Seth the tenets, too, making him memorize at least fifty of them.

One summer day, after failing to shoot neither furred nor feathered creature, Octun pulled out two bottles of wine he had brought back from a campaign as a gift to Saroth. It tasted impotent, flat and too sweet. It didn't seem at all like a drink two men out in the wilderness would share. He found out otherwise.

He talked Octun into drinking more than he should. By doing so, Octun willingly broke a priesthood vow that day. Before long, they laughed, sang and soaked their feet in the River Fon. Of all the times he and Octun had spent together, that day was both the happiest and saddest.

Saroth bragged on Seth. He boasted of Seth's sword skills, his ability to set up a political scheme, his resourcefulness, even his strength. The question he asked was totally rhetorical, "Don't you think Seth will make an even a better king than me?"

"Well, I hope that you are immortal because I think Seth will make a horrible king." He accidentally sprayed a mouth full of wine in Octun's face. Octun's frank answer shook him from his inebriation.

"No...? No...? A horrible king?" Saroth objected.

"No to the first and yes to the second," Octun returned with finality.

"What do you mean 'no'?"

Wiping the wine from his face, Octun replied tensely, "I've never heard you say anything about his faith. Seth repeats the tenet but there is no zeal for them. His prayers are hollow as a log. You give him everything and let him blame others for his misdeeds. He never has to give account for anyone he mistreats. He is your opposite when it comes to the soul."

"Who are you to speak of raising a son? You don't even have one. I know what you are thinking, he's an albino. I didn't think you were so stupid as to believe in fairytales."

"What I believe has absolutely nothing to do with his skin. Albinos are just like any other man. I believe that there are two types of kings: those born to be king, like you, and those born to inherit a kingdom, like Prince Seth."

Octun must have suddenly remembered that he was arguing with the King because, without another word, he turned and strode away.

After Octun left, Saroth saw a rabbit scurry an arm's length away and heard the calls of woodcocks. He stayed and finished off the bottle of wine, plotting how to pay Octun back for insulting Seth. After starting on the second bottle, he fell asleep.

His fury lasted for weeks. He thought of putting Octun in prison. Lord Mernus would not have stood for it. Glynwith, Octun's region, would make a petition before the council citing all Octun's good deeds. Though he was powerful, he was not as powerful as the kings of old, whose words were life and death.

After the fury subsided to a slow burning vengeance, Saroth made Octun's life miserable. From then on, he refused Octun an audience. Octun went through channels just like everyone else. He figured to teach Octun the lesson not to be frank with those better than he.

Octun never attempted to apologize. Saroth sent Octun on campaigns, kept his regiment on the move, and personally got involved in denying his soldiers privileges that others enjoyed. He kept Octun's promotions as slow as possible without upsetting Lord Mernus.

But this sickness has brought me to my senses. Of all that I have done to hurt him, he has only returned good to me, thought Saroth.

Saroth knew that some of his opponents sought to undermine his rule. They solicited Octun's help. He sent them away with simple words. "I will not plot against the King."

One adversary, Lord Faung, Octun actually threatened to put in chains and execute for heresy. Of course, Octun could not legally carry out the threat against such a heavyweight. Lord Faung was a definite heavyweight, physically and politically. Besides, a living Faung was more of a benefit than a dead one. Instead, Octun barred the Lord Faung from all the temples, shrines, and other consecrated places. Stannick used Octun's actions to leverage information from Faung. Saroth used the information to choke the opposition and get them to support the war. In exchange, Saroth got Octun to lift the ban.

"All I have shown him is contempt, Saroth confessed, even by putting him here. Octun's faith transformed my contempt into good for both the kingdom and my son."

He came close to finishing his breakfast and headed for the door. The guard snapped his heels together as soon as he turned the latch. In the corridor, he inquired as to the whereabouts of Keeper Octun.

He was in his study.

"Shall I get the nurse, Prince Seth, or an escort, sire?" the guard asked sincerely.

"No, if I fall I'll drag myself the rest of the way," the King jested, leaving the guard at first confused, then afraid he had offended the king.

The guard went to one knee and bowed his head. "Sire, but the Prince, he gave me charge."

"I am the king. I release you from that charge." Then, with a resigned smile, Saroth thought twice. He knew that he pushed his luck. The feel-good moment would not last. They never did. If an attack caught him and resulted in an injury or worse, the guard stood in danger of Seth's wrath.

"Very well...," snapped Saroth. "Grab a mate. You can be my escort. The other can get the two cases lying on top of the trunk in yonder room."

As the guard reached for the door, it opened. The guard braced his shoulder to protect the king.

Startled, Octun stepped back from the door, bowed quickly and apologized.

Saroth walked past, saying, "Didn't I tell you last night to stop that Iberius? Besides, a sick man has come to make amends." He directed one guard to place the cases on Octun's writing table. The other helped him sit down. Then he dismissed them both.

Octun closed the door.

"Good morning," Saroth grinned, knowing Octun's discomfort.

Returning the greeting, Octun kept his distance and stood by the door.

"I guess I will have to get right to the point," Saroth cleared his throat. "I am ashamed for what I have done to you over the years."

"What you have done to me?" Octun asked naively.

"The campaigns, the denials...," Saroth replied, not believing Octun's ignorance.

"The campaigns were what I wanted. As far as the denials are concerned, I wasn't aware that there had been any, except, maybe my promotions and .... Then, I was appointed here. So, I wasn't sure what to think."

"Have you ever thought about why you were placed here, Iberius?" the King spat cruelly, vexed at Octun's innocence.

Octun squinted in thought.

"It was a half-hearted attempt to put aside my anger," Saroth continued. "Contempt was still in my heart... and there were other reasons, too."

"What reason could there be for putting me so far away from out there... where I am needed," demanded Octun, his finger pointing to somewhere far away from the temple.

Saroth let it pass. He wanted to hold on to the moment, to get that for which he came, affirmation and reconciliation.

"I am glad you are so naive to the deceit and craftiness of the aristocracy, and of your own fame. You don't realize how much power you could have. First of all, think about this. Out on the battlefield, you can command men and influence the outcome of the battle. Here, you have put skillful men in several regiments. They are quickly making their way up the ranks. The priests you prepare for service truly minister to the soldiers. One day there will be hundreds of Octuns mopping up the battlefield with the enemy."

Octun shifted in uneasy consideration.

"Furthermore, one day I must die."

Octun started to speak but, raising his hand, King Saroth quieted him.

"Even if I recover from this sickness, one day I must die and Seth will become king." Leaning forward in Octun's chair and looking him straight in the eyes, Saroth hesitated and hoped against hope. Then asked, "Do you still feel the same about Seth?"

"I ...." Octun reconsidered and decided not to say anything.

"I thought so. I am trying to prepare the way for him. Most everything I do is for him. I have to build his reputation. If we can win this war and he is associated with the victory, it will stay with him. And when he becomes king, everyone will be able to see him for who he really is, not judged by some stupid wives' tale. What if I died and you were in a position that put you in constant conflict with Seth? People respect you and there are many who adore you. I'll bet you don't even realize that you are the main reason the pilgrimages here have increased.

"Yes Iberius, these are troubled times but that's not the only reason. There is a person here that my subjects trust to have the heart of a true worshiper of Obenin. Many of them would follow you in whatever you said. That is why I can't have you on my counsel. As a member, you would have a political voice. The other counsel members, with their suspicious natures, will see you as a threat that can diminish their influence.

"And there is another reason for putting you here." Saroth continued. "You will get the respect you deserve and your needs will be supplied for the rest of your life. Your work is more visible, and Seth will be less paranoid of you if he feels that he can keep an eye on you. In time, he will regain trust in you. Lastly, you must crown Seth king. When the people see you crown him, they will accept him."

"Your council!" Octun's voice lost what warmth it had gained. "I have no desire to be confined in stuffy chambers with those loud windbags who determine the fate of thousands without care. I want to command, to breathe the same air as the men I command, to fight in the same mud, and talk to them as we bind our wounds and spread the glory for Obenin. That is where I belong."

"If you truly feel that way, then you belong here at the temple more than you realize. The men you turn out from these grounds are the best and they always give you the glory. When I look at those who will save us, I see faith in their eyes, faith that you gave them."

"Let your praise go to Obenin."

Hold on to the moment, Saroth thought.

He decided to go for the second mission, affirmation. "Look, Iberius, I am sorry that you feel this way, but right now I need you to do something for me. I want you to lead the mission back to Oracle.

"I know this is a sudden change. Last night it came to me. I can never forget you speaking your mind about Seth, but I can forgive you. I know you don't have any malice towards him even though you are wrong about him not making a good king. Our friendship may never be the same, but I don't want to go to my grave with hatred between us."

"I have never hated you," answered Octun.

Saroth noticed the inflection in Octun's voice. *Alas, thank Obenin, a break through,* Saroth thought.

"My king, I have missed your companionship and if it were not for the wine, I would never have said such a thing. If something were to happen to you, I would never defy Seth, out of respect for you and my own beliefs. And of all the friends I have had, you were the best and the only one who could ever make me really at ease."

"Funny, that was our friendship's downfall. Anyway, this is the first time Seth will be away from my direct protection and this trip may be dangerous if our security has leaked. Take care of him, Iberius, and give him a chance. You'll find out that he has the potential to be great. You taught him more than you realize. He still remembers. Perhaps my greatest mistake was to take you out of his life. Instead, I probably should have assigned him to your regiment."

Octun's entire countenance changed. The defensiveness fell from his eyes. His palms turned outward and he rested on his heels.

"I will take care of him Saroth and I will keep an open mind and minister to him."

But there was something else. Curiosity stirred in Saroth. Octun's voice went a little hollow. None of the previous zeal presented itself. He only showed enthusiasm. For Octun, that was a big difference. Saroth decided not to digress and end on this strong note. Octun affirmed his decision. There was not a better priest in all the order to hold the position of Warrior High Priest, Keeper of Obenin's Primary Temple.

Saroth prepared to leave. He got what he came for though he wanted more, much more.

"Is there something else, my liege?"

"No," he lied, wishing he had not been so obvious. "Time to go."

"Obenin forbid... your.... If am high priest, I will crown Seth king," vowed Octun.

Saroth felt better at hearing it.

Octun retrieved the king's escort, who directed his comrade to retrieve the cases.

Saroth interrupted, "Leave them, they are for the Keeper."

"My Lord, such gifts, it is not proper for me to receive these things."

"I am the king, I say what it proper. It is not a request from a friend but an order from your king who happens to.... Take them." he finished.

Saroth leaned on the guard and walked out.

Boarding his coach, King Saroth looked across the front of the stables at Seth and the Hands of Obenin as they busied themselves to leave. His goodbye to Seth had been short, too short. Seth, overly anxious about the journey, let his attention drift. He nodded his head, but Saroth doubted whether he had heard a word. Saroth's nurse tried to comfort him. From experience, she knew an attack threatened.

The coachman opened the door and poked his head in, "Is there anything else, me Lord?"

"No, Hofas. You may leave at Keeper Octun's command." The King directed his attention back to Seth.

He tried to relax and prepare for the bumpy ride into the city. He was late already. In order to draw attention away from Octun and Seth, he had arranged a ceremony in the village center. Brock Stannick did a good job in raising the anticipation. Seth and Octun could get to the barge and float away without anyone taking notice.

The coachmen took the seat and spat darkened, snuff-filled spit on the ground.

With a lash of the reins, he ordered, "Giddyup, Jiataro! And be good or I'll turns ye into shoe leather."

The coach lurched forward. They were off toward the southern gate to wait for the word to leave. Saroth nursed the bottle of elixir. While the elixir slightly eased the grinding pain in his gut and chest, worry raised his anxiety and kept complete relief at bay. The nurse tried to take the bottle from him. Clutching it like a precious thing from which he could not part, he hissed at her. The pain rebounded twofold, doubling him over in royal agony.

Meanwhile, Octun uncovered two rectangular cases. He ran his hands over the gold leaves of the vine running along the edges and met again just above the latch. He looked at his name and touched the king's crest, which the craftsman recessed into the wood. By this, whoever saw it would immediately know this as a clear sign of his cherished connection to the king.

He unlatched the first case and opened it carefully.

"Al Kenoir, from a gentle breeze to a violent storm," whispered Octun respectfully. "How did an Obenite king come by this?"

The onyx scabbard fascinated him. Silver vines, similar to the gold one on the case, ran along the tube like scabbard all the way to the tip. He wrapped his fingers around the hilt of the sword with his right hand and exposed the blade. His eyes sparkled at the sight as he pulled it out completely. The sword had one cutting edge and tassels dangled from the leather- wrapped hilt.

Octun tested the sword, making a quick lunge. He held the sword out, watching the tip.

"Good balance, steady, strong, the work of a master. Saroth will never be able to tell me how he got a new sword from a rebel craftsman."

Guilt pricked at Octun's heart. He certainly would not have parted with such a thing even if he had more than one. Not only that, if others found out, they would think he had been bought. Valuable contraband is something no one showed in public. Octun decided the sword would have to be a private treasure. Otherwise, he foresaw unnecessary fights with someone who might insult Saroth.

He opened the second case. The plain oak case also bore the king's crests and Octun's name inlaid into the wood. The scabbard and sword lay side-by-side. He thumped the thick leather grip and ran his index finger along the throat. He picked up the sword and grasped the hilt firmly, a perfect fit. The leather grip felt comfortable in him hand. From the pommel to the point of the blade, this weapon's master made it a lethal weapon of beauty. The pommel was small enough so as not to get in the way but large enough to knock heads when necessary. The guard curved upward, away from his hand. He judged the blade about the width of four of his fingers, both edges hardened, and a fuller.

Octun held the sword over his head and brought it down with quick chopping motions while advancing with quick short steps, then made a lateral sweep across what would be his victim's mid-section.

Saroth had bridged the gulf that separated them and Octun felt joyous about it. He no longer just served the crown as a duty-bound Keeper, but, once again in a mutual bond that he vowed never to let escape again.

"Ye gift from good King Saroth, ye battle sword, I name thee *Romala*, the charge for me to bring Prince Seth back to faith."

CHAPTER 17
Leaving The Primary Temple

Parmos did not want to leave the temple, let alone travel to Oracle. He wanted to stay right at the Primary Temple. He sat quietly in the coach feeling guilty and scared. The last minute change that placed Octun in charge of the mission comforted him. How he got ready so quickly amazed them all.

"This feels strange," remarked Ictheos. "We are leaving the temple."

He pulled his coat up around his neck.

"I know," returned Jared, keeping warm by pressing against Ulthea. He pointed at Prince Seth who pinned his muffler to his hood, keeping his face warm. "I tossed and turned all night long."

"We all did," Ictheos agreed.

Parmos cleared his throat in denial.

Ulthea, teased, "There are two things I don't think Parmos could ever lose, his appetite or a wink of sleep."

Parmos did not laugh. He replied, "Here we go to who knows what."

"Obenin will take care of us," reassured Ulthea. "He has not brought us here to hurt us."

Jared screwed his lips in displeasure.

"Do you doubt?" Ulthea confronted.

"You have so much faith. I don't like feeling guilty," Jared remarked.

"He will give us all faith," she reassured.

Parmos butted in, "Here comes Keeper Octun."

He squinted then rubbed his eyes to make sure he wasn't seeing things. "He looks different," pointed out Parmos.

Octun approached them. Charge Horep listened and nodded his head reassuringly as they walked.

Octun stopped, pointed here and there. Horep pointed likewise. Levid loitered on Octun's left looking around but listening all the same.

"Is he smiling?" asked Parmos.

Ictheos remarked, "Someone doused him in happiness."

"It fits him," added Ulthea.

Parmos watched as Octun walked away from Horep and Levid and towards them. When Octun opened the door, they almost tumbled to the ground.

"Good morning," Octun greeted.

"Good morning Keeper Octun," they all responded not quite in unison.

"Are you prepared?" He smiled broadly and then continued. "After all, it will be some time before I return."

Now he's grinning, thought Parmos.

"Does anyone need anything or need to visit the outhouse? Do you want anything else to eat, Parmos?"

Parmos gawked at the others in disbelief. A pun? He never heard Keeper Octun make anything close to a pun.

"If not, we shall be off. Remember, keep the blinds down until we reach the dock." Octun slapped the door shut.

"What's come over him?" Ictheos asked, scratching his head.

"Maybe he's excited, just like we are?" Ulthea posed, scratching her scalp with her index finger, not quite believing her own assumption.

Jared rubbed his chin. "No, I don't think excited is the right word, more like, tickled to death."

Parmos let the black cloth swing down to cover the window and tied it to the little peg driven into the side of the coach.

The coach moved forward. Every now and then, Parmos peeked from behind the blind. He did not see Seth and Octun but he imagined them riding out front. He could not imagine either of them bringing up the rear. About halfway down the hill, Parmos saw a man dressed in beggar's clothes walking hurriedly down the hill. When the beggar looked up at him, he let the blind drop.

The coach descended into the valley to meet the rising fog. They passed no other travelers save the one vagabond. King Saroth's stop in the village insured clear streets.

They crossed over the River Edge and headed down shore, passing piers with flat barges and small boats docked at them. Finally, they passed the last of Ethenia's boathouses. They were in the very outskirts of a few small trading posts and mills along the waterfront. The party halted at a simple landing that looked seldom used.

Parmos chanced another glimpse from behind the blinds. The fog clearing, he saw two men approach Octun. He made out a couple of small barges tied to the dock. Octun greeted them but they did not return his greeting. Instead, alert, they placed their hands on the hilt of their swords. At which, Octun unpinned his muffler and rode closer. They recognized him instantly and greeted him with a salute and a bow.

When Octun swung his mount around, Parmos let the blind drop.

Octun knocked on the coach and ordered, "Get out and follow me. Stay close."

They got out of the coach. "No time to look around," Octun corrected Ulthea, who scanned her surroundings.

A short man with a snub nose and fat lips approached and grabbed the harness of Octun's horse. "Good Morning, sir."

"Good morning, Lieutenant Amaris," Octun returned. "Where were you?"

"Instead of sending my men, I made the checks, sir. I needed a change."

"All secure?"

"It has been still all morning. Our men have watched the shores all night. One of the corporals reported an incident but it turned out to be nothing, some boy arguing with his girl. We ran them off."

"Have you met Prince Seth?" Octun nodded his head in the Prince's direction, to his left.

Amaris knelt before Prince Seth. Seth unpinned his muffler and watched Amaris' face.

"You may rise," directed Seth.

Parmos watched Octun untie the rope and cast off. He marked how Octun busied himself. By the effort he put into the physical labor, he differed from no other soldier. He addressed his soldiers with respect and they respected him. He gave simple orders, he didn't lord over them. In the temple, all he really ever saw was the vigilant and brooding Octun. He spent time instructing them, teaching them rituals, leading them in the various prayers and observances they needed to know. Never before had Parmos observed this side of him.

Seth hardly said a word to anyone the entire morning. He stood around looking princely. No one bothered him. Octun gave Seth as much space on the barge as possible. So did everyone else for that matter. He waited around a lot as if he expected something. No one knew what he wanted. Parmos noticed the only thing he really said was, get this or get that. After a while, Seth sat down and remained in the same place, dead center the barge.

As the fog lifted completely, Ethenia revealed itself. Parmos followed the shoreline, panning northerly toward the village. Somewhere in there the king held the attention of the villagers while Parmos and the others stole away downstream.

The city sat high above them in levels. Homes looked like terraces along the hillside. Brittle and dry evergreens dotted the landscape. Nothing looked new, but the buildings stood in good repair and appeared as strong as the first day the carpenters and stonemasons built them.

Then he saw it, high above the city. A lithe ring of cloud obscured the view.

"Look!" Parmos shouted, pointing off into the distance.

The others noticed too. Atop the plateau, watching over the village stood an immense and intimidating structure. "Is that the temple?"

"It must be," Jared reckoned. "But it doesn't really look like the paintings."

"It looks even bigger than it feels!" Parmos declared.

"The towers, Obenin's name," expressed Ictheos.

"I will be glad to see it again," sighed Ulthea.

"I want to come back soon... real soon," Parmos breathed.

"We will see it soon enough," Octun broke in. "Soon enough."

The river jutted southwesterly. They lost sight of the temple momentarily. After passing by a near peak, the temple appeared briefly in all its glory, rising between the smaller hills of Ethenia. Parmos tried hard to form its essence in his mind, the feel of it, the dusty damp smell, and the crackle of burning wood in the fireplace. He felt homesick already.

The Hands of Obenin, that's what the king called them. It sounded important. Last night, he found comfort in it. Now, the thought chilled him to the bone. He sighed a prayer for their safe return and encouragement for their little band of ten.

Humming drowned out the gentle lapping of waves. He looked up to see Octun taking a deep breath, as if he was about to sing? Manning the rudder, he looked steadily downstream toward their destiny, Oracle, in the Barren Lands, wherever that was.

"My mother birth me to
father's hands
To win glory for the land
To find the faith so others may see
and suffer the cause until I'm free.
Free to serve Obenin's cause.
Free to serve without pause. . . .

Octun returned to humming, singing a few bars here and there whenever it suited him.

Studying Prince Seth, seeing this different side of Octun, Parmos saw how Saroth and Octun became close. However, he wondered how such a free spirit as Saroth could have fathered such a cold fish. Saroth opened himself up so much to them. Seth erected a wall of stone, surrounded the wall by a moat full of crocodiles and pits full of poisonous serpents.

Stirring from sleep, Parmos felt someone stroking his hair. He rolled over to see Ulthea's hand hovering over him. He tried to focus.

"What did you do that for?" he asked.

"I just wanted to touch it," she admitted, then retreated to Jared and Ictheos, who were pointing and chattering excitedly.

Parmos sat up. The barge moved a little swifter than before. Smoke from the fire blew toward him. The warmth it gave was well worth putting up with the smoke. Octun still manned the rudder. His face took on the more characteristic seriousness.

Ictheos' hands moved in a fashion indicating that whatever he saw was huge. Jared agreed. His hands and arms indicated something even larger. Parmos really didn't care to find out what they were so excited about. On the barge behind them, soldiers burst out in laughter and songs. He could not hear the subject of all their ruckus. Their light spirit made him desire to be a part of them instead.

Seth sat closer to the bow of the boat. He found it odd that he actually moved further from the fire. He looked all the others over occasionally. Within the last few moments, the frequency of his glances increased.

Finally, Seth cleared his throat. "I want some water. Ulthea, get me some."

She jumped in surprise. After she regained her composure, she replied, "Yes, my lord," and started to get it.

Octun interceded. "My lord, the servants were left at the temple. On this journey, Prince Seth, we shall all be getting for ourselves."

Scowling, Seth retorted, "A prince deserves to be treated like a prince even in the wilderness."

"Indeed you are the heir. But the king has placed me with the care of you all. The tenets say, *serving one another in peace binds us together in war. We must not burden each other with menial tasks we can do for ourselves. Offer to do for others while you do for yourself. Such is the life of the true Obenite.*" He paused, waiting for Seth to reply.

When he received none, he continued, "It binds everyone into a one spirit and we will irritate each other a lot less. If anyone is to be looked after, it is the Hands of

Obenin. It is your father's will and it is because of them that we are on this journey."

Seth stewed. Yet he got up, retrieved a fur skin of water and retreated back to the bow where he glared at Octun. As he opened the skin and let the water pour into his mouth, he cut his eyes menacingly at Octun.

Parmos watched him carefully. He hoped Octun did not anger the prince too much. After all, he was the prince, divine right to rule and all of that.

Moments passed. Parmos noticed a change in Seth. The shadow of conflict swept his face, revealing that he struggled to stay angry.

Seth spoke, clearly, from rote memory, "There is no substitute for a skillful sword and the stamina to wield it from dusk to dawn."

From wherever it came, it was not a tenet. Octun relaxed his normally tight lips. His mouth opened slightly. A smidgen of surprise and flattery sparkled in his eyes.

Was this a compliment or a challenge or both? Parmos chose to believe it a compliment.

Then Seth moved his lips silently. He may as well have shouted it, "I remember." Seth repeated, "I remember."

The river turned easterly toward the Great River. Darkness fell and they spent the night aboard the barges, which they had tied to shore. Prince Seth, forsaking his inhibitions, wedged himself between Ulthea and Jared to steal their body heat. Octun sat at bow of the barge, looking into the darkness.

Why wouldn't he join them around the fire? Was he being vigilant? Was he praying? wondered Parmos.

He wanted to sit with him. The thought of walking over and saying something filled him with anxiety. Octun had no children until now. Three sons and a daughter were his burden. He watched over them, giving to them the only way he knew, his faith, his protection, and his presence. Parmos loved him deeply.

Octun stood and stretched. The bear woke up and declared himself the king of the forest. He prowled over to the fire.

"Keeper Octun?" asked Parmos.

Octun looked at him as if to ask, "Yes?"

"How much longer will we be on this river?"

"We will disembark at Thell's Landing in two more days."

"How long is the trip to the Barren Lands?" Parmos continued.

"About two days' ride before we reach them and another five and a half days to reach Lord Cuere and Oracle."

Jared cut into the middle of the conversation, "What kind of man is Lord Cuere? Though he brought us here, none of us remember him."

"He is a powerful wizard," Seth butted-in. "He has done many great wonders for Father and me."

"Really?" inquired Ulthea, her curiosity rising. "What sorts of things?"

"He makes people disappear and reappear before my very eyes. Pigeons fly from his hands and he makes things levitate."

Parmos' eyes fixed on Seth.

"When someone said something about my skin or mistreated me, my father would have Amrion fix them?" explained Seth.

"Amrion?" Parmos asked, looking as if he had lost track of the story somehow.

"Lord Cuere..., you should know all his names by now," scolded Seth.

"Yes my lord." Parmos fought against his shame. He knew the name. It was stupid of him to ask such a question.

"What do you mean by fix them?" Ulthea asked nervously.

"You know what I mean, put a hex on them, perpetual bad luck, smite them with sickness, curse them so they will never prosper. He even made one man grow a tail."

"Can he really do that?" asked Jared, doubting.

Seth retorted matter-of-factly, "He brought you here, didn't he?"

"That is undeniable," thought Parmos. He glanced at Octun. His faced fixed into an unreadable expression.

"Do we have to live alone with him?" he asked, growing more nervous as they spoke of Lord Cuere.

"Yes," said Octun flatly.

"For how long?" Parmos entreated.

"Until he says otherwise," replied Octun's, sounding dissatisfied with the arrangement.

Parmos looked at Prince Seth. He could answer the question that noone else had answered. They all looked at Seth, who, in turn, smiled guardedly.

"You may as well tell us all," said Octun, obviously curious himself.

Seth hesitated. Then, spoke to Octun, mostly. Parmos' heart thumped in his chest. He did not feel cold anymore.

"You will go back to Oracle. Lord Cuere will use Oracle to cast a powerful spell on you. He will use you to kill the enemy and bring them to their knees. If he says rain, you will make it rain. If he says lightning, you will make it fall from the sky."

Jared cut in. "How can that be? Is that possible? Chancellor Levid taught nothing about that. The tenets don't even teach against such a thing. It is witchcraft. Keeper, isn't that right?"

Octun did not answer.

"Yes, it is possible. Father Obenin provided us a way to defeat our enemy. No one will be able to withstand us. The Benomian Alliance, Aspharia, the lower regions. Anywhere and everywhere we choose to go will fall under Obenite power. This is more than about deciding who will get rain for their crop and fair weather for fishing. This is about nature's power to destroy."

He paused and stared directly at Octun. "With the power we possess in you, we will do more than all of our previous armies have done, combined."

Ulthea broke out in tears of regret. Jared and Ictheos tried to comfort her.

"Why are you whimpering? You should be leaping up and down," returned Seth, his annoyance with Ulthea ringing clear.

"It's. . . just. . . that it seems like we are going to have to hurt people and take things from them. Isn't it enough to keep the enemy back?"

Jared corrected, "It is in the tenets that wherever Obenites go, that if the lands will not acknowledge our god, then they shall be compelled. The king will infuse every aspect of life with Obenite beliefs."

Seth parried, "Actually, you are talking about the Tenet of Destiny. There are two versions of the Tenet of Destiny. I prefer the one in the Disputed Text. It is convenient for what is at hand. It says that anyone who refuses to submit is an infidel and deserves to die. They may be saved by confessing the faith." Seth looked at Octun, then continued. "Surely, Levid and Octun taught you both."

"Obenin, help us!" sniffed Ulthea.

Jared verbalized his thoughts. "We will be like gods?"

The moment he did so, Octun stood up. His voice boomed, "No you will not. You will be instruments of Obenin."

"Forgive this poor servant. I did not mean anything by it," pleaded Jared.

"Mistakes like this give room for heresy. We are servants of Obenin and his people, subjects of the king."

Keeper Octun put his hand on Jared's shoulder in such a way that Parmos jumped. Jared trembled from head to toe.

The conversation from the previous night still haunted Parmos. The way Octun looked at Jared after he made the comment, about them being like gods, filled him with ominous remorse. He felt as if he had made the comment too.

As usual, he left himself out of current conversations. He sat close to them. He directed his attention more to the shoreline than the conversation, giving him the appearance of eavesdropping. He vacillated between daydreaming and observation. He never really had a whole lot to offer to the conversations anyway. He wanted Octun to take them back to the safety of the temple. Life there was simple. He ate. He learned. He slept. He meditated in his dreams and woke up trying to recite tenets. For months, they encountered the exact same things, day in and day out. Suddenly, everything was different and none of them adjusted very well.

The soldiers moved with determination, clearing the camps and loading supplies and gear back onto the barge. In a moment, both barges looked orderly and clean.

"Too much energy for this early in the morning," Ictheos commented.

"Start gathering your gear," ordered Octun.

Parmos wrapped all his belongings in a bundle and stuffed it in his pack.

Octun talked briefly to his men. He called them by name. He listened as they spoke. Parmos observed as Octun rubbed his chin. He nodded and said a few words. The soldiers made a slight bow at the waist and boarded the barge.

Octun walked back across the pier to Prince Seth. He bowed quickly pointing to his men, then to Parmos and the others. Seth pointed to the other side of the river, then downstream. Octun bowed again and walked toward them.

"We will be here for a little while longer," he announced.

Thell's landing was no more than a rickety jetty sticking out into the river. There, three more soldiers met them with horses.

All in hooded cloaks, the moment struck Parmos as a little strange. The soldiers gave them dark brown robes and small round hats. After dressing, Parmos looked around.

Ictheos voiced the comment Parmos chose to keep to himself: "We look like pilgrims coming from the Obenin's Temple," remarked Ictheos.

Ulthea approached him, "That is exactly what we are." The soldiers helped him up on their horse. Parmos climbed aboard. The horse brayed and stepped forward. Parmos clutched the saddle horn.

A soldier patted his horse's neck. "If you are nervous, she will be too."

The road narrowed into no more than a path with grass down the middle and thick underbrush on both sides.

Parmos noticed that one of the soldiers rode up beside him. He looked over at the soldier. The soldier held the reins with his right hand. He put his left hand near his sword. The soldier looked a little older than he, only much tougher. Unlike Octun, this soldier wore his hair in wild unruly thumb-sized braids. No one would think he was a soldier at all or a priest for that matter.

Clank! An arrow appeared to deflect off the soldier's robe.

"At arms!" he yelled, then, made a high shrilling whistle.

Parmos' horse stopped at the command. He could not get it to go forward to the left or to the right.

****

Beforehand, Octun knew something was not quite right when his mount's ears twitched forward. The animal's gait switched from a lazy swagger, in which his head dipped up and down, to alert, head high in the air and ears forward.

He placed his hand on his sword and his men reacted so swiftly and quietly that he had to glance back to see if they had taken position.

Death cries erupted from the wood, close, way too close. Men rushed them from all sides. Yells and shouts from their attackers disoriented him. Octun did let Ulthea's screams distract him.

Octun's mount obeyed the reins. A man, bearing a knife, came at him from his right. He held his foot out and the man ran into the bottom of it. To oppose his other assailant on his left, Octun pressed his leg against his mount's right side. The horse turned and the attacker ran between his horse's buttocks and bounced off.

With sword in hand, Octun leapt from his horse and charged toward the children. He could see that his men had placed themselves in defensive positions around Parmos and the others. Though his attackers tried, they hadn't wounded anyone. One assailant came toward his sword arm. Without breaking stride, Octun slashed the man's chest. His enemy fell. Octun could not see how many attackers there were, but one by one, they fell. He found himself next to Seth, who fiercely beat back an assailant, skillfully wielding his sword to his foe's end.

An attacker dashed toward Octun's back with a sword raised well above his head, chopping downward to split open the top of his head. He was too close and moving too fast. Octun stepped backward and elbowed the man in the face. With his foe stunned, Octun wheeled around and hit the man in the forehead with the pommel of his sword. He fell to the ground and the point of Octun's sword followed.

The young ranger, assigned to Parmos, stood ground and protected him. He used everything as a weapon - his horse, his hands, and his sword. Octun congratulated himself. He chose all of them well. Everyone one fought well, even Seth.

The archer, Octun saw him launch an arrow and duck behind a tree. The chain mail and leather armor under their robes protected them. The arrowheads were not made from good metal. The chain mail did have weaknesses, and a good archer could take advantage of it. Octun picked up a shield from a dead attacker and charged. He heard the arrow fracture off his shield. He glanced from behind it. The archer was fast. He was already pulling the bow back. The arrow grazed his leg. Octun kept moving. He glanced out again. The archer stepped backward, preparing to launch another arrow. Octun leapt to the side. A good thing too, that one barely missed his thigh. He glanced again. The archer turned to retreat. It was over. Octun's shield smashed into him. He needed one alive. On the ground, he kneed the archer in the groin twice, then gashed his firing arm.

Those who could retreat, ran away shouting profanities at the fighting skills of the band of pilgrims.

Prince Seth dashed after them, but Parmos' ranger tackled him before he got too far.

Seth leapt up shouting furiously, "How dare you touch me in such a manner!"

He lunged the point of his sword toward the ranger's chest. The ranger deflected it easily. Seth withdrew and attacked. The ranger blocked him at every turn.

Seth stepped back and glared at the ranger, "Keeper Octun, I demand you punish him right now."

"Punish the man who saved your life, my lord?"

Prince Seth looked blankly at him. "No one touches me like that, no one!"

"You would not have listened otherwise. It is foolish to pursue them alone. It is foolish for us to pursue them at all. This is ground they know well. Leading us into a preset trap or setting a trap on the fly are old tricks but good ones. We have a survivor. Let's see what we can get out of him."

Octun paused. Prince Seth bit his lips. He looked at the ranger as to burn his face into memory.

"The best thing now," Octun continued, "is to see exactly who we were fighting. Were these highway men looking for opportunity or is there more to it?"

He directed Seth to the archer, whom he had dragged from the underbrush. He studied him for a moment and figured that his wounds were more painful than severe. Octun searched him. He found no hidden weapons.

Octun grasped two handfuls of the man's coat and spoke sternly, "Who are you and why did you attack us?"

The archer did not answer. Octun shook him and put his thumb in the man's wound. "How many of you are still hiding here?"

The archer groaned loudly to keep from answering.

Seth, whose hood had fallen back during the fight, knelt at Octun's side. The archer seemed genuinely afraid of Prince Seth.

Octun perceived the man's fear, though he was not sure whether he recognized Seth. "Or, was it something else." He let the archer's head fall to the ground.

"You take him. Maybe he will talk for you."

Seth leaned over the archer. The man squirmed away from him. Seth put his knee on the archer wound.

"Let me have him," Seth urged.

"Afraid of albinos, are you?" Seth continued.

The archer tried again to get away from Seth yelling, "Get 'im off of me. Please get 'im off of me."

"What's the matter," tormented Seth. "You don't believe all the fables about albinos do you? About how all of us were born out of evil and witchcraft, or that to touch one is death. How about the one that says we have no color because we don't have the life of a soul? Or, do you believe the one about us being cannibals?" Seth paused and took on an even more menacing look.

"No, Squire, no." the archer lied. "To say that would be to mean. . . . The Gran' Heir is evil. . . and to say ... that... that would be faithless."

"So your Crown Prince is an albino. I don't believe it. You ever seen him?"

"No, Squire, I ain't never seen 'im, but every one knows it!"

"Liar!" Seth shouted, lifting the archer by his collar.

"Aiiee." the man screamed.

"Well, how do you know he's an albino if you have never seen him?"

"I ain't seen 'im, Squire."

"Then how do you know what he looks like?"

"I told you! It's well known, Squire, that he's a white soul."

"I would like to meet this Prince Seth, he sounds smashing. Maybe we can get together and swap recipes on how to properly cook peasants, tenderize the stringy meat and get rid of the wild taste."

The archer howled in terror, flailing wildly, trying to get away. Octun stepped on the archer's hand, stopping him from grabbing a rock to bash Prince Seth's head.

"So you were going to try and kill me?"

"No, Squire!"

"Liar! You think I'm going to put you in my pot and eat you, don't you?"

The archer cried, "Don't eat me, me lord, I'm just a robber, that's only tryin' to make an honest livin', we weren't tryin' to hurt you much squire, just take your money, that's all, put food on the table, that's all me lord, we have four bands of twelve people each, we work diff'rent paths, there's no one else on this path, Squire, I promise on my poor mum's grave, please spare me, I'm just a poor peasant, loyal to the king, I am, I go on pilgrimage every year, I do..., personal friend of Keeper Octun, I am...."

The guards laughed loudly at the man's suggestion that he knew Octun.

The archer stopped his begging and chanced a rotten- toothed smile, knowing something he said just saved his life.

"Little liar," Seth quipped. "Today, you shall live, albeit, until the gallows."

CHAPTER 18
Peril In The Barren Lands

Parmos stood in his stirrups and looked toward the horizon. Everything was downhill from there. The ground ended in a black mass. One red thread ran through the middle and disappeared in the distance. A small outpost guarded the flimsy wooden gate that marked the entrance to the Barren Lands.

"We are not going in there," he hoped.

Approaching the phenomenon, he saw that it was not the earth that was black, but a thick grove of petrified trees.

They spent the night at the outpost. Parmos sat on one of the four bunks in the room. Normally, Ulthea did not sleep in the same room as the boys. One of their guards placed the fourth bunk there after Ulthea whined so that Octun gave in. She did not want to be alone in a place like this, none of them did.

Ulthea sat on her bed, legs crossed. Jared sat by her. Ictheos, with his back turned to the rest, poked in the fire. Sparks rose up the chimney. He stopped and let them fly out of sight. Then, he started poking again.

Sadness came over Parmos. He could not explain it. He should be happy. His belly ached with food. Tonight, he had a bed instead of the hard ground.

Ulthea got up from her bed and sat by him. Jared didn't say anything but Parmos noticed that he didn't like it. Her eyes, soft with concern, moved him.

"Why are you sad, still hungry?" joked Ulthea.

He smiled. She had a way of making him feel better. She lifted his spirit and made the day a bit brighter. Her manner coerced him to talk.

"I don't know. I don't know anything."

"Yes, you do," Ulthea shot back. "You know the four of us are together. You know Keeper Octun will not let anything happen to us. You know our faith sustains us."

Parmos lowered his head for a moment. Then, he looked at her. "You have faith enough for both of us."

"Her faith cannot sustain you. You must have faith of your own," interrupted Jared shortly.

"Leave him alone, Jared," rebuked Ictheos, his back still to them.

"Jared didn't mean anything by it. This journey makes us all nervous," defended Ulthea.

"Oh, he meant something by it," insisted Ictheos. "But if you say so, I will leave it alone."

"Stop causing trouble," Ulthea warned.

"I'm not causing trouble. This whole place is trouble, if you ask me," returned Ictheos, an uncaring edge to his voice.

"Have some faith," urged Ulthea.

"Yes, have some faith," echoed Jared.

"That black mass of stone trees scares me. I don't want to go in there. I don't see why the soldiers even stay here. Who in their right mind would go into a place like that?" commented Parmos.

"We would. Everything scares you," accused Jared. His eyes never left Ulthea.

Ulthea shot him a look and agreed with Parmos, "It scares me, too. You need to apologize, Jared. Why are you being so cruel?"

"I'm sorry."

Parmos took the apology for what it was, half-hearted. But, it was true. He was a big crybaby and could not help himself. He thought of Octun. He didn't think Octun was afraid of anyone or anything.

****

Seth lay on his side watching Octun move his bunk closer to the fire. He wondered why Octun brushed the straw off the bunk onto the floor. Once it was all off, Octun breathed a mighty "Humph," and rolled onto the bunk and curled up to keep his feet from dangling off the edge.

Seth asked, "Why did you brush the straw off?"

"I prefer the hard surface. The straw gets in everything."

"I will be glad to feel the comfort of a real bed again." returned Seth.

"It is said that, by far, the best part of a dangerous mission is to return home in success."

Seth turned on his back thinking. Is honor still so important to this man? Or has he changed, like those on the Grand Council, speaking of great things, giving oratory of their great ideas, but who often dealt in treachery?

Seth had personally commissioned Brock Stannick to find some well kept secret or dishonorable act on Octun. Since he had to deal with him, Seth wanted something to show that Octun was just like everyone that advised his father, deceitful, self-interested, liars. Stannick found nothing - no pay-offs to favor those not deserving burial in Obenin's Temple, no angry women, no bastard children, no cleverly hidden piles of rubbish to be sniffed out. Was Octun crazy enough truly to sanctify himself to Obenin or was he very, very clever in covering his misdeeds? Maybe, it was simply that his enemies were enemy soldiers and commanders on the battlefield and he had killed them all?

Octun pulled Seth out of his thoughts. "King Saroth told me that this is your first journey without him."

Sitting up, Seth immediately replied, "I have been many places without Father, but if you mean that this is the first critical mission that I have been on, that is true."

"How are you faring?" asked Octun.

Seth scratched at his sprouting beard, thinking, *He is testing me, trying to interrogate me on the sly, trying to pry something from me, but what?*

"I am fine. I will not disappoint Father. Everything Father has done over the years is to prepare me to take over his throne when he dies."

Seth bit his lips. *Take over, that was an awful choice of words. Why am I so nervous around this man? He is proving to be the least of my worries.*

He wholeheartedly expected Octun to center in on his last statement.

"Out here," testified Octun, his tone sounding like a call to prayer, "it doesn't seem like such a long time ago that I was first on my own, away from the love of my mother and the firm, guiding backhand of my father."

Seth stared at Octun keenly, though shadows cast over his features. *I will give him nothing.* He slid further away from Octun.

Seth soften is tone. He breathed deeply and sighed. "I do feel alone."

"But you are not alone. I am here, the Hands of Obenin are here, and the guards are here."

"That's not exactly what I meant," snapped Seth.

"But you are lonely... no?"

"No...I mean yes... I mean, we all get lonely sometimes."

Octun cleared his throat. His pitch dropped. The prayerful tone in his voice turned more personal, "I joined the Glynwith Regiment when I was fourteen. I left my mother crying pitifully and my father waving proudly. At that time, I thought I was glad to leave. My father made me work every minute I was not studying. My mother seemed so overly concerned about me all the time, especially when I sought the priesthood at twelve years old.

"Three of us made the trip to the training grounds. That was the only easy part of the entire matter. From the moment I set foot on the training ground, I was exposed to cursing and swearing that no Obenite should hear. I thought the cadre who trained us were devils and they were there only to torture us. Before we slept, they required absolute quiet. If we made the slightest sound, they charged in, knocked us out of our bunks, and threw our gear and swords outside in the dirt and mud. Then we would have to clean them and put them in inspection order before we returned to sleep.

"For the first few weeks, we had little sleep and less food. Every muscle ached and I must have asked myself a thousand times what in Obenin's name had I done to myself. I wanted to go home and sit by the fire with a big plate of my mother's cooking. I realized that I had it very good back home. Yet, I stuck it out. The cadre' broke us down and built us up again.

"Later, in my first battle, I discovered the cadre were saviors. Everything forged together on that day. The near brutality of the cadre saved my life. We fought as a unit. We fought as an army. It is an amazing thing to attack during the night with a hundred men and your enemy never hears you coming until it is too late.

"I arrived at training a remnant. The cadre sewed me into the larger fabric. That same thread still holds me to the cloth. It holds all the faithful and makes a beautiful robe for Obenin to wear. The faithful are never alone. After I persevered, I felt proud of my accomplishments and my life changed forever."

Seth sat silently brooding. He lost this war of words, but Octun did not play fairly. In fact, he had an annoying perception that Octun did not play at all. Moreover, he found some common ground with Octun. Both of them missed the most important part of his youth, intermingling with other children, taking their knocks and abuse from them. In contrast, though, during his adolescence and early adult years, Octun fought wars. Somewhere in the journey, Octun found himself.

The king had unwittingly kept him from a normal life. His father manipulated his entire world so much Seth did not truly know himself. Seth accepted that Octun suffered the same plight as he. He hated his father for taking Octun away from him with no explanation as to why. If he hadn't, things might have turned out differently.

"What was your first battle?" the Prince asked, bunching up his coat protectively.

My first battle was not actually a battle, more a skirmish. Octun paused. "It was a rescue mission."

"Were you afraid?"

"I thought my knocking knees would give us away," replied Octun.

The Prince waited for Octun to continue. He didn't. Agitated, Seth drilled, "Well don't just lie there, tell me what happened."

Octun hesitated. After a very long pause, he continued. "We rescued Lady Artia, the mother of Horan Mernus."

"Lord Mernus' mother?" Seth was incredulous. "That was the famous mission lead by General Cabal. I was not aware you were part of the rescue." Was he about to catch Octun in a lie?

"I did not steal into the pirates' camp. The general ordered fifteen of us to cause a diversion, then cover the escape. I knew General Cabal intended to leave us if necessary. Our diversions worked, but the pirates recovered well. The general rescued my lady. We could have pressed the fight; however, that was not the mission. Cabal withdrew to secure Lady Artia. The pirates pursued us hotly. The other decoys and I lured the pirates off Cabal's trail. They killed ten of my comrades. Yet, we led the pirates on a merry chase. We evaded capture for a week. We doubled back, burned their ships and stole a small boat. After a few days at sea, the admiralty rescued us."

This Octun was doing before becoming a man on his sixteenth birthday, Seth realized. He got up and left the room. He felt small and that displeased him greatly.

****

About midnight, Parmos sat up in his bed. A cacophony of ear-piercing whistling noises woke him up. It wasn't someone or something, but many things. Octun broke into the room, followed by Seth. They gave Parmos and the others wads of cotton to put in their ears. Soon, as the wind picked up, the whistling evolved into unbearable banshee like screams.

"How can the soldiers of the outpost stand it?" Parmos curled up on his bunk and tried not to cry.

They left the outpost just before sunrise. Parmos wished he could just close his eyes through the entire trip. They left their horses behind and mounted camels. Four pack animals accompanied them. Parmos' fear subsided into downright boredom after a couple of hours. Just after noon, they broke free of the petrified grove and started a steep descent into the dried gulf of blood-red dirt. Down, down, down, into the eerie place that made the camels nervous.

The road could have been straight. Instead, it zigzagged with sharp corners going well out of the way for a long while, only to cut sharply to the right or left. Since they had entered into the stone trees, Octun's men hardly spoke. Even the funny-haired ranger rode solemn as a monk. The only sounds he heard were the steady beats of the camels' hooves, and the squeaks of their saddles.

Parmos looked down at waist-high stone pillars on each side of the road. He noted another about forty paces in front of them. About midway, Octun raised his hand and ordered everyone to dismount. There was a well and a place to tie the camels.

"Is this a shrine?" Ulthea asked.

"No," answered Octun. "It is a haven." He left it at that.

Octun talked to Seth about something. Seth pointed off into the distance, pointing out more pillars that Parmos took as a boundary.

Octun turned back to them.

"Stay on the road. And, no matter what happens, do not go beyond the pillars. Do you understand me?" Octun's tone foreboding.

"Why?" asked Jared.

"Because he told you to," snapped Seth.

Parmos ate his ration of dried meat and bread. Ulthea sat across from him. She washed the dust from her face. One of the guards asked for a drink of her water. She gave it to him. He lifted the skin up and let the water trickle into his mouth.

He smacked his lips, poured some on his finger and tasted it. Without warning, the soldier walked off with the skin.

The guard interrupted Octun and Seth. Seth shook his finger at the guard and pointed back to them. The soldier returned and gave the skin back to Ulthea, stating, "They never give us the good stuff."

The wind picked up and died down frequently. Small gusts softly peppered Parmos' face as if someone whispered too closely.

"Ride," Octun shouted. Everyone broke into a gallop.

Parmos wondered why. He did not see anything different. As they raced along, Parmos held on for dear life. They made it to one of the havens. Octun, Seth and soldiers flurried around. Before he knew it, two tents sprung up before Parmos got his camel to go to his knees.

Then he saw what Octun sensed well before he saw it. A cloud, red on the edges and jet-black toward the center, blew towards them.

"Parmos! Parmos!" Jared yelled. "Move. Didn't you hear Keeper Octun? Tie the camel and take shelter." Parmos stared at the approaching sandstorm. He dismounted and draped the reins over the hitching post.

One of the guards grabbed Parmos by his clothes. He stumbled, causing the guard to lose his balance, too. They rolled in the dust near the camel's hind feet. The camel, already spooked, panicked. He kicked in the air barely missing Parmos' head and raced into the desert. When the camel ran beyond the four pillars, a blue light erupted from the desert floor. The noise made by the light was so loud that Parmos heard it over the howling wind. The camel froze motionless in the desert. Another red flash followed. It started at the camel's head and moved to the camel's tail. When it finished, the light flashed off and the camel disintegrated with a loud zap. The powdery remains blew off in the wind.

Parmos scampered away in no certain destination. The guard grabbed him and focused his direction on a tent.

They barely made it into the tent and secured the flap before the storm hit. Parmos sat in the corner with him arms wrapped around his knees, shivering. Though he covered his face, the sand choked him and burned his eyes.

One of the soldiers moved over to him. "Come now, lad. We will be okay," he reassured Parmos, looking doubtful himself. "When I found out I was assigned to come here, my skin crawled. However, I cannot let fear overcome me. I must overcome my fear. Colonel Octun taught me that. You are a big boy. Cowardly behavior does not look good on you."

Now, fear and shame occupied the same space in his heart. Parmos looked around for the others. He did not see them. In the rush, he got separated from them. Parmos moved for the flap, but the same soldier that rebuked him, grabbed and pulled him back hard.

"Do not put us in danger because you are weak-hearted," he barked.

Parmos saw the soldier's disappointment. His soul sank down to his toes. Parmos thought only of his faithlessness.

"I am not worthy to even admire Keeper Octun. I cannot bear my unworthiness," he confessed aloud.

Parmos buried his face into his knees and wept bitterly. All he ever seemed to do was weep. He thought of Ulthea. She was half his size and so faithful. Where her courage failed, her faith made the difference. If he were to win her respect, he had to pull something from somewhere. Octun was a father, a mentor, an example of what he wanted in his heart to become. Somewhere he had to find the strength to act like him, to be him. The vow he made that day after visiting Obenin's Resting Place came back to him.

Night came before the sandstorm blew over. Keeper Octun decided not to go any further.

Octun stirred them before sunrise. They rode for hours. They came to a dry riverbed and traveled along what would be midstream. At dusk, they stopped and rested for about two hours. Parmos and the others stretched and ate. With glows on long poles and torches, the band journeyed into the night.

After sunrise, Octun pointed out the cliffs of Oracle in the distance. Parmos stirred his courage. He repeated as many tenets as he remembered.

The cliffs, striated with red and white bands like great muscles of the earth, closed in around them. Caves dotted the cliffs from top to bottom. The riverbed ran between them, disappearing underground.

Men ran toward Keeper Octun. They waved and jumped in celebration like children hurrying to meet their father.

A thin, red-bearded man with thick kinked hair from lack of care lead the pack.

Octun dismounted.

"You're a sight for sore eyes. I was about to give orders to austerity ration what supplies we have left. You know nothing lives in this god-forsaken place," the bearded man greeted.

He bowed to Seth and, disregarding custom, shook Octun's hand. Octun did not know him or any of the other men who gathered around him.

"Oh, forgive me, I am Major Gremal of palace security," he introduced himself, still shaking Octun's hand vigorously.

"You obviously know Prince Seth. I am Keeper...."

"Iberius Octun. I am impressed. It's not every day you are brought supplies by a living legend."

"If I am so, it is by Obenin's will."

"Oh, well... yeah, surely."

"Tell me, how long have you been here?"

"Me, personally? Since Lord Cuere decided to make this place his study chamber," Gremal chuckled.

"And you work directly for Stannick?" Octun pulled his hand away from Gremal.

Gremal shot back, "Well, do not hold that against me."

Octun relaxed a little. "What did you do to get here?"

"Let's just say that Sir Stannick doesn't like free thinking individuals.... There is something that I want to know."

"And what is that?"

"Is there a world still out there, and if there is, are the women still as soft and good-smelling as I barely remember?"

"Yes to both of those questions," interjected Seth.

"Good, I want to put my order in for a maiden on the next caravan. Doesn't matter what she looks like as long I fancy her, and she learns to fancy me."

Gremal's merry sense of humor amused Octun. He remarked, "It probably wasn't your thinking that got you here, but your mouth. Fortunately, out here in no man's land, your manner serves as an asset."

Major Gremal laughed outloud.

Unable to resist, Octun laughed along with Gremal. It took Octun a while to recover.

"Tell Lord Cuere that we have arrived," Octun directed, after taking a deep breath.

"Oh, he knows you are here." Gremal pointed up to a level of caves about ninety meters above them. "You will have to climb up to him. He never comes down from there. I think it's because he hates to climb back up."

Looking up the cliff, Octun exclaimed, "Today Lord Cuere will have to wait or come down. I am too tired to go to him."

CHAPTER 19
Power Received

Octun's men and Cuere's men unpacked the supplies and settled the camels. They exchanged glances but not words. Octun saw Lord Cuere descending the face of the cliff through a combination of stairs and ladders. Where the stairs crumbled from corrosion, Cuere used anchored wooden ladders to navigate down each precarious step. When Lord Cuere reached the bottom, he panted to catch his breath.

"You are early," he commented to Octun after several moments.

"We were in a hurry to get here," Octun returned flatly. As Octun gave his report, Lord Cuere averted his eyes in every direction. After Octun finished his report, Cuere's eyes fixed back on him. This habit greatly annoyed Octun.

"Yes, yes, I am sure that was the case. Where are they?" Cuere asked anxiously.

"They are resting," he pointed at the tent. "We rode all night to get here."

"Good, let them rest..." he folded his arms and rocked back and forth with bowing motions, "oh, um, they will need all their strength."

"The books and other things you asked for are over there," Octun pointed to a couple of wooden crates on the ground by one of the pack animals.

"Good, very good, I have some reports for the King I want to send back with you. By the way... how is his health? Is there any improvement?"

Octun couldn't discern any sincerity in his voice. "He still fights as a good king should."

"Speaking of kings, how did our future king fare this trip?"

"He did well," Octun replied, flinching out a smile.

"Splendid. If there is anything my men can do for you, just say the word and I will have them do it." Cuere put his hands behind his back.

"Thank you, but Major Gremal has already been quite the host."

"Well, get your rest. As soon as the lads and lass rest up, we will go up to Oracle."

Octun really didn't want to go, but the curiosity of how this fit in with what he believed as Obenin's will overpowered his resistance. Though he hadn't seen it, he heard what happened to the camel. He didn't want to believe, but Parmos was not the only witness. Two of the guards saw it too. He had thrown stones out to the same place and nothing happened.

"We no longer call them the lads and the lass," corrected Octun. "King Saroth made a decree that we are to refer to them as the Hands of Obenin."

"Figures. So be it. You are dismissed." Cuere turned his back and strode away.

****

Parmos turned over and tried to ignore the person who shook him. He wanted to go back to sleep. When he heard Octun's voice, he lifted his head and rubbed his eyes. Parmos, embarrassed, apologized, his words thick and slow.

The campfire rations smelled good to him. This morning, though, his churning stomach would not let his appetite take control. At breakfast, he picked over his food and avoided the others. Octun sat on a crate well away from every one else. Parmos looked for some excuse to get near him. Finding none, he left his plate, walked over and sat down on the ground at his feet.

Parmos avoided Octun's eyes. He felt Octun probing him, searching for the mystery of Parmos, searching for the tiniest bit of courage in his heart. He knew Octun viewed him as immature for his age and weak hearted. Yet, he seemed to entertain his lingering at his heels and watchful eye.

"Parmos, what bothers you?" asked Octun.

He wanted to say, "I... am afraid." Instead, he said, "I don't know."

Octun reached over and turned his chin. Parmos resisted and glanced away. Octun looked down at him knowingly.

"So am I. We both have to be brave. You must be brave for your destiny and I must be brave for my faith," remarked Octun.

The brief moment shocked him. Octun opened up, then shut himself off just as quickly. Still, none of the others shared a moment like that. He saw it as a small seed of hope and very much wanted it to grow. Octun's words strengthened him. He hoped to know true courage for the first time.

Suddenly, Octun placed his hand on his shoulder and said, "You have faith and you will find the courage to go with it."

Parmos climbed the ladder up the face of the cliff. Lord Cuere led the way. He kept an impatient pace and expected everyone to keep up.

"Just don't look down and keep moving," Parmos repeated Octun's earlier directions.

"What did you say?" asked Ulthea, who was above him.

"Nothing," he insisted.

Ulthea's pace slowed. She lagged behind Jared and Ictheos.

"Keep up the pace," Prince Seth demanded. "We have a long way to climb.

Ulthea climbed faster.

Parmos heard her sniffling.

Cuere led them up the series of stairs and ladders until they reached the proper level.

"Calm down," comforted Keeper Octun. He helped Ulthea off the final ladder.

"I don't want to go, Keeper Octun, I mean I do want to go but I don't want to go. Please don't make me," she begged.

Jared butted in, "Let's get this over with."

"You don't want to go, either," she snapped.

"I don't, either," added Ictheos. "But we have to."

"Keeper Octun, please don't make us," entreated Ulthea.

Lord Cuere stomped over to them. His hand flailed over his head as if he fought off a swarm of flies.

"This has nothing to do with Keeper Octun. We have work to do. Do you want to disappoint Prince Seth? Do you want to disappoint King Saroth? Do you want the Obenite people to lose faith?" yelled Cuere.

Keeper Octun's faced turned cold. Parmos read it cleary, "How dare you invoke the name of Obenin."

Parmos looked at Prince Seth who watched the interaction with amusement.

"Listen to me." Octun walked right in front of Cuere. All Parmos saw of Lord Cuere's was one elbow sticking out.

"I want all of you to put these blindfolds on. There is nothing for you to see here. Now is not the time."

"What do you mean?" pleaded Ulthea.

"Put them on, hold each other's hands and keep walking in a single column."

Parmos put on his blindfold. He reached out for the others hands. Someone, he figured Octun, placed each of his hands in another's.

"Ulthea," he guessed.

She replied with a shaky squeeze.

"Ictheos?"

"Um huh," returned Ictheos.

****

Octun knew of the frozen people. At first, he doubted it but Levid assured him it was not myth. Levid explained everything, but the description severely lacked the reality. Octun passed person after frozen person on the way to Oracle. Ictheos, Jared, Ulthea and Parmos no longer held hands, but clung together like grapes. He wondered if they sensed the frozen figures around them.

As he ushered them from chamber to chamber, Octun grew more concerned. Nothing Levid said prepared him for this.

He wondered, "What sort of evil did they do to die like this, if they are truly dead?"

Octun continually checked the blindfolds to make sure they remained tight.

He denied the Hand of Obenin the sight, but he could not help himself. Someone tried very hard to make the place look natural. It looked too well planned, even the stalactites had a questionable spacing to them.

In certain places, he even noticed ridges in the rocks like those in a stone quarry. The farther down they went, the wall smoothed out. The humidity lessened until the dry air made him thirsty.

Ulthea collapsed, causing Parmos and the others to fall.

Prince Seth and Octun lifted Ulthea to her feet and removed all their blindfolds.

Ulthea repeated, "Must have faith." Ulthea prayed aloud. She mixed the tenets with anything and everything spiritual that crossed her mind in a manner that all made sense.

"Shut up!" snapped Ictheos.

She kept right on praying.

Jared tried to stop. Prince Seth kept pushing him forward.

Parmos moaned in agony, "I'm burning... up inside."

"Cuere, what is happening?" demanded Octun. He drew his sword and raised the glows high. He backed into Parmos taking a protective stance in front of them.

****

Octun threatened, "What evil is this? Undo it!" He started toward Cuere.

Seth intervened, "Lower your sword Keeper. Do not interfere. You will do more harm than good."

"We must get them closer," shouted Cuere. "Hurry."

"This is Lord Cuere's forte. Just do what he says and get this over with!" exclaimed Seth in frustration, showing a case of nerves himself.

Suddenly they broke into a cavern. At the far end was a hole in the wall.

Octun surmised that they had arrived at Oracle. "Is this it?"

"Yes," answered Cuere.

"What will happen now?" pressured Octun.

Cuere picked up a scroll from among the many propped against the wall.

Stepping to the front and facing Oracle, he read aloud. When finished, he directed each of them to stand in a semi-circle around the mouth of Oracle.

Instead of doing as Lord Cuere directed, Parmos and the others reached toward Oracle like children reaching for sweets. They touched the inside of Oracle's mouth simultaneously. A narrow beam of red light swept them one by one. It turned amber and swept them again. It turned green and flicked off. The entire place quaked. Noises echoed within the belly of Oracle.

The sound of hundreds of fluttering wings caused Octun to raise his sword again. As the sounds grew louder, the pitch shifted higher then lower, finally, settling into a low earth-moving rumble.

He moved to snatch the Hands of Obenin from Oracle. Seth stepped in his way again. "This has to finish."

Before he could take a step, a stinking mist spewed from the chasm and engulfed everyone.

Octun could not see a thing in the silvery mist. He reacted to a scream. He bumped Seth out of the way and lunged toward where he had seen Parmos. He knocked someone down in the process. Grasping at the sprawling body, he pulled the person close to his face. It was Lord Cuere. "What did you do?" Octun yelled.

Another belch, black smoke erupted from Oracle.

"Ulthea...! Ictheos...! Parmos...! Jared...!" in vain, he waited for answers.

"What have you done to them?" Though he could not see Cuere's face, Octun knew that events were helplessly beyond his control.

He dropped Cuere. The thump of Cuere's head against the ground satisfied him for now. Cuere cursed him, then groaned.

Octun, on his knees, made his way in the darkness toward Oracle. He groped around, feeling his way. More screams, lasting longer than he thought possible. He adjusted his course and headed for the screams.

Before he reached Oracle's mouth, the darkness retreated, leaving only the silvery mist. Then it also retreated into Oracle's mouth. The Hands of Obenin were gone.

"Bring them back!" Octun ordered, his voice booming and veins popping in his forehead.

Cuere returned Octun's fierce stare with a helpless shrug.

He got up and started toward Cuere. Prince Seth stepped in between them. "We must let the events take their natural course... whatever that may be." Seth put both hands up as if they would stop Octun.

"No, I will not just sit here and do nothing!" Octun objected.

He placed a glows into the mouth of Oracle. He hoisted himself up. He crawled into the depth only to emerge to see Seth and Cuere staring at him knowingly.

Octun tried three more times. Each time, he came back to the very place he started, just as Lord Cuere said would happen. He had no choice but to wait and see. Contrary to Seth's statement, he knew there was nothing natural about the entire matter.

****

Parmos saw darkness. He heard everything but he saw not a speck of light. Voices surrounded him. The clicks, hisses and hiccups sounded like the voices of men. He felt enclosed in a bubble of complete darkness and pressure. Disorientated, Parmos could not tell whether he stood upright, hung upside down or lay on his back.

"Keeper Octun!" he yelled. He received no reply. He called the others, still nothing.

The strange voices grew louder. Panic-stricken, he struck and kicked. The pressure increased and the voices got closer.

"Who are you?" Parmos screamed. "Leave me alone!"

He flailed in panic. An incredible force struck him, as if the bubble suddenly shrank and stripped the flesh off his body, sucking it into a searing ball inside his belly. The pain... he knew he should be dead. He wanted death to take him. Yet, he lived. Instead of life draining from his body, life charged into his body. He burned with power. He screamed in pain. He felt warm and wet, very wet from head to toe.

****

Jared resolved to scream as loudly as possible. Between the screams of pain, he prayed for more pain. If pain was what it took to end this terror, he readied a scream and a prayer for each wave of misery that came his way. He suppressed his survival instinct to fight. Fighting made the beating worse anyway. However, he could not stop his body from wriggling, twisting and squirming like a possessed man. A furnace ignited in his very soul. The deep misery within him spread to the surface, eating him bit by miniscule bit from the inside out. A desire for power and chaos entered and bored in his mind like a screw. Then it was gone.

****

With no more will to scream, Ictheos agonized, "Why has Obenin chosen such a terrible fate for us? Why can't I just pass out and be lost to this torture? Someone should have told us!"

A portal opened in the darkness. An hallucination or real, it didn't matter. He saw the image as clear as day. Unquenchable thirst, hunger, and famine decimated the world. The inhabitants called on him to save them. The scene shifted, he brought life back to the world only to destroy it again. He laughed. The thought amused him, to toy with the fate of others. He found himself laughing. He could not stop.

****

The things behind the voices ate Ulthea alive; yet, she lived through the horror. Ulthea heard no more voices. The nightmarish biting ended. The fire inside her soul died down to a smolder. Only, she thirsted for water. Not just to quench her thirst, but she needed to submerge in it and stay there. As her desire for water grew, so did her hate for it. It confused her. These two opposing emotions existed in the same thought for one single thing, water in any form. Slowly, her body evaporated like dew in the morning sun.

****

Oracle belched and a smoky mist poured out. Octun sprang to his feet.

"Something is happening," he informed the others. They knew just as well as he did.

The mist spewed from Oracle again followed, immediately by the consuming darkness. Then it was gone and at the foot of the Oracle lay a heap of bloody bodies.

"By my name," breathed Seth, "are they...dead?"

Octun's courage overcame the hopelessness of the situation and dashed over. Ulthea lay on top of the pile. He placed his palm on her forehead. It felt feverish. He rubbed the red fluid between his fingers and thumb. Its stickiness reminded him of fresh tree sap. He turned her over and tried to find a heartbeat. It beat strong and fast.

"She is alive," he reported in great relief. "Help me with them."

Neither Seth nor Cuere moved.

"Don't just stand there gawking, help me with them... now!"

They snapped out of shock and rushed to help.

"Lord Cuere, get me some water to clean them up," Octun ordered.

Cuere disappeared from the cave as Seth helped Octun lay the Hands of Obenin side by side.

Octun examined them, looking at their skin, in their ears, noses and mouths. Finally, he looked again for lacerations and punctures on their bodies. He shook his head at Seth. "Where did all this..." Octun paused and then continued. "...blood come from? I do not believe it came all from them."

He stared into Oracle. Not that he looked for an answer, but he looked on it as an evil thing. He noticed something strange. A mass of dark crystals protruded from where the hole had been.

Lord Cuere came back into the cave with water in a vessel, decided it was not nearly enough, and asked Prince Seth to help him with more.

Alone, Keeper Octun prayed. His doubts surfaced into an undeniable force demanding consideration. He could no longer reject his doubts as a lack of faith or test of faith. The bloody bodies lay before him. He tried to sort through all his thoughts, each vying for priority. Everything was in a mess. Clearly, he knew the most important question was whether this entire matter, from conception to fruition, was the will of his god. He was the spiritual leader of his country. If this was the will of Obenin, then why did he not have peace?

This was not entirely a spiritual matter to be determined by him alone. Those who possessed the divine right to rule determined the fate of the kingdom, not the high priest.

Octun thought, *It is not Obenin's will that the faithless rule. Every Obenite knows this. The kingdom is in peril. If the king dies, a man who does not... no, two men who do not display true Obenite values will determine the fate of many.*

Prince Seth's words echoed in Octun's heart. The words struck him the moment Prince Seth uttered them. But, in the moment, he didn't react.

"By my name. That is what he said."

Octun knelt in sincerity, "Obenin, father of us all, great patriarch who has been exalted to live after death, I attempt to understand all that is going on. I am ashamed that I remain ignorant of your will. I am the Keeper of your Resting Place, your high priest. Help me find the truth. Show me the error of my reasoning. I beg. Please let King Saroth live until Prince Seth finds the faith he needs to sustain the kingdom."

As he finished praying, one thought remained strong in his mind. It shined a light that he believed would show him the way to the truth. A thing that turned over and over in his mind: "The faithless shall not rule." Octun's goal of ministering to Seth seemed too distant to achieve. He had to try, though. He had to try for Saroth and for the Kingdom of Obenin. If ever there was anything more dire than the impending invasion by the Benomian alliance, more fundamental to his life as high priest, this was it.

"Prince Seth, I must reach him. I must bring Prince Seth back to faith and these four youngsters will help me," Octun declared aloud.

He lifted his eyes to see Prince Seth staring at him.

Prince Seth ordered, "Keeper, you will leave the Barren Lands tomorrow morning. Your role in dealing with the Hands of Obenin is over."

****

The next morning, Parmos studied the others' faces. He knew they all wanted to talk about what happened. No one wanted to speak first. He remembered some of what happened inside Oracle. Other memories remained sketchy.

And... Octun was gone. He left in the strangest way. He did not say good-bye. At least not the way Parmos expected. He knew there wouldn't be hugs. What he imagined was Octun gripping his shoulder with that vice-like grip. Parmos would have resisted the need to drop to his knees. Octun would have looked him dead in the eyes and given him some word of wisdom. What actually happened was, when he asked for Octun, Prince Seth told Parmos to look out toward the soldiers. He and the others ran to the ledge and looked down just in time to see Octun galloping off.

"Did we do something?" Ulthea asked, rubbing her watery eyes.

"I don't know what we did. We were out cold until just before he left," Parmos objected sadly.

Ulthea proposed an excuse, "Lord Cuere said that he left on an urgent matter. Maybe that's just the way he handles good-byes. He doesn't have a wife and children of his own. Most of his friends are soldiers and you can't expect soldiers to weep when they depart."

Jared rubbed his chin and said, "He's just worried about leaving us with someone he doesn't care for very much."

"That would be all the more reason to show more concern when he left!" argued Ictheos.

"Something must have really been bothering him," assured Ulthea, "or maybe it really was so urgent that he just didn't have time to say goodbye."

"This is just guessing. When we get back, I am going to ask him," declared Jared.

"You mean you are going to ask Chancellor Levid what might have been bothering Octun," Ictheos shot back.

Jared did not laugh.

"Well I know one thing," added Ictheos, "Seth and Lord Cuere's attitudes are different toward us now."

"All I remember is being scared out of my mind," told Ulthea, "and then there was nothing."

They all nodded their heads.

"There are blood stains all over the cave floor," remarked Ictheos.

"Blood, what blood?" said Ulthea, startled.

"All over the floor of Oracle's cave," Ictheos reported. "I overheard Seth and Cuere talking about what to do about it."

"I don't want to go back in there," objected Parmos.

Jared asked very anxiously, "Where did it come from? Did they kill something in there?"

"I don't know and I didn't ask. Lord Cuere found me listening, stamped his feet, pointed his finger and ordered me to get out."

"Well I want to see for myself," insisted Jared.

"But," reminded Ulthea, "Keeper Octun told us to obey everything that Lord Cuere told us to do."

Jared looked at her in dismay as if to say, "You had to remind me, didn't you."

"But that's not all I saw," teased Ictheos. "The blood on the floor is nothing compared to this."

Jared frowned and snapped, "Why are you drawing this out?" "I don't know. Just seems like... fun."

"There is nothing funny about it," argued Jared.

"You won't believe it if I tell you anyway," persisted Ictheos. "You have to see them for yourselves... the reason why Keeper Octun blindfolded us."

All Parmos cared to know is that Octun blindfolded them for a reason. He didn't want anything to do with discovering that reason. Parmos saw Cuere and Seth enter and cut off his response.

They all bowed to the Prince.

Cuere scowled at them. "Oh, um, are you ready?" he asked impatiently.

Parmos looked at Jared, who nodded his head.

Cuere beckoned them to approach. The others got within an arm's reach, while Parmos kept his distance.

"Do not be alarmed by anything you see here," Cuere advised. "I have uncovered many mysteries in the Barren Lands. Oracle is only one of them. Listen to me and I will teach you many things, wondrous things."

Seth added, "Just stick close to me. Do not touch anything and don't run off. We may never find you."

Parmos lagged behind the others. When they saw the first of The Barren Lands' frozen citizen, he moved to the middle of the pack, joining Ulthea. Ulthea kept her face buried in Ictheos' shoulder. She refused to look anymore.

"I don't want to be here," she moaned.

Parmos forced a glance, the looked down toward the floor. No wonder Octun chose to blindfold them. "If we had seen these things, we would have run back the other way."

The thought, accidentally, surfaced to his lips. "What are they?" he asked thoughtlessly and too loudly.

"They have been here for centuries at least," replied Cuere. "They are one of Obenin's best-kept secret and a great treasure. No one knows where they came from or how they got this way."

Parmos didn't want to hear anymore. That was enough courage for one day.

Shielding his eyes with his hand, Lord Cuere looked up at the sky. Two clouds hung like mountain peaks in a thin haze. "This shouldn't be too hard."

"What shouldn't be too hard, sir?" inquired Jared earnestly.

"Prince Seth wants to see for himself the wonders I can perform through you. I will teach you how to control it and wield it so I can destroy the enemy."

"Well, Oh, um." He continued. "Let's see what you can do. Gather around me and lift your arms to the sky like so.

They reached for the sky.

"Good, good," coached Lord Cuere. "So you will know the meaning of what you are saying, I will translate. 'Oh mighty clouds of the sky, bring forth your rain.' The words are not Obenite so you will have to listen closely and repeat exactly what I say...."

Parmos stammered over the words. He found the pronunciations very difficult. He looked at Jared, who shrugged his shoulders.

"No! No! No!" barked Lord Cuere. "Repeat exactly what I say, the way I say it and in unison. Now let's try it again."

Murmuring, they tried it again.

"Louder, say it louder with command and authority and in unison... and do it with your eyes closed."

Jared whispered in Parmos' ear, "Why didn't he tell us to do it with our eyes closed the first time?"

Parmos repeated the spell at the top of his lungs. He felt better about how he said the words. After several more tries, everything seemed right to him but nothing happened. Not a drop of rain fell. He opened his eyes and peeked at the sky. The mountain peak of clouds were breaking apart and drifting away.

They kept it up for a long time and Parmos' throat ached. He wanted to stop for a little while but Lord Cuere had other ideas.

"There is something you all are not doing right!" He stomped around kicking the air, avoiding Seth's glare.

"Do it again with more feeling, mean it in your hearts. Don't plead with the elements, command them.... Command them as Octun commands his men," Cuere ordered.

Still, nothing happened.

"How can I make anything happen when you all aren't doing what I command?"

Parmos felt the burden Cuere placed on his back.

"Lord Cuere, we are doing the best we can. We are trying to do everything you say!" objected Jared, with an edge.

Seth spoke out, "Lord Cuere, we will stop and resume later."

Cuere put his hands on his hips and marched off into the cave like a spoiled child who could not have his way. Trying to comfort his sister, Ictheos stroked her hair.

"How much longer are we going to be with him?" She clenched her fingers in her bangs and pulled.

Ictheos answered, "Forever."

That evening, Cuere brought them back on the ledge. They chanted, danced, knelt down in prayer, jumped, shouted, screamed, whistled, ran around in a circle wavering as if the wind blew them, and shivered spasmodically. Finally, Cuere made them lie on their backs with their feet touching. Then, with their hands touching, they chanted more of the strange verse.

Lord Cuere threw up his hands angrily and scolded, "Just go to sleep, you obviously aren't up to it today."

Seth scowled at them.

Downcast and hurt, Parmos trudged out of the cool night air into the cave and sat near the fire. Ulthea sulked.

Parmos sat by her. "I will tell Keeper Octun when we see him, how Lord Cuere treats us. He will do something... I know he will."

That seemed to comfort her a bit.

She sighed, "I wish he had never left us here!"

Jared looked around the cave. Lord Cuere and Seth were off somewhere.

He motioned for them together in a huddle. "I don't think Lord Cuere really knows what he is doing."

"Amazing discovery, I would have never guess," chided Ictheos.

"But he is the one who brought us through Oracle and he made Oracle give us the power we are supposed to have," Ulthea argued.

"Yes, that's true, but he seems to bumble through everything," retorted Jared. "He is making us feel guilty and unwilling, but he is the one with the problem. Why can't he just say that he doesn't know how to bring the power out of us?"

"But how can we do anything without him? We don't know what to do. I can't even say the words right," Ulthea protested.

Parmos nodded his head, hoping his agreeing would help her feel better.

Jared smiled and then laughed. "Maybe in his bumbling he will bumble upon something that works."

Parmos resisted laughing. The situation seemed too grave. After the others kept laughing, he laughed too, welcoming the light-heartedness.

Lord Cuere and Seth came back into the chamber.

"What is so funny?" Cuere asked.

Parmos' eyes sparkled. They all tried to stop laughing but, none of them could withhold a chuckle here or there.

Seth walked up to them. Parmos bowed. Jared and Ictheos bowed deeply and Ulthea gave a quick curtsey.

Seth looked at them one by one.

Tight-lipped, he held up his index finger, "Do not test us."

He turned to the side and walked by them. Looking down at them over his left shoulder, Seth laid down his expectation. "I am not Octun. Lord Cuere is not Chancellor Levid. This may not be a good thing as you see it, but it is a very good thing to us. Do not even think you can get away with not showing either one of us proper respect."

Parmos swallowed hard. Here, for all practical purposes, neither Octun nor Levid existed. They all needed to remember that and get used to it.

****

Cuere came back to the anterior chamber. He slapped a piece of the black crystal, chiseled from the dead oracle, in his palm. He had broken a sweat just to remove a piece about as thick as his thumb and just longer than his middle finger. He noticed how the Hands of Obenin all tossed in their sleep.

At first, he thought they were waking up and went back to studying the crystal. He stuck it in the fire and touched the tip gingerly. It did not hold much heat. He sat down and used the crystal to flick charred bits of wood from the edges of the fire back into the dying blaze.

The hot blade of rationalization cut into him. He did not like the way that felt. Parmos slept right next to him. He wanted to pick up a rock and bash his head.

"Just when I am so close to getting what I want... if I fail I will be an embarrassment to the King and Prince Seth. I will be executed to atone for their loss of face."

He banged the crystal on a rock. "But I knew that from the beginning. There is still hope. Just like when I first invoked Oracle, I overlooked that the staff needed power for the glows. There is something that I have overlooked. Maybe there is some link to the glows with this, too."

He decided to go study the scrolls again.

Ulthea suddenly cried out and sat up. Her fingers opened like flower petal. She waited. Jared sat up. His eyes opened but he did not look awake. The others did the same.

Lord Cuere watched in amazement. Parmos and the others sat perfectly still. The scene reminded him of his frozen citizens. They moved to their knees and then their feet. They locked their arms around each other and made noises that remotely sounded like drunken friends singing drinking songs. He thought they were in a trance. As he looked closer, he saw they were awake and aware of everything. Cuere deciphered the chant. His heart raced.

Seth ran into the chamber. "What's happening?"

"No time to explain," Cuere shouted. "Just keep out of the way."

Parmos broke free and fell down. He tried to dig an escape route through the cave floor.

Lord Cuere dashed over and grabbed Parmos by the arm. "Join with them!" he yelled. "There is no way I'm going to let you ruin everything I've worked and hoped so hard for. Now get up and join with them."

His adrenalin flowing, Cuere dragged Parmos across the ground, "Now, lock arms."

"No!" objected Parmos vehemently.

He tried to force Parmos' hand. Cuere was not strong enough.

"Look at you. You are almost big enough to break a horse's back and you are sprawling on the floor like a coward. Maybe you are a coward. Are you a coward, Parmos, a big, hulking sniveling coward? If I were your father, I would be ashamed of you!"

Anger flashed in Parmos' eyes, causing Cuere to take a step back. Parmos closed his eyes and clenched his teeth. Tears rolled down his cheek. His lips trembled. Cuere stood undecided whether his words accomplished anything. A lifetime passed, from death to reincarnation. Cuere witnessed the paltry face of a peasant child finally melt away and reshape into the glowing semblance of a young man with purpose. He hoped that purpose was not to do him harm.

Parmos opened his eyes and firmly grasped Ictheos' and Ulthea's shoulders.

Running out to the ledge, Cuere looked at the sky. Dark and threatening clouds amassed over the entire valley. The wind picked up and red Barren Lands dust stung his eyes. Lightning flashed across the sky immediately followed by thunderclaps. Straightway a deluge of water gushed from the sky. The winds raged.

Cuere exclaimed, "This is getting out of hand."

Rushing back into the cave, he jumped and leapt, flailing his arms wildly in the excitement. "You are losing control!" he yelled. "Concentrate. Don't get lost in your power... gain control!"

He saw desperation in their sweaty faces and their songs clashed disharmoniously.

"The scrolls say listen to each other. They say you can read each other's thoughts. Work together. Listen to my voice. Calm the storm. We want rain, only rain."

Cuere ran back out to the ledge, made a quick judgment about the storm then ran back inside.

He reported to Seth, "The storm lulls. It is doing my bidding. Come see."

He led the prince outside. "We have rain. We will practice starting and stopping before I have them to move on to something else."

"Very good," commended Prince Seth. "My place is assured and so is yours."

Cuere continued to coach the Hands of Obenin. As their chants became clearer and more harmonious, he noticed the position of their heads: tilted back as far as possible, their mouths gaping open, and their lips no longer moved. As he listened carefully, he heard each individual voice. Even so, the chants seemed to originate from somewhere else.

"They speak the language of the scrolls?" he surmised. "Alas, alas, the purpose of my life has come together."

CHAPTER 20
Power Revealed

Octun looked down from the temple's sixth tower. Thousands upon thousands from every Obenite kingdom jammed into the village of Ethenia. From the temple steps to across the River Edge, Obenites gathered to see the Hands of Obenin. Brock Stannick and his men stirred the multitude into a zealous mob. Rumors of great power from Obenin started to spread like wildfire over dry plains within days after Cuere's return from the Barren Lands.

Obenin had bestowed a special power on Lord Cuere. Prince Seth is the reincarnation of Obenin and all the great fathers in one body. Saroth had been healed by four children. Octun doubted them all.

He existed outside Saroth's fellowship again and would find out the truth just like everyone else. Seth barred his every attempt to see Saroth.

In thought, Octun figured that maybe that was best. How could he face Saroth with such a failure? Seth seemed even more absorbed in his power over people.

The names of Saroth, Seth and Cuere echoed from the hills. None of the mob knew what to expect. No one wanted to miss anything, either.

Merchants made money by the wagonloads. Artists and musicians entertained the crowd. Bells and horns erupted from everywhere. The fact that only a few hundred actually saw the ceremony did not matter.

Saroth chose the temple for obvious reasons. The council, the powerful families, the rich merchants, they all gathered at their patriarch's grave. Lord Mernus had previously approached Octun about the rumors. The only thing Octun could tell him was the balance of power shifted completely into the hands of the royal family. Saroth had not compelled anyone to attend the unplanned event. They wanted to be there, to know how this shift in power affected their fortunes.

Octun opened the door and walked down the stairs. The time approached for him to take his place.

Octun took his place until the trumpet flourishes sounded, signifying his turn in the ceremony. He performed the Ritual of Sovereign for Saroth, customarily affirming the Bedowyn right to rule. Octun finished by kneeling at Saroth's feet and kissing his hand. He panged at the thought of releasing it.

Unexpectedly, Saroth muttered something to Octun and beckoned him closer. The unusual gesture brought an inquisitive look from Seth but he did not interfere. Saroth's words were all but unintelligible, wet puffs of air on his ear. His hand shook as he lifted it to shield his lips from onlookers.

"Forgive me" or "forgiven", though he did not truly know which one the king said, Octun believed Saroth meant both. He kissed Saroth's hand again. Saroth rested his hand on Octun's.

Octun choked out the words. "I remember my oath, my liege, my friend. I will crown Seth King to carryon in your name. I will not oppose him."

Trumpets blasted out the familiar fanfare announcing the king's address to the crowd.

The mob responded by lifting both hands, palms outward, each time they shouted, "Saroth! Long live the Grand Monarch."

They roared the king's name, in unison, over and over again until Seth stepped forward. He raised his hands to calm them down.

Just as the people started to settle, someone shouted, "Long live the king!"

Octun suspected one of Stannick's men.

Seth held up his hands again.

Finally, he announced, "Obenin has smiled on my father the king, and upon this nation. He has revealed to us a great power by the hand of Lord Cuere, Master of the Barren Lands."

Octun noted Seth's pause, letting the name soak into the minds of the mob. The masses murmured but remained attentive, waiting to cast their judgment with applause or condemnation.

Seth continued, "I present to you a gift from above, a manifestation of Obenin's power and godhood, The Hands of Obenin."

When the Hands of Obenin took center stage, the entire crowd took a breath, then let out a crestfallen sigh.

"How can these four saplings help us?" someone shouted.

Octun looked over at Mernus who stood stupefied.

Though the crowd scoured him with boos and hisses, Seth brimmed with confidence.

Lord Cuere moved to center stage. He held up a large silver orb with inscriptions covering its surface. He turned to the king and bowed. He bowed to Prince Seth.

Cuere spoke to the orb and it glowed with blue brilliance. He levitated, his feet about shoulder high. The crowd gasped and drew back in fear.

When he let go of the orb, it hovered an arm's length above his head. He directed the Hands of Obenin to gather in a circle. They locked arms around one another. The orb drifted over them, casting the blue aura that defied the daylight.

Lord Cuere spoke to them and they responded.

"Concentrate." As Cuere spoke, the globe reacted to his words.

The halo emitted translucent waves that spread through the crowd. Cuere's volume hardly decreased as his words flowed down the mountain and into the valley.

Snow," directed Cuere.

Within moments, light flakes fell. It grew into a white, light-hearted flurry.

"A miracle!" one of Stannick's men shouted. His voice cracked with nervousness.

"Long live Saroth!" another shouted.

The crowd responded with confused murmurs.

"Wind," Cuere said.

The wind picked up.

"More, stronger."

Stannick's men went to work stirring the people, assuring the crowd of a miracle and not an omen.

Octun watched. He wrapped himself in his cloak. He saw Cuere in a different light. Saroth was not mad after all. It was he who underestimated the man's ability.

"Hail," directed Cuere.

Rice-sized hail pelted the crowd. The jubilation turned back to apprehension.

No matter what Stannick's men shouted, the crowd grew more and more concerned about their own safety.

The sky darkened. The crowd drew back. The hail grew to the size of peas. The sky looked like dusk. Many started to run away. The council members headed for the safety of the temple. Octun protected Saroth with his body. The hail grew into the size of a man's thumbnail-- a stampede followed.

"Clear it all," directed Cuere. "Comfort the people."

Sunlight broke through the clouds. Most of the crowd stopped in their tracks. They looked up, marveling at clouds racing away.

The crowd turned back toward the temple.

"Saroth! Saroth has saved us! Long live Saroth."

The kingdom erupted with cheers.

Octun watched the mob cheer and celebrate. With such power, they were beyond challenge. Not only would the Benomian Alliance be defeated, the glory of the victories to follow were beyond comprehension. A part of him wanted to let go of his apprehension. But he could not.

The mob's celebration changed. The mood shifted from jubilation to one of a war-hungry people.

The chant started with a few. Others joined and then the crowd in unison, "Seth, Seth long live Prince Seth. Long live King Seth!"

"The kingdom is saved," concluded Octun. "That is all that matters."

Mernus seemed happy. The council seemed happy. The crowd behaved like dogs jumping for meat on a string. Octun appeared to be the only one not celebrating.

The soldiers kept the crowd at bay, while the rich and powerful on stage thronged to flatter Seth and Cuere.

He looked at the king, whose head started to slump. Octun rested him gently against the back of the throne. Saroth fell forward. Octun cradled him against his chest.

In the mass of bodies, no one paid attention to him yelling for help. He kicked the person closest to him.

The man turned and glared angrily.

"King Saroth... he.... Get Seth, now," Octun yelled.

The man pushed his way through the crowd and came back with Prince Seth in his wake.

Octun picked the king up and carried him inside.

Saroth opened his eyes. They fixed somewhere beyond the ceiling. Taking a shallow gasp of air, he tried to speak. Seth leaned close to his father's lips. Twice more Saroth gasped then, with a hollow rasping, expelled his last breath.

Octun placed his hand on Saroth's head and closed his eyes.

"My lord has gone," choked Octun.

Seth leapt up and threw a chair against the wall. He picked up a piece of pottery and shattered it against the wall. He slammed the flat of his fist into the table again and again.

Octun let him rage. He wanted Seth to purge himself of the anguish of loosing his father.

Seth lashed out at everyone, "Get out," he bellowed.

Octun remained behind.

"You defy the king?" Seth railed, "How dare you."

"No," returned Octun. "I am the high priest. It is my duty to stay with the king until his body is prepared for burial."

"Is that all you care about priest, duty?"

"I loved your father. In life, in death, it is my pleasure and duty to serve him. I am honored to serve such a man. There are only two people for whom I owe so much, your father and Lord Mernus. King Saroth was a great king, a good man, and a true Obenite."

"A good man, a good king? How about a good father? Can you speculate on that? Do you know if he was? Well I do?"

Octun faltered, then recovered, "He cared for you. He did what he thought was best."

"If he had done what was right, he would not have burdened himself with me. He wanted to make everyone love me but they won't and it killed him. I have killed him."

Seth buried his face in his father's chest. "I am sorry, Father."

He wept bitterly, "I am sorry. Absolve me father of this guilt and I will bring such glory to the kingdom. I will make it more than you ever imagined. It will be glorious. The world will not love me. The world will only accept and fear me, or they will perish for what they made me do to you. Where Saroth's name was great, the name of King Seth shall be greater. Oh! Father, they will accept me willingly or they shall perish."

Seth glared at Octun. After such a passionate plea and vow, Octun saw no zeal, only twisted, grief-fueled, cold-blooded determination. Seth accepted his loneliness and defied anyone who attempted to share his suffering.

"Leave me, priest. Leave me alone with my father, my victim."

****

The next morning, Brock Stannick stood outside the council chamber of the Grand Palace. He watched Seth approach. He thought Seth's manner odd. He tried to saunter like his father, but his steps were too high and stiff. It looked more like a drunken march than anything else. He even dressed in his father's favorite robe, a garish thing his father used only to warm himself in private chambers.

Stannick bowed, "You wear the crown well, my lord."

Seth flashed a viciously twisted smile that lowered his brow and cast his eyes in shadows. "Are they all in there?"

"Yes, my lord, they are and Keeper Octun is on his way back to the primary temple."

"Do they suspect anything?"

"They are always suspicious, but I'm sure they know nothing of your plan. They kept their families here for the coronation. Now that it is over, I told them that all other ceremonies are canceled, security reasons, a threat on your life. They believed that. I directed them to remain on the estate until everything and everyone is checked. They gathered in here even without my asking. I think Lord Mernus has something to discuss with them."

"Do you have the objects?"

"I have not parted with them since my men brought them to me."

"Good, give them to me."

Stannick handed over the bag tied to his belt. He stepped a few doors down and knocked. Two men stepped out.

"Guard the chamber door. Position the men. When I knock twice, enter, swords drawn," Stannick ordered, with bravado.

Seth stood in front of the door and brushed himself off as if he were about to enter into a woman's quarters. Stannick opened the door and King Seth entered into the council chamber for the first time.

Fourteen of Obenin's wealthiest and most powerful families sat at a horseshoe-shaped table.

The murmuring ceased. Everyone looked up. Their eyes widened.

Seth walked up the steps and sat on the throne, looking down at the council. The head of the horseshoe was farthest from the throne. A large chair, slightly smaller than the throne but clearly larger than the rest, marked a position of power. Lord Mernus sat there.

Seth marked each council member one by one as he met their stares. Their expressions ranged from abhorrence to culpability. Finally, his eyes settled on Lord Mernus, a gray-haired, distinguished-looking man. Stannick knew that if the pot stirred against Seth, Mernus would be holding the spoon.

Lord Mernus rarely supported King Saroth fully. Seth needed a viable threat, arm-twisting and blackmail to get him to fall in line.

Mernus wanted compromise with the enemy. He sought to remove the power to tax from the king and place it in the hands of the council. At every opportunity, he used his power and popularity to stir up trouble.

But..., reckoned Stannick, *he is not ruthless. Seth will undo him because of that weakness.*

Seth rapped his knuckles hard against the arm of the throne, "Your support will be rewarded."

Eight of the fourteen men stood and walked out. They averted their eyes from the questioning gaze of the remaining council members.

The remaining six reeled with astonishment.

Stannick gloried in the moment with his new king. The game was up and there was nothing Mernus could do about it. After this day, the name Brock Stannick would be synonymous with treachery.

Where Seth did not have their respect, he would have their fear. After Seth got what he wanted, he expected an order to arrange their deaths.

He gave the signal. Guards, armed to the teeth, burst into the room.

"What is the meaning of this?" Lord Mernus demanded. He stood with his knuckles grinding into the table. "This is a disgrace. You dishonor your father's memory and blaspheme the name of Obenin."

"Oh," tested Seth, the whites of his eyes turning red, "you have my father's honor in mind, do you? Or is it just my presence that truly provokes your outrage? Keeper Octun kept his promise to my father. He anointed me king and crowned me before the people."

"Even though we did not always agree with Saroth," stated Mernus, "we of the council always concerned ourselves with King Saroth's image and what the council projected to his subjects."

"Well if it is honor, then why have you held one thousand five hundred and twenty five soldiers from Father's ranks?"

****

Lord Mernus straightened himself and crossed his arms. He wondered how the Prince had found out such an exact number. He realized this plot existed long before the King's death. Stannick had been constantly on the move.

Stannick had made several previous visits to him and to those remaining at the table with messages from the King. The King had not sent him to discuss anything. Through Stannick, the Prince had made it appear that Mernus and the others were in the King's favor. In reality, Stannick was covering his dealing with the traitors.

How could I have been such a fool? Mernus thought.

Regardless, he had to play the hand dealt.

"To keep order in my region and to protect my possessions," Mernus retorted vehemently.

"Oh, who could be after your wealth?" Seth waved him off. "Did you really expect to keep a force of that size hidden? You even have conscripts in reserve, raised from the vagabonds and peasants to overthrow me when I eventually came to power."

Lord Mernus inadvertently looked at those who conspired with him.

One hot reflection illuminated his mind. Brock Stannick must have had other spies, spies they did not know about. *I told them that we should revolt earlier, but they said we should wait out of respect for Saroth. Now it's too late.*

Purposely this time, Lord Mernus sneered at the others. Seeing they were not about to say anything, he slapped his hands against the tabletop. He wanted the others on the council to see the great disappointment and disgust in his eyes. All of them were blowhards. Now that they were up against the a beheading, they sat silent and gutless.

Lord Mernus spoke as if for the entire Obenite nation. "My lord," he stumbled over the words.

Taking a deep breath, he started again, "You are the king, now. The power of the Hands of Obenin is under your control. There is a matter of peace of which you should be aware."

"And what is that?" asked Seth smugly.

"Allowing any one person to wield the power we saw on the day of Saroth's death is far too dangerous. We have been bartering a treaty with the Benomian Alliances. If you hand over the power to tax, let us confirm all future appointments of Keeper of the Primary Temple, and to make certain laws to allow the council to control trade, there will be peace. The people are wary of war. Even with the power of Obenin with us, our soldiers still face many battles."

"I assure you, Lord Mernus, there will be no peace. There will be only victory, total, overwhelming and brutal subjection."

"And what will you do with us--try us for treason? Treason of aristocracy is the duty of a grand tribunal and not the sole decision of the king. We can manipulate who is on the tribunal. All of us have men in reserve, and if you think your army will choose to fight their brothers for you... well, we shall see."

"Oh, I have a much simpler method than the tribunal or civil war."

Seth got up and swaggered into the horseshoe. He emptied the contents of the bag on the table. He sorted through the pile.

"Recognize this?"

He tossed a ring to Mernus carelessly.

"What have you done? If you have harmed her, I will... I will...."

Mernus watched helplessly as Seth placed rings, bracelets, locks of hair, and other things taken from their children and wives in front of the each council member. Brock's men soon closed in around them to retain a maddened order among the remaining council members.

"Your loved ones are not harmed. You see what you have brought on yourselves by plotting against me. I realize some of you participated in this conspiracy only under duress. I will remember that when the time comes. But right now, this is what all of you will do."

Mernus did his best to hide his vengeful thoughts. Dying for what he believed was one thing. If Seth was capable of this, there was no telling what else he could do. The threat of what Seth might do to his family kept him silent, for now.

No one breathed as Seth delivered the terms. He did not want money. He ransomed for power and for their public support of him. They must approve and take his plans back to the people. Mernus felt the clock ticking. If the Benomian Alliance of Tenzia, Bardia and Carden fell, Seth did not need any of them anymore.

Seth continued, "The power of the Hands of Obenin will defeat the Benomian Alliance. I know there are those within my own kingdom who hate me, if not because of my skin, then for other reasons. I want to know where you are and what you are doing. All of you will march with me to these victories. I will not let anyone interfere with them in any way. There is no room for the thought of a rebellion...Lord Mernus. The troops you have in reserve will go to the front. You will show unequivocal support for me with public statements to the people tomorrow.

"All of you, with your hopeless imaginations, have underestimated me. Now submit or pay dearly. Submission is life. Betrayal is death. When you see the glorious victory I have promised my father, you will accept me. You will prosper. We all will prosper and this little incident will seem insignificant."

Seth directed the latter at Mernus, who bit his lips so hard that he tasted blood.

CHAPTER 21
The Spectacle of War

Across the Plains of Gath, as far as Octun surveyed, the Obenite army and citizens covered every rolling hill like a blanket of black snow.

This is the beginning of the victories Lord Cuere promised," Octun thought. Magic and heaven's power to rout the Benomian Alliance here at Gath, the plan, Cuere's plan, came to life before him. He saw no chance for their enemy. Commanders already held their orders for movement into the mountains, even though this day's battle had not been fought; invade and conquer Bardia to split the Benomian Alliance. Break Tenzia and Carden. After that, turn attention to the south and make firm the hold on Aspharia.

Before I am old and unable to fight any longer, we will have conquered all the great lands of the civilized world.

Farmers and old men with only staves or garden tools lined themselves behind the ranks of the regular army. Behind them, women and children danced and sang in celebration. Sometimes children made their way to the soldiers' camps. Soldiers spent as much time tracking down parents as they did sharpening their swords.

Hundreds of tavern keepers sold spirits and ales out of wagons and tents. Madams moved their brothels so close to the soldier's camp, the soldiers made muster just as quickly as they could from their own tents. Craftsmen fashioned wares and wandered around selling them. Artists set up tent galleries and painted portraits of the noblemen who wore new armor and swords made for the occasion. The Obenites turned the plains into one mobile market.

Parents dedicated babies to Obenin. Men and women tried to conceive children; they believed the days especially blessed. Couples married in hopes that their marriage would be as assured as the victory.

Octun's men stood ready at his flank. His roan steed dug his front right hoof into the dirt. His ears pricked up. The impending charge excited the horse.

Octun disapproved of the perpetual celebration that followed the day the Hands of Obenin displayed their power before the crown.

The kingdom did not truly mourn Saroth's death. No one remembers him, thought Octun.

If this was Cuere's promise fulfilled, Obenin made whole again, why did he feel despair?

Octun spoke to his captain. "All this is not necessary. They should have stayed at home."

His captain spoke with an effeminate voice that Octun learned to ignore and those soldiers under his command learned not to make fun of within the captain's earshot.

"They all want to be able to say they were here or took part in the greatest victory this kingdom has ever known. After all, the alliance outnumbers our actual fighting force two to one."

Trumpets sounded as troops tightened their formations around the banners, swallowtails and other flags wavering in a stiff breeze.

"That is no excuse."

"Yes, Colonel Octun, but remember there are four hundred years of bad blood. I believe this whole thing has been staged to put a certain impression into everyone's mind, especially the Benomian Alliance. Sending an army against us will avail to nothing. When the news of this battle gets to the world's ears, it will dishearten those who would seek to defeat us. For if the Benomian Alliance fails, and they are by far our most bothersome foe, who has a chance? We have never been able to keep an army on their soil. Now, we will move eastward across the ocean and soutward, beyond Aspharia."

Octun could not deny this. At least he was back on the battlefield. Only this time a sense of irony filled him.

****

"Everything else was just show. This is really it," remarked Parmos. He stepped away from Lord Cuere, who stood too close.

Visibly nervous, Jared elaborated, "The very reason that Obenin brought us here is now at hand. Everything that Lord Cuere and the rest of the kingdom hope for weighs on our shoulders."

"Where is Keeper Octun or Chancellor Levid?" Ulthea asked, wrapping both her arms around Jared's left arm. "One of them should be here."

"Their part with you is finished. They have done all that I directed them to do. I told you this before. Why do you keep whining about them?" Cuere snapped.

"I just wish they were here," complained Ulthea.

Parmos smoldered. Lord Cuere's treatment of them worsened each day. Keeper Octun wasn't warm, but he was not rude or cruel. He took care of them the only way he knew how. At the moment, Parmos missed that dearly. He glanced at Ictheos who quickly wrinkled his nose at Lord Cuere. Ulthea giggled under her breath.

Finally, the signal came.

"Oh, um, this is it. Come outside and listen to what I say."

They went outside. From their vantage point, Parmos saw the distance between the Obenites and the Benomian Army. The children prepared themselves while Cuere went into his normal hysterics, arms flailing wildly.

CHAPTER 22
On The Other Side Of Things

The Benomian army stood on edge. Gol Feth, a corporal, refused to believe the rumors that gods were among the Obenites. The rumor spread through their camp like a fiery plague, setting their ears ablaze. Now, a black mass formed, where before clear skies prevailed. There were so many Obenites.

"Where did all the people come from?"

Slowly, the churning omen rumbled towards them.

Years of hard fighting, the terrifying raids during the last winter, deathly conditions in the mountains; finally, they stood on Obenite soil only for power from heaven to thwart them.

Gol, along with some of their officers, tried to put some courage back into their troops, saying, "They invaded our land first. We drove them out. Now, we will have justice for every woman and child they have killed. King Saroth is dead. His son carries own his evil dealings. The Obenites boast that their god has saved them from our wrath. But, what have we seen from their army that we have not conquered with an irresistible force? If there were truly gods among them would they not have saved the Obenites by now?"

Premature gray streaks in Gol Feth's black beard made him look older than twenty-five. Before this war, he considered himself handsome. The last time he saw his wife, she turned away from him to hide her horror.

"She had no tears for me, only for herself."

His nose, once kingly, was flattened and twisted like that of a tavern brawler. An awful scar from a burn left the right side of his face a melted, bubbled mess.

Gol, originally, did not want to take part in this war. His main reason for joining the army was to fight off the marauders who lived in the mountains. Though the Obenite king did not officially sanction the marauders, he armed them secretly. The Benomian Alliance knew it. The Obenite people knew it-- some secret.

He and the others of his fighting group, who lived near the mountains, had grown tired of the constant threat. They formed a militia to seek out the Obenites and kill them. When the leaders of the Benomian Alliance saw their success, they sent forces to join them. They chased the marauders far into Obenite territory. The Obenites declared their actions an act of war. The conflict escalated into another phase of an endless war.

Once they beat the raiders back, he wanted to stop. The orders he received contradicted his desire. The Benomian Alliance pulled an invasion force from all the nations lying north of Obenin. Even the High Northerners from the frozen wastelands joined them. He was no deserter. He swallowed his thoughts. He had killed his share of men and planned that this day he would kill more than he had done in all the battles before.

Killing, war, mothers of widows and orphans. Sires of contempt and ill will..., and he planted himself on the front line.

Gol's anger surged. He believed the Obenites forced him into the situation by invading his homeland. There were always sporadic battles between them, but they chose a full-scale attack during his lifetime. Normally, a man only lived a little passed fifty-five; couldn't they have waited until time judged him too old to endure the combat? They, the Obenites, turned him from a man into a rogue animal that viciously murdered his guilt every day.

Yet, every night Gol's guilt resurrected itself. Dreams haunted him. The desperate screams, the panicky faces, the smell of blood and death as he slashed his sword or plunged his pike into other men's bodies, by the dozens. He hated the Obenites for this. He saw himself on death's table.

His family prepares his body for death. No matter how hard they scrub, they cannot remove the stains on his hands. How can men, in an attempt to obtain their own evil goals, be so ruthless as to force a man's hand and change him into an animal? he thought.

Gol stood with his men. The black mass churned toward them, consuming his stalwart exaltation from the previous night. He faced gods, after all. His body felt strange and his ears popped, yet, he stood.

"Steady," he commanded. "Prepare for the advance."

The advance given, he started forward. His armor clanked. A weak chorus of war cries filled his ears. He wished the Obenites were closer. By chance, if the gods drew something awful down from heaven in the thick of the fight, they might accidentally kill their own and give the Benomian Alliance the edge.

Gol charged with all his might. Hail the size of a man's knuckle pounded him. He saw sunlight glinting off the Obenite's helmets. Freezing rain poured from the sky. It chilled him to the bone, soaking his heavy clothing and weighing him down. Lightning reached from the sky and struck a few soldiers. The Obenites seemed twice as far away from him and getting farther. But, he knew they stood firm, waiting for the gods among them to weaken him and his comrades and kill off as many of them as possible.

Some of those near him cast down their weapons and fled. Gol kept moving forward. Without warning, he found himself face down in the mud. Moments before, the ground was dry and dusty. Everything was lost. He would never see his wife again, to kiss her lips and snuggle next to her on frosty mornings. Then he thought, on the other hand, he would not have to see her trying not to look at his face. She did not have to pretend anymore. She would be free from him, his ugliness, and the pity she felt for herself.

He tried to get up but someone in retreat stumbled over him, burying a knee into his back. Others followed, trampling him. Suddenly, blackness surrounded him and the cries of his men diminished.

CHAPTER 23
Octun Shocks Everyone

As the Benomian army fled, the trumpeters gave the charge, and a great roar went up. First, the knights and cavalry charged, their lances leveled. Those who brought nags covered with crude homemade armor followed.
Next, the foot soldiers ran mightily. Last, the old men who were better off warming their bones in front of a crackling fire limped along the best they could.

With the wind at his back and the weather still foul by the waning spell, Octun charged toward the frantic enemy line. He rode into the midst of the relatively few soldiers who did not flee. He raised his sword to hack one of them. The enemy soldier, who held no weapon, froze dazed with fear and confusion. Octun raised his sword higher. The soldier cringed backward with his hand up. He recognized that, like many other enemy soldiers, this man ran amuck, blundering into harms way. Only a few actually fought. Pockets of resistance fell one by one. They had no chance against the Obenite's merciless onslaught.

Moved deeply, Octun returned his sword to its scabbard. The frightened enemy soldier ran for his life. An old man wearing a helmet made from a bucket and riding a mule galloped past Octun. The old man threw a spear at the soldier catching him in the back near his kidney; after which, he caught up with him and finished him off. For a while, Keeper Octun rode slowly watching the behavior of his people. A killing frenzy seized them.

I'm a soldier, a warrior high priest. Isn't that part of my purpose?

He halted his horse. Others rushed by him, excited to take part in the massacre.

I killed for a reason... to conquer for the gain of my people and to carry the teachings of faith to the world. A soldier kills because he must. He kills in hope of a greater purpose. Pleasure has no part in it. Octun tried to justify himself, to put a difference between what he did and events all around him.

He watched as the last old, self-appointed knight, whom the foot soldiers had passed, dug his heels into the side of his ox. "Giddyup!" he yelled, "Or I'll skin ye and hang ye up for jerky!"

Octun turned his steed and galloped back to camp. *Everything is going as planned,* he thought, *there is no need for me here!*

On his way back to camp, he saw a child, about eight years old, on the battlefield. The child tormented a fallen soldier with a stick. The soldier covered his head, unable to move from the child's reach. Octun leaned to the side, swooped up the child and sat him in front. Suddenly, he pulled back on the reigns and turned around. He threw his canteen of water down to the fallen soldier. The soldier managed to turn on his back. He opened the canteen and washed the mud from his face. Octun saw a terrible burn and twisted nose. A veteran of many wars like himself, caught up in something more terrible than either one of them imagined. Octun turned and continued back to camp.

****

Observing the battle through a spyglass, Parmos watched Octun return from the battle. It shocked him. He expected Octun to return last. He certainly did not expect to see him carrying a screaming brat in front of him.

"Why is Keeper Octun returning?" asked Parmos.

"Maybe the battle is too easy for him," jested Ictheos, his eyes stuck to his own spyglass.

As he rode into the camp, Octun broke his mount into a spirited trot.

Ictheos offered the spyglass to Ulthea.

"It is him," she remarked in disbelief.

They ran to meet him, waving for him to stop. Octun spurred the horse from a trot into a gallop and rode right past them.

Ulthea cried, "What have we done? Why is he mad at us?"

The others were speechless.

Without much thought, Jared's anger took hold of him. "Keeper Octun," Jared yelled out, "Come back here. I don't care if you are under orders not to talk to us."

Lord Cuere stormed over to them and told them to get to their tent.

"You must forget your feelings for Keeper Octun," he warned. "You are my responsibility now and that's what matters. Your work today is not done. We have one more thing to do. At dusk, most everyone will have returned to the camps. You will bring terror to the Benomian Alliance."

"Can't we rest, Lord Cuere," pleaded Ulthea.

"You can sleep later," Cuere retorted.

"But can't we at least sleep until dusk?" Jared pressed. "The spell exhausted us. We are drained."

"Well I guess that is acceptable," Cuere gave in.

CHAPTER 24
The Dead and the Dying

The next day, only the regular army advanced into the mountains. Their intent was to press through to the northern empires and claim it for Obenin. As they traveled, Ulthea rode through the prior day's battlefield. Bodies spoiled the ground. Squawking vultures hovered over the human debris of battle, hurrying the Obenites army from amidst their feast on the dead.

Ulthea saw men gathering bodies and putting them into mass graves. The highway men, King Saroth's body, nothing prepared her for this kind of death: stiff, hacked, bloody, trampled, mouths open, crawling with insects, birds picking the flesh of corpses, the stench of blood and dead souls. She tried to turn away, but there was nowhere to turn. She could not help but look at each body she passed. So much death caused by the hands of soldiers, caused by her. This raw face of death never crossed her imagination until this moment.

The great slaughter of men littered Obenite text. Octun taught about it. Levid pontificated on it in such a way that made battle seem so distant and grand. Here, up close and personal, she saw the carnage brought upon the retreating army. Trapped by chaos and panic, they never stood a chance.

She refused to shed a tear. "Faith keeps me. This is Obenin's will. This is his wrath," she reasoned. "He has given us the power of righteousness. The Alliance did this to themselves."

She spurred her mount to catch up with Parmos. Once there, he greeted her sadly.

"What's wrong?" she asked.

"This is wrong. I am wrong?"

"What are you talking about? We did what was necessary," Ulthea replied.

"Someone should have told us. Levid and Octun should have made us understand what killing is like."

"And how would they have done that?"

"I don't know. But," he nodded to the field of bodies, "this makes me very sad."

"Then why aren't you crying," she pressed.

"I don't know. That is the worse part of all."

CHAPTER 25
An Attempt To Restore Bonds

The chill from the snow-capped mountains made the early spring night feel like winter's approach. Ulthea wrapped up in another quilt. She hated the arguing. Yet, she wanted to hear every word. Jared fussed at Parmos in hushed tones. None of them wanted to bring Lord Cuere out of his tent. Jared challenged Parmos at every turn. Parmos did little to defend himself. Ictheos threw in a word or two, purposefully stirring the pot.

Who'd have thought that Parmos had his own mind?" Ulthea wondered.

"I don't know what I expected but it was too much for me," Parmos said, pitching a piece of bread into the fire. "It's hard for me to believe we took part in all the killing."

"What did you expect it to be like?" Jared rebutted coldly. "Didn't you listen to Chancellor Levid's lectures? He taught us about the number of people who died in the battles."

"That's right, Parmos. Don't you remember?" chided Ictheos.

"That's not what I mean," Parmos objected. "Besides, Keeper Octun never bragged about the number of men he killed.

"Jared, you sound like you don't care," Ulthea commented without thought.

"I don't. Why should I? Why should anyone? They are the enemy," snapped Jared.

Ulthea looked into the fire. The corners of her lips loosened in submission. She actually meant, you sound like you don't care about what Parmos thinks. Only she knew Jared's answer, again, "Why should I?"

"Jared is right," Ictheos spoke out. "I do feel sorry for them but this is Obenin's will and if the Benomian Alliance doesn't surrender, there will be more of it."

Parmos stood up. His eyes narrowed in thought as he looked at the others. "So, I guess I will have to get used to it." He turned, took two steps and swung back to them. "How many will I have to kill to get used to it?" Not waiting for the reply, he moved quickly to the tent and threw the flap back angrily.

Ulthea stared into the fire. Parmos' words left them all silent. She considered them. Mostly, she wondered about Parmos. That moment touched her. Parmos touched her. She looked at the tent flap with a blossoming appreciation of Parmos.

The full moon loomed overhead. The horn for final checks sounded. Celebrating soldiers quieted down as they put away their gear. She watched the commanders leave Seth's tent. They all chatted merrily. King Seth stood straight and broad- shouldered. He moved stiffly as he talked at his generals and commanders. She determined that the Benomian Alliance presented very little opposition. She scanned their faces. In the torch light, she hoped to see Octun's face. She watched the commanders bow and leave, no Octun. Somehow, they had to find him. He was a soldier. He killed for his beliefs. Even though he seemed angry at them, Octun could talk to Jared and Parmos, solve their argument, and comfort them all.

`Dread. It crawled up from her belly like a tiny spider. If she had not been watching, she wouldn't have noticed. But, since she was, she wanted to swat it off of her and step on it. Only she felt hopeless and helpless. And as the tiny spider crawled towards her heart, it grew larger. So did her dread.

She needed Octun to knock the spider off her and crush it under his huge boot. If Lord Cuere had a problem with them disobeying his order, Octun would protect them from his wrath. She... they had to find Octun.

****

The Obenite army moved deep into the mountains. Patrols still rooted out pockets of resistance here and there. Once the patrols checked in, Jared and the others brought havoc down upon the Benomian Alliance. Lord Cuere taught them to use their power to affect the weather far beyond their vision. Their personal guards constantly changed. None lasted over a couple of days.

Jared studied one of his guards who cleaned and checked his gear near them. Occasionally, he looked up at them, surveyed the area, then went back to cleaning his gear.

As he cleaned each item, the guard placed it in his pack. He left the weapons for last. Jared noted that guard looked just old enough to marry and start a family. Maybe he had a family already.

The guard treated his weapons with reverence. His sword, knives, and a dangerous-looking chain, he placed in his clothing, which appeared tailored specifically to hold each weapon.

Jared approached the guard. When the guard realized that Jared was actually approaching him, he leapt up and bowed.

"Master?" he stammered over the word. He did not look up from the bow.

Jared smiled. He put his hand over the guard's head as the king did.

"Bless me master, and I shall prosper." The guard overflowed with sincerity.

"Good servant, I shall bless you. But I require something of you first."

"Name it, master of the sky, and if it is within me, I will give it."

"Where is Keeper Octun's camp?"

"But Lord Cuere will punish me if he finds out I told you."

"I will not tell him, if you don't."

The guard glanced up. He kissed Jared's hand then pointed down the mountain slope. "Go that way to the river. Go upstream. The only hard part is knowing the different ensigns and coats-of-arms. All regiments are grouped together and their boundaries are marked by their banners. The largest flag tells the region. The smaller banner tells the regiment or family. "Careful though, the mercenaries also bear the emblem of the family who pays them. The swallowtails under the smaller banner gives the charge, that is, the infantry, archery, cavalry, knights and so on. The cavalry flies the winged sword. Colonel Octun is with Glynwith, a lily on a white field. When you find it, watch for the temple guard. Four times a day, he calls the regiment for prayer and rituals. The priest always ends up in the temple tent. It is also Keeper Octun's quarters."

"Why doesn't the Keeper camp with us? He is the high priest and should minister to the royals."

"No one knows, master. It vexes everyone. No one ministers to the king's encampment. We find the nearest priest." The guard paused. "Master? My wife and baby, bless them so they want for nothing, save my company."

Jared touched the soldier's shoulder and chanted melodiously. As he did, a stiff wind picked up. A slither of sunlight broke through the clouds.

The guard cried, "Oh, thank you master! Thank you."

Back in front of their tent, Jared stood with the others as Lord Cuere instructed them. He started earlier than usual and kept them going far longer than any previous time. When they asked about the men who might still be out in harm's way, Lord Cuere barked, "They don't matter."

After Lord Cuere let them go, Jared and the others collapsed in their tent. He hardly finished telling them his plan to sneak out to see Octun before Parmos started snoring.

Before dawn, Jared felt someone shaking him. He tried to ignore it. The pestering continued. He, finally, turned over.

"Parmos, I must be dreaming," he thought.

"Jared... Jared, wake up. This is your plan," persisted Parmos.

Jared relented, "All right! All right! Just give me a moment. Are the others up?"

"No."

"Well, get them up."

Jared pulled up the side of the tent, where Ictheos had previously loosened the stake. They stole into the darkness. Jared barely saw where he stepped. Ictheos led them through brush like a creature of the night. He moved instinctively, seemingly aware of every other thing that moved. He stopped them, started them and redirected them.

Once at the river, they headed upstream finding as much cover as they could. About an hour and a half passed before Ictheos spotted the torch-lit Lily of Glynwith. There they waited until the temple priest announced prayers.

The priest walked slowly through the camp singing and waving a glows suspended from chains. A small group of soldiers followed him.

"What are you doing sneaking around in our camp?" a voice grunted angrily.

With a start, Jared turned to see a soldier bending over them. He put the glows right in their faces. Jared shielded his eyes.

When the soldiers saw their faces, he immediately apologized. "The Hands of the Obenin. Forgive me I did not know who you were. Please forgive me." He knelt on both knees.

Jared looked at the others. They looked back at him as to say, "You got us into this mess, say something."

Jared, quick to answer, said, "Arise, servant of Obenin. What is your name?"

Parmos' mouth dropped. Jared answered as if they were supposed to be here.

"I am Corporal Ihnan, acting Sergeant of the Perimeter Guard, master." He kept his gaze toward the ground.

"We are going to see Keeper Octun, why have you stopped us?"

"You appeared to be sneaking, master. With no escort, I didn't realize who you were."

"We don't like to draw attention to ourselves. It causes disorder. Are you one of Lord Cuere's men?"

"Lord, no," he spat. "I'm with the Glynwith Cavalry."

"The Glynwith Cavalry," repeated Parmos. "Then could you tell us where Keeper Octun's tent is?"

"Of course, master, I would be honored to show you."

"And the price would be a blessing, I assume?" asked Jared.

"No, master, it is an honor. I ask not, but if thou be merciful?" Ihnan returned humbly.

"Thank you," Ulthea blurted out. "Alas, someone of faith."

CHAPTER 26
Octun Puts Everything On The Alter

Jared did not want to wake Octun. They gathered around each side of him. The temple tent was large enough for ten or twelve soldiers to stand with their gear. An altar, idols and religious artifacts sat in perfect order. Octun rested uncomfortably, evidently disturbed by the sound of his own snoring. They closed in around him and, for a moment, watched the covers rise and fall with each breath.

Jared nodded to Ulthea. She grabbed his arm and shook him gently. "Keeper Octun... Keeper Octun."

"Um..." he rolled over to his side and curled up like a babe in the womb.

"I have made arrangements. The minor priest will cover prayers," he mumbled, a great amount of irritation in his grumbling.

"Sir...." Ulthea beckoned more loudly. "Keeper...."

Octun snapped awake when he recognized the voice.

"What are you doing here?" asked Octun, quickly scanning the area.

"Keeper Octun," Ulthea began, "we are very sorry to just show up like this, but what else can we do?"

Ulthea swallowed hard. Octun's harsh tone surprised her. "We need your help," she pleaded

"There is nothing I can do for you. Get out of my tent."

Ulthea teared up.

Parmos spoke out, "Why are you doing this to us?" Jared disapproved. As Parmos spoke, Jared realized how Parmos felt about Octun. The way he spoke, the manner in which he gestured, Parmos emulated Octun. Though Ictheos often teased Parmos about it, he had rejected it as comical. In this show of courage, Jared changed his mind completely. A jealous shiver ran through him. He looked at Ulthea. She fixed her gaze on Parmos. This maddened Jared.

". . . why do you reject us?" argued Parmos.

Jared drew back. Anger filled Octun's face. Jared expected Octun to hit Parmos. Instead, Octun took a deep breath. He still looked angry, but the anger seemed redirected away from Parmos.

"We are victims of evil men. You are not acting for the good of the kingdom. My heart is changed, yet I groan under the weight of my guilt."

Octun paused. He looked at each of them. The others dropped their eyes. Jared did not. He saw brutally raw truth perching on Octun's lips.

"What do want to know?" asked Octun.

Jared's gut turned, "Ulthea wants to know why you avoid us."

"Is that all that bothers you?" asked Octun, trivializing Jared's worries.

For a moment, none of them responded. Octun's rebuke filled them with guilt.

Parmos got up and walked to the other side of the tent. He kept his back turned, separating himself from the conversation.

"I don't believe any of this was ever the will of Obenin, but conspired by those who seek their own gain, with utter disregard to the people," accused Octun.

"Don't believe it to be the will of Obenin!" Ulthea shrieked. "But what about all the things you told us and taught us."

Octun hesitated. "I am sorry, but I thought it all a test of my faith."

"How does that explain why you avoid us," Ulthea

continued, not willing to let the question go
unanswered.

Octun repeated himself again. "I don't
believe *any* of this is of Obenin."

"If not Obenin's will," Jared returned angrily, "then
whose?"

"I don't believe it is Obenin's will that you are in
our land. I do not believe he gave you the power to
control the elements."

"But how could we have done all that we have done
if it were not?" Ictheos objected.

Octun drove his fist into the ground. "I don't
know!"

"Keeper, why are you saying these terrible things
about us?" Ulthea moaned, tears pouring down her cheeks.

He reached out and grabbed her face. His hand
covered her chin and cheeks, forcing her to look at him.
"What do you think is going to happen to you?"

She wrestled against his grip. "You are hurting
me."

The fierceness in Octun's eyes terrified her. For the
first time, she witnessed the warrior side of the high priest
directed at her.

"What do you think is going to happen to you?"

"I don't know!" she sobbed, slapping at Octun's
arm.

"Prince Seth and Lord Cuere will make your lives a
sentence of hell and death. You will do their every bidding
and your lives will be to serve their whims... their motives
are not pure. And, there are those who are beginning to
see you as gods and that takes away from the glory of
Obenin. That is heresy and blasphemy."

"But we will never seek glory upon ourselves. We
will always be servants of the king and the people,"
objected Ulthea.

"And whose servants are you now? Whose purpose do you serve? If you are not the offspring of righteousness, then whose offspring are you?"

Jared pitied Ulthea. Angry, scared and trembling, Ulthea looked like a blade of grass against Octun's massive body. But, he dared not interfere.

****

Ulthea could not bear any more. With all her strength, she clawed at Octun's fingers until they bled. She pried her way from Octun's grasp and ran from the tent, stumbling into the dawn light.

Her heart shattered. This man fathered their faith. He taught them that the king's divine right to serve is beyond their questioning. He assured them that to serve the king faithfully is to serve Obenin faithfully. The very basis of the tenets rested on some of these principles. He told them Obenin ordained their purpose. Now, he was telling them, not only was their purpose vain, but they themselves and the power they possessed were evil. They all looked up to Octun as a pillar of faith and fatherly figure. Now, his own faith waned.

Ulthea marched back into the tent screaming at the top of her lungs.

"You are wrong. We will do all that we are supposed to do. We are not evil, and we will not let ourselves be used by anyone who makes us do anything against Obenin's tenets."

"So you believe," returned Octun unaffected.

"What are you planning, Keeper Octun?" Ictheos asked.

"Don't do anything that will get you in trouble with King Seth," Parmos added, unexpectedly. "Even if you hate us, don't give up everything you stand for."

Before he could get an answer, someone snatched open the tent flap.

Lord Cuere entered, flanked by two of his men. His normally yellowed cheeks reddened with anger.

"What are you doing here? I told you not to go wondering off without my permission. Now get back to your tent!"

More soldiers entered the tent. Octun recognized them immediately. The shorter of the two wore the mantle of junior regimental officer; the taller, a senior lieutenant. Both came from Glywith; both trained on the temple grounds during Octun's tenure.

Cuere continued undeterred, "Keeper Octun, I ordered you not to have anything to do with the Hands of Obenin. I will strip you of everything, your rank, your position. What were you telling them?"

Colonel Octun rose to his feet. His eyes riveted into Lord Cuere. His tone, frigid and numb, carried the potential volatility of a volcano.

"My position as high priest, you can have. My rank," he looked at his epaulets. ". . . try to take them if you dare. What I said this morning should have been said long ago. I won't tell you what I told them, but I will tell you this, Cuere," he spoke the name with disdain and contempt.

"I loathe the sight of you. You are an insecure little child driven by revenge. A dabbler in things that you don't fully understand. I don't know how you tricked a good king like Saroth into following your blasphemous plans. You have used me and everyone else to obtain your own goals and now the kingdom is in peril."

"In peril!" assailed Cuere. "In peril... you are an idiot. I have just handed this kingdom the greatest victory in its history and set the course for the next millennium. Your praying has made you mad!"

"You are as short-sighted as a mole and without a shred of common sense," scoffed Octun.

Putting his hands under his cloak, Cuere moved toward Octun.

"Boo!" shouted Octun and flung his arms outward.

Lord Cuere jerked back, dropping a silver ball, which rolled into Octun's boot. He kicked it across the tent. When it landed, it made a weak whizzing sound, ending with a puff of smoke.

Ulthea wanted to laugh but she realized the gravity of the situation. She found comfort in the way Octun spoke to Cuere.

"Out of tricks?" taunted Octun.

Cuere ordered, "Arrest him and take him to the King."

The Glynwith soldiers drew their swords as Cuere's men took an offensive position.

Octun shook his head quickly at the Glynwith soldiers. They gripped their swords more tightly and took a step forward.

"At ease," he ordered. "Stand and witness. Tell everything you see no matter what you see. Do not hide anything just to protect me."

The soldiers looked at each other. Reluctantly sheathing their swords, they rested on their heels.

Cuere's men took a careful step forward.

Octun stooped down to retrieve his gear from under a table. To Ulthea's amazement, it was already collected and bundled up for travel.

"Arrest him or you will be executed for cowardice."

Ulthea saw fear and indecision in the eyes of Cuere's guard. Two of them were not enough. The rumor that the few years of comfort at Obenin's Temple had softened Octun spread throughout the army. His early return from the battlefield at Gath perpetuated it. She knew this day promised to bring an end to the rumor.

Cuere's men positioned themselves in front of him on either side.

One of them tried to work his way behind Octun. He glanced down, trying to avoid some of the temple's sacred icons. The guard never saw Octun move. All he felt was a solidly packed pack smash him in the face-- he never got a chance to make one thrust with his sword.

The other soldier attempted to thrust his sword into Octun's chest. Octun moved to one side and smashed his opponent's knee with his foot. The second guard fell on his back swearing and holding his knee in pain. Suddenly, the first guard leapt up, spitting blood and vengeance. Lord Cuere's eyes went wide when he realized he stood too close to the altercation.

Too late, Cuere wriggled like a fish out of water, trying to loosen himself from Octun's iron grip. Octun pulled Cuere close to his face and turned to put Cuere's back to the one standing guard. Nose to nose, Octun sneered at him with pure disgust.

"It is only my oath to Saroth that keeps you alive. I swore to him that I would not oppose Seth. Seth, evidently, thinks he needs you. Cuere, you are not worth spit." He paused. "Then again, maybe you are."

Octun spat in Cuere's face, then pitched him through the air into the guard. They both fell crashing onto the small temple altar. It shattered into splinters.

Octun recovered his gear as Ulthea and the others watched in wonderment.

"Where are you going?" Parmos beseeched, his voice cracked.

Octun spoke with dismay, "I don't know. I only know that I will not go back to the temple. What little I want from there has already been retrieved for me. Going back would only disgrace it."

Octun took off his high priest mantle and ripped it in half. He tossed the pieces out in front of him.

Slapping the tent flap back, Octun stormed out. He looked around. It seemed that the entire Obenite army rushed toward the Glynwith camp. Ulthea and the others followed like children whose mother was leaving them, begging her to stay, promising to change if she would only give them a second chance.

Despite her feelings, Ulthea knew Octun had to leave for now. Seth and his men would soon arrive. She and the others, unwittingly, thwarted Octun's plans to steal away. They caused this mess. This was not supposed to happen. Wherever Octun went, she hoped Obenin would help him.

Cuere came from the tent cursing, calling out for someone in the crowd to arrest Keeper Octun. In a flash, the soldiers spread out, getting out of danger's way. Putting his hand on his sword, Octun looked for anyone who might step forward.

"Why are you all just standing there? After all that I have done for this kingdom. King Seth will execute you all."

The crowd murmured against the words.

****

A soldier pushed his way through the crowd to challenge Octun.

The crowd jeered, "Traitor to the Lily of Glynwith. You bring shame to your family."

Tossing his pack into the crowd, Octun drew Saroth's gift, the battle sword, Romala. He held it with both hands. He never imagined fighting a fellow soldier with it. For a moment, he studied his adversary's face. He had seen him around the camp, a braggart and an arrogant man. Some might say he was handsome. His skin was darker than Octun's own and he was younger. He reminded Octun of an overgrown bear cub.

"Surrender your sword!" he ordered Octun.

"King Saroth gave me this battle sword... a dear friend, a great king. I have lost him. I will not lose the sword, too. Step aside and let me pass."

"Oh! I can't do that. Didn't you hear Lord Cuere? You are under arrest." He swished his sword through the air.

"I have not done anything that did not need to be done. Step aside and let me pass."

"I think your age is showing old man, you being thirty five and all. First, you return to camp before the battle even started good. Now your hearing is going. I'll speak louder and slower so you can read my lips, if you still can't hear me. Drop... your... sword.... You... are... under... arrest."

"Your inexperience is no excuse for your stupidity, but I have no quarrel with you. Step... aside."

The soldier lunged toward him, swinging his sword with some skill. Moving to one side, Octun tried only to wound him but missed the soldier completely.

"Getting slow in your old age?" the bear cub taunted.

He's a bit clumsy, but in a dangerous way," Octun thought, hoping he would not have to kill the man.

Of all the robbers and soldiers of foreign lands he had killed, he had never battled another Obenite soldier to the death. Some commanders used tactics that purposefully ended in a conscript's death. Octun used other means for instilling discipline. Those commanders dared not so carelessly sacrifice a knight in training. Why do so to a commoner?

The bear cub charged again, bringing his sword-bearing paws down on his head. Octun countered, blocking him, metal clanking. He continued on the defense as his opponent tried to force him to one side.

His attacker stepped back and assaulted him again with a

flurry of strokes. Octun recognized his attacker's frustration. He had tried his best, to no avail.

What will he try next? Yes, he will try to tie me up at close quarters and hope his younger strength can disarm me or throw me," figured Octun.

Indeed, that was the bear cub's next move. Octun felt the soldier trying to force him to the right.

All right, if the bear cub wants to go to the right, the bear cub will go to the right."

Smartly, Octun pushed against the bear cub. The bear cub, not about to be outdone, pushed back with all his strength. Octun gave way and tugged on his opponent. When the bear cub realized his feet were off the ground, he tried to tighten his grip on Octun. Too late, Octun flipped him. He hit the ground so hard the crowd winched. Octun placed his sword at the soldier's throat.

"Do you want to die today, bear cub?"

The soldier caught his breath and rested in the dust, thankful for his life and cursing his own over-confidence.

Other soldiers, not from the Glynwith regiment, attempted to break through to the fight. The regiment packed closely together and buffeted them to cover Octun's escape.

****

Ulthea saw Octun last. Someone tossed his gear to him and he was gone, lost in the mass of bodies that engulfed him.

With a rushing impulse, Ulthea tried to run after him, calling his name until her throat ached. She worked back to the others. Soldiers barked and insulted one another. Anger raged through the crowd like spring lightning, ending with thunderous roars and cursing.

Seth and his generals arrived. They argued with the Glynwith commanders. After about an hour, other generals and commanders pushed their way through the mob to join the argument. The shouts for Glynwith and Octun overpowered shouts for the king. The words of Glynwith leaders held such sway that discourse threatened to fracture the Obenite army. Suddenly, a new and greater commotion arose as if bearable terms had been reached.

Ulthea looked up. The lily banners atop the tents lowered. Glynwith headed home and no one dared stop them, not even King Seth.

Before sunset, the last lone soldier of the Glynwith Regiment, a man known as Bear Cub, began marching back to the Obenite side of the Abringian Mountains.

CHAPTER 27
The Taste Of Being Worshipped

Over the next several weeks, the remaining Obenite army pressed through the mountain passes. They targeted Bardia first. Parmos noticed a general agitation in everyone. Lord Mernus had disappeared; no one knew where he was. Seth did not seem worried about it. Many wondered if Mernus remained among the living.

Lord Cuere treated them more hatefully than ever. To Parmos, he seemed to take out his impotence in handling the situation with Octun out on them.

After that day, Cuere spent much of his time in his tent studying. Morning, noon, and night, he mulled over his artifacts, holding them up then reading from scrolls.

Parmos noticed a difference in himself as well, a difference he withheld from the others until now. Sitting, Jared lowered his head to his knees. Parmos moved closer to him. Normally, he could feel the others during their storm song, especially Jared. He sensed his intent and emotion. This time, he felt only himself and the torment of the song.

"What happened to us tonight?" Parmos asked Jared.

"I don't know. It was not normal."

"I was so scared," Ulthea revealed. "I almost lost control."

"No," Jared cut in. "I wanted to loose myself. Then, there was this vision or something."

"What do you mean?" Ictheos asked.

"Well... for a moment, I saw. . . or I thought I saw something," Jared returned.

"Like what?" insisted Ictheos, as if he were waiting for someone else to say it first.

"I thought I saw myself in the storm... or part of the storm... or something. I was up in the storm, then I saw a terrible whirlwind smashing down everything."

"I thought I was seeing things," Ictheos confessed with a sigh of relief.

"Then I remember struggling, trying to bring everything under control, trying desperately to bring myself back. Some part of me didn't want to come back," Jared recounted.

"I know," Parmos agreed. "Things started just like they always do. After a while, something happened. Instead of having to use a hammer and all my might to break a stone, all I need now is the power in my fist. I think it has something drawing me to the. . . the . . . well, something drawing me..., no calling me, from that way." He nodded his head easterly.

"What 'drawing'?" Ictheos asked, this time in ignorance.

Parmos picked up a large twig and tossed it into the fire. "I've felt strange for twelve days now," Parmos revealed.

"So have I," Ulthea replied.

"Well, why didn't *you* mention it sooner?" Jared asked as if it were important.

"Why didn't you mention it?" argued Parmos.

"Do I have to bring up everything?"

"Wait a minute," Ulthea interrupted Parmos' reply. "You all are getting off the subject. We'll get nothing done by fussing at each other."

Parmos squinted his eyes and bit his lip. He tried to get back to his point. "I think we must be very careful from now on."

"Careful?" Jared parried, continuing in the argumentative mood.

"Yes, careful. If we are not careful, we might hurt ourselves."

Twisting his body and gritting his teeth, Jared admitted the inescapable. "Okay! Okay! We should be careful. There is something about these mountains that makes us more powerful and we shouldn't take any chances."

Ictheos patted Parmos on the shoulder, "Nothing will go wrong, but you know... someone ought to tell Lord Cuere."

"You must be losing your mind. There is absolutely no way I'm going to tell him anything," spat Jared.

Ictheos stared at Jared and laughed, his eyes sparkling with mischief. "I have you."

The others laughed at Jared.

"As each day passes, I get more and more fed up with him," continued Jared.

"I think that we should talk to the king about him," Ulthea suggested.

"Yes," declared Jared finally, "we must talk to King Seth. When we see him tomorrow, we will tell him how Lord Cuere treats us."

A shiver ran up Parmos' spine when he saw Lord Cuere walk toward them. By his prideful strut, Parmos knew that the scouts reported no meaningful resistance in Bardia.

The next morning, Parmos got the immediate impression that everyone watched them very closely. Even their personal guards seemed disembodied spirits drifting about them. Everyone in the camp moved in his direction.

Parmos tried to grab Ulthea and run, too late. The mob trapped them, touching them, yelling and shoving. Men cried for Parmos and the others to bless them, to bless their land, children, wives or parents. He did not know what to do. If he did not do something, the soldiers adoration might kill them. He touched as many of the soldiers as possible.

He shouted whatever came to his mind, as long as it sounded like a blessing.

Each man, who thanked them, tried to withdraw, but others pressed inwardly toward him, preventing any outward movement.

Jared reacted in turn. "Go in peace. May you prosper. Your children grow strong. May your wife grant you many sons."

The blessed soldiers ended up forming a protective cushion around the four. They needed help, quickly. The soldiers nearest them started to beat the crowd back for their own safety.

From the outer perimeter of the crowd, men cried out in pain. King Seth's personal guard brutally beat a path through the throng of soldiers. They used shields and short spears. Lord Cuere followed in their wake carrying a sleek metal staff. The mob shouted insults at the king's guard, who shouted back at them. The jostling renewed. The king's guard did not yield any ground. They braced with their shields and waited for reinforcements.

"Enough!" shouted Cuere. He gripped the staff with both hands and chanted something none of them understood. He lifted it up in the air and thrust it downward, burying its end into the ground. Then he leaned the staff toward the crowd.

"Move aside," he commanded. Some of the king's guard did not move quickly enough. The staff rumbled like the sound of a landslide. From where Parmos stood, the staff formed the air into what looked like a huge ball of water. As he looked through it, everything appeared larger and warped like a bad dream. When the bubble hit the soldiers, it knocked them up through the air over the heads of the mob.

Cuere repeated the words. Again the staff rumbled. Three or four soldiers and one of the king's guard went flying through the air again.

Cuere leapt up and swung his staff over his head. "Move back or suffer the same fate."

"The king!" someone shouted. Everyone scattered.

"Get back to your duties or to your tents," Seth ordered.

Backed by reinforcement, he yelled, "Now!"

"King Seth. I am glad you are here. What's happened to these people? They act like they have never seen us before," Cuere shouted.

"Get into my tent!" ordered Seth, his manner terse.

Once in his tent, King Seth sat behind a long table covered with brightly colored cloths. He looked very displeased.

"More scouts returned this morning. What they reported shocked me," began Seth. "As they approached the village of Das-chein, a helpless group of people met them, begging to appease the gods among us."

"I don't see anything so unusual about that. Each night I bring some sort of devastation on them," Cuere boasted.

"This is different. Nothing but walls are left. The cattle and sheep lay scorched and are still smoldering."

Lord Cuere shot a disapproving look at Jared and then Parmos.

"You didn't tell me they held such power. Why were you keeping this from me?" Seth studied Cuere's every inflection and movement.

"Well... my lord... I just wanted to be sure. Better to be conservative. The danger would be in overestimating their power."

King Seth stared at Lord Cuere for a long time.

Finally, he said, "In the future, don't bother to speculate about what I want, just do what I tell you. Now though, as you see, we have a problem."

Seth got up and walked over to the Hands of Obenin. He looked down his nose at each of them as if to perceive some subtle change. All except Jared looked down when Seth eyed them. Their gazes locked. Finally, Jared lowered his eyes.

"The soldier's attitudes towards them have changed. We need to come up with some sort of plan where we can use this to the utmost advantage. My father would have it no other way." Parmos glanced at Jared. What was he thinking by staring King Seth down? Octun's words came back to him. "Who do you serve?"

King Seth's face brightened with cunning. Parmos, for the first time, witnessed any discussions about their fate.

"We will make Lord Mernus pay for his desertion. Once we finish here, he and his region will suffer."

"But my lord, what of me? You have promised me certain things."

"I have no intention of reneging on my promise to you... as long as you serve father and me well."

Cuere swallowed hard.

"Remember, Lord Cuere, it is I who decides who is to live and who is to die. The fate of the kingdom is in my hands and I will not share the glory with anyone. My father will be magnified in me."

Who is going to speak for us? Parmos wondered. *It's certainly not going to be me.*

He saw a certain futility in addressing the king about the matter—Seth had mentioned Saroth one too may times.

"My lord, I have something to say," Jared ventured, stepping forward.

Cuere's eyes widened. His mouth dropped open. "You have nothing to say to King Seth that you do not say to me first," Lord Cuere challenged.

Jared did not stop. "That's just what I mean."

"I said, shut up!" Cuere raised his stick.

"I don't think we are being treated very well for people who are supposed to be heroes."

"Shut up, you!" Cuere raised his staff higher and started chanting.

Seth stopped him.

"Let him speak," directed Seth.

"You, still, treat us like prisoners. We have no freedom."

"You have not been treated any differently than you have always been."

"But, my lord, we don't exist until you need us," Jared emphasized. "I see everyone's gain except ours. Lord Cuere has servants and soldiers tending to him. We have nothing."

King Seth looked at him as if to say, "Is that all?"

"It seems the rest of our lives will be this way. The hope of what shall become of us is dim."

"Take them back to their tents, Lord Cuere. But, before you go, remember this, my spoiled lad. You are here to serve me and me alone. Whatever is to become of you is my choice. Trust me, you will be in my service for a long time. Wherever there are land and people, I shall rule over them and you will be the weapon which I wield.

"The world will say that a terrible and strong king rules in Obenin. Eventually, the name of Obenin will fade and only the name of Seth will remain and my father's name will be glorified.

"So, I will take good care of you. If your own companionship is not enough for you, I will order Lord Cuere to find you some servants and to put more 'care' in his caretaker role." He waved his hands and dismissed them.

Before they left the tent, Seth added, "And search the spoils, give them a trinket or two. Give each of them their own quarters."

Lord Cuere withdrew from the tent, bowing deeply. Outside of Seth's earshot, Parmos listened to Cuere's angry tirade.

"The king should have treated me better. I am the true hero, the man who saved this pitiful kingdom from destruction. No matter what I do, someone always belittles it. No one ever gives me all the credit I am due and I am tired of it. I should be planning the new empire, not serving others. I will not take any more abasement or ridicule from a spoiled brat. When the time is right, I will teach everyone a lesson in humility, even King Seth."

Parmos and the others settled back in their tent. Jared raged. He spoke loudly, with a higher pitch than normal.

"He never listens to us. The only thing King Seth cares about is his quest for power," Jared argued. "He did not even hear what we had to say."

"We have to try," urged Ulthea. "He will listen to us if we make him realize what we mean."

"We are doomed," declared Ictheos ominously. "Doomed, doomed, doomed. Lord Cuere wants vengeance on everyone. King Seth want to rule everyone. We are caught between them. We're doomed, doomed, doomed."

"I don't think it would have been like this if King Saroth was alive. I don't think he would have let this happen to us," Ulthea rationalized.

"But he is dead and he can't help us now. No one can. Not even Father Obenin," Ictheos objected. "We can't even help ourselves. Octun was right. Look at what Jared asked for: mammon, spoils."

Ulthea would not have it. "How can you say that? Just because we want a little more for ourselves does not mean we are bad."

"If you say so, but I think Keeper Octun was right."

Parmos puzzled over Ictheos' comments. Ictheos' soul accepted the inevitability of Octun's admonishment as prophecy. Seth and Cuere charted an unalterable course for them and they may as well get used to it.

Jared came to Ulthea's aid. "Remember, we read that sometimes when the faith of others is in doubt, someone has to take a stand for what he knows is right!"

Ulthea brightened. "The tenets, yes, that is the answer. But, what should we do? How can we bring them back to faith?"

Jared motioned for them to gather closer. "What I am saying is that we should refuse to do anything, use our powers, that is, if they don't agree to give us what we want."

"And repent of their hypocrisy and selfishness," added Ulthea.

"What?" Ictheos laughed. "All that's going to do is cause trouble. We can't order the king around like that. We don't have the... power."

Jared clenched his fists in determination. "We do have the power... and the right."

Ulthea added quickly, "If they aren't looking out for the kingdom then someone must. Maybe that is the reason we were brought here, to bring the throne back to faith, to take Seth's eyes from his self interest, put them on Obenin."

"That's not going to work. But... go ahead anyway. I don't have any better ideas," Ictheos relented.

"Why don't we just leave?" Parmos injected.

"Do what?" Jared laughed.

"Leave."

"And go where?" Jared asked, rolling his eyes.

"To where we are being led, toward that 'drawing' we all feel."

"Why should we leave?" Ulthea asked, trembling under the snuggly blanket at the very thought.

"Because I don't think King Seth will do anything other than what he wants. He's proven that he will have his way no matter what. Ictheos is right. Keeper Octun was right. Just as he left, Lord Mernus left, the entire Glynwith Regiment walked out, we should leave. Anywhere is better than here."

"Well, there's an idea." Ictheos whistled.

Parmos could not tell whether he agreed or disagreed. He gave no clue. So, Parmos asked.

Ictheos just looked at him with one eyebrow raised.

Parmos kept his eyes on him and added, "Keeper Octun believes those two are capable of anything. If we confront them, there is no telling what might happen."

"I really don't believe anyone could be that cruel. After all, they need us," Ulthea surmised.

"How could he afford to hurt us? It's by the power we have that he was able to have this victory. But, Parmos, if it will make you happy, we will do that as a back up plan," declared Jared.

Ictheos looked at Parmos. Both knew that Jared believed his own plan would work and there would be no need to leave the comfort of the camp and venture into the cold mountains.

That evening, Lord Cuere and Seth entered their tent. Parmos became suspicious. This was unusual. Seth did not ever come to see them.

"Come with me, now. We have more work to do," Cuere snapped his fingers at them motioning toward the door.

Parmos tensed up. He could not move even if he wanted to.

"What is the meaning of this?" Cuere put his hands on his hips.

Choosing his words carefully, Jared spoke with determination, "Lord Cuere, we cannot participate in this mockery of Obenin's will. You will not listen to us, so we must do something to get your attention."

Cuere directed his guards to lift them. Parmos wrapped his arms around his knees and locked them. The guards lifted him though Parmos refused to drop his feet to the ground. The others did the same. The guards shook him harshly, attempting to shake loose his legs.

"If you don't do what I say, I'll make you regret that you ever crossed me," threatened Cuere.

Prince Seth cut him off, "So Master Jared, you speak for everyone?"

Jared stood and brushed himself off stalling for the time it took for his courage to build. He bowed deeply and said, "My Lord."

Parmos' heart pounded in his throat. Jared had spoken boldly to Lord Cuere. That was the easy part. Parmos feared for them all. He whispered a quick prayer for Jared to take courage.

His blustering bravado faded. Jared bit his lips, forcing the undeniable fact that he possessed great power to the forefront.

"My Lord," he started again, "we are worried. Ulthea reminded us we are not acting according to the tenets. The will of Obenin has been cast aside for other motives."

Jared took a deep breath and expelled it, declaring, "And... and we don't want to do anything else or cause any more destruction until we know our purpose still follows Obenin's Tenets."

"Oh," said Seth calmly, "you are trying to tell me how to run my kingdom? Or do you doubt my divine right to rule?"

"Well... sire... no... the tenets... that's all... we are concerned about the tenets," he stammered.

"Concerned. Does your concern merit treason?"

Jared did not answer.

"Well, remember you serve me and what I say is law. What I say is Obenin's will. I say what the tenets mean. Everything falls or rises by my word, even your very lives." Seth turned to one of his men.

"Take this one out and lash him before the camp. That way all shall know that even these who control the heavens are under my rule."

The soldier hesitated. "Move now or you will join them.

"Jared struggled. The guards carried him out effortlessly. The others followed close behind, restrained by more guards.

Jared sobbed before the first lash hit him.

Ulthea's scream anticipated the lash. Each time the man drew his arm back, she let out a short gasping yelp. Each time the lash hit Jared's back, she screamed.

Parmos felt Jared trying to stir the weather. He sensed Jared's desire to make the lashing stop even if it meant destroying them all. The excruciating pain and Ulthea's screams broke his concentration. Jared prayed aloud for Obenin's immediate wrath on the soldier who beat his back open, and on Seth and Cuere.

The crowd seemed truly amazed to see blood. The fact that no wrath of god fell despite the prayer only served to give credit to Seth. Seth got his point across. Heaven was truly on his side.

Seth raised his hand to stop the punishment. The entire camp kneeled when he did so.

As Seth walked away, he jested, "Guess there will be no storms tonight."

Jared lay on his stomach. Seth's personal physician dressed his wounds for the second time. Jared winced each time the physician dabbed the cloth on his wounds.

"It burns like fire," grimaced Jared.

Ulthea squeezed his hands tightly, saying over and over again, "It will be fine."

On the far side of the tent, Parmos and Ictheos looked on, simmering with hate.

Finally, after the doctor bandaged Jared and departed, Ictheos exploded, "Why did Seth do this! He didn't have to beat Jared. Is this all we have to look forward to?"

"Shush!" Parmos waved his hands quieting him. "Things are bad enough. Do you want them to come and beat you, too?"

"I know, but I feel so helpless. All the power we possess, and we can do nothing to right this? If we do something here and now, we will destroy ourselves, too."

"But we can do something..." Parmos whispered. "We can escape."

"We could destroy everything and ourselves, too," Jared spat.

"Jared, how can you say that," Ulthea rebuked.

"I don't know. I don't think I was serious, but I hurt and I want to hurt those who hurt me."

Parmos advised, "Well save your anger. You are going to need the strength it will generate."

"We don't have much of a choice, do we," stated Ictheos.

"How," asked Jared, winching as he tried to adjust his position, "are we going to pull this off."

"First of all," Parmos stated. "I don't think we should trust anyone. Lord Cuere said he would make us pay. I know he must be planning something. Tonight, I could have sworn I saw him add something to our food. I don't know what it was, but I didn't eat mine. I started to say something, but when I saw none of you had an appetite either, I decided not to take the chance and tip him off. We should be careful of what we eat or drink. I am convinced that if we can get some place and find a haven from King Seth, we will have him at our mercy. He will have to do what is right."

Ictheos scratched his head. "What is right? I'm kind of lost on that right now."

"The tenets are right. They will lead the crown back to faith," reminded Ulthea.

"Yes, the tenets." Itheos rolled his eyes at her.

"Where will we go? How will we live?" quizzed Jared.

"Any place is better than here," Ictheos interceded with a rather early committal.

"We have to find the source of the calling. It is as if something is calling my name. Sometimes I can barely resist it. We have to find it," persisted Parmos.

"What do you think, Jared?" Ulthea asked. "Do you agree with Parmos?"

Instead, Parmos answered, "He shouldn't say too much. After all, it is supposed to be the back up plan."

CHAPTER 28
Power Evolving

Six days passed. Their preparations seemed too easy. The guards and servants were all too eager to bring them things they needed to survive in the wild. Parmos and the others collected all they wanted and more than they could carry, glows, clothing, gold coins, a bow with a quiver full of arrows, all done without question. All the guards and servants wanted in return were blessing. Jared swore each of them to secrecy.

They went along with everything Lord Cuere told them to do without so much as a worried look. They bowed and showed humility that satisfied Seth.

Moving about one day behind the main armed force, they were one day from emerging from the mountains. Parmos scoffed at Ulthea's lack of commitment. Jared seemed eager but unfocused, giving Parmos reason to wonder about his motives. The lethargy of the long trek through the mountains disappeared, and anticipation of a full-scale invasion crackled through the air.

Ictheos said very little. He didn't have to. In comparison to Jared and Ulthea, he moved with zeal and determination. Ictheos made fun of Jared because of his laziness in preparing for their escape. Lately, Ictheos' tone had become sharper.

That night, huddled together in Jared's tent, Parmos whispered, "We have to go now. The calling grows weaker instead of stronger."

Jared objected, "I am not sure now is the time."

Ictheos lashed out. "Listen," Ictheos argued in hushed tones. "What do you hear?"

"Not much," answered Jared.

"That is what I mean. The gambling and drinking is stopping. The soldiers don't fight and argue as much. Their vigilance is returning. We have enough provisions. If you want to stay here, you can. But, I'm leaving with Parmos before we clear these mountains, with or without you. And that includes you." He looked at Ulthea and shook his finger. "Jared," Ictheos continued. He lifted his chin and cut his eyes toward Jared. "Why do you hesitate? Or, did the lashing make you a coward?"

Jared leapt for Ictheos. Parmos grabbed him and wrestled him down.

Ulthea pleaded, "Ictheos, what is wrong with you?"

"At least I got a reaction from him. I was beginning to wonder."

"Don't ever call me a coward again," threatened Jared. "I have reasons for what I do. Reasons I do not care to share with you."

"And I don't care to know them. All I need to know is whether you will stay or go."

Jared gritted his teeth and resisted giving an answer. "Let me go, Parmos."

Parmos released Jared. Jared sat up and looked at Ulthea, whose eyes pleaded with him.

"Going," he replied.

Scattered clouds dappled the night sky. Patchy fog rolled in. The soldier's turned in for the night.

Parmos gave the signal. Ictheos slit the rear canvas of Jared's tent and slipped through. Parmos fed the four bundles in which they carried their provision through the slit. One by one, they slipped through. Parmos took one look back and slipped out.

With Ictheos in the lead, they crept stealthily, feeling their way along the terrain. Parmos and the others scrambled to keep up with Ictheos.

Parmos' heart pumped hard. He prayed that in the darkness, they would not happen into some diligent sentry or sleepless royal guard, or that Lord Cuere or Prince Seth would not get an itch and come to look in on them. The fact that neither of them had ever done that did not comfort him.

Only one thing did, Ictheos' sure-footed movement and keen sense of direction. He sped up, slowed down, came to a stop in mid-stride, then crouched, a predator in his element.

First, they traveled down the same hill they climbed earlier in the day to make their camp. Then they followed a stream, just narrow enough to leap over. Next, they steadily climbed upward.

By this time, some of the clouds and fog drifted away. The thick forest covered their movement and kept them out of the moonlight. They skirted the edge of fire-lit camps. Ictheos pressed them forward all night long. Finally, they broke free of the main camps.

Ictheos warned them they were not in the clear. He pointed out things he barely saw. Ictheos stuck his finger in the dirt. All Parmos saw was dirt. Ictheos saw the hoof prints of oxen and horses, the probable number of men, even how old the tracks were.

Wild animals, even the stray Benomian soldier, all posed a threat. Ictheos seemed pleased with himself, joking about reaching their destination alive. Parmos let him have his moment.

"Wait a minute," pleaded Ulthea, "let me breathe again."

"We can't tarry," Ictheos reminded. "I'm sure Lord Cuere is stomping around as if he is trying to kill a thousand crawling insects. We are not that far away from the encampments. I am sure they know we are gone by now. Word of our escape and orders to find us will spread quickly."

In minutes, Ictheos had them up again, moving quickly along the mountain pass, trying to stay in the most worn trails to conceal their direction.

Ictheos held up his hand to stop them. He hustled them into cover, signaling for them to keep low and keep quiet.

They hid in the brush for a while. Jared lifted his head in doubt. Immediately, Ictheos threw a stick at his head,

making him duck back down. He started to speak. Ictheos scowled and put his finger to his lips, then cupped his ear and pointed up the trail.

In the distance, Parmos heard the first sign that someone was approaching, the sound of laughter. A band of men and pack animals came toward them. The men sang drinking songs to keep their spirits up and to keep from arguing with each other. Parmos watched them closely. He knew better. He hoped, anyway. He wanted to see and hear Keeper Octun walking and singing among them.

Ictheos gave the all clear. Before he started, Jared stopped them.

"Wait," directed Jared. "We don't know how far they are behind us and we can't keep this pace up forever. We are far enough away that we can do something to stop the soldiers without slowing ourselves down. That will give us more time."

They gathered together. To Parmos it seemed a bit strange fouling the weather simply because they chose to.

The spiritual presence of the others differed. They acted chaotically. Their rhythms did not match. Parmos sensed Jared surge-- anger drove him. Parmos felt Ulthea trying to restrain him.

Jared resisted but she kept him in check. Before long, everything behind them was wet, fogged in, and freezing.

For days, the four continued traveling the same mountain pass covering their trail for as long as possible. They did not encounter any more caravans before leaving the pass and venturing through more treacherous mountain terrain. They headed as straight for the snowcapped peak of Mount Kaob as possible. Ictheos' forest-dweller instincts returned to him fully. He decorated his bow and waited for the opportunity to use it. A rabbit scooted through the underbrush.

"Get it," Ulthea shouted, excitedly.

Ictheos did not get a good shot and scoffed at the slowness of his reflexes. Later, they saw a young buck ahead of them, standing still, his nose in the air. It smelled them. As the animal sprang forward, Ictheos' arrow hit his mark. The buck stumbled. Ictheos reloaded and let another fly. The animal fell and tried to get back to its feet.

Parmos bounded over and pounced on him, wrestling the animal to the ground and keeping the small rack away from him. Jared joined him to finish it off.

As they skinned the deer, Jared shook his head in doubt. "Maybe you shouldn't have done that. It might give us away."

Ictheos shrugged. "I was in the moment." After considering Jared's statement, he said, "Well, it is too late for that now. Anyway, we haven't covered our trail since we left the supply line. They will find where we left the path. If we don't get where we are going fast, they will catch up with us anyway."

With his belly full, Parmos' first inclination was to sleep. In the morning, Ictheos would be on them, demanding that they keep their pace.

Ulthea took first watch. She peered sadly into the fires. Her homesick gaze affected Parmos.

"Are you asleep?" she called to them.

Jared and Ictheos grunted at her.

Parmos answered, "What do you need?"

"How far do you think they are behind us?"

"Don't know," answered Parmos.

"What do you think they will do to us if they catch us?"

"I don't want to even think about that," answered Jared, stirring from his nodding at the painful memory of his lashing.

"What do you think Keeper Octun is doing now?"

No one moaned or groaned in return.

"Do you think he is in any danger?"

Parmos sat up.

"I think," Ictheos, replied, "...that Seth will strip him of everything even his position as Keeper."

Ictheos turned his attention to the fire and threw a couple of broken sticks on it.

"He said he wasn't going back there. He ripped up his Keeper mantle," reminded Parmos.

"But where else would he go?" asked Ictheos. He picked up another stick and stirred the fire until it burned brighter.

"I would go home," Ulthea declared, nodding her head to emphasize her statement.

Parmos frowned. His thoughts instantly became troublesome. "Home, where is home?"

"Glynwith," answered Jared, turning to his left side. "You know that."

"No, I don't mean for Keeper Octun. I mean for us." Ictheos and Ulthea looked at him. Jared grunted.

"Where are you going with this?" asked Ictheos.

"I feel," Ulthea said hesitantly, getting comfortable with her words, "that home is Obenin's Temple. At the same time, I feel that home is somewhere else. But at the same time, I don't feel anything about that other place."

"No place is stranger than home, and nothing is more confusing than what you just said," jested Ictheos.

"'Misplaced' is the word you are looking for," Jared rang in. "Doesn't matter, though. This is where I belong. My destiny is here."

Ulthea tried to comfort Parmos. She asked him whether he regretted leaving the Obenite camp after all.

"No, that's not it. I just remembered something," Parmos said.

"What?" asked Ulthea.

"I don't know," he lied, then changed the subject. "Anyway, we still have a problem. We know they are tracking us."

"There is something we can do about that," replied Jared, taking a greater interest in the conversation.

"Like what?" Ulthea yawned; now she was sleepy.

"What can we do other than what we have not already done?" Parmos asked.

"We could make sure they stop following us for good," threatened Jared.

"Are you suggesting that we kill them," Parmos interrogated.

"They showed us no mercy!" Jared argued.

"You are mad because your plan failed, and you were punished for it," retorted Parmos.

"Of course I'm angry. What do you expect me to be? You would feel the same way too, if it they had beaten open your back!"

"We left with a specific purpose in mind, bring the King and Lord Cuere back into the will of Obenin. If we hurt those that we are suppose to be helping then we will be just as bad as Cuere and Seth," Parmos argued.

"You two seem to be getting on one another's nerves a lot lately," Ictheos threw out. "When are you just going to fight and get it over with?"

"Ictheos," chastised Ulthea, she shot him a disapproving glance.

She interceded, "I can see Jared's point. It's hard not to think of revenge when we have been treated the way we have. Hurting those who are innocent, though, will not help. We shouldn't hurt hundreds just to strike back at two."

"I don't think we should seek revenge on Cuere or Seth. Seth is king and has a right to be ruler," insisted Parmos.

"He has a point there," said Ictheos, egging on the argument.

"Why don't you all just go to sleep. I hate that I brought up the subject," spat Ulthea, putting an end to the argument.

The next day, they continued to move with a greater sense of urgency. Ulthea fell asleep without waking anyone to take watch. They lost precious time. For weeks, Mount Kaob loomed in the distance. Though it seemed to move further away instead of closer, they kept moving. Ictheos let them take nothing for granted. He kept them from assuming their occasional fouling the weather stopped anyone. They had no scouts to send back. They had to assume it had no effect. The fact that they saw or heard nothing of soldiers behind them only seemed to make Ictheos move faster.

Mount Kaob, finally, covered their entire forward view twelve weeks after they had escaped. They broke through the forest to see a clear mountain lake. The reflection of the peaks and the sky upon the lake made the world look upside down. Jared wanted to stay. Ictheos did not let them stop until they were on the Mt. Kaob side of the lake and on higher ground.

Ictheos saw the fires first. In turn, he quickly doused theirs. "Look," he whispered as if the soldiers could hear him from the distance.

"The search parties," whispered Parmos.

"I don't want to hear another complaint about how fast we move," quipped Ictheos.

"We have to do something," said Ulthea. "They will catch up to us in a day or so if we don't. We have to slow them down," suggested Ictheos.

"Slow them down," barked Jared. "No, we have to stop them. I am not going back, ever."

"What do you want to do?" Parmos asked, suspiciously.

"Our power increases as we get closer to the mountain. I can feel it," returned Jared, leaving the question open.

"I do not want to hurt them," complained Ulthea.

"What do you think they are going to do with us if we do not go with them? Have you ever thought of that?"

"Ask for a blessing in exchange for some food, clothes, and freedom," joked Ictheos.

"This is nothing to laugh about," scolded Jared.

"It isn't now," Ictheos shot back. "But give it a day or so."

"I am tired of this. I am tired of holding back. We have to send Seth and Cuere a message: *Do not pursue us or else*. If these soldiers are the only way of sending that message then we have to do it," persisted Jared.

"Who made you leader?" confronted Parmos. "It is not enough that Ictheos keeps us running like rabbits, but at least I can understand that. Every time we turn around, you are ordering us around. Ictheos make the fire.

Parmos gather the wood. Ulthea cook the food. I think you believe only your ideas are good ones."

"What has gotten into you, Parmos? Or are you an imposter conjured up by Lord Cuere," interrupted Ictheos.

Jared's face grew stern and he clenched his fist. "Ictheos, I am not in the mood for your jokes. And Parmos, do you think you can do better?"

Ictheos moved out of the way and sat down to watch.

It sounded like a challenge to Parmos. He stood quiet for a moment. He realized that, at this moment, Jared verbally asserted himself as their leader.

Parmos stepped closer, his size advantage over Jared apparent to him for the very first time.

"Wait. Just wait. What are you doing?" pleaded Ulthea.

Ictheos responded, "Looks like a fight to me. It may give our position away, but who cares."

"Listen to me." She shook Jared's shoulder.

"You two need to remember, you are brothers of the spirit. The tenets say to be patient with your brother and to give ear to his complaint."

"They also say a matter that cannot be resolved may be challenged by duel if both parties agree," injected Ictheos.

Ulthea marched over to Ictheos, took off her gloves and slapped his face with them.

Ictheos blinked at her, then laughed out loud. Jared and Parmos could not help themselves and stopped arguing.

They sat in a circle. Ulthea sat between Jared and Parmos; Ictheos separated them on the other. Growing in the storm, minds colliding with harmony, each took turns with the melody, composing a symphony with nature itself. They were learning to control their power without Lord Cuere.

Parmos became aware of his surroundings. He did not know where he was. Disoriented and confused, he looked around. All he saw was Mount Kaob, which did not look so imposing anymore. He looked down on billowy clouds.

"This isn't right," Parmos thought. Then it hit him. In a panic, he looked around for his body. He didn't see it but he sensed it. A thin thread of awareness tethered him to his boulder of a body. He existed in two places at the same time. His body existed, barely aware of anything but his immediate surrounding. He heard. When he opened his eyes, everything directly in front of him focused. Everything to his side view blurred.

Parmos' body felt weak. He tried to stand but failed. In his wind form, power surged through him like a fiery stream of lava. It burned him and he loved it. He swooshed through the clouds. Freedom gripped him. He felt no restraint and it exhilarated him.

Where were the others? Did this happen to them?

He reached out in his mind as Cuere taught them to do. There. He heard Jared. Though he did not actually hear a voice, he knew it was him. The others were there, too. He sensed their form and feelings just as easily as he recognized their faces and voices.

Ictheos delighted in his power. His mirthful spirit carried mischievousness. Nothing bothered him. Nothing worried him. Everything was something for him to meddle with, and he did.

Ulthea confused Parmos. Her dark thoughts did not seem capable of originating from such a usually happy person. Ulthea brooded over the lake. It pleased her. It disturbed her. She wanted to play in it. She wanted to dry it up into crusty earth. She craved water insatiably, yet she loathed the desire within her.

Parmos could not assure himself if whether what he perceived was emotion. A cool sensation ran through him whenever he thought of Ulthea. A pattern of vibrations accompanied the sensation. The sensation warmed or cooled as the patterns changed. From this phenomenon, he got a general impression of what he knew only as emotion. Her thoughts entered into his mind. He found it difficult to separate them from his own. For the most part, they did not conflict with the sensation she projected to him.

Parmos sensed chaos, power and destruction emitting from Jared. Even more, the desire to control radiated so powerfully that Parmos struggled to resist its subduing force.

"Spread out!" Jared ordered.

Parmos repeated his earlier argument, "Who made you leader?" As he rushed through the tree, Parmos realized he had no feeling of touch, no taste, and no depth perception.

There they were, a small band of men looking worriedly upward. Parmos knew that they were only part of several bands sent out to search for them. What would he do to them? He didn't want to harm them. They were pawns, just like the four of them had been. These men fought ignorantly for what they thought best, just as he did, possibly just as he was doing now. He increased the force of the wind within the camp below. He used freezing rain to put out their fire, and hail to pounce on them. He hoped they would get the message. This was not just a freak of nature.

One of the soldiers yelled, his mouth open all the way to his tonsils. Parmos headed straight for him. He brushed the soldier's entire face all at once. He stopped and watched the soldier, who shuddered and looked around, sensing his presence. Instantly, the soldier sprinted off into the woods, stumbling along in the darkness.

Parmos did the same to each soldier he encountered. Some of them swatted at his unseen force. He watched as one soldier swung his sword through him. He swirled around the man and brought the force of the wind against him, knocking him off his feet. He buffeted the soldiers until they all scattered in retreat, leaving their gear behind.

****

Ictheos floated down into a camp of men. He felt like a feather rocking back and forth, twisting and turning on a gentle breeze. He thought of putting out their fire but thought that too common. The others would think of that.

He floated over to the sentry who sat on a rock, fighting off sleep. Ictheos let a thin stream of wind blow on his face. The sentry brushed it off, like shooing away a bug. Ictheos did it again, giving the wind a definite rhythm against the sentry's face.

The sentry leapt off the rock. He drew his sword and spun around wildly.

Ictheos let him wait. Soon the soldier calmed down, attributing the strange occurrence to being half-asleep. The sentry stretched and took a drink of water.

A few pea-sized pellets of hail hit the sentry. He stopped drinking and looked up into the sky. He looked around but saw nothing. He took another drink of water. A few more pellets hit him.

The soldier said something. Ictheos perceived it as calling his comrades out for playing a trick on him. Others in the camp stirred sleepily. The sentry scoffed and shook his fist.

Slowly, Ictheos let the hail start again. He steadily increased its size and rate. He followed the sentry as he ran for his helmet. The other soldiers wakened.

The sentry tried to shield himself. The hail rang off his helmet. Ictheos blew it sideways until it pounded the sentry in the face. He shouted in pain and Ictheos pelted him harder.

The other soldiers watched their comrade's torment in wonder. No one tried to help him. When he approached, they withdrew. Some drew their swords to keep him at bay. He finally ran off into the forest. Ictheos let him go.

"Now it is time for the campfires. In an instant, the fires were out. When he left, not one soldier stood. Ictheos laughed at their agony, but they were all alive.

****

Jared swirled in the storm. Power and vengeance tormented him and his mind. He found pleasure in that torment. He pulled the clouds into him until they were black and dense. Thunder rolled and lightning flashed. Moving further into the forest, he wanted to seek out the search parties one by one. He looked down at the campfires and moved toward them.

He hovered over the camp. The soldiers, about ten of them, knew something unnatural threatened them. Scrambling, they gathered their gear quickly and tried to take cover. There was no place to go. Jared blew down the thin tents. Two soldiers sought shelter from the wind behind a huge boulder. Jared changed the direction of the wind. He pulled down lightening. It struck several trees, splitting them. The crash sent the soldiers diving. When they got up to flee, he knocked them all down again. They were hopeless. He lifted them up about the height of a man and let them fall.

A voice called to him, "Jared, what are you doing?"

He did not answer. He didn't have to.

"Stop, you are killing them!" she shouted.

Reluctantly he moved away.

Together, Jared and Ulthea moved back toward their bodies.

"The mountain," Jared thought.

"Yes, the mountain," echoed Ulthea.

Jared cleared the sky. The moon shined brightly. Ulthea and Jared played together, whooshing up and down the side of the mountain, looking for some sign of the source of their urge. Neither sensed it any longer. Something not present in this wind form guided their physical bodies. Their search came up empty.

At the very moment Jared returned to his body, he became disoriented. He was fully aware of both forms, the power of his wind form and weakness of his human body. Once, back into his body, his other form dissipated. He was not aware of anyone else but himself. Sheer exhaustion overcame him and he fell asleep.

****

At the lake, the snowcap of Mt. Kaob appeared an almost perfect cone, so smooth that one could slide from the pinnacle back down to the base on an even blanket of snow. From where they stood now, the top disappeared into the clouds and the sides weren't smooth at all, but a formidable pile of cliffs, sheer faces, and overhangs. This was a challenge that the wind forms could not overcome. They must haul flesh, bone and blood up the treacherous terrain. Just before sunset, they collapsed from exhaustion.

Parmos looked back over their travels, thinking, "I thought we had traveled farther than that."

He looked ahead to their first obstacle, an overhang that looked ominous in the moonlight. They had no choice but to go around it.

The next day, Jared led them in the opposite direction that Parmos' wanted to go. The overhang proved the least of their worries. After a half days travel, an unsurpassable crevasse dropped off into snowy oblivion. A ledge hugged the mountain, leading farther. Parmos did not see its end. It was too narrow for them to use, anyway. They were forced to double back. Just after dark, they returned to the camp where they spent the previous night. They used it again.

A wet snow fell, making the night colder and more miserable. Parmos took a glows from his pack and wrapped it up. He banged it vigorously until it burned his hands. He placed it on a rock at the base of the overhang. It melted the snow off the rock and they all warmed their hands and faces.

He checked his ration of food. Having no way of judging how much they needed, he hoped it was enough. The thought surfaced.

Without thinking, Parmos spoke aloud, "I told you we should have gone east. When I was in my wind form, I saw a place to climb. I know I did," reminded Parmos.

"How could you really tell if we could pass? The size of things is really hard to judge," Jared debated. "Even if we went the way you said, there is still no way of knowing if your way is passable. I thought the same in my wind form."

At daybreak, they traveled east. They made good progress. Jared didn't even look at Parmos. Parmos wanted to see the look on his face so badly.

The sheer rock face offered no place to climb. The endless trudge along the sheer wall wore on their minds. Trudging through the knee-high snow wore on them physically. Parmos, for the first time, thought they were actually better off with Seth.

Then he saw it, a fissure in the rock that split the mountain. Chunks of the mountain lay strewn about. The crack ran from the base dozens of meters up until the mountain took shape again.

Only wide enough for one of them at a time, Parmos squeezed through the fissure first. After seeing the way was clear and that there was indeed a place for them to climb, he beckoned the others to enter. Apple-sized crumbs of the mountain littered the area.

Parmos was awed at the power of nature to reshape or destroy itself. The sight humbled him. Stepping over jagged rocks, they climbed into the mountain. Farther ahead, the path inclined and they crawled on hands and knees. The farther they went, the darker it became. They chose not to use the glows until the fissure became almost pitch black. Finding a place level enough for them to gather closer, Jared suggested that they spend the night.

Parmos had no way of knowing whether it was night or day. Ictheos had them off again. The climb grew steeply. Jared reached down to help the others. Parmos brought up the rear, pushing them up.

Parmos lost track of how long they climbed. It felt as if he had been climbing since his birth.

They reached another ledge and rested there. Looking around, Parmos saw a little speck of light reflecting off the rock. This spurred them on. They broke into the light shielding their eyes. A light fog covered the area.

The calling urged him stronger than ever. The others felt it, too. They were close to the source of the calling, very close. Surveying the distance, he saw that part of the mountain had collapsed, leaving a wasteland of huge boulders. On the other side, there stood another seemingly unsurpassable rock face. To his left, a denser cloud of fog prevented them from seeing anything beyond.

"Look!" Ictheos drew their attention to something strange. There were tracks in the snow. Faint but they were there. "Two types, the hunter and the hunted."

"There must be another way to this place. But why would an animal venture this far from the tree line and water?" asked Parmos.

Ictheos brightened, "Hopefully, this means something good."

"What if we meet the beast?" Ulthea asked worriedly.

"We have heaven in our hands, surely we can handle some beast," boasted Jared.

They rested in a field of boulders. Ictheos kicked up snow. With each kick he said, "Parmos will die of hunger. Jared will die when his temper freezes. He can't live without it."

"You can die and go to the underworld. I will not die. I cannot die," returned Jared.

His comments drew stares from all of them.

Ulthea asked, "Do you know how that sounded?"

"I am not dying out here, and I am not going to let you die. What else could I have meant?"

Ictheos laughed.

Parmos did not reply. He studied the tracks and surroundings."

"Hey!" shouted Ictheos, pointing in front of them.

A buck limped towards them.

"It's wounded..." Jared remarked. "At least something will be easy for us."

Just as Jared moved to finish killing the wounded animal, a huge bear roared over the hill. Stunned, they all froze in their tracks. The bear lifted its bloody head into the air and stood on its hind feet, towered over the deer, then brought it down. Then, it turned towards them.

Jared, for the first time, gave no orders.

"Run!" shouted Ictheos. "unless you want to test your immortality."

Leaving their gear, they retreated down the pass. The bear, hesitant about leaving its prey, bounded after them.

"Can't we use our power to do something!" yelled Ulthea.

"You can stop and give it a try," returned Ictheos.

On hands and knees, they scrambled back into the fissure. Parmos pushed Ulthea up first, then he pushed Ictheos up, who quickly helped him up. They had Jared by the arms. The bear was coming too fast.

"Get me up, get me up!" cried Jared.

Just as the bear snapped at him, the others pulled him to safety.

On its hind legs, the bear tried to get at them. It gnawed at the ice and snow. Its hungry mouth sprayed foul spit.

In the blink of an eye, they evolved into their wind forms. They rushed through the fissure, bringing a blast of snow behind them.

Sensing the unnatural presence only made the bear angrier. He swatted at them and bit at the air. The wind became so fierce that Parmos grew concerned about their bodies. Whirling around the bear and pummeling it with blasts of air, they forced it to flee down the mountain.

Carrying as much of the deer as they could, they continued on their journey late into day. They reached another craggy obstacle and started to climb. Keeping as close to the rock face as possible, they made poor progress. With short side steps, it took them about an hour for the rock face to give way to a ledge on which they rested.

"We can't go any farther this way," Ictheos stated the obvious. "The only way is up."

They climbed about five minutes then, moved left into the fog bank.

"Do you feel that?" asked Ictheos. "It's getting warmer."

CHAPTER 29
New Oracle

Jared pressed close to the mountainside, careful of each step. The snow gave way to a slippery ice. Suddenly, he lost his footing. Ulthea, who was immediately behind him, reached to catch him and fell, too. Down the path of snow and ice they slid, rolling, unable to catch a grip on anything. He landed hard in an icy rut and continued to slide. Picking up speed, he slammed side to side against uneven lumps of ice.

Though he tried desperately, Jared could not stop himself. He heard Ulthea shouting behind him. He knew the slide would end somehow. Jagged rocks, careening headlong off a cliff, his previous thoughts of immortality may have been premature.

He shot out of the tunnel like an arrow from a crossbow. He spun along the wet slimy surface, ending up sliding on his stomach, facing in the opposite direction of his slide. Slowly, he came to a stop. He felt the weight of another body crash against him. He gasped to regain his breath. Though in pain, Jared didn't think he was hurt badly.

"Ulthea, are you okay?"

She didn't answer, so he asked again.

"Ugh, I think so, but I hurt all over."

"I can't find my pack, do you have yours?"

"Yes, hold on." Anticipating what Jared was going to ask for, she untied and lifted the flap on her pack. She took out the only glows she carried.

She charged it and fashioned a sling to carry it. She held it up to get a good look around.

"What do you think?" Ulthea asked.

"I ... I feel warm air and, look here on the ground, we are sitting in mud."

"Where do you think this is coming from?" asked Ulthea.

"Well, we know it can't be coming from back there." He nodded back from where they had come. "The only thing I can think of is a warm spring." He scratched his head. "Maybe this mountain is volcanic."

"Volcanic!" Ulthea exclaimed as if it would erupt any moment.

"Yes, it must be. How else could this be?" Jared stood up and tested his legs. Other than a few bruises and scrapes, he was fine.

Ulthea gave him the sling. The caverns were more jagged and irregular than those of the Barren Lands. Nothing appeared manmade. It hinted of the same disastrous force that made the fissure through which they crawled days ago.

"I wonder where this leads?" Jared stepped forward. One jagged edge protruded toward the tunnel. A little longer slide and his outcome might have been much different.

Ulthea felt the surface of the rock. "What is this stuff?"

"Probably some kind of moss or something that grows in places like this... dark and wet, I mean."

Jared walked off from her.

"Wait," begged Ulthea, "shouldn't we wait for Ictheos and Parmos?"

"We won't wander off too far. I'm sure we can find a way to signal them."

"But who knows what might be in here?" She pointed. "Wait a minute. Look over there."

"What, what?"

"Light reflecting off the wall."

"It's probably from the glows," Jared assured.

Ulthea breathed a sigh of relief.

Jared swung the glows back and forth.

"No, the reflection doesn't shift when I move the glows."

They followed the light into the open air.

"Obenin's name," Ulthea breathed.

Jared smacked his forehead in disbelief. "How is it that this oasis exists in the middle of desolation, trees, water, birds? This is incredible."

"Looks like they are going to find us," joked Jared when he heard the yells of Parmos and Ictheos echoing through the cave.

When he and Ulthea found them, they were rubbing their sore spots. They retrieved most of their gear from the icy slide and set about making camp. They collected wood and made torches to save the last of the glows.

Sleep lingered in Jared eyes. He welcomed the warmth after trudging through so much snow. He used the heavy clothing as a pillow.

Ulthea gasped. He sat up. She gawked at him wide-eyed and breathless with excitement.

"It's gone!" she exclaimed.

"What's gone?" he asked.

"The calling, it's gone. It drove me for months now it is gone."

They lit the torches. Jared led the search through caverns careful to mark their path.

They came upon a place clearly marked, laid before them like red carpet for honored guests. They followed a line of animals drawn on the wall of the cavern. As they walked, the entire animal kingdom followed: man, then mammals, all sorts of birds, then salamanders and frogs, then fish, all leading the mouth a familiar gaping hole in the wall-- another oracle. Even Parmos saw the drawings represented someone's belief that all life came from the mouth of this New Oracle.

Clicks filled the cavern the moment all of them stepped in front of New Oracle. A narrow strip of light swept down all four of them simultaneously. Jared could not tell where the light came from. A voice spoke to him. The words comforted him, though he felt another presence stirring inside his body. Jared responded with words similar to those Cuere spoke to his artifacts. He did not understand the words he spoke. Yet, he felt they were right.

A second light went over his body. It went over the others too. Only, this time, the light alternated in color. Slowly, clear jagged crystals filled the entire face of New Oracle. As more crystals appeared, its face got brighter and brighter. Jared shielded his eyes.

The portal changed and the night sky appeared in front of them. Stars covered the face, appearing so close Jared believed he could touch them. The fabric of night sky split. What looked like black smoke covered the stars. Ulthea disappeared into a bright spark, and a crackle. Jared watched the others disappear one by one, until he was the only one left.

CHAPTER 30
Octun Meets Kerwal and Tok

The horse lathered as Octun approached the rendezvous point. He pitied the poor creature. The ride reduced the beautiful stallion to a frothy, smelly mess. But, if he must ride a hundred more into the ground to get to Lord Mernus' side, he would. He thought it ironic that the first conflict of his military service was for Lord Mernus' family. Now, here at this new age, this new pilgrimage, he embarked on yet another rescue mission for Lord Mernus. The mission renewed his hope. He hoped others of the council fared so well.

Lord Mernus' staunch support of King Seth had puzzled him. Now he knew the truth. Strangely, Mernus' troubles relieved him. Not as many of the council members truly aligned with King Seth, after all. Charge Horep had brought the word of Seth's treachery concerning Lord Mernus. The Grand Council no longer existed. The jury was still out on whether it was ever to reform.

Horep told him the Hands of Obenin had escaped Seth. The traditional lines of power wavered. New alliances formed. Old houses fractured. All attempts to capture or kill the Hands of Obenin failed because their power grew beyond anything they had seen them do. Even so, Seth still controlled most of the army. His vicious tactics secured obedience. Ruthlessness, torture, murder, more kidnappings, and terrorizing villages that had even a hint a opposition, Seth used them all. Octun cursed the day he granted Saroth's dying wish.

He slowed the horse. The poor creature, it may not survive the night. It grunted with every breath. He approached the hunting lodge. It was larger than he expected. The lodges were usually a hut for spending the night and dressing the kill. This one could house a small family comfortably.

Two men approached him. They grabbed his horse's rein on both sides. He recognized them, and they him. These men grew up in the service of Lord Mernus. Their parents, their grandparents, great-grandparents, all of them served Mernus' forefathers. To a great extent, though, the relationship remained one of allegiance rather than serfdom.

Kerwal stood a head over Octun, his chosen instrument for most occasions, the hammer. He swung it like a mace or jabbed it like a short spear. Every once in a while, Kerwal flung it freely through the air. He followed it with his massive body charging like a rogue elephant through a crowded market.

Tok specialized in light and lethal special weapons of every sort: knives, daggers, darts, razor-tipped chains, light swords, star-shaped metal objects that he threw, and armor- piercing devices. He sometimes used a funny looking awl by which an assassin could get through chain mail. The man loved daggers. He possessed enough daggers to arm a small army.

Octun greeted them and dismounted. His next order caught them off guard. "There appears to be no stable. Take the horse into the lodge. Dry him off. Keep him warm."

Octun entered the lodge flanked by Kerwal, Tok and his horse. Lord Mernus turned to greet him. His mouth dropped at the sight.

"Iberius, what is this? Bringing this stinking horse into the lodge?"

"If I don't, it will suffer and die."

Octun sipped hot tea. Lord Mernus spat fire against Seth. Obenin stood on the verge of civil war. Never in a millennium would he have thought it possible. Mernus laid all the fault at Seth's feet.

"Once my family is free, Seth will pay dearly."

Brock Stannick had kept Lord Mernus' family on the move. Twenty men guarded them. With word of Mernus' escape, Stannick moved them to places easier to defend. With the gloom of civil war hovering over the kingdom, Stannick had too much to do, and his vigilance in this particular task faltered.

They needed to act swiftly before Seth returned to Obenin. Now that the Hands of Obenin were no longer under his control, he needed to keep Mernus from causing more trouble.

Mernus told Octun of an inside man and how he feared Octun would not receive word. Mernus seemed truly amazed how Octun just disappeared in such a manner.

"It was as if you died, and the army buried you in a foreign country," quipped Mernus.

The spy got word to Mernus of the location of the next hiding place and the maximum time they were going to be there.

"We must strike quickly. Hit hard. Grab my family and escape," directed Mernus.

Mernus' rescue force crept through the wood until it reached Bedowyn Manor. Leaving three men near the front entrance, the remainder made their way to the northwest corner. There, Mernus' inside man placed a sympathizer as guard.

Circling around, they spied the guard. Tok made a call. It sounded so much like an owl, Octun wondered how the guard could tell the difference. He called again. The guard returned it.

Scampering out of the wood, Octun helped them over the wall. They huddled in the garden behind tall shrubs until everyone reported to Octun.

Without a sound, they moved toward the manor. Octun halted everyone when he spied four guards looking vigilant.

The guard who let them over the wall gave another call. The men Octun left near the front gate started a diversion. Two of the guards rushed toward the ruckus, leaving two on either side of the entrance. Tok removed a blowgun from his quiver. He took a dart out of a small wooden box. With a quick puff, he hit one of the guards in the neck with the dart.

The guard winced and went to his knee. His comrade rushed over to aid him. The man looked at him and pulled the dart from his neck. Too late. Tok hit him also.

Kerwal dragged the bodies into the kitchen. He stuffed them in the huge stone oven and shut the door. From the kitchen, they moved into the servants' quarters. The rooms gave them access to secret passages leading to key places within the manor. Through these passages, servants kept out of sight as they provided for their master. Sometimes the King spied on his quests from these spaces.

Mernus led them through the passages as if he had personally traveled them many times.

When asked, he simply whispered, "What better way to know your enemy than through his mistresses."

It was time for them to separate. Mernus went alone to rescue his family from the cellar.

Octun, Kerwal, and Tok moved through the manor with impunity. The guards were scattered throughout the manor, placed as layered protection against any rescue attempt. Six soldiers came toward them down the corridor between the library and the main reception hall. Kerwal charged, his hammer ready to crush his enemy. He raised his hammer and swung it around his head. He set his target on one of the guards, who faded back. The hammer hit the door of the reception hall. It burst open. The guards arrayed themselves, barring Kerwal's advance. Octun drew Saroth's gift and slashed through the air.

Tok caught a glimpse of it.

"Someone loves you," he remarked. "An Obenite wielding a sword from an Aspharian master-- I cannot even steal one of those."

This sword was narrower than his battle sword, perfect for an assault like this one.

In response to Octun's sword, Tok pulled out two narrow thin, pig skewer-like blades. "This is as close as I can get to that sword."

Tok charged into the fight, careful to keep well out of Kerwal's way.

A guard attempted a crossing maneuver. Kerwal dropped the head of the hammer and blocked him. Then in an upward motion, he caught the soldier in the chin with the butt. He followed with a foot to the man's midsection. Kerwal's foe reeled back against the wall. He swung the hammer at the guard's head. His foe ducked as the hammer knocked out a chunk of plaster so large it exposed a beam. Kerwal recovered from the failed attempt. He regained his balance. The guard brought his sword down with both hands. Again, Kerwal blocked with the hammer's head. The metal clanked against the rock, sending sparks flying. The sword bounced to the left. Kerwal saw a clear shot to crush his foe's chest and delivered a fatal blow.

Tok struck with lethal quickness, lunging out and recoiling after he buried the skewers in his victims. His skills amazed Octun. He was art in motion. He locked one soldier's sword after the other with the skewers. Before they knew it, he disarmed them and the point of the skewers found their mark. Tok spun, kicked and flew through the air, off tables, off the chairs and off the wall. He downed two men while Kerwal smashed everything in sight. The skewers slashed through the air like flashes of light.

Assassin. Octun wondered why Mernus needed such a man, then thought better of it.

Kerwal's roars motivated Octun. Octun wielded his sword against his opponents' broad swords. He moved quickly, keeping on the offensive. He faced two men. They fought hard and with skill. One tried to flank him. He did not let it happen. Each time the soldiers attempted to maneuver, he countered and kept himself in front of them both. He fended them off, forcing them back with quick blocks and counters. He fought back and forth between the two until frustration drew their mistakes.

The more Octun fought the more his anger rose. He molded it and made it a reflection of what he felt in his soul-- gloom, void of spiritual guidance, and filled with nothing but vengeance. Blood, he needed blood to atone for the sin he brought upon his kingdom.

"If my own blood must run, so be it," he yelled.

Octun blocked a joint attack with his sword and kicked a guard in the chest. The guard fell backwards. He slashed the other across the face and dealt him a lethal wound.

The plan worked: between the diversion in the wood and their breach, chaos prevailed. More men rushed toward them. Mernus could make his way to his family.

"There are too many of them," Octun yelled, pretending they attempted to escape. In truth, he wanted to draw the guards away from the house, away from Mernus.

Fighting their way back out of the reception hall, Octun, Tok, and Kerwal retreated down the corridor toward the library, soldiers in hot pursuit.

They smashed through doors that looked like giant shutters into a courtyard bordered by the high manor wall.

The three turned their backs against the wall.

"Ah," grunted Kerwal, "room to work."

Soldiers poured out the door. Kerwal charged into the crowd. Open space gave him room to whirl his hammer and increase the force of its blows. Close indoor fighting made him think too much. The open space freed his mind to rage. It wasn't so much about precision, rather covering as great a space as possible and clearing out anyone in it.

Octun looked at him. Kerwal fought as if it were his time to die, a disgraced hero trying to regain his honor in one last battle in which he wished to perish.

The guards were all traitors as far as Octun was concerned,

shiftless men paid by Stannick and kept in check by a

ridiculous code of thieves and cutthroats. Octun let out a

mighty battle cry and smashed his way into the midst of the

fight, making sure he kept well out of Kerwal's way.

****

Lord Mernus put his key into the lock. He knew two men guarded the other side of the door. Fortunately, his inside man told him their names and nicknames. The captain of the guard had locked them in with his family. The captain thought he had the only key.

The lock clanked. Mernus opened the door and shouted down to them. "Horse, Chungie, we're under attack. Report to the east gate." He heard them bound up the steps.

Near the top, he met the first man with a boot to the face. The guard fell back into his comrade. Both tumbled down the steps, recovering on the first landing. The guard tried to block Mernus' assault but was out of position and off balance. Mernus parried once or twice, then plunged his sword into the soldier's gut. The second guard was trapped and helpless.

"You would keep my family hostage for a price of a few fish in the market." Mernus exacted his revenge, delivering a fatal gouge with his sword. He stepped on them as he continued on his way.

Mernus found his wife and grandchildren locked in two separate rooms. Though relatively comfortable, they were poorly kept and living well beneath the manner to which they were accustomed. His wife's dress was soiled and frayed. The children looked thin and like they had not washed in days. This gave Mernus little comfort. Seth still abducted them. He imprisoned them. That alone deserved death.

His wife fell into his arms and kissed him. His grandchildren wrapped themselves around his legs so tightly he could not walk.

"Where is our son?" his wife asked.

"He was injured during a clash with Stannick. We tried to capture him but he escaped," replied Mernus.

"He is responsible for this. Find him, my love, and make him pay."

"He will get his just due, sooner or later. Whether by me or someone else, he will get his."

Mernus led his family back up the stairs. Lady Mernus spat on the guards as she walked over them. She herded the children close behind her husband. Mernus peeked out the door to make sure the coast was clear. They found their way back to the kitchen. He motioned to his wife to keep the children quiet while he checked the way out. He saw no one and stepped backward. He felt a knifepoint in his back.

His attacker's thick Heno accent carried the smell of too much liquor. "I don't know who you are, but tonight is your last."

He felt a little jab and another. He turned. The guard fell forward. He stepped out of the way. Lady Mernus held a large kitchen knife.

"You talk too much!" she snapped.

Crash! The Mernus grandchildren ran screaming from the house. Lord Mernus let them pass and stepped forward to protect them.

"Get them over the wall," he yelled. "I have men waiting."

Octun, Kerwal and Tok came out of the house into the shadowy night.

"The manor is secure," Octun reported.

"This was supposed to be a hit, rescue, and run mission," replied Mernus, stunned.

With a quick push of the hammer's head with his shoulder, Kerwal let the handle fall into his left hand with a smack. He chuckled, "I guess we just hit too hard."

CHAPTER 31
Power Realized, Jared's Ultimatum

Jared watched Ulthea soak up to her neck in one of the hot springs. Steam hung motionless is the morning air. A month after they dragged themselves from New Oracle, she complained that her body still ached. The warm water from the pools helped her. Ulthea spent more time in the springs than any of them. It eased her mind. He figured, at the least, they were gone only a moment. At the most, he figured, a couple of days. It felt like an eternity.

Jared didn't mind in the least that she spent so much time in the springs. The more she bathed, the more he watched. At first, Jared hid from her. Now, he only partially shielded himself from her view. All she had to do was turn around. He didn't care whether she saw him or not.

Stress and conflict infused his relationships with the group. Every exhale provoked a disagreement. Every inhalation fostered resentment. They spent more time apart than ever before, especially since the experience in New Oracle. Ulthea liked to sit in the springs and mentally isolate herself from everything. Ictheos explored every little nook and cranny of the cave. Parmos meditated too much.

Jared shifted his position from stooping to sitting on a small boulder. Sooner or later, she had to get out of the water. He had nothing else better to do but watch and think about their power, and about narrow-minded Parmos.

Ulthea acted as a buffer between them. She sided with him in nearly all the arguments, leaving Parmos sullen and brooding.

This gave Jared the advantage. Ictheos, with his noncommittal sarcasm, usually followed him after Ulthea made her decision. Parmos submitted begrudgingly and only after Ulthea and Ictheos took sides. Parmos held his ground until then and always made snide remarks afterward. Parmos delayed all Jared's plans.

Parmos did things for Ulthea, too, things that Jared felt she should do herself. Jared liked her, but why should he cater to her. Though she flirted to make Jared jealous, she showed no romantic interest in Parmos. She was either unaware of Parmos' feelings toward her or she ignored them intentionally. Either way pleased Jared.

Parmos' commitment to turning Seth back to the faith deeply disturbed Jared. That one thing bothered him most. On this one matter, Ulthea agreed consistently with Parmos. Sooner or later, Jared knew that he had to find a way to change her mind. He had to make her see that they were the ones who should be worshipped.

****

Ulthea groaned; her body weighed ten times more than normal, or so it felt to her. She didn't want to move a hair but she was getting hungry.

The boys got on her nerves, even Jared. Yet, she liked him. He was arrogant, self-centered, and a bit cold at times, but she liked him. She couldn't help it.

Parmos treated her better, but she didn't like him that way.

Then there was Ictheos. He went off by himself. No one could ever find him. He would just show up seemingly out of nowhere.

"You're sitting there minding your own business and suddenly there is a hand on your shoulder. He draws pleasure from harassing everyone," thought Ulthea.

Ulthea reached for her clothes. Jared was getting bolder, but she still allowed him only the usual glimpse. Sooner or later, something was going to happen. She leaned forward to expose her bare back.

Crack! Something splintered on the rocks very close to her, an arrow. She ducked beneath the surface.

****

Jared turned as another bowman released an arrow. The arrow never met its mark. The air became so dense in front of the bowman that the arrow stopped in mid-air. Jared increased the density of air around his attacker. He entombed the soldier, crushing him from all sides. He squeezed and squeezed. He laughed at his attacker's excruciating pain.

Four other soldiers charged them. The soldiers yelled loudly and bravely.

"Ulthea!" Jared shouted.

A waterspout rose from where Ulthea dipped under. Ulthea rose from the midst of the waterspout. The water covered her like an evening gown. With the wave of her hand, more water slammed into the soldiers with such force that it knocked them off their feet and rolled them backwards. None of them got up. Ulthea returned to the ground and quickly gathered her clothing.

From somewhere across the crater, thunder clapped and men screamed dreadfully. One of the others was under attack. From the sound, Jared knew the only danger was to the attackers.

Jared held his archer firmly. He toyed with two others who got up after Ulthea struck them. He lifted them high into the air and spun them around. He dropped them one by one.

"You think you can kill us? We who control the heavens, no one can stop us," he boasted.

He lifted them up again and flung them far away. Jared didn't care where they landed as long as they were far enough away that he would not smell their rotting stench.

The archer, he still held captive. Jared drew him closer. "So the King sent you to kill us. Look at me. We are no longer children. I am a man now. Look at her!"

The soldier dared not look at Ulthea. This pleased Jared.

"She is a woman. Tell Seth that he is no longer king. We are the kings, now. And tell him that praying, if he has learned to pray, is useless unless he prays to us. If he doesn't honor us, the usual storms that wash away crops and the freezing weather in the middle of summer will be nothing in comparison to what we will do. He must bring us gifts and build three temples in the very place I put you down. If he does not, everyone will suffer for his lack of faith in us and the Obenite kingdom will end tragically."

Jared waved his hand and shifted to his wind-form. The archer found himself high over a village near the foot of the mountains. Passersby were astounded at the sight of a man dropping from the sky. They expected the impact against the ground to dash him to bits. Just before he was to crash, the archer stopped falling and landed as softly as a feather.

"You told them what? What do you mean, giving him an ultimatum like that? We all agreed to keep the calamities minor and give King Seth the ultimatum to make him turn his will toward Obenin," Parmos argued, his face red with anger.

"We decided that because we were ignorant and afraid of things we couldn't see," disputed Jared.

"What are you talking about?"

"Look at us. Aren't we like gods? Everyone and everything is under our mercy. No one can stop us. We can do what we want and no one will dare object," declared Jared.

Parmos looked at Ulthea and Ictheos. They showed no alarm at Jared's claims.

"What is wrong with you all? What have you been scheming? We still bleed and we still have the needs of men. There has been no change to us."

"How do you know? Those are only physical things. Look at the power we possess. In comparison to ordinary men, we are gods. New Oracle has transformed us. I don't think we need our flesh and blood when we reach out in our wind forms." Jared pointed toward the oracle's location.

Parmos paused, searching for a reply.

"New Oracle may have transformed Father Obenin into a god. You will only stir his vengeance," offered Parmos.

Jared did not reply. He could not deny the possibility. But the matter was far from over.

CHAPTER 32
Octun Disappoints Mernus

Lord Mernus clenched his fists. Muscles in his face flexed. Anger and disappointment drew his lips into a tight ball that made him look as if he carried a pit between his teeth and lips.

"Why do you resist? The kingdom needs you to resume the priesthood and take your place as Keeper of the Primary Temple?" Mernus demanded of Octun.

The position meant something, now. Perhaps more than it had since the priesthood's inception. For those who fought against Seth, Octun would serve as the inspiration. He was the first to outright defy Seth and Lord Cuere. Though they hunted him, he still survived, showing up here and there like a spirit and disappearing again, leaving behind a sense of blessing to the people.

Mernus and the others needed that. Glynwith was not fully committed to the rebellion. They supplied arms, a few men, and other types of support, but their hearts were not with Mernus' alliance. The rebellious forces perceived that Octun supported Mernus. Still, he needed more visibility. Mernus needed Octun to set the hearts of Glynwith afire, to pick up arms and fight alongside him.

Seth's march back into Obenin proved he still wielded great power. Even after all his treachery, the number of Obenites who sided with Seth shocked Mernus.

Seth treated his opponents with inhuman viciousness. Any village within his reach that appeared to support Mernus, he attacked and burned. Anyone who did not manage to flee the onslaught suffered the same fate. He spared no man, woman, or child.

Seth held from Heno to Bedowyn and all the Middle Kingdom except Glynwith. Mernus held the Southern Kingdom. Southern Gath switched hands more times than a coin in the marketplace.

Mernus dismissed Octun's reasoning before he heard it. Octun spoke with distant determination. "And commit the same atrocities in the name of freedom from Seth's tyranny? Between the two forces, there will be no one left. And what if you win? Will there be another king? Will it be you? Will I be asked to crown someone else who destroys the kingdom?

"My service to the people as Keeper was a dismal failure to the kingdom and to myself. Ultimately, as Keeper, I am bound to serve another man rather than. . ." He paused, not bringing himself to say the words. He continued, ". . . a god. I will not reclaim the High Priesthood. That is over and done with."

Octun turned and looked out across the lake. The wind carried a sense of woe.

The changed weather patterns brought chaos. Animals behaved strangely. Sometimes certain birds migrated out of season. Bears went in their caves to hibernate and came out again in a few days, confused and dangerous. When the ground dried and cracked, the Hands of Obenin made it rain so hard the ground could not absorb the water fast enough. Flash floods washed fertile topsoil away. Winter became a slushy mess; then, the Hand of Obenin would freeze it, making sheets of ice stretching hundreds of kilometers. Thousands of acres of forest were stripped of its branches.

Not only did Obenin suffer, other kingdoms did as well. The one good fortune about the weather, no one could attack them in the midst of their civil war. Bardia, Carden, Tenzia, the entire Benomian Alliance, suffered the same fate. Even to the far south, across the sea, Aspharia encountered weather changes.

The Hands of Obenin made Mernus wonder why any of them fought. Instead of hands of help, they turned into fists of malice, sky demons they had no way of exorcising. Yet, the Obenites fought.

Lightning flashed here and there in the distance -- long continuous bolts, which made the sky appear to walk on legs of lightning. Thunder rolled in from across the lake. The gentle rumble comforted him. Trees swayed gently in the wind. This storm seemed natural, nothing conjured.

"I deserve more than silence," Mernus snapped. He still stood behind Octun, waiting for something.

Mernus cursed and swore at Octun, who did not move an inch figuratively or physically until he was ready.

Octun turned. He wore the same, nothing more to give, expression.

Mernus broke in.

"If I give you a regiment to command will you take it?" Octun chuckled.

"You laugh at my offer?" Mernus leaned forward as if he were ready to attack.

"Not like you think. It is the irony of the matter. I thought of King Saroth, one of the last conversations we had. I desired a regular command, to lead troops against the Benomian Alliance. He denied it and kept me as Keeper. Now you offer a command to me and I cannot take it."

"Will not, you mean!" Mernus stormed away. He slammed the door leaving Octun alone on the balcony. Mernus wanted to say more but held his tongue. He did not know what part Octun would play in this war. It puzzled him. He somewhat understood Octun's reasons, including the deathbed oath he made Saroth. Deep down, a hunch nagged at him not to push any further. Octun's role was written but not revealed.

Somewhere in this historic moment, the name of Iberius Octun would find its way alongside his. Mernus knew that, above all, Octun could not allow himself only to watch and do nothing while his nation perished.

Mernus took a deep breath, held it, and focused on the next series of battles.

CHAPTER 33
Power Abused, Sky Demons At Play

"Jared is right. Why should we worship anyone?" The field of corpses at the foot of the Abrigian Mountains came back to her. The count of dead enemy soldiers had brought smiles and satisfaction to the Obenite commanders. She had not drawn a sword but she had killed them nonetheless. Obenin's tenants, Levid's teaching, even Keeper Octun's position as high priest, killing was all part worship, all a part of religion, something necessary to protect the god you believe in and the way of life you want. *Then, if we are to be worshipped, killing is part of that.*

She played in her wind form. The water fascinated her. The water tormented her. In her wind form, water was the first thing she sought. Energy surged through her and ebbed slightly, then surged again. The overall effect built up in her. She skimmed over the surface of the water in the lagoon, attempting to form waves. Large waves formed and moved away from her. Slowly, the waves built up until they were as high as a man. She moved out to the sea, gliding across the waves. She hated the sea. It gave her energy but it did not obey her. It was too large. A few times, she tried to go beneath the surface, to immerse in it and gratify her insatiable appetite. When she hit the surface, her form spread out over it. She had no sense of touch. Yet, she experienced a sensation that reminded her of pain and mental horror.

She tried repeatedly but nothing happened. She swirled over the spot for hours, just looking at it. A fishing boat came upon her. They pointed and shouted at the water where she moved. They sailed up to the spot, disturbing the very site that denied her entrance into pleasure.

"How could they, don't they know how beautiful it is. They have no right."

Ulthea buffeted the boat in warning. The sudden shock caused the men to grab the sides of the boat. She buffeted it again, causing the boat to pitch wildly. The fishermen's fear gratified her. She whipped winds around the boat, rocking it violently as it spun around. Water splashed over the deck. The four helpless fishermen held on for dear life. She hit them repeatedly with wind shears from every direction. One of the men tumbled overboard. The small mast came crashing down.

Pulling herself away from the boat, she hovered far above it. The last man standing on the boat looked around. He said a quick prayer and looked toward the sky. Thinking the strange occurrence over, he helped his friends. Another fisherman swam back to the boat and used some of the collapsed rigging to get back on board.

Ulthea flew out to sea until she reached the limits of her power. No matter how hard they tried, the limit always jerked them back, painfully. She turned, gathering the wind and rain behind her, making it more and more dense.

Jared was right. She was wrong. Parmos was wrong. These fishermen were fish themselves in comparison to them. The man named Obenin lay dead in a stone coffin for centuries. They were here, now, and powerful. "If a dead man can have an entire kingdom, why can't we have the world?" she thought.

Faster and faster, until she could build no more speed, she crashed into the boat with indifference. They never knew what hit them. The boat splintered, sending the men flying into the sea. She watched the two surviving fishermen struggle to reach the debris. One tried to help his friend, but he barely had the energy to save himself. He let go of his friend, who sank into the murky depths.

Ulthea turned and blew the lone survivor far out to sea.

****

Ictheos allowed the farmer to think himself blessed. Ictheos found pleasure in the farmer's adoration of his wind form. For this adoration, Ictheos awarded the farmer with favor. No other farmer in the valley had a bountiful harvest. Their plants perished under Ictheos' will. Other farmers envied Ictheos' farmer, but they did not dare harm him or his property. Whatever god he served would surely take vengeance on them if they did. They were right. No one else had the right to destroy what Ictheos made. Ictheos provided the farmer with just enough rain and just enough sunshine for an abundant harvest of corn.

Ictheos watched as the farmer went merrily about his daily business. He had no friends, no wife, no children, and apparently no concerned family. No one visited him. The farmer's only companion was one red dog with a mutilated ear and a bad disposition. The dog kept onlookers at the edge of the property. They resorted to pointing at the thriving greenery in the farmer's fields. Eventually, Ictheos stirred up some sort of weather that drove them away, adding to the image that the gods protected this man.

With the other farmers' crops mostly ruined, this farmer could name his price. Ictheos figured this was one reason the man was so merry.

As the farmer walked to the house, he stopped suddenly and snapped his finger. He had left his hat on the side of the trough. Ictheos stirred a stiff breeze and blew the hat toward the farmer. The farmer picked up the hat and dusted it off. After going down on both knees, he mumbled what Ictheos took as a prayer, then got up and went inside.

Ictheos went in through the open window. Forcing his way through small openings like the crack under the door disconcerted him. The act always blocked his sense of location and time for a while and truly terrified him. The other three found it just as frightening.

The farmer lit two lanterns. Ictheos looked around the room. This was his first time inside the farmer's house. Junk littered the house. It wasn't filthy, though. The farmer used it as a living space, kitchen, bedroom, and as a workshop for minor repairs.

The farmer looked around. Something unnatural was about. Ictheos knew the farmer had grown used to his presence. After all, he played the part of the good spirit sent to watch over this lonely old man.

The farmer's dog yapped and growled. The hair stood up on his back. He snapped and tore at the air. The farmer swatted him on the nose with his hat. The dog trotted to the corner and looked nervously around the room.

Ictheos floated over to one of two lanterns. He doused it by putting a fast stream of air down the glass. The farmer went over and relit it. Ictheos spread out across the shack. The dog scampered to the door, whimpering and scratching for the farmer to let him out. Ictheos doused both lanterns simultaneously.

At dusk the next day, Ictheos visited his farmer. He found him in the barn piling corn in his wagon. Ictheos figured that he must get the eating kind of corn to market before it hardened. He stood to sell out before he even got to market. It would take several trips in his wagon to deliver all of it. Then the farmer would start bringing in the kind of corn planted for livestock feed.

Ictheos swept down. He knocked a few shingles off the farmer's shack. Then he left.

His next visit came mid-morning. The farmer clenched a nail in his teeth as he hammered away. Ictheos caused a light rain to fall. The farmer looked up and shook his head, then continued to work. The rain stiffened. Eventually, the farmer stopped working and scooted down the roof to the ladder.

Swoosh. Ictheos swept the ladder away just before the farmer stepped on the first rung. The farmer missed his step and fell into the mud.

He lay on his back for a moment. He wiggled his feet, then his fingers. He sat up and twisted his back. Nothing was broken. The farmer looked up at the sky worriedly and shook his head.

Ictheos chased the dog past the farmer. Suddenly, the dog stopped and ran around as if chasing its tail. When it found nothing, it sprinted off, snapping at the air and snarling like a wild animal. Befuddled, the farmer stood with his mouth gaping open. Finally, with a whimper, the dog high-tailed to the edge of the corn, where it turned back to the farmer and yapped.

Ictheos continued harassing the dog. It barked louder, dancing toward the corn then toward the farmer, beckoning the farmer to follow. For a moment, Ictheos thought the farmer was about to follow.

The farmer's eyes went from the barn to the dog. He tried to call the dog back. It would not leave the edge of the corn.

Concerned, the farmer walked down the hill to see about him. He petted the dog on the head sadly. It lay down at his feet whimpering. The farmer picked him up, but when he started back up the hill, the dog wriggled out of his arms. It bit the leg of his britches and tried to pull the farmer into the corn.

The farmer kicked him off.

The dog barked twice. The farmer threw up his hands in exasperation. At that, the dog fled into the cornstalks.

Two days later, Ictheos visited the farmer at night. The farmer slept in his bed. Ictheos blew all the shingles off the house and made a downpour that left the house and everything inside waterlogged.

He sensed dread and vexation from the farmer. In the darkness, the farmer found his way to the barn. Ictheos watched as he lit the lantern. He moped about, carrying stones from a pile near the back of the barn and stacked them near the barn doors. Once finished, he sat and whittled little figurines. He placed the figurines by the stones and wedged a pick ax into the middle of the stones. He took some twine and dangled the figurines from the blades of the pick ax. Finally, he put several armloads of the corn onto the stones. Kneeling, the farmer kissed the idols and prayed fervently.

Two more days passed before Ictheos visited him again. The farmer had fixed his roof. The farmer surveyed the roof from the ladder. Ictheos could not tell if he was looking for something or inspecting the roof. Ictheos saw the farmer's barn door open and went inside. The wagon was full and ready for the market. The horses were rigged and in the barn, as well.

Ictheos hovered over the barn, the house and the fields. The farmer looked at the sky. Before the farmer made it to the barn, Ictheos amassed mountains of dark clouds over the area. Sheets of lightning flashed from the sky. The barn erupted into flaming splinters. The farmer fell backwards to the ground. The first of his harvest burned. Lightning flashed. The farmer rolled over and covered his head. Ictheos struck the house repeatedly while the farmer cringed in fear.

The horses screamed in pain, caught in the fire and destruction. The farmer rolled under the edge of the watering trough for protection while Ictheos laid the cornfields to waste. Ictheos shook the earth as he electrocuted the farmer's livestock with explosive attacks of lightning. The farmer covered his ears. As a finishing touch, Ictheos washed away the topsoil with torrential rain. Once satisfied, he swept the weather away, leaving a clear blue sky.

Ictheos watched the muddy farmer finally come to understand that he suffered a devastating lost: no harvest, no livestock, no barn, no way to replant, all gone. Laughing sarcastically, Ictheos satisfied himself with the tears from the hollow shell of a man he left. As he departed, he saw the head of the red dog battling the current of the swollen stream. The dog reached the shore, made his way over to the farmer, and lay down beside him.

CHAPTER 34
Still A Hero If Not A Priest

Burning green wood popped embers onto the hearth of Octun's uncle's cottage. His uncle, Ryhad, one of his father's two surviving brothers, had practically forgotten about the cottage. Ryhad's age and physical condition made traveling hard. His children were not interested in the isolation it offered, especially in these bizarre times. Obenites felt comfort in groups of people. The rumor of the poor farmer along the Great River spread like wildfire. Some thought both the story and the farmer crazy, but Ryhad knew the magistrate who investigated the matter. The magistrate's report stated that the entire incident was isolated to one farm. The magistrate wrote of personally witnessing a lightening bolt turning the farmer's red dog into a smoking carcass.

Octun appreciated Ryhad making the exception and coaxing his creaky body into a wagon to see him. Uncle Ryhad brought one of his ten grandsons, Nineo. Though Octun hid his movements from friend and enemy alike, recently he felt free to move around. King Seth had much more serious matters to worry about.

"I escaped Seth over sixteen month ago. No one inquires of me anymore?" Octun shoved the iron rod that served as a poker into the fire sending sparks around the black pot and up the chimney.

Ryhad scratched the one black patch in his silvery beard. "No strangers have been askin' about you in the village and nobody followed us. I think the King is more worried about Mernus and those demons in the mountains than you. Everyone is scared. No one knows what to believe in or who to worship. Some believe the world is comin' to an end."

"What do you think?" Octun looked at his Uncle and then at his cousin's soft features.

Ryhad leaned back thoughtfully. Nineo looked scared.

"They want somethin'. It is a guessin' game as to what. I believe the king knows. I believe that he knew soon after they escaped." Ryhad paused. He took out a pipe and a pouch of tobacco. He shook the pipe at Octun. "I knew King Seth would mess things up. He was too spoiled, a sheltered brat."

He finalized the subject by tapping the pipe firmly on the table to clear it out. Ash fell out on the table. Ryhad swept it away with the back of his hand.

The years had mellowed his uncle. Even at Octun's induction as Keeper of the Primary Temple, the man's mouth knew no tact. Saroth chastened Ryhad by making him leave.

"You didn't answer me," insisted Octun.

"I don't really know what to think. All I can go on is what you tell me and how I see those actin' around me."

"How do they react?"

"It's enough to make you want to piss on them all."

Ryhad looked at his grandson. "If you say a word to your grandma, I'll tan your hide into next week."

This Ryhad he remembered. As a child, he had both feared and loved his uncle. Ryhad had made him laugh despite his mother's disapproving glares.

After a long draw on his pipe that made Octun cough in sympathy for his uncle's lungs, Ryhad exhaled the smoke in short puffs that lingered about his face.

"Some people I know have started worshipin' toward the mountains. Others say the Hands of Obenin are a godsend from Obenin to bring justice to the land. Their name among Glynwith is no longer *Barapk*

Alanom but *Neve Usentes.* Instead of the Obenin's Temple, many Obenites pilgrimage to the foothills of the Abringian Mountains. They carry food, gifts, and gold."

"From Children of the Wind to the New Ones," interpreted Octun. "Do you think they are gods?"

"I think the Heno people have it right, Sky Demons of Obenin. But, from what you tell me... they don't seem to be gods or demons, but mortal. If they aren't demons from the spirit world, I think their intent is demonic. Why bring such calamity on the innocent?"

Octun told Ryhad about the ultimatum delivered by the sole survivor of the nearly successful first attack on the Sky Demons. This contradicted against Ryhad's belief that Brock Stannick created the rumor to take pressure off Seth. Octun assured Ryhad that it was not a rumor. The Sky Demons, that was fitting, wanted to be worshipped. Every attempt to kill them since was assumed a failure because no one ever returned.

"King Seth has known for almost two years, now. They have rejected Obenin and my teaching. They want the kingdom, but they will not stop there."

"You knew them?"

"Yes, I taught them. I was their caretaker."

"What were they like? I was in Ethenia that day they showed their power. I met you on the temple grounds a few days before, but I never got a glimpse of them."

"Three of them had skin and hair different from ours. The other is one of us. It is confirmed that he is from a prominent family in the Yan Free Territories. The family has denied him."

"I don't blame them," shot Ryhad coldly. "People will surely take their anger out on them for this evil."

"Something has happened to them. I don't know what. Seth and Cuere did not count on it. I spoke with them the day I forsook the keepers. They looked to me for help but I had nothing to give. I had failed them long before that day. The oath I swore to Saroth on the day I leftfor Oracle, then affirmed on King Saroth's deathbed, not to oppose Seth..., made worse by crowning Seth as King..., those were the moments I both failed and buried myself in that failure."

"It surprises me that King Saroth had anythin' to do with this business. That Seth and Cuere must have put a hex on him or somethin'," remarked Ryhad.

Octun leaned back in his chair and stared into his uncle's eyes and then into the eyes of his cousin. From their expressions, he saw that their belief in the tangible overrode the Obenite faith, the memory of Saroth, and the tenets. Octun thought of Seth's fit of sorrow.

"He cried at his father's bedside. He was distraught." His defense of Seth did not set well within himself.

"Humph," Rhyhad scoffed and went back to smoking his pipe.

Ictheos, Jared, Ulthea and Parmos, the New Ones, Sky Demons of Obenin, threatened all Obenin and the Benomian Alliance. The kingdom could not see the power of their god, Obenin, but the Sky Demons' power brought the known world to its knees. Seth proved himself as an ineffective and incapable leader. There was no way the kingdom would ever prosper again as long as he remained in power.

Octun knew Ryhad saw his doubt, yet said nothing so far. After all, his nephew was still officially the Keeper of Obenin's Temple as far as Glynwith figured. King Saroth appointed him spiritual leader of all the kingdoms. King Seth did not appoint anyone to take his place and had not even bothered with defrocking him. Seth simply sent men after him. The Primary Temple suffered from attacks from the Sky Demon. It still stood. They probably wanted to claim it for themselves. Several dedicated priests still cared for it.

Ryhad's eyes grew sly. Octun felt he had something for him. Ryhad meant his stories to help the younger generation; most often, they left the listener in a quandary as to what they were supposed to mean.

When asked, Ryhad would simply reply, "Meditate on it. You can't become a man by me telling you everythin'."

"You know, Keeper. I am glad that you decided to come home. You don't come home enough. And I am glad this talk about religion came up," he said, closing his slyest eye.

"Home is the best place to come when you're troubled or tryin' to find somethin', or when you just do somethin' so foolish that you got no place else to go."

"Where do I fall?" Octun's tone blustery, he did not want to hear some concocted fact or story that his uncle tried to make into a profound point. Octun already pondered too much. So much raged in his mind, he doubted he could figure it all out in ten life spans. He needed to find answers quickly. His deathbed oath to Saroth choked the life out of him. The fallen spiritual status made him sick with indecision.

"I don't know what they did to you, Keeper. But my few hairs went straight with anger when I first heard the many rumors about you. I didn't believe a one. You have been up here for months, and it's not because you are afraid of bein' captured by Charge Stannick's men. So, maybe you are tryin' to come to some decision, eh?"

Lifting his eyes to the ceiling, Octun apologized to heaven for what he was about to say. He let it pour out of his heart.

"Ever since I learned of King Saroth's plans, I doubted. The whole matter didn't seem scriptural. But I said nothing and was able to dismiss the doubt because, above all, we are taught of the divine right of the king to rule and he is guided by Obenin's will.

"At first, I was able to accept it all, but now I realize that I was always concerned that something would go wrong. I guess that was why I was so efficient. Maybe I could prevent the inevitable. I vowed to restore King Seth's faith. At Oracle, when I saw the children lying in a bloody pile, I knew this was evil. My heart went from all that was happening around me. And after the death of King Saroth, I knew that somehow he had been corrupted, too. Maybe he erred because he was sick, probably because, as you said, Lord Cuere did something to him. "The whole matter brought sourness to my mouth and I started to abhor the fact I had been caught up in it. I prayed hard, like I did before and after every battle, but there was no help. I have been in solitude here reading, praying, waiting and wondering what the difference is between a lack of faith and judging whether your beliefs are the truth. Is all the good that has happened to me in life brought about by prayer, or was it coincidence, luck, or something else?"

Octun's eyes watered. He wanted to smash something. If he did, he hoped Nineo and Ryhad would get out of the way.

"You know, Octun, your mother was not Obenite."

"What do you mean by that?" Octun snapped.

"Well, she was Obenite by marriage and conversion, but not by ancestry."

Octun's eyes narrowed. His temper seethed.

"I know I am a half-breed, part-Aspharian part-Obenite. What has that got to do with anything?"

Normally, Ryhad had nothing to fear. Now, he dealt with a troubled man whose world crumbled around him, and Octun sensed his past was about to crumble, too. Ryhad knew he was too far into the story to stop.

"Yes, you know your father worked for his admiral after he got lame. He kept the place runnin' while the officer was out fightin' wars. One day the admiral brought back men and women as slaves and servants. Your mother was one of them. Your father saw her, and loved her and after five years bought her freedom from his lord."

"Where is this leading Uncle?"

"Your mother had a secret which she kept from almost everyone, even your father for a while. She was a strong, quiet woman, yet submitted to your father. But her mind would not be changed about one thing, her personal beliefs. I know all these things because my wife was the only person she would talk to openly. There were a lot of women and men who treated your mother badly, mostly out of jealousy. Women sought after your father, even after he married. But he always remained true, and I ought to know."

"You are rambling."

"Give some space to an old man, will you? I have lots of stories up here, and sometimes they all try to come out at the same time. Well, anyway, she was not Obenite at heart."

"What do you mean?" Octun shouted, leaping up from his chair and smashing it against the wall.

Nineo scampered out of the cottage.

Reaching over, Octun lifted Ryhad from the chair to his face.

"What has my mother done to deserve this from you in her grave? She went on the pilgrimages, she taught me how to pray, she read me the words of Obenin..."

"Think about it, son! Think about it!" his uncle shouted in one breath. "She taught you the words of Obenin at the local shrine. It would have looked bad on your father if she hadn't. What did she read to you when the two of you were alone? Think about what she wore man. Her clothin's were proper for an Obenite woman, but wasn't there somethin' that always adorned her dress? Why did she pray over you long after your father had gone to bed, and over you in the mornin'?"

Suddenly, all of it came back to Octun. The memories stung like walking barefoot on the rocks after a long winter. She would take the book from her secret place. Not a book really, but papers that she had kept bound together with yarn. He thought they were stories and sayings, but his uncle implied they were much more.

Octun remembered the embroidery and patterns that adorned her dress, almost like a sword with the hilt upward. Even the sweaters she knitted for him had these patterns. He had thought nothing of it. His mother did pray a lot more at home than at the shrines. She always seemed to have an air of guilt that saddened her beautiful face.

"Why are you telling me this now? What good will it do me?"

"I don't know," his uncle confessed, "but it seems like the right thing to say."

He sat his uncle back into his seat. "I am sorry, very sorry, please forgive me."

Ryhad breathed deeply. Maybe in his rambling he had said something after all.

"My mother told Aunt Ruth all this?"

"Yes, and your Aunt Ruth told me, and that was as far as it ever got."

"Tell me something about her religion."

"At the time, I wasn't concerned much about what or who she actually believed in. The manuscripts she read to you was mostly things that she remembered from her own teachin's, which she wrote down. From what I understand, even in her own land, her religion had few believers. The numbers increased when we invaded. Ruth can tell you much more than I can. I'll brin' her with me next time and maybe, just maybe, we might be able to dig up those papers. Oh, and she kept diaries, too."

"There is no need to bring her. I am leaving with you."

Ryhad glowed with pride. Octun rode beside him right through middle of town to the inn Ryhad owned. They dismounted at the front door. Already, a small crowd followed them through the streets. The name *Scourge of Namiberro* hung over the door of the inn.

"That is a long name for an inn, and a strange one at that. When did you change it?" Octun asked, knowing his uncle took advantage of his reputation to bring in customers.

Ryhad deflected the question. "If you know what's good for you, you won't ask that question around your Aunt Ruth. She is already gonna beat you to death then feed you to death."

"If I tell her that you knew I was near but didn't tell her, you will be the one she beats," Octun quipped.

As he walked into the inn, Octun's mouth dropped open. He looked at his uncle and shook his head in disbelief.

Ryhad slapped him on the back jovially. "Can't a man honor his family?" quipped Rhyad.

Ryhad separated the war hero from the high priest giving the inn a profane edge. The war hero, he exalted. The high priest, he mentioned only when it benefited him.

"How can a person get drunk celebrating the war hero without defiling the high priest?" asked Octun.

Ryhad returned, "But you said you left the keepers."

Octun looked around the foyer. "Is that supposed to be me? Where did you get that statue?"

"I know a man who knows a man who worked for Saroth's sculptor."

Octun stood in front of his life-sized stone image. Patrons knew who it was, though the face was narrower and the neck was longer than his.

Ryhad smiled slyly.

"What else can I expect?" asked Octun with a smirk.

Patrons turned to look at their noisy entrance. Astounded, Octun put his hand on his forehead.

"This is not an inn but a museum," exclaimed Octun.

The tavern area praised every campaign or skirmish he ever fought. His uncle even managed to acquire parts of the ship he stole during the Mernus rescue. He had attached the wheel right in the middle of the bar. Loaso, Namiberro, Mpolu, the sub-Aspharian wilderness, they were all there. Ryhad used everything Octun ever sent home, or he finagled someone into finding what he wanted. No wonder he had guests when their kingdom faltered. This placed served as a reminder of the glorious days of triumph and riches.

Octun admonished his uncle's selfishness in taking advantage of his fame.

"Times are hard and competition is stiff," Ryhad rebutted. "A proprietor needs as many edges as he can get if he wants to be legitimate. "And Ruth insists on bein' legitimate."

A shout erupted from the back. His Aunt Ruth hurried toward him shuffling her feet as fast as she could. Her body bounced in objection.

"Whew, whew," she bellowed in long breaths, her excitement getting the best of her.

She stopped and put her hand over her mouth in disbelief and excitement. In a flash, her eyes turned into little coals of trapped fire.

"Oh, you are in for it now! Draw sword and defend yourself or run the other way," jested Rhyad.

"Iberius Octun Ruben Marchus, get over here."
She pointed to the floor about a hair away from the toe of

her shoe. Her strong contralto voice carried over the patron's laughter.

"Don't do it man or this place is going to be your tomb, too. Here lies the great warrior high priest, Keeper of Obenin's Primary Temple, beat to death by his aunt," Ryhad proclaimed.

The crowd roared with laughter.

Octun stepped helplessly in front of her.

"Bend down," she ordered.

Octun bent his back.

"Lower." She patted her foot impatiently.

He stooped a little lower.

Her eyes softened. She grabbed him and hugged him with the strength of a mother bear. Squeezing and releasing, she wrung his clothing. For a second, he thought she was going to pick him up by the scruff of the neck and carry him back to her den.

Then, the beating started. She squeezed him with her right arm and beat his back with her left fist. She switched, beating him with her right fist. Next, she wrapped him in her embrace. Alternating hands, she pounded his back even more. His back resounded with the booming thump, thump, thump of a large drum.

Then she wept. "You game rooster, you! It's 'bout time you come home. It's 'bout time you come home. I know you troubled, boy. Let Aunt Ruth get you back on the mend."

She grabbed his ear and pulled him into the inn's enormous kitchen.

"Sit!" She pointed to a chair at the head of the table. One of the barmaids complained when she took another guest's plates right out of her hands and put them in front of Octun.

"This will whet your appetite. She moved to the stove, bumping one of the cooks out of the way with her hip.

"Stoke the other, I got this one."

Octun leaned back in his chair, with his feet stretched under the table. He unbuckled his belt. Ruth smiled and plopped another plate in front of him.

Octun's family came in and out all night. Little children sat on his knee. He told them stories and they marveled. Some fell asleep on the floor in front of him. Other children objected with cries and tantrums as their mothers came for them. Everything seemed distant and familiar at the same time. He missed this place.

People whom he had not seen for decades came to visit. Children were no longer children. Most had families of their own. Some asked if he thought they should join the war or which forces they should join. He put the questions off. He talked that night more than he did in the last four years.

The next night, Octun opened the first of his mother's two trunks. He found them in the room when he returned from a meeting with some of the village leaders. The chests were crammed full. He sat on the top to unlock one. He thought this unusual. His mother kept such a neat house, arguing with his father to throw out things he had no intention of ever using or looking at again.

The first thing Octun saw, lying atop a quilt as if it kept everything safe, was his father's favorite pipe, his mother's favorite, too. After his mother died, he never saw it again. His father didn't really smoke all that often, but his mother liked to see him with it. He obliged her. He figured his father placed it there before giving the chest to Ruth.

Octun slid his finger along the ivory mouthpiece. Where the mouthpiece met the wooden stem, symbols adorned the good-sized bowl. They were clearly Aspharian. If he remembered correctly, they represented an ideal in which some Aspharians believed, especially those of the southern coast, in the region called Namiberro.

The inside of the bowl was shaped like any other pipe. The outside was another matter. The intricate workings told a story. Octun looked closely at the tiny figures. On the side closest to the smoker, a crown set around the peak of a mountain. On the opposite side, the craftsman carved a lioness and cubs encircled by the same crown. He had no idea what it meant.

Picking up the quilt, he spread it out across his bed. It used to be his as a child. His mother covered him with it to protect him from the dangers of the world.

Memories of his mother and his father filled him. They were happy. Their house was filled with hard work, good food, occasional bouts of laughter, and the frequent hard knock. His father, a stern disciplinarian, sometimes argued against his mother's rebuke about his punishment.

His father always replied, "You have no idea what he has to face out there. It might hurt now, but it will help later."

The words were prophetic.

He pulled the folds from the quilt and ran his hands over it. Large, heavy and square, the patchwork contained nothing fancy. Most Obenite designs were meant to be big and impressive, not intricate; mostly symbols, crests, names, and occasionally, a flower or two. He brushed his right hand across the symbol in the middle of the quilt. It made a crossing pattern. The longest of the stitching pointed from head to toe. The shorter, about half the length, ran from left to right.

He remembered this as his mother's favorite pattern, the one of which his uncle spoke. She used it over and over again, even in the clothing she made for him. Only his were not so bold. His mother never explained it.

An eternal spirit inspired the heroes in mother's stories. He remembered one particular story about a man who hit the water with a piece of cloth. The water parted before him and he walked across on dry land.

In those days, he thought the stories were Obenite, but none of his other mates had ever heard them. He passed them along to the other children. Until, one day, his mother came to him and told him that, if he wanted to keep hearing the stories, he had to stop telling other children. He asked her why. She cried and he never asked again. His father seemed troubled for a long time about the matter. He sat with them some evenings as she read the tenets to Octun every night for about a month. Later, she continued to tell him the stories. His father knew. Octun never retold the stories to his friends again.

As an adult, he looked at the things from his childhood in a different light. As a child, he took everything for granted, especially that his parents would always be there. His mother was too good to die, his father too ornery. As an adult, he realized nothing in nature was permanent.

Octun left the quilt on the bed and went back into the chest. He saw something that made him shiver. Octun picked it up with both hands. It was the first gift he remembered giving to her. His father helped him make it, a basket for a bed warmer. Together he and his father heated and beat the metal into shape and polished it. The metal tarnished but there was not a charred area on it. She had never used it.

He found other objects in the chest. He assumed what some might have meant to his mother, for others he had no idea.

He did not find the stories his uncle spoke of, but he found something special. At the bottom of the chest, he found his mother's diary. He thumbed through the bound pages. Bound pages cost money, more money than his father made. Yet, he held them in his hand. It was an expense showing how much his father cared for his mother. Bound and treated pages like these were mostly found in official business, never in the personal diary of a commoner. Most commoners did not even write except to make their mark or sign their names.

Looking in the second chest, he found more diaries. Evidently, his mother wrote volumes. He knew she was bright and had some education. He realized there must be much more he did not know about her.

She must have been highly educated before her captivity and kept it a secret from almost everyone. Those who knew kept the secret.

He read the first couple of pages of the first diary, which started about five years after his parents married. She wrote flawlessly. The first passages contained a love letter to his father about the diary itself. It meant the world to her.

"Levid would be jealous," Octun whispered. Her handwriting looked like a work of art, and very readable.

Mostly, his mother captured her daily life and a few private thoughts. She wrote of his Aunt Ruth and Uncle Ryhad. Octun read about their kindness to her despite her previous slave status. She and Ruth became like sisters. Also, she wrote of him as a small boy.

Octun was not prepared for the flood of emotions the memories brought back. Those memories were the reason he had not come home since his father's death. Every excuse he ever gave came to nothing. One thought racked his mind: he avoided home to avoid his loss and to avoid his guilt.

His mother's death lingered as Saroth's had. Her slow and painful slip into the afterlife made him feel hopeless to help her. He came to visit her when he could.

Each time, he longed to see her and dreaded to see her. The sickness emaciated her. Each time he beheld her face, she looked thinner and weaker, wasting away from a full round face into a wisp of flesh that covered rattling bones.

Each time he came home, she asked about Aspharia. She did not want to hear of the war like everyone else. She wanted to know about the people, the land, the weather, the smell, anything. He wanted to stay in Glynwith, but she kept sending him back. When he refused, she grew feverish, going into weak rantings until he agreed to go back to the life he made for himself.

He received no word of her final days, only that she had died. He came home to a grave upon which the grass had taken root. His father still mourned and accepted no attempts of comfort. He never remarried. Once she died, Octun and his father never really spoke of their mutual loss.

Occasionally, they visited her grave together, both standing silently, looking down at the grass, projecting strength to the other by not allowing themselves to cry. He wanted to, so much.

His father died just over two years later. The estate hands found him alive in the woods, lying under a tree in the rain, as if he was taking a nap. He never recovered. Again, Octun came back to a grave.

The admiral set aside land for Octun. Ryhad kept it up. Octun sent money home. He sent trinkets and spoils from war, everything and anything but himself.

His delusive lies confronted him.

In this moment of cold hard truth, he confessed out loud, "I am afraid to face my guilt."

Octun wept.

With all the power to take a life as he did in numerous battles, he had no power to stop death when it got ready to take someone.

Guilt came in heavy sheaves these days. Fate bound it all together, his parents, Seth, the demons in the mountains, the war. The war brought him home to face his first guilt. His mother helped him from the grave finally to morn her death and his father's death the way he should. What would help him face the other guilty burdens?

He flipped the pages, reading passages of her diaries here and there. Tiring, he put some of the diaries aside and picked up the last one. His mouth dropped. His mother had drawn a much better picture of the carvings on his father's pipe. He could not read the writing under the drawing. He stared at it. Page after page of Aspharian writing covered the paper. How had she kept it up after all the years? He recognized the style but he could not read a single word. Though it was Aspharian, it differed in such a way that made the writing indecipherable. Octun searched backwards through the books. The Aspharian writing started third from the last diary. He needed someone to translate them.

Chancellor Levid could translate them. There was no way he was going to ask him, though. He held bitterness toward the man. Levid may have been a victim, too, but his coziness with Stannick made him untrustworthy.

Octun searched for his Aunt Ruth. He found her sending one of her maids into the streets.

"We run a good place here, not a brothel. Go over to the *Smilin' Traveler*. Sell yourself for a pretty dress, for all I care, but you ain't goin' to do it here."

Ruth slammed the door. "The little hussy," she grumbled.

Turning to see Octun, she smiled. "Evenin', darlin'."

She gave him a hug that took his breath away.

"Sit down let me get you somethin' to eat."

She rang a bell. Another maid came in. The maid listened but kept her eyes on Octun.

"All right, little missy, I'll send you right out after the last one if you don't keep your eyes and everythin' else to yourself. Now scat and get the man somethin' to eat."

Ruth patted Octun on the shoulder. "All the lasses have been talkin' bout you. So, you better behave. You understand me."

She shook her finger at him. "But you oughta be married. There ain't no rule against it in the priesthood. Our local keeper is married with three younguns. Some of the warrior has gone out the priest but he's a good man."

Octun didn't say anything.

"I ain't kiddin', boy."

"Yes, Aunt Ruth."

"You'll find someone, wait and see, a good southern girl."

In another life, he thought.

"Aunt Ruth..." he started.

Ruth noticed the turn of the conversation. For a change, she looked at him quietly.

"Mother's diaries. I am not accusing you. But, did you read them?"

"Course not. I didn't have to. She told me everythin' anyways, except close to the end."

Ruth pulled out a chair and sat down across from him.

"Why didn't I ever know about them?"

"She gave them to me, not to you. You gallivantin' all over creation, one war after another, no place to settle down until King Saroth appointed you as Keeper, you would have lost them or damaged them. Your mother wouldn't have it. She knew and I knew, in time, I'd give them to you."

"Did she tell you anything about the last four diaries?"

Ruth teared up. "Milla was such a good soul. Some people treated her so bad 'cause they were jealous. Her kindness and your reputation was her revenge on them. You brought such glory to the kingdom and to Glynwith. Nobody ever spoke bad about her once you became a hero. It was shameful. Most never apologized, they just started invitin' her over and treatin' her like one of their oldest friends. It helped your father conduct business, but she didn't like it one bit. She remembered who her real friends were."

Ruth dried her eyes with her apron.

Sniffling, she continued, "She kinda clammed up on me sometimes, though. I think she wanted to go home. When I reminded her it was forbidden for her to write in her native language, she didn't care. Besides, it's not like she was puttin' her diaries in the market. What could they do to her? What could they do to Ruben at that point? She just kept writin' until she just couldn't anymore. She never told me the meaning of the words she wrote in her tongue, only that it was for you and it would help you through some tough times."

The maid came back with a platter of food large enough to feed three men. She set it in front of Octun, curtsied, flitted her dress as she turned, looked at him over her shoulder, and fluttered her lashes.

"Lasses nowadays, floosies every one," snapped Ruth.

Octun prepared to go to bed. His Aunt Ruth's words made him feel better. The entire experience did. Ruth and Ryhad surely did put him back on the road to mending. It promised to be a long one.

A hurried knock on the door took him from his thoughts. He unlatched the door. Ryhad peered into the room as if he expected someone else to be there. He stepped in and took another look around. Ryhad shut the door and spoke in whispers. Ryhad made Octun get dressed and follow.

They went down the stairs and exited the back way. Ryhad led him along footpaths between buildings. Meeting conspicuous men along the way, Ryhad gave signs and code words. He spoke to the men briefly. Each let them pass and stepped back into the shadows.

"Why are we sneaking about?" Octun asked.

"Who's sneakin'? That's just how we greet each other around here at night."

Octun scoffed.

"There are things honest folk just don't need to know," Ryhad replied finally.

They came upon a small house at the end of a narrow road. Octun recognized it as the old place where people went to get letters read and to have things explained to them. The previous owner was a crook, and the magistrate finally ran him out of town.

Cloaked men lurked in the shadows. Ryhad whistled. Octun and Ryhad hurried to the little porch and knocked twice on the door.

Someone returned the knock.

"Guard the goose," said Ryhad.

"She is well protected," a heavy voice behind the door answered.

The door opened. A small fire and a single glows dimly lighted the room. The man in front of the fire turned around. Octun recognized him immediately. He reached for his sword.

"Hold on," his uncle intervened, locking his arms around Octun's sword arm.

Gremal stepped closer. He reached inside his vest and pulled out a letter. He turned it over and moved it so that the light revealed a seal. It carried Lord Mernus' secret seal.

Octun found the fact hard to believe. Major Gremal was Mernus' inside man all along.

Major Gremal answered Octun's question without being asked. His jovial manner was gone. He spoke quickly and urgently. "When I heard what King Seth did to some of the Grand Council's families, I got a message to Lord Mernus. I am not proud of the things I had to do to gain Stannick's confidence. The fact that we rescued Mernus' family does little to quiet my conscience. There is one thing, though, that does, something unexpected, something that involves you."

Gremal led him to a back room. There, two men kneeled, looking after a woman who waved her arms in the air disturbingly. Spasms ran through her body. She rambled despairingly.

Kerwal and Tok turned to face Octun, then turned again to the poor woman. She coughed harshly. When Kerwal sat her up, she spit up blood.

"What ails her?" Octun asked, frowning, not really wanting to get too close.

"Her conscience. She wants absolution for her sins," Gremal replied.

"I am no longer a priest."

"She doesn't care, but it has to be you," Gremal insisted.

"Is this why you called me out and gave secret signs?" his frustration raising his volume.

Gremal put his hand on Octun's shoulder. "It is our good fortune you are here tonight of all nights. Hear her confession."

He approached the bed. Kerwal laid her back against the pillow.

For a moment, she did not look at Octun, then she turned to him slowly.

Weakly she asked, "Don't you recognize me, my Keeper?"

He looked at Gremal.

"It's King Saroth's nurse. We had to bring her to the heart of Glywith. Her family has been running from Seth for a long time. We found them, and her, by luck. Her mind will not let medicine heal her."

Octun looked down at her and leaned down to her lips.

She whispered, "I killed King Saroth. I killed him. High Priest and Keeper Obenin, forgive me. I killed him."

Though she wept a thousand times already, she wept again.

She told Octun how Seth and Cuere gave her the potion to give Saroth. She gave no excuse, only that she regretted not facing death rather than having submitted to them.

She turned and gave a deep gut-cleansing sigh. Tok touched her forehead and felt for her breath.

"She sleeps," Tok reported.

Octun simmered in thought. Seth's grief... no, not grief, a confession racked with guilt... the journey to Oracle, concern for Saroth's health, the coronation, all guile!

Octun got up from the floor. His thick husky vow to Saroth became chaff. He peeled it away and cast it to the floor at nurse's bedside. Immediately, a feeling came over him, like the wind blew against his back, replacing Octun's burden and sweeping the chaff away. The burning need to punish evil men replaced his guilt. His lethargy of purpose moved away from view as he closed his eyes and clenched his fist. His purpose became clear. He must take a leading role in deposing Seth.

"Uncle Ryhad, have someone get my gear and meet me at the stables. Stir every man in the village and countryside. Send word to the Glynwith Regiment."

Octun kicked the door off its hinges and stormed from the room. He barked, "Gremal, Kerwal, Tok, are you coming?"

"Where are we going? It is dark." Gremal asked. "And the nurse?"

"Uncle can take care of her. There is nothing I can give her. The moon is full and you are taking me to Mernus. The regiment can catch up later."

CHAPTER 35
Octun At War

Repel the enemy from the borders of Glynwith, reclaim everything north of the Barren Lands and swing westward toward Bedowyn Lake to join with Mernus.

Six weeks after Octun broke his vow to Saroth, he meant to retake and hold the Middle Kingdom. This would split Seth's forces. The Southern Kingdom would fall to internal rebel forces and Seth's men would have no place to go. Next, move into Gath, on to Grand Palace and finally Ethenia. Octun thought it a good plan.

The first great battle that held promise to turn the tide and reunite Obenin started with him. *Repel the enemy. Recapture and hold all the land north of Glynwith to the Great River.*

Fearing a trap and the proximity of Glynwith, had deterred Seth from coming any farther. Instead, he had turned west and fortified Bedowyn. So much for not drawing Glynwith into the war. Now that Glynwith had chosen sides, Seth had nothing to lose by invading. Octun had to win or Seth would surely rule.

The entire Glynwith Regiment flanked him. Reinforced by men who had fled the Southern Kingdom and the Primary Kingdom, twenty-five thousand well-armed men joined other commanders to the north and south of him. Evidently, many of Seth's potential opponents had been waiting for Glynwith, waiting for Octun. Octun took command of the lead forces. The Glynwith standard flapped in the wind. Tok and Kerwal rode up beside him.

Seth's forces covered the hills before them. The front line positioned itself in mass, one solid line that did not seem to end. Octun faced an uphill fight. Seth's army put ranks of pikes on the front lines. The enemy forces waited for them to move.

Spies reported the wizard, Lord Cuere, fought with this particular force. Octun dismissed the idea. He knew Seth would not let Cuere this far from his side. If they ever approached Heno, that would be a different matter.

Tok's horse snorted. The fur on his neck twitched. He tightened the reins to steady him.

"He smells blood," explained Tok.

"The blood of Seth's army," roared Kerwal.

"It is still Obenite blood, the blood of our brothers. History repeats itself," protested Octun. "And we must wade through history and blood until we release the kingdom from Seth's evil."

"And what about those devils in the mountains?" asked Tok.

"This is the task before us," stated Octun.

Octun straightened his back and checked his armor. He put on his helmet and drew Saroth's gift, the sword, Romala. As Octun brandished his sword in the air, the army advanced behind him. The soldiers beat their weapons against their shields.

Octun released his rage and embraced life, death, and every doubt between them. The anger at Seth, at his god, himself, and the pity for Saroth fed his rage. Today he would work his anger out in horror and death.

Octun looked at Kerwal. Octun whirled Romala like a madman.

"Battle your brothers. Save them from the evil that seizes them. Save Glynwith. Save our kingdom and restore the name of a good king, King Saroth!"

Octun charged. The regiment followed, sending up a roar heard for miles. This was the most important war of his time. Octun would leave the battle only as a victor or dead.

As they charged, large round stones catapulted over their heads toward the enemy lines. The stones crashed into the enemy's front line, softening up the ranks of pikes. Showers of arrows soared over their heads in both directions. Octun raised his shield. Seth's archers miscalculated. Because of their elevation on the hill and the speed of their charge, the arcs of Seth's archers were too high. The point of their advance rode under the arrows.

As they attacked up the hill, the last stone landed and rolled down the hill. The last volley of Glynwith archers struck the frontline. They were cutting it close. The enemy tried to close ranks but the line fractured and the cavalry charged through the holes. Octun kept moving, slashing his way through, careful not to isolate himself.

The cavalry moved skillfully, causing a general disarray of Seth's forces. Seth's army focused on them and not the advance of the foot soldiers.

Though his foot soldiers fought mightily, Octun felt a forward surge from the enemy. They were regrouping and putting up a good fight. Glynwith answered, bringing the enemy surge to a halt.

Cold anger drove Tok. Every thrust targeted some part of the body meant to end a life quickly. He conserved his energy that way. He needed to go the distance.

Kerwal grunted and mashed his hammer into the enemy. Kerwal, Tok, and Octun watched each other's flank working as a team, moving forward always forward.

The series of battles went on for weeks. Seth's army did not go down easily, retreating to alternate fighting positions and reinforcing their lines a number of times. They did not retreat westward toward Bedowyn but eastward toward the Barren Lands. Retreating to the north took them too close to where Mernus battled for the

Bedowyn stronghold. The smaller force could hold on in the thick forest and keep Seth's army occupied.

Octun tried to turn the battle toward Mernus but couldn't. Seth's generals knew Octun attempted to wedge them between Mernus and Glynwith.

After thirty-four days, the Great River lay one day away. Seth's army had to fight or withdraw a little to the north to cross the estuary of the great river. Octun smelled a trap. He consulted with the generals, only to find himself promoted to general. They toasted. He received quick instructions from a senior commander of Mernus' forces and took off back to his own command.

Octun advanced his forces but did not hotly pursue the enemy. Instead, ships of soldiers came from the ocean and moved up the Great River, cutting off Seth's army. Then they prepared another front in southern Gath.
Seth's army had no choice but to move further west and join the forces that battled Mernus.

During the battle of the middle kingdom, Octun received word of a great sea battle. Seth's naval officers still controlled the best ships and held the most experience in the admiralty.

Octun and the generals struggled for a plan. If Seth won the sea battle, his marines would follow. Mernus' forces might need to hold Bedowyn without him. If the forces in Gath failed, it meant a dead stop to their advance.

Octun decided to split his forces between Bedowyn and Gath. He sat down at his table to draft the orders when a messenger walked in with an incredulous report.
The previous report was wrong. The Kingdom of Carden, a member of the Benomian Alliance, came to aide the Obenite naval force and defeated Seth's previously superior naval force. This was how Mernus' forces were able to create a front in Gath in the first place.

Octun sent emissaries to make sure of the Cards' intent and to coordinate further the effort to fortify Gath. After which, he turned west again to help Mernus.

Bedowyn proved to be a stubborn stronghold. Most people there traditionally remained loyal to the royal family, even during times of despicable rulers.

Octun met up with Mernus, whose men were tired and bogged down in a stalemate. Octun's arrival boosted their morale. They fought with renewed vigor. Day by day, they moved through the dense forest, clearing it of Seth forces, holding ground, and advancing again.

Upon reaching the fortress, they surrounded it. Octun pounded it with fire, stone, and animal carcasses. He wanted to make the castle as unlivable as possible. Daily they offered Seth's forces terms for their surrender. Daily Seth's commander denied the terms. Octun delivered the final ultimatum himself.

Octun directed his forces to assault the castle. Showers of stones and arrows flew over the wall before the soldiers stormed. The catapults battered the ramparts demolishing, fighting positions. Before the ladders rose, Octun spotted the white flag. He relaxed. The fighting ended. The surrender spared Obenites lives.

Independent rebel forces had freed the Southern Kindgom. The Middle Kingdom was under Mernus' control. Octun knew the Primary Kingdom, with its terrain and allegiance to Seth, presented an even more bloody and difficult ordeal.

The Obenite generals met in Mernus' tent. When Octun walked in, four men he did not recognize were speaking casually with Mernus. By their dress and markings, he recognized them as a Carden general and two commanders, and one other who was probably the King of Carden.

For the first time ever, Cards and Obenites ate together and shared a common purpose. Octun eyed them cautiously. The Cards eyed him cautiously.

"Sit Iberius," offered Mernus. "Meet King Hallib."

Hallib, King of Carden, led the discussion. Mernus seemed impressed by Hallib. So was Octun. Hallib, barely twenty years old, with locks of deep brown hair down to his shoulders, spoke with sage wisdom. Enthusiastic, his hazel eyes brightened with questions as he separated fact from fiction concerning the rumors that raced through his kingdom.

King Hallib told how he chanced the move to support Mernus. His advisors thought him foolish. Many of the wealthy Cards did, also. Octun listened as Hallib explained how he defied his advisors and threats of the rich and powerful, even many of his subjects. Before Seth's treachery with the Grand Counsel, Hallib had been one of the main proponents of the peace Mernus wanted to offer. While the Carden counsel debated, King Hallib gave his navy and army orders and moved out with them. He left his advisors befuddled.

Hallib's original plan was to anchor off the coast and send emissaries secretly to offer support to Mernus. When he happened upon the battle between Seth's fleet and a few beleaguered ships supporting Mernus, he took a chance. His effort saved the Obenite ships. Hallib submitted the command of some of his forces to the Obenite commanders. The alliance caught Seth off guard.

After sunset, the communion continued. Hallib spoke of how Obenin's mistake affected the entire Benomian Alliance. Until a few months ago, the Cards thought Seth still controlled the Sky Demons. They believed the havoc brought on them was completely Seth's doing. When the word came that the Obenite civil war did not involve the Sky Demons, Hallib took heart.

Hallib's understanding of things he had not actually witnessed fascinated Octun. Octun rubbed his chin and scratched his head in wonder and amazement.

As Hallib spoke, the entire group listened. He fished for answers about the godlike inhabitants in the mountains. The Obenites simply observed stoically and let him continue, waiting to see how close he came.

Hallib believed there were three different minds at work. According to reports, he developed a theory that, at one time, they may have needed one another to perform the wonder of controlling the heavens. Hallib now believed they no longer did.

One of the demons brutalized everything. He believed that to be the one named Jared. The destruction carried a cold-blooded hand of revenge. He destroyed buildings and killed people. He seemed hell-bent on making everyone accept his ultimatum.

Hallib believed another demon became a vicious practical joker. Octun marveled as he related an incident similar to that of the Obenite farmer near the Great River. He spoke of times where no one could build past a certain height. Each morning when the carpenters returned, something had knocked the wall down. Even after days of labor, this sometimes happened.

Then, there was the water spirit who was always in a bad mood. Hallib attributed this to the sullen Parmos. He did not dismiss Ulthea, though, because the situations had the feel of a scorned woman.

Octun thought carefully on this. So, where was the other one? Either, Parmos or Ulthea was out of the picture. Why?

Mernus finally gave in. He told Hallib how Seth slowly murdered his own father, the escape, Lord Cuere, Oracle and the attempt to kill the demons in the mountains.

Hallib drew back, putting his hands in the air, it all made sense to him.

"We know where they are. Seth tried to kill them. I tried to kill them. Every attempt has failed. There was only one near success. That was the first attempt," reported Mernus.

"Sometimes it makes me doubt what we are fighting for," added Octun. It was the first word he had uttered in a while.

"You know where they are?" Hallib asked.

"The way is inaccessible," contended Mernus. "They keep the mountains impassable. With their spirits, they reach out great distances."

"Well, where is it?"

"They are holed up in a hot springs in Mount Kaob," Mernus answered.

"I have heard of this place. The old smugglers used it long ago but something spooked them. It is taboo. So you have tried?"

"Many times, secretly from the Bardian side and from the Obenite side." reiterated Mernus. "What are you getting at?"

Hallib thought for a minute. He looked to the left, then up, then to the right as if he examined the inside of his skull. He leaned forward to Mernus, "But you haven't tried for the Carden side."

Mernus and Octun cocked their heads.

"The Great Rift!"

They all nodded in agreement.

Octun dispatched forces to the north. The object was not to attack but to prevent escape. Octun joined the remaining generals and marched into Gath. Seth sacrificed some of his forces to stall and allow him to fortify Ethenia and the Grand Palace. Octun needed to drive Seth from Ethenia and make him retreat into Obenin's Primary

Temple, which promised to be the last stand and a vicious one at that. Even damaged, the temple's high walls, towers and elevation gave Seth the advantage.

Additionally, Seth flew ensigns over the temple and placed idols there, attempting to give the Sky Demons the impression he worshipped them. It worked.

Seth used this deception to avert disaster and enslave the Ethenians in a hurried attempt to fortify and repair the temple for the battle.

Seth's army dug in there. They all knew the stakes. Seth wanted a long drawn-out battle resulting in terms. For he no longer fought to retain the kingdom -- he fought for his life. Mernus demanded a fight to the death.

Octun witnessed an act even Mernus never really believed would happen. Instead of the prior plan for a simple truce, Mernus signed a pact of mutual protection and trade with Hallib. Also, he met with emissaries from Tenzia and Bardia but did not allow them to join in the war. They were only to stay on their side of the mountains and, if perchance Seth or his cohorts made it through, capture them if possible. Kill them if necessary. Mernus made the Benomian Alliance swear to bring the bodies to him.

CHAPTER 36
The Assault on the Grand Palace

Cuere paced back and forth along the southern rampart of the Grand Palace. He waited for Mernus' army to deliver the terms of surrender. He wore a long oiled skin coat with a hood to protect him from the steady drizzle. The soldiers accompanying Cuere on the rampart watched with disdain, stepping aside as he walked passed. Metal objects clanked under his coat as he paced. One of the soldiers pointed in his direction curiously.

The cloud of doom hovering over Seth's army angered Cuere. Hopelessness soaked the army to the core. The hopelessness stagnated and the reek of defeat emanated from each soldier that defended the Grand Palace. The soldiers might not live through the battle, but Cuere's resolve for his own survival did not falter. This was his day of power incarnate, no proxies to demonstrate his power, as were the Sky Demons, no using his power to strengthen a fledgling king. Today, in the next few moments, he sincerely needed to burn somebody, preferably to a crisp.

Finally, a muddy rebel soldier with a white flag rode up to the wall and stood up in his stirrups defiantly.

The rebel soldier cleared his throat and spat on the soupy mud. He shouted, "Lord Mernus, leader of the Obenite Rebellion, fights to free the land from the evil King Seth and his sorcerer Lord Cuere. He demands your unconditional surrender and that you turn over King Seth and Lord Cuere immediately."

Cuere looked down at the rebel soldier and threw open his overcoat, revealing all sorts of artifacts inside.

He detached an object that looked like a reed with a seedpod on the end, made of silver and about twice as thick. He spoke to it and pointed toward the emissary who had turned his horse to flee. A stream of fire erupted from the seedpod, grazing the emissary and causing the horse to rear up. The blast from Cuere's reed left the once muddy ground smoldering. Cuere fired again with one long steady stream of fire. The blast hit the rebel emissary square on. Only a charred patch of dirt remained. Those who could see Cuere gawked at him. Those who could not see turned in Cuere's direction anyway. Cuere saw respect and wonder in their eyes as cheering broke out.

Cuere thought, "Finally, this is the respect I deserve. They cheer my name and no other."

Mernus' army stormed the walls. Cuere held an artifact in each hand. With his left hand, Cuere protected himself from the arrows with an invisible shield produced from a glowing ball. With his right hand, he spoke to and shook the reed, releasing searing blasts that struck charging soldiers two or three at a time.

Seth's army took courage. Hundred of arrows swooshed toward Mernus' forces. Cuere wondered from where all the archers came; they didn't seem to be there moments earlier. Cuere ran along the ramparts flinging destructive bolts until Mernus' forces withdrew in fear. Mernus' army never got a chance to raise ladders in an attempt to scale the walls. Cuere stood on the wall watching the retreat. They were out of range of his reed. The soldiers cheered and gathered around Cuere. He raised his hands and yelled at them. They drew back with a gasp.

Cuere chuckled. He could not stop himself. The chuckle turned in a full-hearted guffaw. He never laughed so hard in all his life. The soldiers looked at one another and began to chuckle, too. Finally, they laughed with him, keeping a careful eye and putting even more space between themselves and Cuere.

Three weeks later, about noon, a soldier knocked on Cuere's door. When told to enter, he came breathlessly into the room and reported a new attack. Cuere gathered his things and rushed to the wall. Mernus' army tried a new tactic. They approached with a rolling tower, shielded from top to bottom with metal. Four wheels allowed rebel soldiers to move the tower. Cuere did not know what was inside the tower. He did not want to find out, either. He used the reed. A blast hit the shielded tower. Some exposed lashing started to burn. Other than that, Cuere's blast had no effect.

Everyone looked at him for an answer. He left the rampart and returned shortly.

"Behold," Cuere boasted. "the power of your master."

He lifted a jet black orb-like head with both hands. Cuere possessed nothing else like it. Jagged teeth filled the open mouth. Flattened nostrils flared and four short horns jutted out of the forehead.

He held it up to the left and then the right. The men drew back. He turned toward the attacking army and spoke to the artifact. A red beam erupted from the head. The thing sounded like a dragon's roar. It hit the structure and pulverized the top half. The head took several moments to recharge. He directed it at a few exposed soldiers. The beam hit them. All that remained was a hole in the ground from the impact.

Careful to take cover because he had nothing but the wall for protection, Cuere ran from place to place trying to keep the attack at bay from all sides. Frequently, he chanced exposing himself to make sure he actually could hit something before he fired. Cuere struck the advancing line repeatedly, but the rebels kept coming.

The captain of the guard approached Cuere. "There are too many of them. You can't kill 'em all by yourself. Give us a way to defend ourselves. Put a man on each wall with one of those magic reeds or a dragon's head like that one. Teach them to use it."

"No," Cuere yelled selfishly.

"If you don't, the palace is lost," argued the captain.

Cuere submitted, but he had only one artifact he could teach them to use quickly. Reluctantly, Cuere took the reed and separated it in two lengthwise pieces. The range and power decreased but it still remained deadly. Cuere turned to the captain and pointed. "Get your second and meet me over there.

Cuere reasoned, "There is no degree of dead. Whether it burns them to a crisp or simply kills, dead is dead."

Once safely behind cover, Cuere gave each man one half of the reed. Cuere spoke to both pieces of the reed, "Cintpyursee nakocvsee dsee vakocz atyurvsee." He then addressed the captain and his second. "Both of you repeat these words, "Intn, dakocs, trolimes, test ujetsu."

The two officers attempted the words.

"No," Cuere snapped, "the first two are correct. Listen carefully; tro-lim-mes, test, u-jet-tsu."

The two officers tried again. Immediately, they both grimaced in pain.

"It appears you got it right," Cuere smirked.

"Now..." Cuere moved their arms gingerly away from his direction. "I have given the... magic reed permission to recognize and obey you. All you have to say is..." He leaned and whispered in their ears, "Seetyurve." They both repeated the words. The magic reeds fired. One blast burned a black spot into the rampart, the other hit an archer who fell from rampart screaming and in flames.

"And do be careful," Cuere added.

Mernus' forces withdrew. All night long, Mernus' forces felt out Cuere's defenses. Cuere became exhausted and beleaguered. By morning, their enemy fought from a distance, out of reach of his magic reeds and dragon's head.

The siege went on for weeks. Cuere resisted revealing any more artifacts than those used to purify water, and to fuse metal for repairs. Cuere used the magic reed to disintegrate the dead animals flung by the enemy catapults. He needed to hold the base of the Heno Plateau for as long as possible. Mernus could go around him but the treacherous passes made ambushes very likely. A relatively few soldiers could cause serious harm to Mernus'forces.

A mighty crash knocked Cuere from his feet. He rushed outside only to see soldiers fleeing for cover, retreating from the wall. Several more crashes shook them. He grabbed one of the fleeing soldiers. "What is going on?"

"They have a new weapon!"

"What kind of magic is this?" asked Cuere.

"No magic, sir. Stones flung from something that looks like a catapult. The stones are thrown from a greater distance and faster, though. The attack is beyond the range of the magic reeds. The walls are buckling. Everyone is retreating underground for the last assault."

For a moment Cuere thought of riding out with his artifacts and single-handedly taking on Mernus' army. Next, he considered taking an attack force to act as additional shielding for him. As he thought, the image of one of the huge stones hurtling through the air down on his head discouraged further contemplation. He did not have any artifact that could stop that...yet.

"Go get your captain and his second," Cuere ordered.

Cuere retrieved his reed from the two men, then led them through the palace. They carried a trunk with them.

In the king's quarters, Cuere opened a secret passage that led down into a newly completed tunnel. They waited at the exit until nightfall. Cuere imagined the palace was overrun. Now that there were gaping holes in the walls, his direct involvement in the fight was an unnecessary danger. After all, though powerful, he was only one man. Besides, he needed to buy time, not for Seth, but for himself.

He understood more of the ancient text than ever. It all opened up for Cuere. He needed to get back to Obenin's Temple where Stannick protected his scrolls. He needed time to sort out the ancient numbers that told the location of things. Cuere needed money, a ship and an escape route. Once he had that, he wouldn't need King Seth or Charge Stannick anymore.

Cuere gave the captain a glows to hold. He hid his face menacingly behind his coat. When he lowered it, they gawked in disbelief. Before them, Cuere stood disguised as a man twice his age, with a red beard and a crooked back. They exited the tunnel and fled in the darkness.

CHAPTER 37
Seth and Cue're Under Siege

Seth slouched on his throne in the Primary Temple, looking at the back of his hand. His fingertips lightly brushed the hair just over a thumbnail sized brown spot on his albinoid skin. Brock Stannick stood a couple of paces away.

"Is this a sign from you, Father, that you have forgiven me. Will I be like everyone else?"

He loved the brown patch of color on his skin. It appeared just after breakfast below the knuckle of his ring finger.

"It is a good omen among this tragedy," Seth continued.

The battle for Heno left his forces scattered and disorganized. His forces fought well but many saw the sudden departure of Lord Cuere, the captain, and his second as desertion. As a result, Seth's co-conspirators deserted him as well. After such bold talk and grandstanding, they wasted away like yesterday's breakfast.

Previously, he tried to woo Glynwith just as much as Mernus did. Appeasing them seemed to work. For a while, their half-hearted support for Mernus eased.

His search for Octun turned up nothing. Deep within his homeland, searching him out proved harder than finding a shadow in the dark, virtually nonexistent. Those loyal to Octun killed his spies, male and female alike. He need not look any further, Glynwith and Mernus threatened his doorstep.

He regretted not hitting Glynwith with everything he had. Even if he had not completely conquered them, the fight might have caught them off guard. The attack would have weakened them and he would be far better off than he was, even with Carden in the fight.

"Fortunetelling must not be a part of Cuere's bag of tricks," he fumed at the thought.

"Where can I go? We cannot escape over the mountains. The Bards, Cards, and the Tenzians hate me." He held his hand up to the light to get a better look at the little brown patch.

"Aspharia is no good, they hate us more than all the Benomian Alliance put together. If there is bad blood between our relatives within the Benomian Alliance, there is bad body, soul, and spirit with Aspharia... except in Mpolu," he paused considering his words.

Radiating pain spread from the base of his neck to his temples, watering his eyes so much that a tear rolled down his cheek. He put his head on his knees. Covering his head with his hands, he barked at Stannick, "Is any more left?"

"No, my lord, there is no more potion left. Maybe Lord Cuere can help."

"Ha," scorned Seth. "After what he did, do you think I would let him give me anything? He seeks power now. He tasted it at Heno. He will not let it go." His eyes squinted, studying Stannick as if to perceive some tiny change in him. The way Stannick returned the look caused him to question.

"He is trying to kill me, too, the one person who never failed me save that dog, Gremal. Yet, he laughs at me whilst plotting my doom."

Seth squeezed the sides of his head with his forearms. Thousands of tiny strands of wooly yarn pulled it in every direction, rending his brain to bits. His vision blurred.

Though Cuere and his general challenged every inch of ground, he wanted them to fight harder, to sacrifice themselves for him.

"To let Mernus beat them at every turn is unforgivable," he accused out loud.

The demons in the mountains wanted him to act as a puppet. He hated thinking of them. Every morning he hated looking up to a sky he could no longer trust. Mernus wanted him dead. Cuere should be fighting, not cowering in the temple.

"I defy them all," he grumbled.

Thoughts of Cuere made his skin tingle in warning. A sixth sense nagged at him, trying to keep him from danger.

"The seasons have no meaning." His head throbbed. "The demons are out to make a mockery of me. They want my body, my soul and my kingdom. Why can't you kill them?"

Seth waited for an answer.

"Answer me, Stannick."

"We have all tried," replied Stannick, uncertainty ringing in his tone. "We have all failed."

"We are doomed to desolation unless we worship them. Pestilence and famine persist. Whoever heard of famine when there is rain. Nature rises to spite me."

Stannick rebutted, "Nature has very little to do with anything anymore. A dangerously monotonous routine controls everything. Some already worship toward the mountains. Obenites and Benomians alike have tried to appease the Hands of Obenin by building a temple in the Abringian Mountains. Despite the war, your subjects worked feverously to complete it. When the rest of the kingdom noticed that the area suffered less than the rest, altars and small buildings dedicated to them sprung up all over the place. It is how we survive here at the Primary Temple."

Seth got up from his throne. He looked at his hand again. He stroked the hairs above the spot. Turning toward the huge portrait of his great-grandfather, he regretted not ordering the royal artist to paint a portrait of himself with the crown upon his head. He thought there would be ample time after his victory over the Benomian Alliance. Now, he had no victory, only defeat.

He looked at Stannick, scowling, "They are just sitting there. What were they waiting for?"

"They... you mean Mernus, sir?"

"Who else would I be talking about," Seth yelled.

Seth rubbed the back of his neck and then massaged his temples firmly.

"My lord, you must eat something."

"They will poison me. They tried before."

"I will prepare it for you, if you trust no one else."

"Don't tell me what to do," Seth ordered.

Seth eyed Stannick's uncertainty.

"Then what, how shall I serve you?" asked Stannick.

"Where is Lord Cuere?"

Stannick shrugged.

"Go and fetch him."

Stannick called the guard.

"He will want to know the reason he is pulled from his work."

"Tell him his king demands it."

Lord Cuere entered the room. He carried a scroll and a knurled rod he used like a walking cane. It made very little noise when it hit the floor.

"Look at this," he held his hand to Cuere. "Do you think it is a sign that Father forgives me?"

Cuere looked at the spot curiously.

"Or is he after me? He knows what I did to him, what we did to him," his eyes distant as he looked at his hands again.

"Sire, I have served you well," Cuere returned, picking up displeasure in Seth's tone.

"You served yourself," Seth accused.

"You supplied the ambition. I supplied the means."
"Failed ambition, failed means. It is fate for our crimes. Or did you lie to me from the beginning?"

"I did not lie! What happened could not have been foreseen by anyone. I had them under control and then Octun interfered. He defied our authority in front of them. It affected them, causing them to escape. He is to blame for this calamity."

Cuere's words struck something in Seth. "Octun, he loved my father. He loved me once. I think he loved me more than Father did. Octun taught me. He corrected me. Then, in a flash, he vanished. Father sent him away."

Cuere stated, "We are alike in many ways. Both of us are victims of others' incompetence. We are visionaries limited by those who have sworn to support us and even by those who raised us."

Not knowing how to respond, Seth brought his hands to his face. With his fists clenched, he pressed his temples as if trying to keep his head from exploding. His signet ring dug into his skin. His eyes did not look into this world. Blood trickled down his face. "My skin... my skin, it is not yellow like yours or black like Octun's."

"My lord, it is only a nick," lied Cuere.

Seth touched his face. "See my blood..." He wiped it with his finger and offered it to Cuere.

Lord Cuere withdrew.

"It is red... just like any other man's...," Seth whined. "There is sin in it, just like any other man's.... My mother, she was the cause... my father... his love did this to me.... I am alone.... This is his revenge from the grave... the spirits told him what I did.... Children, they are so cruel, children can be. But soon it is forgotten and they are friends again...we blame everyone else for our failure don't we?"

"Don't despair, my lord. Here in the scrolls, there is an answer, the word of a southern oracle. I understand everything now. This is not over. We must find a way to escape."

Seth's jaw did not move as he spoke the words. "It is over, Cuere." Finality bent his words eerily.

"My lord, listen to me. There is a way. It is all here in the scrolls. The artifacts are the key. The scrolls tell you what to do. It is plain to me now. I don't see why I did not comprehend it before. We have to find a way to escape this place. We have to find the courage. You are courageous, my lord."

"It is too late." Seth's eyes narrowed. Veins popped in his head.

"I should have been so brave as to take vengeance out on my father like you. My plans were too complicated, too ostentatious. I should have used more base means to do it. Just as you did," Cuere said, trying to sound sincere. He approached Seth, put one hand on his shoulder and raised his staff slowly.

Seth ground his teeth in painful recollection. *Perhaps this is the only thing that Cuere is totally right about,* he thought.

Instead of comfort, it brought rage. He wanted to take it all back.

"There is nothing I can do!" Seth shouted.

"Lord Cuere, can't you see the king is disturbed? Leave now," ordered Stannick.

Cuere wheeled around threateningly. "I am Lord Cuere, master of the unknown. I understand mysteries you never will. You do not order me."

Cuere's staff sprung to life. Stannick tried to draw his sword. His head still toward the ceiling and feet toward the floor, Stannick ended up spread-eagle in mid-air, gagging and turning blue.

"There is nothing I can do but avenge him," roared Seth.

Cuere's blood ran cold.

Seth could not stop himself. As Cuere fell, Seth was on top of him, plunging the dagger into his hands, arms, face, neck and chest, purging himself of every ounce of guilt, every sinful deed, every bit of treachery. He wanted all of it to transfer from his heart into the blade and into Lord Cuere. Seth stopped in exhaustion and wept bitterly.

Stannick stood dumbfounded.

Seth, still on his knees, moved away from Cuere. He looked at the blood on his hands and then on his body. It was all over him, from head to toe. He removed his cloak and attempted to wipe the blood from his hands.

"Bring me water," he yelled.

Stannick retrieved a basin of water from the other side of the room and placed it by Seth.

Seth scrubbed his hands, sobbing all the while.

"The spot," he lamented. "It is gone. I am not forgiven."

Seth grabbed the dagger, threw his head back and put it to his chest. He pushed with all his might but the dagger would not move. He could not do it. Though he tried several times, suicide was not possible.

He lamented, "Kill me. Kill me."

****

Stannick pitied Seth and hung his head only to see fresh blood on his own britches and boots. He had not escaped the stain.

"Burn it," Stannick ordered.

The palace guards looked shocked.

Stannick answered the question in their eyes. "I did not kill Cuere. King Seth did it himself."

"But why, sir?" one of the guards asked.

"Someone had to atone for this. Just be glad it was not any of us."

Staring pityingly at Seth, the guards gathered Cuere's remains.

One asked, "And what of the king?"

"Clean him up and take care of him. Tell the generals what has happened."

"They will not believe us."

"Show them the king," returned Stannick. "It is over, they can give him over in exchange for their lives."

"And you?"

"I am afraid there in no bargaining for me."

CHAPTER 38
Parmos and Jared, Power Unleashed

Trying hard to find some solitude, Ulthea closed her eyes and breathed deeply. She wanted to clear her mind, to push back the world that closed in on her. It had been over five years since escaping together. Parmos and Jared had been fighting ever since. The conflict between Parmos and Jared made everything too small. She tired of playing mediator between them. Usually she agreed with Jared, even though his brash manner made her want to slap him sometimes. She spent a lot of time in her wind form just to get away from them, so much time that it weakened her physical body.

The kingdoms on both sides of the mountain worked on their temples with religious dedication. So far, they saw a total of five, more than they asked for. Solid white flags flew over every place that worshipped them. Groups of women dressed in white carried on at the temple sites as if spirits possessed them. She thought of how each of them would soon have their own place to live and not be bothered with each other.

She put on her clothes and walked off. She thought clearly now, but she must talk to Ictheos first. She climbed on all fours up the ledge that ran along the mouth of one of Ictheos' hiding places. Not that she had to, but she needed time to focus her thoughts. Ictheos became difficult at times. His sarcasm and twisted sense of humor made talking to him very challenging. Getting a straight answer was like trying to pull a tooth from a crocodile.

She faced another uphill climb. She checked her footing; slowly, she climbed until she felt a hand on her wrist. She let out a little gasp.

Ictheos pulled her up.

"You must really want to see me," he quipped.

She sat down on the edge of the smooth, narrow, oval-shaped tunnel that sometimes sucked things into it. The tunnel sloped slightly downward. This made it very hard to navigate when using her power to move her body short distances. One wrong move and there was no time to recover before you bashed against the rocky ledges below.

Ulthea looked at the scattered debris that disappeared into the darkness. "Probably why he chose it," she figured. "It has the leave-me-alone feeling to it."

She looked out over the warm springs. The view over the treetops wasn't bad. The entire west end of the area was in view.

Ulthea knew of at least four of these openings. It looked manmade, very similar to the Barren Lands.

Sighing deeply, she said, "We have got to do something about Jared and Parmos. I didn't think it could get any worse, but it has."

"We. Who is this *we* person? Anyway, they don't bother me. I've been waiting for the fight. So far, it is just words and more words, years and years of words."

"Ictheos, I am serious." She pushed his shoulder.

"And I'm not?"

"Ah! Men, a curse on all of you."

Ictheos got off his knees, sat down and crossed his legs. She turned to face him.

Ulthea placed a hand on his calf.

"Why does Parmos hold on to his desire to change the hearts and minds of the Obenites. The rest of us gave that up already."

Ictheos nodded, "We surely did."

"And Jared, I agree with him. We have to sustain ourselves. We can't live here forever."

"Sure can't."

Ulthea scowled at him.

"What do you want from me? I'm here. I'm listening," returned Ictheos.

"But, Jared, ah! His head is like a rock. He treats me like he owns me." Ulthea pointed her finger. "I know, you said it before. If I let him, he does."

Ictheos smirked, then threw in, "When are you going to confess that you love him. He knows it. We all know it."

Ulthea slapped his calf and smiled. "What if they are really fighting over you?" he asked unexpectedly.

It caught her off guard. The thought both scared and amused her.

"Do you think it is really about me?"

He looked at her. "Isn't it obvious?"

"Parmos, he is so wild looking."

Scratching his chin, Ictheos' faced twitched in vexation. He replied, "We all look wild."

"You know what I mean. He is wild in every way. Jared, he is so confident, dashing, even."

"I'd like to dash his head in with a rock, sometimes."

"Ictheos!"

They sat quietly for a few minutes. Ictheos looked out over the treetops. She studied his face. `His hair was much longer, down around his shoulders. The curiosity and brightness of his face left a year ago. A long sullen look of dissatisfaction replaced it.

"What's that?" asked Ulthea.

"What's what?"

"You know what I am talking about, all that hanging around your neck."

"You tell me." He leaned over to her.

She held the figures in her hand.

"Can I see?"

Ictheos took them off and gave them to her.

She separated the necklaces and looked at them one by one. Each fascinated her.

"What do they mean?" She paused knowing his answer. "Figure it out for myself, I know, I know."

The old piece of leather had a tree etched in the middle. At first, she thought it was the same as Levid wore around his neck. Only this had curvy lines on both sides of the tree. A word rose from her lips. A foreign word that sounded familiar.

"Lompolasona," she whispered. "This is for Lompolasona, the balance of good and bad spirits."

"Home, our village, like Father said, before anyone came." He said it warmly, as if he wanted to be there.

She did not know how to reply.

The next one puzzled her for a while. She looked at it and thought. Then, she realized what it was suppose to be, a blazing sun. "It looks like a flower. This is supposed to be a symbol for Obenin."

She held up another. She turned it and looked closely, trying to detect something special about it.

"I give up. What is it supposed to be?"

"I don't know."

"What do you mean, I don't know. You made it," she chided.

"It is us. I just don't know what to put on it yet."

"Us?"

"Yes, the four of us or the three of us since Parmos still isn't convinced."

She decided to talk more about this later. After all, they needed more than a white flag, maybe a symbol, a statue, or something on their temples.

The last necklace hung lower than the others. When she asked why, he stated, "Just seemed like the right thing to do at the time."

She recognized it as the symbol of the Spirit Men; they called it a cross and always spoke of it reverently.

Later that day, she heard Parmos and Jared arguing. She started to walk away. Instead, she found herself running toward them. From the tone of their voices, she knew this was the one. When she saw them, she immediately knew something bad was about to happen. She tried to intervene.

Ictheos stopped her. "This has to happen. It is the only way to settle it. They have to fight."

This time, Ulthea relented.

Parmos confronted Jared defiantly. Jared did not back down.

Ictheos framed the argument. "Neither one cares for right or wrong. They care only about winning."

"We are not gods," argued Parmos, his fist clenched in emotion. Standing as tall, he stood a head above Jared.

Jared moved closer to Parmos and poked him in the chest.

"I don't care what you think. Ulthea and Ictheos both agree with me. Why don't you come to your senses so we can do what we must?"

"Must!" Parmos raged. "The bad things that you do are wrong. It destroys hope."

"And I suppose those soldiers we often find hiding in the mountains are just coming to play hide and seek."

"They fear us."

"And they should," retorted Jared. "You are stupid enough to believe all those lies. Let me show you what a real god can do."

Ulthea watched in dismay. No more would they be four, but three if any of them made it through this day.

Jared swept his hands over his head. Air swirled around Parmos, then thickened. Grimacing, Parmos struggled to breathe. He closed his eyes and summoned his concentration. Slowly the air mass loosened. Then, with a push outward with both hands, it broke. The shockwave knocked Jared down to the ground and sent a wave of air howling through the trees.

The move surprised Ulthea. Then she smiled. Parmos turned out to be more capable than she expected. Jared was not about to beat him without some bruises of his own.

"This is turning out to be more interesting than I thought it would," remarked Ictheos, his amusement obvious. "Evidently, while we have been practicing mischief, he has been practicing for a fight."

"Octun did not lie to us," argued Parmos.

Jared glanced at Ulthea. Jared blurred from her sight. Parmos came into view. She smiled coyly at Parmos.

"You're a villain. Why did you do that?" Ictheos joked.

"I don't know. I just couldn't help myself. You are a bad influence."

"Now Jared is going to be really mad," chuckled Ictheos.

Jared stood. He patted the dust from his clothes in stiff hard strokes.

"They were still lies," his words in time with the swat of his hands against his clothing.

"The Obenite god is dead, a slimy, mummified mass of putrid flesh preserved in a sarcophagus. I will show them whom to serve."

Jared took his wind form. His body grew weak. He fell down and rolled over on his back looking upward.

Ulthea ran over to him. His eyes were still open.

"He should not have done that so quickly." Ulthea felt Jared's cheeks.

As if he were preparing to meditate, Parmos squatted with his legs crossed. His body slumped.

"There they go," remarked Ictheos looking up into the sky.

"Ictheos, stay here and guard us," directed Ulthea.

"Why do I have to miss all the fun?" replied Ictheos.

Ulthea followed Jared and Parmos. In her wind form, she sensed them and saw their aura in the distance.

Jared headed into Bardia. She questioned why. They traveled a great distance. Then she saw it, a large city teeming with people.

Jared caused the clouds to amass over the city until the sky looked like a deadly dawn. Thunder rolled across the sky. Long tentacle of lightning flashed. The people fled indoors, pulling their shutters. They believed it would help.

Lightning struck Parmos' wind form. It had no affect. She sensed that he was fine.

Parmos struggled with the storm, trying to resist Jared's power. The power from New Oracle started to radiate. She felt it as never before. Jared and Parmos were like fires needing wood. New Oracle stoked them.

By solidifying the elements and the shear speed, Jared battered the south wall of the city until it buckled.

Parmos swarmed around Jared, who kept up the attack.

For a moment, Ulthea lost sight of Parmos, but still sensed him. He spread himself through the clouds. Parmos became a part of the storm. No matter how hard Jared tried, he could not make the storm any worse. The lightning strikes decreased. The driving rain eased.

Jared left the area, leaving Parmos to deal with the storm. With no interference from Jared, Parmos was able to break the cohesion of the storm, freeing him to follow Jared.

Ulthea lingered and watched. How the people scattered from Jared's approach. Even during the somewhat brief encounter, one of the walls lay in ruin. For a moment, she considered helping Parmos. Instead, she found comfort in the destructive power they controlled. The people in the city might give anything to keep that sort of damage away from their city. They could have anything they wanted... anything.

Jared attacked another city. The deluge of rain swelled the river. People fled the threatening flood despite the driving rain. They did not have time to take anything with them.

The swelling river fascinated Ulthea. She flew across the cresting river waves. She wanted more. She wanted it to bathe her. Spreading herself out, she desired the river to cover her, but it did not. As the water level rose, so did she. She wanted Jared to make it rain even harder. But the rain was stopping.

"Parmos!" She smote the surface of the river.

She tried to increase the storm and make the flooded river cover her form. Maybe if she helped Jared, it could happen. She felt Parmos fighting them both.

****

The ground moved under Icthoes' feet. Then it shook violently, causing boulders to fall from the cliffs. He sweated profusely. His whole body tingled and itched. Screeches erupted from the caverns.

Maybe fighting was not such a good idea after all, thought Ictheos. *They are tearing this place apart.*

****

Frustrated, Ulthea did not believe how well Parmos fought them off. The rain minling with her wind form bought her gratification as well as torment. She danced in pleasure. She writhed in pain. Yet, she wanted more.

Parmos denied her more of her obsession. He locked them in battle for hours. The storm lost its momentum, and she and Jared could not bring it back.

Jared moved on again. The water compelled her. She found it hard to move away. Jared and Parmos left her behind. With all her will power, she finally pulled herself away from the tormenting river and followed.

Lightening flashed in sheets. She knew that the known world would remember this night as the night the world almost ended.

Jared attempted to cut a path of destruction from Bardia to the Aspharian Sea. He wanted to spare no one from the grief.

Over Obenin's Primary Temple, Jared bristled at the sight of it, despite seeing their flags. He tried to strike the north tower. Ulthea stopped him. He didn't try anymore but moved on toward Glynwith. Parmos, in hot pursuit, countered Jared's every turn all the way to the Yan Free Territory.

Ulthea sensed a shifting dark purpose in Jared. He left Parmos to dissipate the latest storm. She knew Parmos understood Jared's intent; still, he did not follow. Parmos did not want anyone else to suffer.

She followed Jared for hours until she saw the Abringian Mountains before her. She deduced his plan.

"No, Jared, don't," she begged.

Jared hovered over Parmos.

Ulthea entered into her physical body.

"Itcheos," she moaned. "Help me."

Ictheos helped her to her feet.

She motioned him toward Parmos.

"Jared, don't hurt him."

She flopped down on Parmos, knocking him over. She wrapped her arms around him with all her failing strength. Ictheos put a protective pocket of air around them. Parmos moaned under her weight. She looked behind her.

"Jared no!" she screamed.

She sensed Jared's hate for Parmos. It penetrated her being. For a moment, she thought he might go through her to get to Parmos. He hovered around them for a long time, then stormed away. She had saved Parmos for now.

She held Parmos' head in her lap. "Parmos, you have to give in to him, or you have to leave. Please, I don't want anything to happen to you."

Back in his body, Parmos touched her cheek. His hands felt cold and wet.

Ictheos looked at them both. He did not say anything. Ulthea expected some joke or wisecrack. Instead, Ictheos removed his necklaces and placed them all around Parmos' neck.

Over the next few days, she and Ictheos helped Parmos collect supplies and moved him to a completely separate area of the caverns. The morning after the new moon, Parmos left.

CHAPTER 39
The Personal Test of Godhood

Small rocks crumpled down the side of the mountain. Jared hesitated, then walked on. Instead of turning into the caverns, he walked along toward the springs where Ulthea bathed. His pace slowed and he lowered his head, pretending to be in troubled thoughts. He headed toward a little group of trees. Though he walked, at one point his feet no longer touched the ground.

Once in the trees, he moved quickly to flank his attacker.

"How dare you enter into my domain. You will never leave," Jared shouted.

Jared's eyes grew wide with impossibility. His mouth gaped. No one was there. Too late, he had fallen for the ruse.

He wheeled around. Something hit his chest, just to the left of his right shoulder. He looked at it. A short arrow with a thick shaft, buried up to its vanes, stuck out of him.

Jared looked at his blood streaming down his chest. With his wind form, he soared upward. Power surged in him, then lulled, leaving him disoriented. Vengeance blackened his waning thoughts. He tried to crush his assailant. The wind whirled. He mustered only a gentle breeze that stirred the dust, making his attacker shield his eyes. After the arguing and fighting, Parmos was right, after all. No transformation, no godhood, no existence apart from his body, only emptiness and a painful immersion into darkness, death met him without absolution.

****

Again and again, Ulthea dipped herself in the hot spring. Maybe they had not done the right thing by Parmos. Right was such a relative term these days. Was it really their only choice?

She dipped again, staying down, holding her breath. The thought crossed her mind that, of all the great power she possessed, especially in her wind form, she could not do the simplest things -- easily judge how big or how small something was, or dip under the water.

The pressure in her lungs increased. How long could she stay under, not long enough. She shot to the surface. Her mouth gasped in air to rescue her aching lungs.

She grew dizzy. Her world spun. She closed her eyes to try to steady herself. When she opened them, someone stood over her.

It took her a second to focus. Despite the gray-streaked beard and clothing that made him look like a wild animal, it was Octun.

"Why was he here?"

Then she saw it. Octun lifted his crossbow. He aimed it at her. Before she could say a word, she felt herself growing cold in the warm spring water.

****

Octun devised the entire plan. He put it into action. Once he heard Carden's king imply that the Great Rift gave covered access into the deepest parts of Mount Kaob, he knew what to do. Though his enemy was powerful, they were inexperienced and predictable. They did not alter their routines. Forest animals went into burrows, birds roosted until certain times, when the Sky

Demons patrolled the mountains. He concealed himself during the times he might have been exposed and moved with patience. His Carden guide had taken him to the entrance of the warm springs and turned back.

Not once did they detect him. This was his first opportunity to get them all. He knew where they all were. Now was the time to strike.

He pulled Ulthea out of the hot spring. It was not deep enough to conceal her entire body.

"Aaahhh!"

Octun reached for his dagger. Before he could, he found himself unable to move. He struggled with the invisible force. The more he struggled, the invisible vice squeezed him more.

"What have you done? What have you done!" Ictheos screamed. "Ulthea."

Octun felt himself falling. He slammed into the ground. The jolt knocked the breath out of him. He writhed and wriggled trying to break his bonds. He was not finished. He had to hold on. He hit the ground again. He felt his thighbone break.

Everything blurred. He wondered where he was. The last thing he remembered was watching Jared and plotting to kill him. That was it. Ictheos. He heard sobbing. Octun moved his right arm, no pain. He moved him left arm. Pain racked him but he could use it. He slipped out his dagger, slid it under his body and put it in his right hand. He hid it as best he could.

Octun moaned weakly.

Someone turned him over. Ictheos came into view.

Octun watched his features change from anger to shock. Ictheos recognized him.

He yelled at the top of his breath, "How could you do this Keeper?"

Octun coughed. He tasted blood. He hoped he would not drown in it; then again, it may be better than

suffering for hours or days until death took him. Or
would Ictheos finish the job?

He tried to speak. It came out weak and mumbled.
For a moment, he closed his eyes. Then he smelled
Ictheos' breath. He coughed again and tried to speak.

He moved his left arm a hair at a time. He winced
in pain, but remained determined. He moved his right arm
trying to get just the right angle so as to not lose grip on
the dagger.

"Because. . . you . . . are evil ...."

Ictheos tried to pull away, too late. With his left
arm, he pulled Ictheos down onto the blade. It plunged
into his side. He held Ictheos onto it, digging and twisting,
hoping to hit something vital. Ictheos wrestled off the
dagger. Octun pulled him back creating a new wound.
Ictheos went limp on top of him.

Dying seemed such an easy thing. All he had to do
was lie there. With most of his body numb, he did not feel
much pain. Death, his death, differed from how he
imagined it or for what he hoped. As a soldier, he never
imagined getting old. Each day was potentially his last.
Fate did not spare others he thought stronger and better.
Yet, here he lay.

An idea struck him. This war ended at the hands of
one hero who saved the known world from servitude. He
reconsidered; this promised to be a much better death than
he ever imagined.

"Ryhad's Inn will swell with business. A name
change was appropriate. Namiberro was such a small
matter compared to this."

For once, he let himself gloat in his own
achievement. This time he surely had the right to do so.

Hold on. Finish the job. Parmos is coming, resolved
Octun.

Octun opened his eyes. A campfire burned. The stars twinkled at him. "They are waiting for me. What is taking so long?"

Someone was crying. He could not see who it was. Involuntarily, his eyes opened as small slits. He forced them open wider and turned his head.

A mass of yellow hair came into his view.

He moaned.

Parmos looked at him. Parmos was saying something. Whatever he said sounded whiny. He wished it would stop.

Octun fought off a blackout.

The fog in his mind lifted and he saw through it. He did not know how long it would last, so he had to act.

He managed to whisper, "Parmos."

Parmos wept bitterly, "I am so sorry. I tried to help. I tried to stop them, but I could not. I tried to stop them."

Octun worked his fingers to get the blood back into his left arm. It still worked.

Bit by bit he inched upward.

Parmos repositioned himself to look into Octun's eyes. Octun stopped his movement.

Something rubbed across his face. What was it? "Necklaces," thought Octun.

Then he saw it. The pattern Ryhad spoke of, the one he remembered from his childhood, his mother's favorite pattern, it dangled right in front of his face.

With a sudden move, he grabbed for the necklace. Parmos struggled to get away. The string broke.

Octun held the necklace up and looked at the little cross. He put it on his chest, and took a deep breath.

****

Parmos kneeled beside Octun. The scene smacked of distant pain, on his knees, alone, with those who were supposed to care for him fading away, leaving him alone with an uncertain destiny.

Parmos returned here only because he really had no place else to go. He could not blend in with the people of the land. Coming back would give him time to make a better plan. Then he saw this. He could not believe his own eyes. After so much death, Octun's face looked peaceful, no worried lines, no concern, just peaceful. Parmos rubbed the back of his neck. A growing sense that he was not alone nagged him. Had Octun not acted alone?

He spun around and raised his hands to attack.

"No. I will not let you activate your energy form."

Parmos could not even blink an eye. Whatever the figure did sent a vicious pain coursing through his torso. Someone stood in the middle of a bright light. The light brightened and ebbed with the patter of his words.

"Calm yourself. I am not here to hurt you."

"Doesn't feel like it," Parmos thought.

He tried to use his power to release himself from the trap. Nothing helped. His powers did not work.

"We apologize for your turmoil," the figure remarked, his tone was monotone and worn out. Parmos noticed, that as the figure spoke, a warm sensation filled him.

"I am Vector Technician Serion Carrico Platt. You may call me, Serion. I have come to disable the portal."

"Portal," thought Parmos.

"The phenomenon in yonder cave," Serion responded.

Parmos realized, *He is reading my thoughts.*

This Serion kept him from moving. He knew everything, his every thought. *How can I fight this?*

"There is no reason to establish a conflict between us. I can disengage. If you attempt to activate the energy spectrum, I will immobilize you again," answered Serion.

Parmos picked up on Serion's frostbitten seriousness. Though he did not understand everything the man in the light said, he understood enough to know he meant business.

A series of clicks and buzzes came from the light. Parmos ended up on his knees. The sudden release left his entire body stinging, not enough to be excruciatingly painful but enough for Serions's warning to keep Parmos very conscious of his actions.

"Who..., what are you?" Parmos asked, afraid to look directly at the light.

The light dimmed. "Serion," He seemed frustrated to Parmos. "I have come to disable the portal."

"Portal?"

The light dimmed more. He could almost make out the man's face.

"The portal in yonder cave."

The light brightened. A bar of light covered Parmos from head to toe, then turned into a small dot and disappeared.

"The big hole in the wall from which your energy comes."

"You mean New Oracle?" entreated Parmos.

"Why do primals give it some mystic name? And Oracle, that's the worse," spat Serion.

The same light scanned Octun. A small device that looked like an iron rat floated out of the light. Parmos moved out of the way.

The device floated over to Octun's head and landed in his hair. Spindly legs emerged from the iron rat. They moved down Octun's neck, chattering like a squirrel.

"The others are dead, that is less work for me," remarked Serion. "But, the big guy here, I have plans for him."

"What do you mean? Leave him alone, he must be buried."

"Power down, immobilization is eminent."

A jolt hit Parmos so hard it knocked him head over heels. He landed flat on his back.

"I granted you one warning more than I usually give."

Parmos cleared his head. He looked over at Octun. The iron rat moved to Octun's neck.

"What is it doing to him?"

"He should live. The rest is not your concern."

The light moved away from him.

"Wait!" Parmos shouted. He considered snatching the iron rat off Octun.

"Don't touch it. It has less patience than me."

Parmos halted. Serion's responses to his unspoken intent and thoughts were getting the best of Parmos.

"Then I will stop pre-empting your questions," Serion stated. "Follow me if you want to ask questions. I have one hour to do five hours of work."

Parmos took one final look at the iron rat. It moved away from Octun's neck back to his head, leaving tiny tentacles buried into various parts of his body.

Parmos followed Serion to New Oracle. Never once did the aura of light fade enough for him to get a good look at his face.

Shiny metal boxes were stacked in front of New Oracle. Serion busied himself opening them up, saying only, "Stand clear out of my way."

Parmos watched him. Serion moved with the assurance of a task performed many times.

"Why did you allow them to bring me here?" Parmos finally asked.

"Them? We were not a part of, or have any knowledge of why you were teleported here."

The warm glow ebbed.

"I don't understand." Parmos' head ached from Serion's last warning. Serion's lack of answers made it hurt worse.

"Long-range scanners detected an active portal. We received attenuated signals and my instruments could not locate its source. For some reason, the signal and energy properties of this portal differ from all others. It wasn't until some time ago that the portal's activity sent out enough energy within the frequency spectrums we can consistently detect and track back to the source."

This man spoke the Obenite language clearly but in such a way that Parmos did not understand it. It was ten times worse than talking to Chancellor Levid.

"We just located this... oracle and it took a while to get here. The universe is an unfathomably immense place."

"So you made the Oracles?" asked Parmos.

"No, we did not construct the portals. Some other intelligence made them long before we discovered them. They were a viciously mischievous bunch at that. We no longer deploy through them, either. Law strictly forbids it. Thousands of years ago, we made examples of those who used the portals. It was a horrible way to somewhat die, locked inside your body like that."

Parmos thought for a moment. Realization set in.

"The Barren Lands."

"What?"

Parmos thought it funny that Serion asked him a question.

"The Barren Lands, that was the oracle. . . I mean portal that brought us here."

"How much can one technician do? What is its location and status?"

"Status?"

"Is it active?"

"Active?"

Serion's glow changed color. It had a red hue.

"What does it look like?" he snapped.

"It has dark crystals sticking from it now."

The glow remained the same hue. "What transpires on the planets of this sector?"

Parmos didn't answer. He knew he was not supposed to.

Serion set up lights and moved the cases to one side.

Serion arranged the seemingly indistinguishable cases in an order that made sense only to him. He opened the first.

He took out an object that looked like an awl. Serion looked at it, spoke to it, then gripped it with both hands. Light shot from the end of it in short bursts that bounced off the rock face of the portal in brilliant sparks. With sparks flying, he moved the beam in circles as he progressed clockwise around the opening. Serion waited, then started the same motion little wider from the mouth.

"What is going to happen to me?" Parmos raised his voice over the noise.

"It depends," returned Serion.

The answer caught him of guard. Uncertainty about Serion's truthfulness in doing him no harm started to gnaw again.

"If my directive was to terminate you, I would have done that already."

"There are things far worse than death," spat Parmos.

"Like this assignment."

Parmos heard something that sounded like a laugh. Serion stopped the circling motions and turned to address him.

"I have everything under control, trust me." He paused, then added, "Of course you don't." He returned to the circling motion.

The device chirped like a cricket and the light changed to a purplish color. Serion moved the beam in tighter circles. The light changed to red and the awl emitted a steady tone. He let it stay there for a while. When the light stopped, it left a small glowing spot on the wall.

Walking back to the case, he looked over the remaining instruments to make sure everything was there. He took out a cloth, wiped the awl and put it back into its place. He closed the case, carried it to the other side, put it down, walked back, and opened up the next case.

Parmos asked again, before the next commotion started.

"What will happen to me?"

"The spent portal may have been linked to this one. I assume it is. Your coordinates of origin are probably stored in here."

Serion pointed to the spot he marked on the wall.

"There should also be a detailed signature recording of the energy form that integrated itself into your human system. It cannot survive outside the environment provided by the portal without a host, which is one reason I wear this." The aura flickered.

Parmos thought for a moment. Serion waited a second, as if he expected Parmos to ask a question. Parmos said nothing. Serion returned to work.

This tool looked like two stable grooming brushes attached to a metal bar. The aura radiated more brightly. It seemed to rotate around him as he floated up into the air.

Serion attached the instrument to the cave wall and centered it on the mark. His aura stopped rotating. Serion floated away, and the brushes started to turn, slowly at first, then more quickly.

He retrieved the brushes with a piece of the cave wall attached to them. The aura rotated again, Serion floated down with both. The chunk of rock was as thick as the distance from his elbow to the tip of his fingers.

Serion left the brushes on the rock and moved to an entirely new case. They looked like nothing Parmos had seen before, but so did everything else, including Serion himself. Looking at the long black ropes, Parmos observed they were not woven at all, but one solid black piece with round metal ends. Serion floated up with two of the ropes. He connected them in the hole left by the brushes and floated back down. He closed the case, moved it to the other side, and walked back.

After which, he opened a third case. He connected the other ends of the ropes to the case and poked something inside it.

"You will call it a computer in about one thousand seven hundred years." He kept poking at the machine with one finger. The case clicked and whirred.

Parmos wanted to run away, but he found it impossible. Somehow, Serion kept him from running away.

Dust flew around the cave.

"I know it is not you," Serion commented, without even looking up.

Serion stopped his work. "Watch your energy level. This time, it is not me you will have to deal with."

Parmos didn't know he had started to use his power. Nonetheless, he took a deep breath and kept himself in check.

He hesitated further, waiting for Serion to give him the answer before he asked.

When he did not reply, Parmos asked, "What is this place? Is it magic? Is it cursed?"

"They are all cursed, every last one of them. Where ever they are, no matter how many there are, they are all cursed."

"Who cursed them?" responded Parmos.

Serion's laugh was clear this time. He answered, "The portals were the primary means of transport eons ago. I am repeating myself... again. Infractions were punishable by indefinite suspension of mobility while keeping the conscious active. Your body could live immobilized for eons but your thoughts and emotions were not affected."

Parmos shivered.

"The Barren Lands you referred to, that is what happened to them. This must have been their escape plan, their intended tunnel to safety."

"Will that happen to me," he asked uneasily.

"No. You will be sent back to where you came from minus the energy form."

"What if I don't want to go back?"

"That is not an option, and beyond my directives."

A definite shift in his aura occurred and the warm sensation dwindled. He felt cold, even.

"The data from your journey is recorded in this portal."

Serion continued to talk, though only to himself. "This is odd. In every case, transport coordinates are always linked only to one other portal. Good Fortune! This one contains the locations of at least... yes,... fifteen other portals."

Then to Parmos, "This is good news for me. We cannot find the portal unless the energy spectrum is within the known range and at a certain level. The technology to completely disable the portal beyond restoration without destructive results was available only within the last century. With this information, I will definitely be at base station from now on, and not roaming the galaxy."

Serion poked the case with finality.

A loud sound like a giant key unlocking a giant door struck the cave.

The entire face of the portal started to move and come to pieces in organized fashion. The sides moved away like removing pieces of a puzzle.

Parmos saw the nature of Oracle. Now, he had really seen it all. Neither Lord Cuere nor anyone one else he knew had ever witnessed such a sight.

"Whoever originally built it, vanished a long time ago to some unknown dimension or part on the universe. They left a riddle of altered physics for the rest of us to deal with."

Serion went back to work, taking out equipment and moving cases. He never stopped for a break. Parmos could not help but watch. Parts of the exposed portal chirped, flashed and whirred. Serion checked his cases often, his aura brightening and faded consistently.

Finally, Serion approached him.

"You must return now."

He pointed to a place he marked in front of the portal.

Parmos hesitated. The aura turned red, and the warm sensation faded. He felt a little twinge. The longer he hesitated, the more the twinge hurt.

Reluctantly he got up and walked over to the spot.

"Stand still. Do not move. Do not talk. Do not change your energy pattern," ordered Serion.

"But what about Octun and the others?"

"I have insured that none of the energy forms survived on the bacterial matter of the body.

"Can I at least say good-bye."

"Say good-bye to whom?" refused Serion.

His fingers flew across the controls.

Parmos kept in his tears. He didn't need to cry anymore. He needed the courage he showed the day he faced down Jared.

The portal leapt to life. Parmos faced the portal. The entire face filled with stars in an endless void. He listened as Serion spoke in a strange language. The devices beeped at him and a large figure flashed into view.

"Your home planet," Serion announced. "Which... happens to be..."

For a moment, Parmos felt Serion's vexation. Suddenly, whatever mental and emotional connection Serion had established, dissipated.

"That is very odd. But that is impossible. The coordinates of this planet are not what I set on my instruments!"

He turned to Serion. A flash from the portal dimmed Serion's aura. His equipment blared audible alarms and red lights flashed. With alarming speed, his hands ran expertly over the console canceling the alarms one by one.

"That was not supposed to happen. Some sort of interference from the portal!" He looked at Parmos in despair.

A cold wave moved from Parmos' head to toe. He panicked. He tried to move, but could not. He tried activating his powers. Nothing worked. Serion dashed about checking the ropes, checking his cases and throwing them open frantically. He took out objects and threw them aside, then left to go look in another cases.

The entire cave faded from his view. Something was happening to him. Something unexpected, and he knew even Serion was absolutely powerless to help him.

****

Serion panted, trying to catch his breath. He checked and rechecked his preparations. Everything was perfect. He misconnected nothing. The original settings read perfectly: energy levels, tolerances, positioning, navigation, all perfect.

After examining the interference from the portal, he ruled out random phenomenon. The anomaly implied intelligence. It deleted Parmos' travel coordinates and erased every recorded parameter since setup. This portal contained centuries of data. Just before everything went wrong, the meter pegged. The energy coursing through the portal sent his equipment into over-range protection, showing only the highest possible readings, even though he could measure the output of a quasar with that thing. Now all of the portal's data was gone in a flash.

Serion tried using the portal's playback function to review the coordinates and other information to give him some clue. That did not work either. Someone had hacked into his equipment despite the most complex security protocol known.

"It just all goes to show that I need more help. If they won't give it to me, I guess I will have to acquire some myself." Serion packed up his gear. He took one case with him as he went to retrieve the iron rat.

www.ingramcontent.com/pod-product-compliance
Lightning Source LLC
Chambersburg PA
CBHW071305200626
46813CB00015B/44